PRAISE FOR
SHIFTING PLAINS

"[Johnson] luxuriates in a level of world-building few authors investigate. I truly love Jean's books. Her characters have plenty of depth and personality. Her tone is playful and her sizzling-hot sex scenes are inventive and fun."

—*Errant Dreams*

"An enjoyable romantic fantasy." —*Midwest Book Review*

"I really enjoyed this book. In fact, I read it twice in one day."

—*Fresh Fiction*

"[Johnson] blends the fantasy and romance together seamlessly and brings you into brand-new fantasylands that are filled with wonderful characters and environs. This is definitely an author to keep your eye on."

—*Night Owl Reviews*

PRAISE FOR JEAN JOH[illegible] AND THE SONS [illegible]

"Jean Johnson's writing is fa[illegible]ic, and wildly entertaining. Terrific—[illegible] utterly engaging. I loved it!" —Jayne Ann [illegible] *Times* bestselling author

"Cursed brothers, fated mates, prophecies, yum! . . . Jean Johnson spins an intriguing tale of destiny and magic."

—Robin D. Owens, RITA Award–winning author

"What a debut! I have to say it is a must-read for those who enjoy fantasy and romance. I so thoroughly enjoyed [*The Sword*] and eagerly look forward to each of the other brothers' stories. Jean Johnson can't write them fast enough for me!" —*The Best Reviews*

continued . . .

"Enchantments, amusement, eight hunks, and one bewitching woman make for a fun romantic fantasy . . . Humorous and magical . . . [A] delightful charmer."

—*Midwest Book Review*

"A paranormal adventure series that will appeal to fantasy and historical fans, plus time-travel lovers as well. It's like *Alice in Wonderland* meets the *Knights of the Round Table* and you're never quite sure what's going to happen next. Delightful entertainment . . . Will leave you dreaming of a sexy mage for yourself."

—*Romance Junkies*

"An intriguing new fantasy romance series . . . [A] unique combination of magic, time-travel, and fantasy that will have readers looking toward the next book. Think *Seven Brides for Seven Brothers* but add one more and give them magic, with curses and fantasy thrown in for fun. Cunning . . . Creative . . . Lovers of magic and fantasy will enjoy this fun, fresh, and very romantic offering."

—*Time Travel Romance Writers*

"The writing is sharp and witty, and the story is charming. [Johnson] makes everything perfectly believable. She has created an enchanting situation and . . . is off to a flying start. She tells her story with a lively zest that transports a reader to the place of action. I can hardly wait for the next one. It is a must-read."

—*Romance Reviews Today*

"A fun story. I look forward to seeing how these alpha males find their soul mates in the remaining books."

—*The Eternal Night*

"An intriguing world . . . An enjoyable showcase for an inventive new author. Jean Johnson brings a welcome voice to the romance genre."

—*The Romance Reader*

"An intriguing and entertaining tale of another dimension . . . Quite entertaining. It will be fun to see how the prophecy turns out for the rest of the brothers."

—*Fresh Fiction*

Titles by Jean Johnson

SHIFTING PLAINS

BEDTIME STORIES

FINDING DESTINY

THE SHIFTER

The Sons of Destiny

THE SWORD

THE WOLF

THE MASTER

THE SONG

THE CAT

THE STORM

THE FLAME

THE MAGE

Theirs Not to Reason Why

A SOLDIER'S DUTY

The SHIFTER

JEAN JOHNSON

BERKLEY SENSATION, NEW YORK

THE BERKLEY PUBLISHING GROUP
Published by the Penguin Group
Penguin Group (USA) Inc.
375 Hudson Street, New York, New York 10014, USA
Penguin Group (Canada), 90 Eglinton Avenue East, Suite 700, Toronto, Ontario M4P 2Y3, Canada (a division of Pearson Penguin Canada Inc.) • Penguin Books Ltd., 80 Strand, London WC2R 0RL, England • Penguin Group Ireland, 25 St. Stephen's Green, Dublin 2, Ireland (a division of Penguin Books Ltd.) • Penguin Group (Australia), 250 Camberwell Road, Camberwell, Victoria 3124, Australia (a division of Pearson Australia Group Pty. Ltd.) • Penguin Books India Pvt. Ltd., 11 Community Centre, Panchsheel Park, New Delhi—110 017, India • Penguin Group (NZ), 67 Apollo Drive, Rosedale, Auckland 0632, New Zealand (a division of Pearson New Zealand Ltd.) • Penguin Books (South Africa) (Pty.) Ltd., 24 Sturdee Avenue, Rosebank, Johannesburg 2196, South Africa

Penguin Books Ltd., Registered Offices: 80 Strand, London WC2R 0RL, England

This book is an original publication of The Berkley Publishing Group.

PUBLISHING HISTORY
Berkley Sensation trade paperback edition / May 2012

Library of Congress Cataloging-in-Publication Data

Johnson, Jean, 1972-
The shifter / Jean Johnson.—Berkley Sensation trade paperback ed.
p. cm.
ISBN 978-0-425-24733-4
I. Title.
PS3610.O355S53 2012
813'.6—dc23
2012000563

PRINTED IN THE UNITED STATES OF AMERICA

10 9 8 7 6 5 4 3 2 1

Acknowledgments

Many thanks to Alienor, Stormi, NotSoSaintly, and Alexandra for their constant efforts on my behalf. While no manuscript ever arrives at a publishing house with a perfect shine the very first time, with all rough edges removed and scratch marks buffed away, these ladies do help polish my work well enough that at least some reflections can be seen. I do what I can myself, but it's always good to have extra sets of eyes looking something over. Together, these four women make for a fabulous beta-editing team.

My thanks also to you, my readers. You're the ones I write these stories for. If I have made you smile or giggle, blush or tense, or just made you eager to keep reading, then I've done my job right. Here's hoping I keep doing it right, just for you. If you want to see what I'm currently up to, or just want to drop me a note, come see me at www.JeanJohnson.net. I'm always happy to hear from you!

Jean

ONE

"Married?" Traver hissed, leaning close as he reached over Solyn's shoulder to hang yet another sprig of greenery on the drying lines strung in her mother's herb-room. "I mean, I like you as a friend, but not like *that*. It'd be like . . . like marrying one of my sisters!"

"I panicked, alright?" Solyn hissed back as the young man mock-shuddered. She elbowed him lightly, more as a warning not to harangue her than as a warning at how close he was standing. "Let's see how clear *you'd* think with the stink of Tarquin Tun Nev fouling each breath! And you're not exactly the kind who makes my heart race, either," she conceded, gently shaking more herbs over the lower lines. "At least we like each other as friends. I certainly don't like him."

"True." Traver scrubbed his knuckles over her wavy brown locks. He resumed the task of hanging more herbs overhead.

"Besides, all you have to do is get someone to *listen* to you while you're off trading tea. Once we get this . . . thing investigated," she whispered, lowering her volume even further, "then they can take everyone involved away, and you and I won't have to get married."

"Unless, of course, what I saw wasn't him at all, and Tarquin *isn't* involved," Traver muttered. "Then he'll still be around, flexing his muscles and pressing for your hand. But I doubt it."

"Ugh." Solyn made a face. She stiffened and grimaced again as the silver band of her ring squeezed her middle finger twice. "Shh. Someone's coming."

"I don't think Tarquin smells all that bad," Traver stated quietly, hanging the last of the hyssop over her head. His body bumped against hers, but neither of them paid it any attention. They had been friends too long to notice such things. "He buys and wears the perfume you make. You should be grateful for his coin, at the very least."

"Buys and wears too much of it, if you ask me," Solyn muttered back. "I don't think he bathes, which is why he drowns himself in it. Hello, Aunt Hylin."

"Solyn, Traver," the older woman greeted them. Like her niece, she had wavy brown locks and hazel eyes, though her hair was streaked with gray. She dropped two baskets of yet more herbs on the worktable. "Hang these up as well when you're done with those, and don't dawdle. Your mother says the hedges in the upper pasture are finally ready for clipping, and we're just about done with the garden herbs, here. Your mother wants to pack some fresh tea in with the dried."

"Yes, Aunt," Solyn murmured. If one wanted a stimulating tea, one picked something grown in the hotter lands down by the southern coast. If one wanted a delicate tea, one drank the kind grown in the mountains. Fresh tea carried the most nuances and was highly prized, but it was difficult to transport, compared to the bruised, fermented, and dried varieties more commonly traded.

"And no twining around each other when you're supposed to be working," Hylin added, giving the closely standing Traver and Solyn a pointed look. "You're not married yet."

Blushing, they quickly separated. Solyn gave Traver a guilty look, while he struggled not to look awkward. Clearing his throat, he asked, "You, ah . . . know about that?"

Hylin raised her brows. "Huh. So it's *not* a jest . . . That Tarquin boy was complaining that you'd lied about an engagement to this lout, but from the looks of you two, it isn't a lie, is it?"

Traver cleared his throat. "Ah . . . no. Not a lie. As such. I mean, I haven't asked Ysander for his blessing, yet . . ."

Hylin snorted. "Then you'd better get to it, hadn't you? Those teas get sent off in the morning, and so do you—and no twining in here!"

Plucking the emptied baskets from the side table, she flicked a stray stalk of hyssop onto the tabletop and left the herb-room. Solyn sighed and lifted the plant toward one of the few empty spots on the strings stretched over her head. Taking it from her, Traver draped it on the highest line with the others, then squeezed her shoulder.

"Guess I'll have to visit your father tonight, instead of when I get back," he muttered. "The, ah, living arrangements will have to be discussed, since neither of us have a home of our own."

Holding up her palm in caution, Solyn tapped her ear with her free hand, then nodded when the silver band on her left hand twisted of its own volition around her finger, indicating no one else was close enough to eavesdrop. Traver was exempt from the spell on the ring, thanks to a special, hidden loop of metal he himself wore. If anyone tried to imitate him without it, she would know; the ring would warn her that someone was trying to impersonate her friend.

"Sorry about that. As I said, I panicked. I guess I'm only good at one subterfuge at a time," she sighed. "I'm more a woman of action. Except I can't take any actions. I can only sit here, study what little I can, and wait to react to everything."

Shifting his hand to her other shoulder, Traver gave her a one-armed hug. "We can't all be perfect. Once we get down into the hills, I'll head north as fast as I can go, and I won't stop until I reach the Shifting City and find someone who will listen to me."

"Remember, it's not paranoia if they really are out to get you," Solyn quipped, before turning serious. "Be careful, Traver. I don't want anything to happen to you on the journey."

"I'll be careful. You be careful, too," he warned her. "Now . . . what's the next category for when I see you tonight, if we get a moment alone?"

"Um . . . colors, and be opposite—blue to orange, yellow to purple, that sort of thing," Solyn said. "Though I don't know if we'll have another chance to be alone before you go."

"Then if I don't see you tonight, when I get back, I'll talk about how blue the sky was down by the Morning River, and you'll tell me how you prefer orange sunsets up here among the mountains." Hugging her again, Traver reached for the herb basket. "Let's get these hung up, then I'll help you clip tea leaves for the trip."

Kenyen Sin Siin did not like the way the cave smelled. Nor did he like the nervous way their guide, Bellar Sil Quen, kept looking at him every time he sniffed at the mound of stones at the back of said cave. Unfortunately, a tiger's sense of smell was not nearly as good as one might think. Kenyen couldn't quite tell if the smell came from the rocks or from something behind them. He thought it might be the latter, but most of the rocks were fairly large; a tentative touch with one large, tan-and-white paw proved they would not be easily budged.

"Hey!" The warning came from Bellar. "Get away from there, young man. Those rocks don't look stable—you don't want to get crushed, do you?" the middle-aged man challenged him.

Kenyen quirked his brows but obediently lowered his paw. Sitting on his haunches, he watched the shapeshifter from Family Dane, Clan Dog, stare at him for a few moments more, then turn back to the work of the others. A coalition of twelve shapeshifters, three of them travel-experienced princesses, had been sent by the Queen to look for signs of a "Family Mongrel" along their southern borders.

Supposedly the band was a group of banished outcasts, shapeshifter men who had turned their back on nearly two hundred years of civilized behavior, choosing instead to rob travelers, abduct women, and worse. Kenyen and the others only knew about it because one of their victims, a woman named Ellet Sou Tred, had managed to escape during a great wildfire. She had run to the river valley of the Mornai, where a scribe had taken care of her and her newborn child, writing down the woman's words before she succumbed to her lingering injuries.

That book had been brought to the Plains by that daughter, who was now Kenyen's sister-in-law. Her fears that the Shifterai were like the men her mother had described had dismayed the true shapeshifters, prompting them to send an expedition south into the hills and mountains described in the book. This cavern, nestled among the northern foothills of the Correda Mountains, was one of the few signs their group had seen that anyone had camped for extended periods of time in these hills, ex-Shifterai or otherwise. Similar caverns had been described in the book, making this one a very likely candidate.

Kenyen couldn't get that scent off his mind. He sniffed again, whiskers twitching. Something dry, something dusty . . . but not enough of it to really tell. It didn't help that the others brought their own scents, stirring up the ashes of the long-abandoned fire pits, poking at moldering rubbish from discarded animal bones and bits of clothing, so on and so forth. At least the light illuminating the chamber came from the three brightly rapped lightglobes they had brought, shedding a steady blue white glow across the large cavern.

Giving in to his curiosity, he shifted his shape. Muscles shrank, fur grayed, and claws turned blunt, no longer retractable. Pausing just long enough to scratch behind an ear with one hind foot, Kenyen stood and sniffed again at the pile of rocks. *Much better*, he thought. *A wolf's nose is definitely superior to a tiger's for sniffing out clues. And that scent . . . is . . .*

. . . Bone? Further sniffing reassured him it was indeed bone. Bone, and something else. Bone and . . . decayed flesh? *Is that . . . dead human I'm smelling? Is there a body trapped under these rocks?*

"Hey, I said get away from there!" Bellar ordered. "Why don't you come over here and sniff at these old ashes and bits of cloth, if you simply *have* to smell something? It'd be more useful."

Bellar had seemed interested in helping the party look for any signs of outcast activity among the foothills marking the end of the Shifting Plains and the start of the Correda Mountains, but now Kenyen wasn't so sure. Bellar's own brother had been one of the men banished around the same time as the reported actions of Family Mongrel. This expedition to find that so-called Family had almost missed this cave, despite Bellar's supposed familiarity with the area from his many trade expeditions into the mountains to the south. *So was it a deliberate avoidance of this area, or simply an accidental one?*

Settling onto the ground, Kenyen crossed his wolf paws and lowered his head. His ears still flicked, listening to the others murmur over the years-old evidence that this cave had once been occupied by a group of people, but otherwise he feigned disinterest in the proceedings. Idly studying the rocks, it took him a few moments to realize that there was more to the rock fall than just a pile of rubble.

One of the larger, deeper clefts between the rocks at the bottom had two peculiarities to it. The first was that it was fairly large, about the size of his head, and deep enough that he couldn't see anything blocking its shadowed depths. The second thing he noticed was the faint impression of tracks in the gritty dirt lining the cavern floor. The animal tracks he expected, since many other items in this cave had been investigated by wandering animals through the years, but drag marks, he did not.

Drag marks? Kenyen almost lifted his head off his paws. Forcing himself to relax, he glanced at the others. They were discussing the moldered contents of what must have been an abandoned food basket. A quick glance showed that Bellar wasn't looking his way. Shifting shape again, Kenyen slithered cautiously into the hole, tongue flicking to taste the air hidden in those shadowed depths.

Grass viper eyes weren't particularly adapted to seeing in the dark, but the path was wide and straight, and he could tell it opened into a larger space. Determining it was large enough, Kenyen transformed into a fourth form once he was beyond the tunnel, changing into the shape of a hunting cat. Once he did so, he could see a few details. Light from the front part of the cave seeped through a couple of gaps in the rocks—which had been deliberately placed, he now saw, for there were no signs of smaller chips or dust resting among the larger chunks on the backside of the pile, only on the front, as if to make it look like a true rock fall.

Those faint beams of light allowed him to see the bones lying on the packed earth of the alcove. Most of the flesh looked like it had been picked clean by insects or small animals; what little was left had dried along with the bones themselves, and nothing large had disturbed the lay of the body. More disturbing, it looked like rodent-chewed remnants of leather had been looped around the wrist and ankle joints of the body. A pile of desiccated waste lay to one side, and a bucket to the other.

". . . Kenyen? Kenyen Sin Siin, where are you?"

This time, it was Ashallan Nur Am who called to him. One of the many female shapeshifters of Family Lion, Clan Cat, the princess wasn't a particularly strong shapeshifter—five pure shapes at most—but she was an experienced warband member and huntress, and the nominal leader of this expedition.

Since there was enough room for him to take human form again, Kenyen reshaped himself and responded to her call. "I'm back here, Highness! Behind the rock pile. There's a path big enough for a small cat, and from this side, the lay of the stones looks like they were deliberately placed."

"What are you now, a stonemason?" Bellar called back. Kenyen couldn't see his face but could hear a slight edge in the older man's voice, the barest hint of upset. "I told you those rocks are unstable!"

"Stop playing around, Kenyen." Ashallan sighed. He interrupted her before she could order him back out.

"There's a dead body back here, Princess," he told them, raising his voice a little to make sure he would be heard. "It looks like he or she died in here as a prisoner."

That caused an immediate uproar. The others called out questions to both Kenyen and Bellar, some merely confused, some accusatory. Ashallan's voice cut through the others, sharp and hard.

". . . *Enough!* Bellar Sil Quen, you seemed rather eager to keep us away from that rock pile. If Kenyen's words are true, then such eagerness is suspect. Manolo Zel Jav, I brought a Truth Stone in my right-hand saddlebag. Fetch it for me."

"Of course, Princess," the older shapeshifter murmured.

"Narquen Vil Shem," Ashallan continued, "you have a rat form, do you not? See if you can find that tunnel Kenyen used. Anyone else have a form small enough?"

"There's only enough room for one other, Princess, before we crowd this place too much," Kenyen called out through the wall of rock separating them. "As for where I went, I passed through it as a snake, so you should be able to see my tracks. But there's enough room for a rabbit to hop through—actually, if you could bring the smallest of the lightglobes, that would be great. The light back here isn't very good. Only a cat or better could see some of these details in the dark, but not all of them."

"Narquen, take it and go," Ashallan ordered.

"Well, if you'll forgive me for not using a pure shape, Your Highness . . ." the shifter in question murmured.

Some of the light gleaming through the gaps in the rock pile shifted. It grew stronger down at ground level, shifting with the shadow of the ratlike creature pulling it along. Narquen had taken on a largish rat form with extra muscular limbs and an elongated, prehensile tail, which he had wound through the netting their people used to carry and hang the precious, enchanted spheres.

Kenyen moved out of his way, giving him room to expand back into his natural form. Picking up the netting, the other shifter lifted the globe to one side, letting its light fall on the body, the bucket, and everything.

"He's right," Narquen confirmed after a long look. The slightly older shifter raised his voice so that he could be heard through the wall of stones. "These rocks were piled deliberately and stabilized on this side. The bones of a human are also back here, with signs that it was bound and kept here for a while. What looks like a water bucket, and a corner of this little pocket-cave where he voided himself . . . Wait—Kenyen, does that look like writing under the body?"

Frowning, Kenyen crouched along with Narquen, peering as the other shifter angled their source of light for a better look. The soil back here was thin, some of it hard-packed, the rest just smears on the hard stone of the cavern floor. Though the letters were smudged in a few spots, words had been scratched into dirt and rock alike.

He wasn't as scholarly as his older brother Akodan, but Kenyen wasn't illiterate, either. Few were, on the Plains. Squinting, he studied the markings carefully. "Yes, it's definitely writing . . . From the position, I'd say . . . *this* rock was used to scratch it into the ground one letter at a time—yes, you can see the scratches on the pointier end, here."

"Yes. And the letters were scratched several times to try and deepen them," Narquen agreed. He hesitated, then gingerly lifted one of the arm bones. "But why are they only *under* the body? Why not elsewhere in this place?"

Kenyen scratched behind his ear, then shrugged. "Maybe he didn't want his captors to see what he was writing, so he lay on top of it?"

"Help me move it—Father Sky, Mother Earth, forgive us for disturbing this unfortunate person's resting place," Narquen added in wry reverence. "But—careful with that bone—it's pretty obvious he was a prisoner, here. Or maybe it was a she. If that book of your sister-in-law's is right, they were more likely to torment women."

"It could've been anyone," Kenyen agreed, grimacing as they carefully shifted the corpse. Once the unpleasant task was complete, they peered at the letters again. It didn't take long for Kenyen to figure out what the words were, smeared spots and all. "*I . . . am . . . the real . . . Tunric Tel Vem? . . . Tel Wem?*"

Narquen shrugged. "Looks more like a *W*, maybe? It's hard to tell with some of the scratches laid over each other. What's this word here?"

Kenyen shook his head. "Too smudged to tell. *This* bit could be either *of Nespah* or *of Mespak* or something between the two. If I remember the maps right, those sound like two of the valley-holds, places with more tea plantations than actual villages or towns to the south. Neither location looked like they were all that close to the Plains."

The other shifter shook his head. "I only know a little bit about the kingdom of Correda, and I only glanced at the maps. We'd have to check the ones we brought."

"Speak up!" they heard Ashallan order. "What have you two found?"

Kenyen answered her, raising his voice again. "It looks like this body was a man named Tunric, which I've heard is a common name for men in Correda. Tunric Tel Vem or Tunric Tel Wem. He was from either Nespah or Mespak, we're not sure which."

Narquen rubbed his chin, murmuring, ". . . That's rather an odd thing to say, isn't it? That he's the *real* Tunric?"

"If he was worried about people finding his body, he'd just say he was Tunric," Kenyen agreed equally as quiet, frowning. "But to emphasize he's the *real* one means he feared his identity was in doubt. Which means he feared someone was going to try to pretend to be him. But, the magics for casting an illusion spell are very complex and taxing. With magics in this whole region deeply weakened by the Shattering of Aiar, a mage that strong would have had to come from very far away."

Narquen put his hand on Kenyen's arm. "Not a spellcaster, Kenyen. It could have been a shapeshifter. If these Family Mongrel types were cruel enough to brutalize women, then what's to stop them from perverting their abilities from the purity of animal forms to the atrocity of echoing human faces? We may have done it as children when learning how to make small shifts, but we don't go around pretending to be each other once we move on to animal shifts. These curs have no such honor."

"Atava isn't the sort to lie, and apples rarely fall far from the tree," Kenyen replied, thinking it through. "The scribe who raised her would therefore have been equally honest, particularly one entrusted with writing legal contracts for his fellow Mornai. The only doubt lies in the words of Atava's mother. Did she tell the truth, or did she exaggerate and even lie? With her long dead, we can't ask her directly . . ."

He fell silent for a few moments, thinking, then voiced his thoughts aloud.

"There are plenty of different animal tracks layered with human ones in the dirt of the main cavern, enough to say that shifters lived here for a while," Kenyen reasoned out. "So many different wild animals would not mingle openly with humans. So shifters stayed here, and a man who feared his true identity was being stolen died here. Which implicates dishonorable shapeshifters."

"Then she was most likely telling the truth," the other shifter agreed.

Narquen's agreement confirmed Kenyen's own thoughts. The Shifterai were nomadic most of the year, but they were not an ignorant, uneducated people. Logic was prized among their kind.

The other shifter nodded at the desiccated corpse. "The men who left this body here were not above extreme cruelties, to imprison and leave a man to die behind this wall. The words in that book have a solid kernel of truth within them, between those tracks and this man's demise—when I dragged the lightglobe in here in one of my smallest forms, it looked like others had dragged supplies in via the same route. The bucket probably held water, which they'd bring in via skins."

"A little water, a little food . . . enough to sustain him for days, maybe even a turning of Brother Moon. Long enough for them to interrogate him, until they had wrung all the information they needed to try to take his place in the greater world. Long enough for him to realize they were probably going to kill him once they were through." Kenyen sighed roughly, rubbing his forehead. "So then the important question is, is someone still impersonating this man? And why? And how long ago did this man die, and was he really from the holdings of Nespah or Mespak, and if so, did his impersonator go back?"

Narquen chuckled under his breath. "That's more than one

question, you know. But good ones all the same." Raising his voice, he called out to the others. "I have verified what Kenyen has seen back here. It indeed appears that someone was kept back here as a prisoner . . . and was either slain back here or simply left to die."

"How unpleasant. If you two are done back there, we have the Truth Stone, now," Ashallan called through the rocks separating them from the main cavern. "I want you to help us question Bellar, here."

Both men shifted shape and made their way back through the small tunnel, bringing the lightglobe with them. Once in the main cavern, they both returned to human form, loins covered in modesty-preserving fur long enough to don the clothes they had folded and set aside. As he dressed, Kenyen noted that Bellar Sil Quen didn't look happy to see the white marble disk in Ashallan's hand, standing with his arms folded across his *chamak*-covered chest. Bellar reluctantly pulled one hand free, accepting the stone the middle-aged woman held out to him.

"You know how this goes," Ashallan reminded him. "State a lie, then state the truth."

"My name is Marro," Bellar obligingly muttered, clutching the palm-sized disk. A shift of his fingers revealed blackened imprints where his fingers had touched the surface. They faded after a few moments, leaving nothing but white, unblemished marble. Gripping it again, he cleared his throat. "Look . . . he may have been banished from the Plains, but there is nothing in the law which says I cannot talk with my brother. And yes, I've met with him over the years. Always *off* the Plains."

A shift of his fingers revealed the unblemished truth of that statement. Ashallan nodded, her expression neutral. The other two female shifters watched him with a mixture of curiosity and wariness, the same as most of the males. Kenyen finished clasping his pectoral collar around his shoulders, and wondered if he should shift his nose to something sensitive enough to pick up whether or not

Bellar was nervous about these revelations, perhaps hiding something by omission, if not through a lie.

"Nollan . . . we disagree on several things, but he's still my brother. And for the last ten years, he's made a life for himself in Correda as a tea farmer," Bellar told them. "When I heard about this expedition being planned this last winter, I flew into the mountains to meet with him, to see if Nollan had anything useful to tell me. He . . ."

"Go on," Ashallan urged quietly when Bellar hesitated.

Bellar looked uncomfortable, nose wrinkling and brow furrowing, but continued. "He gave me a funny look. Kind of like I was a bug and he was debating whether or not he'd squish me for it. He'd never looked at me like that before. Then he sighed and . . . and he just told me to keep people away from this cave, particularly the back of it. But I don't know why, and he didn't tell me why, and I *didn't* know about the body back there. I swear it on this stone."

Opening his fingers, he showed the all-white disk to the others.

"Where do you meet with your brother, when you go into the mountains?" one of the other princesses, Anaika, asked him.

"I used to meet with him near here, but not for the last half-dozen years. These days, I leave word at a tavern in the town of Teshal, and he gets back to me within a day or two. I've never asked where Nollan lives—he has a right to make a new life for himself, even though he's been banished," Bellar added defensively.

Kenyen frowned in thought. "If I remember the map right, Teshal's nowhere near either the Nespah or Mespak valleys. It's off to the east."

Manolo, from the same Family Tiger as Kenyen, dug into the saddlebag he had brought into the cave. Within moments, he fished out a folded map. He flopped the worn parchment over his hands so that it could be seen by the others and nodded. ". . . Teshal isn't near either; you're right."

Ashallan looked at Kenyen and Narquen. "Do you have any questions?"

Kenyen nodded and lifted his chin at Bellar. "Did your brother Nollan ever mention Nespah or Mespak?"

"Not that I can recall." He displayed the stone again, proving his words true.

"What about the name Tunric?" Narquen asked.

Bellar shrugged. "Not that I can recall."

"Well, if you *do* recall, let us know," Ashallan ordered him tartly, the same tone of voice a mother would use on a son who had disappointed her. Considering Bellar was close to her age, her tone made him flush.

"What about this Family Mongrel, did he ever mention that name?" Manolo asked him next.

Bellar frowned in thought. "I think he mentioned it . . . but I can't remember much. Mostly in the last few years, we've talked about him being a tea farmer, and he'd sell me some of his tea, and I'd give him the occasional bit of news about the Family and the Clan. He's not a *bad* man."

"Your brother was listed as banished for forcing himself on a maiden," Ashallan countered bluntly. "That's hardly the actions of a *good* man."

"Well, he never committed *murder*, as far as I know," Bellar defended. "He might know something about that body back there, but if he ran with this Family Mongrel, it was probably one of the others."

"Well, we'll just have to go question him, won't we?" the other princess, Asellah Lu Nish of Family Mustang, Clan Horse, stated. She was the oldest of the female shifters selected for this expedition, but with only two shapes to her name, her greatest contribution to the group lay in herb-healing and her years of trade experience with the Corredai. "And anyone he knows."

"We'll go to Teshal, question your brother, and see what he has to say," Ashallan decided.

"Just in case he doesn't know anything," Narquen offered, "perhaps we should send a couple of us to the Nespah and Mespak valleys to scout around for this Tunric Tel Vem or Tel Wem."

"We've already spent half the summer looking, Highness," Kenyen agreed. "Winter in these mountains is supposed to be as unpleasant as winter on the Plains. I can head to Nespah, if you like, and cut down on our overall travel time?"

"And I'll head to Mespak," Narquen offered.

"One of us should also report back to Her Majesty that we've finally made some progress," Ashallan murmured. Anaika raised her hand, and Ashallan nodded. "You have a fast enough bird form, cousin; you go to the capital and let the Queen know what we're doing. As for *you*, Bellar . . . the fact that you held secret your knowledge of this Family Mongrel is a black mark against you. Cooperate, and you may erase it. Withhold much more information, and you may end up needing to ask your brother for room in his home."

Bellar gave her a glum look. "I *didn't* want my brother persecuted any further."

"And if he is free of further crimes, he will not be," Ashallan said, shrugging. "Those that are guilty, however, will need to be attended to properly . . . even if they commit their crimes in another kingdom," the princess added grimly. "It's *our* fault we didn't take stronger measures to stop their wicked ways from continuing.

"Of course, it means sending a delegation to His Majesty if there *is* something in need of prosecution, since we're officially within Correda's borders. But first we need proof there is still wrongdoing happening, and whether or not our kind, exiled or otherwise, had anything to do with it." Sighing roughly, she raked her gray-streaked locks back from her face. "We'll handle that once we have a need for it. A dead body, however incriminating, isn't enough, since we still don't know *who* hid it back there. We are here merely to make sure this so-called Family Mongrel is no longer committing crimes against women—against *anyone*—and thus bringing dishonor to the real ways and the good name of the Shifterai."

"I'd be careful, though. If one of the banished shifters perverted his powers enough to take on the identity of this dead man," the other princess of Family Lion stated, "then just asking about his name might make the name-thief wary, or maybe even chase him into hiding."

Ashallan turned her attention back to Kenyen and sighed roughly. "I do wish your brother were here. We could really use a strong *multerai* to help us with this. Whoever these murderers are, they're frightfully strong, if they feel they can imitate others and get away with it, but I guess we'll have to make do with what we have."

Kenyen hated the way she put that. *As if I'm nothing more than a straw-snake, only good for frightening little children, and only for a brief moment at that. I may not have ten or twelve or more shifts, but I am good at the things I can do.* He kept his reaction hidden, however. The only way he could prove himself was to show his competency in other areas. *I'm not helpless, and I'm not useless.* Instead, he spoke lightly, chasing the topic at hand.

"A good point, Anaika," Kenyen agreed, nodding at the young woman. "I think Narquen and I could learn whatever we need just by perching in trees and listening to the locals speak. It would take longer than a direct inquiry, but it would be safer—Bellar, I have another question."

"What else do you want to know?" Bellar asked warily.

"According to the book of Ellet Sou Tred's suffering, on two occasions a new shifter joined Family Mongrel. Both of them were marked with the Banishment scar, just like the others," Kenyen said, tapping his own unblemished forehead briefly before lowering his hand. "Did your brother ever ask you to tell anyone else about his location? In specific, other banished men?"

Bellar gave him a sour look. “Would you like me to bring back Elder Brother Moon from oblivion, too? Or perhaps give you the secret to eternal life?”

“Answer the question, Bellar,” Ashallan ordered him.

“Well, of *course* he did. He knows that if you have the Banished mark on your forehead, it’s hard to find work, outkingdom,” Bellar admitted gruffly. “He figured he could help them, maybe give them a second chance.”

Manolo eyed Bellar, asking shrewdly, “Did he give you a special phrase or word to give to them, or tell you to have them say something specific when going to him to look for work?”

“Why would he give them a special saying?” Anaika asked, giving the older shifter a puzzled look.

“It’s fairly obvious to me, and I think to Kenyen,” Manolo told her, “that whatever else this Family Mongrel has been up to, they’ve been trying hard to avoid drawing attention to their activities. The Corredai aren’t like us in culture—few outkingdoms are—but they do have laws against the beating and raping of women just as we do. Laws against brutality of all kinds, and laws against theft. Laws against murder.

“Given how much the writings said that the men of Family Mongrel enjoyed their violent, brutal ways, and how many pains they took to avoid being found or tracked by anyone, it’s clear they knew their actions were illegal, and clear that they enjoyed doing them anyway,” Manolo stated, returning his gaze to Bellar. “Yet it’s also clear they took in new members at one point. Your brother might’ve joined Family Mongrel, or may have simply known about their activities. If your brother wanted to keep people away from the back of this cave, then he likely knew about the dead body bound behind these rocks, and that’s the sort of thing they might’ve done.”

“He’s *not* a murderer,” Bellar muttered stubbornly.

“Bellar, if he knew about that body being back there, why didn’t he report it to the authorities in Correda so they could come and bury it in accordance with their traditions and contact the missing man's family?" Kenyen asked pointedly. "There are too many questions here, with many of them pointing at potentially ugly answers. So we are asking you, did your brother tell you to say anything to banished Shifterai, or give them anything, or direct them to approach him in a specific way whenever you might have the chance to point another banished man in his direction?"

"Use the Truth Stone," Ashallan added as Bellar hesitated. "If your brother is simply helping the banished to find legitimate work, then he has nothing to fear from us. All kingdoms honor the Truth, be it by stone or by wand or by spell. But all kingdoms revile murder, and we have a body behind that rock fall that was apparently bound and imprisoned and left there to rot . . . and your brother knew *something* about it. Something unpleasant enough he didn't want others to find this cave, nor explore it beyond those stones."

Sighing roughly, the middle-aged shifter gripped the marble disk. "Nollan told me that . . . that if I knew of anyone—any male, that is—who was being banished from the Plains, I was to point them into the mountains toward him, and instruct them to tell him they were looking for work."

"Anything else?" Manolo asked when Bellar displayed the unblemished stone.

Bellar shrugged. "Just that they were to be honest with him as to why they'd been banished . . . and that he particularly wanted me to encourage them to go looking for him if they were strong shifters, and that if I thought they'd get along with him, they should bring him a gift. But he didn't tell me what kind of gift. That's all he said on the matter."

Again, he displayed the stone, showing it was white.

Manolo eyed Bellar. "Well, whatever your brother has been up to, at least he's done his best to keep you ignorant of it. I'm not sure if that's more than a single point in his favor, since he might be concealing more crimes than those which earned his banishment, but he kept you innocent of it."

"He made a mistake, and he was banished for it. He doesn't deserve further persecution just for that," Bellar argued back.

"If he's innocent of further wrongdoing, then he won't be. We just want to ask him some questions. But first, we'll tear down the rocks and bury the body with respect," Ashallan instructed the others. "Then we'll split up in the morning."

"We'll meet in the town of Teshal at the inn after, what, two weeks? That should be enough time to look around and ask questions, right?" Narquen asked, glancing at Kenyen.

"I suggest three weeks," Manolo told the others, lifting the map in his hand. "A lot of these roads are switchbacks. Distances are longer on the ground than they might look on the map. Flying straight there would be a lot faster than riding for those of us with the forms for it, but I think the locals would prefer to deal with people wearing clothing, not just feathers or fur. Perching in a tree might be alright for eavesdropping, but you may still have to ask people questions . . . and if there are lawbreakers at work, hiding themselves among the Corredai, best if you look like a non-shifter while doing so. Though I'm not quite sure how someone permanently branded with bluesteel *could* hide their Banishment scars."

"Well, at least our clothes aren't that far off from what the Corredai wear," Narquen muttered to Kenyen. "We might be able to blend in a little."

Kenyen snorted, muttering back, "You should've seen the shapeless rags my sister-in-law wore, back when she abandoned her old life among the Mornai."

"Enough chatter, you two. We'll take three weeks to look around and ask questions," Ashallan told the two men. "Bellar's brother is our best lead, but your pursuits may prove fruitful. If there is more than one inn, then we'll meet at either the northernmost or westernmost inn, in that order. And if we don't hear from you within four weeks, we'll come looking for you. Hopefully we can find what we need in Teshal. When we do, we'll send messengers to you—to the northernmost or westernmost inn of each valley, Nespah or Mespak. And don't take any big chances. Neither of you have all that many shapes."

"As you wish, Princess," Kenyen agreed, dipping his head respectfully. At least, outwardly. Inwardly, he griped again. *Seven shapes is a* respectable *number of shapes for a Shifterai male—the average is five, after all, and mine are as pure as any Shifter Council has judged. What I* can *do, I do* well, *thank you.* Moving to the rock wall, he shifted himself taller and stronger, hoisting the first of the rocks from the top of the pile forming the makeshift barrier between them and the body of the man in the back. *I love my brother, I really do . . . but there are times when I am tired of being compared to him.*

Manolo joined him, and the others formed a chain toward the cavern entrance, passing the rocks one after another to get them out of their way. Knowing his brother and sister-in-law would want details of whatever they found, Kenyen set himself to remember everything about this cave, and everything about the body they were unveiling.

Atava's existence was one of the few pleasant end results of the atrocities her mother had suffered at the hands of the so-called Family Mongrel. But Atava herself wasn't interested in vengeance against the men who may have fathered her so much as she just wanted justice. Like her, Kenyen and the other shifters wanted such things stopped and needed to know if they were still happening.

He and Manolo were here to represent her interests in this hunt. Kenyen didn't know exactly when the man in the back of this cave had died, but he was willing to bet that it happened after his sister-in-law was born. Those bones didn't look two decades old, and there had been no indication in her mother's ramblings that the shapeshifters calling themselves Family Mongrel had harbored a male prisoner.

For the first two months, their search had seemed fruitless. The only signs they had found were smaller versions like those in the front half of this place, years-old evidence that a group of people had once lived sporadically in the cave-riddled hills of northern Correda, which lay along the southern edge of the Plains.

But now we have a lead. Where it leads to, I have no idea, he admitted. *All I can do is hunt down these curs and see that Family Mongrel, if it still exists, is scattered beyond both moons . . . and maybe avenge the death of this Tunric fellow, whoever he was.*

I do know I'll have to be extra careful in going about it. Someone murdered this fellow back here, either deliberately or through cruel neglect, but I cannot take the chance it was through neglect. They might not hesitate to kill again, particularly if this Tunric fellow held a position of wealth or importance. His impersonator wouldn't want to give that up.

TWO

The water was cool and sweet, partially shaded by the aspens and pines growing along the riverbed. The side-trail leading down from the main road to this grassy bank had been steep but worth the detour. Eyeing the rippling liquid, Kenyen debated stopping for lunch as well as water. The way his brown mare tugged on the reins a little, pointing her nose from the stream to the tufts of grass off to their right, made up his mind. Pulling a lead rope from one of his saddlebags, he clipped it to her halter, then unbuckled her bridle, freeing her teeth so she could eat.

Tying the other end of the rope around a nearby tree so that the mare could reach both grass and stream, Kenyen removed the tack while she grazed. He gave her a cursory brushing, then turned saddle upside down to air-dry while the two of them rested. Once his horse's needs were tended, Kenyen pulled bread and cheese from one of his saddlebags.

Tunric Tel Vem, or Tel Wem, was long dead. There was some

urgency to find out if his murderers had been caught, yes, but not enough to prod him into racing his mount past her endurance. That meant Kenyen had time to enjoy the shade of the forest and the flow of the small river on this trip. The landscape around him looked nothing like the slowly undulating hills and rills of the Plains, with chest-high grass, low bushes, and broad horizons. No, the mountains surrounding him were high, the foothills close, the steep valleys cluttered, and the profusion of foliage almost exotic.

Dipping his wooden travel mug into the river, he nibbled on the food and debated taking the time to go on a hunt, stretching his provisions. He had coins with him and had passed more than one place where food could be bought each day, but hunting was fun. Relaxing, in an exciting, tense way. Plus there were always new kinds of tasty game to be found and flushed out. *Hm . . . maybe I should go hunting closer to dusk, when it's easier to creep up on my prey? Of course, letting the gutted game bleed out while I travel might work; that usually improves the flavor a little.*

Just as he bit into the herbed bread he had bought two villages ago, Kenyen heard water splashing. Not the trickling and rippling of the river but actual splashing. Rocking forward from his hip to one knee, he peered through the bushes lining the edge of the broad stream. The noise increased, until a tired man riding an equally tired pony came trotting and stumbling and splashing into view.

The slight limping of the pony concerned Kenyen; a good horseman wouldn't ride his mount until it foundered. Nor would he force it into a fast walk through a mountain riverbed which was more rock than mud along its bottom. Not unless something truly important, maybe even dangerous, pressed the young man.

"Hey." Rising from the bank, he caught the young man's attention, raising his voice a bit more. ". . . Hey!"

Brown curls bounced as the youth jerked up his head, eyes wide and searching the bank. The moment he spotted Kenyen, he flinched, then frowned. Craning his neck, he looked all around, then cautiously guided his short mare closer. When he stopped her, she hung her head and snorted at the water. Without the splashing of the mare to get in their way, normal conversation was now possible. "Ah, yes? You wanted . . . ? Wait, are you Shifterai?"

Kenyen lifted a hand self-consciously to the pectoral draped around his shoulders and neck. It bore seven rows of animal-carved beads, one each for the pure shapes he could form. His plan had been to hide it in his saddlebags when he got closer to the valley of Nespah. "Yes, I am."

The relief on the young man's face puzzled Kenyen. "Thank the Gods—wait, where are you from?"

Kenyen rolled his eyes at the pony rider. Either the other young man was exceptionally scatterbrained or there was something far more pressing on his mind. "The Shifting Plains, obviously? Kenyen Sin Siin, of Clan Cat, Family Tiger," Kenyen told him. "Your mount looks like she has bruised hocks, or maybe a stone in one of her frogs. Why don't you bring her ashore and rest for a few minutes? I'd be happy to take a look at her hooves for you."

Again, the other man peered all around them. "Is there anyone with you?"

"No. I split from my companions two days ago—this is the right way to get to the Nespah region, isn't it?" Kenyen asked.

"Yes." Twisting in the saddle, he pointed upstream. "I just came from there. It's a day's ride uphill, maybe a little more. If you follow the river, it's the right-hand fork. You'll see where the road crosses it on a covered bridge—are you really from the Plains?"

"As sure as I can shift shape," Kenyen told him.

The young man frowned for a moment in thought, then glanced behind him once more, as if expecting pursuit of some kind. Looking back at Kenyen, he nodded and lifted his chin. "Prove it. Something big, not tiny. And no hiding your head."

That was an odd request. Lifting his brows, Kenyen lifted his hands as well. Pulling the collar of wooden beads over his head, he set it on the ground, then unfastened the buttons stitched down the side of his *chamak* tunic. Toeing out of his riding boots, he pulled on the drawstrings of his gathered trousers and let them drop, revealing a modesty pelt of brown fur from hips to thighs. Without hesitation, he curled down and twisted his flesh, molding it into the orange, brown, and cream figure of a stripe-cat, his Family's namesake.

His mare ignored him, accustomed to the ways of the Shifterai, where forty-nine out of every fifty men and one out of every fifty women born and bred on the Plains could take on at least two animal shapes and usually up to five, or even more. When the old Aian Empire had shattered not quite two hundred years ago, magic at the heart of the continent had shattered as well, affecting most strongly those who had survived the cataclysm that had wiped out the old capital city at the heart of what was now called the Shifting Plains. All of their livestock were used to shapeshifters.

The man's mountain-bred pony, however, was not accustomed to his kind. She nickered and reared, or tried to. The young man wrestled the short mare back down to all fours, then nudged her over to the bank. Since it was away from the stripe-cat, the pony nervously complied. Tying her reins to a tree limb, he dismounted and came back. Kenyen, raised to be polite, sat on his haunches and waited patiently. He quirked one fuzzy brow as the youth gingerly touched him, but sat still as a thumb scrubbed over his flattened forehead.

"Shift back!" the stranger commanded. Kenyen complied, still seated on the ground. The other man nodded, then swallowed. "And again—to a different form. Nothing small!"

Since he only had three large forms, and only one was larger than his tiger-shape, Kenyen stood and shifted onto all fours, taking on the form of a brown-coated stallion. He whuffed as the other young man rubbed again at his forehead, and blinked when the Corredai youth sighed.

". . . Thank Cora. You *aren't* one of them."

Taking that as a sign the odd examination was over, Kenyen shifted back, loins once again clad in fur for decency's sake. "One of who? And what's your name?"

Breathing deep, the youth squared his shoulders. "I'm Traver Ys Ten. I'm from the Nespah holdings. And for the last . . . I don't know how many years, at least twelve . . . we've been plagued by shapeshifters. Only they're not shifting into animals. They're—"

"—Shifting into other men," Kenyen finished for him. Receiving a startled gaze, he shook his head and folded his arms across his naked chest. "I don't know whether the Gods are laughing or just smiling today. I'm actually here in the mountains for the same reason. Tell me, Traver Ys Ten of the Nespah region, do you know of a man named Tunric Tel Vem, or maybe Tunric Tel Wem?"

Traver blinked, visibly startled. "Yes, Tunric Tel Vem! That's like one of the meanest of them! Sure, he *acts* nice in public, but . . . How do you know who he is? I mean, isn't? Or both?"

"I don't," Kenyen admitted. "I just know my companions and I found a body in a cave that looked like it had been kept there as a prisoner, and the prisoner had scratched his name into the rocks in a way that made us think someone wanted to imitate him. Have you ever heard this Tunric mention a 'Family Mongrel' or something along those lines?"

Traver bit his lip for a moment, then shook his head hesitantly. "I'm not sure . . . maybe, but . . . Wait, who are your companions, and why did you split from them?"

"Well, we're actually trying to track down criminals banished from the Plains, some of them from over twenty years ago. As for *why* we're looking for them . . ." Kenyen reached for his trousers, pulling them on as he explained the tale of his sister-in-law's mother. By the time he finished, the Corredai was giving him a sympathetic, grim nod, half understanding, half agreement. Kenyen finished the tale with, ". . . And so when we found the body of Tunric in a cave, but weren't sure if he came from Nespah or Mespak, we split up.

"If you do have shapeshifters impersonating people here in the mountains, then we need to know about it," Kenyen told Traver. "It's not because they're criminals, though their new crimes are enough to condemn them again. It's because they've banded together to coordinate their crimes. This has to be stopped, and my people are willing to take on the responsibility of stopping them. As soon as I've looked at your mare's hooves and she's had a few bites of grass, we can go join the others at the town of Teshal. Ashallan will want to hear this."

"*A*shallan?" Traver asked, the corner of his mouth quirking up wryly. "You really *are* from the Plains. Tunric and the others like him won't even refer to Her Majesty with the honorific *Ai*, let alone give any female the *A* of a princess. They *really* don't like women. Tunric's wife divorced him a decade ago, claiming he abused her, and he didn't seem to care. He used to be a kinder, gentler man, but in the last dozen years . . . Polite in public, but only if it's truly public. The rest of the time he's arrogant at the very least, and unpleasant whenever he thinks he can get away with it."

"That would fit with what we know about this Family Mongrel," Kenyen agreed, thinking of the things he had read in the book. Coaxing the now-calmer pony farther up on the bank, he checked each of her hooves in turn. "Easy, girl . . . just let me check . . . Ah, good. No stones are lodged in the soft tissues of her hooves, but she's bruised around the ankles and the frogs of her hooves are tender from the rocks in the stream. If you'd pushed her much more, she would have foundered or broken a leg."

"I didn't have a choice. I couldn't be sure if one of the others in the trading party was a shifter or not—I don't know all their identities," Traver added as Kenyen looked up sharply. "I just know there are a lot of them, and that they're impersonating more men than just a handful in my own town. I would've gone to a Magister, but there aren't any large enough towns in the direction we were going. And I would've waited, except one of the men, I'm pretty sure *he* was a shifter, and he was giving me looks I just did not like. They made the hairs on my neck crawl, so I left early. Just took off, to get away as fast as I could."

Kenyen narrowed his eyes. "How do you know so much about these . . . these man-shifters?"

Traver shrugged, looking at the cheese and bread abandoned on the ground. "It was about six years back, when I was still a kid. I'd just gotten a new bow for my birthing-day gift and was dared to go deer hunting at night with it—I have good night sight, you see," he explained in an aside. "But then I got a bit lost and saw firelight. I snuck up on them, since I didn't know who was out there, and saw a clearing with a small bonfire and several men around it. Their faces . . . their faces kept *melting*."

Kenyen, unfastening the pony's bridle so she could eat as well, looked up at that. "Melting?"

"One minute it would be Tunric and his boy Tarquin, the next they were each somebody else, and they didn't look related anymore. Then they'd go back. The others, too. And they had hand mirrors, and they were looking into them. Now that I'm older, I realize they were practicing or something. And joking and laughing, and saying things about who they thought would make a good 'replacement candidate' next. I didn't know the names at the time, but later I learned some of them were men like Tunric, merchants and landowners. Powerful men in their communities."

"That doesn't sound good, but it does sound like something Family Mongrel would do," Kenyen muttered grimly. Grunting, he pulled the saddle from the pony's back. It was damp with sweat, not river water, and would need airing so the beast didn't gain any sores.

He wished his brother was here; Akodan was better at thinking strategically, at figuring out how to outflank an enemy. *All I can think of is the horror of not knowing who all the man-shifters might be and how many of their victims died in caves like the original Tunric did. I have no clue how to find all of the shapeshifted curs from Family Mongrel, nor how to stop them. I know something will come to me, but at the moment . . .*

"I didn't know what to think, or what to do about what I saw," Traver muttered, his voice barely audible over the stream. "They scared me. They shoved each other, talked coarsely . . . and there was this woman. I hadn't seen her before. She was dirty, and barely dressed in rags, and she scuttled about like a . . . like a timid mouse, and they hit her if she didn't move fast enough. And . . . other things." He shrugged, hugging his arms to his chest. "I told a friend of mine, and sh . . . well, they said they believed me, because of some things that were happening that they'd seen, too. But it was late, I was young, I didn't dare get close at the time, and I couldn't find anything out after that. Nor could my friend.

"Everyone seemed so normal. But . . . little things kept adding up over the years. Until I was hunting through the hills again and found another bonfire. I didn't dare get close enough to see much, but I saw enough to know they're still out there, and one of them is definitely the man calling himself Tunric Tel Vem."

Kenyen didn't miss the way the other young man kept looking at his food. "You want something to eat?"

Traver nodded. Scooping the bread and cheese off the ground, Kenyen dusted them off, then broke each in two and gave the younger man the cleaner halves. Taking a bite himself, he chewed and thought. Both his mare and the shorter pony cropped at the grass growing along the banks, feeding while they rested. Finally, Kenyen swallowed and asked, ". . . Why did you want me to shift shape twice? What was that about?"

"They have these marks on their forehead. Bluesteel scars," Traver told him. "They have a way of covering it up when they're pretending to be a human, but it shows up when they've shifted into an animal shape."

Kenyen eyed him, then snapped a twig off the nearest aspen tree and drew a swirling, line-crossed mark in the dirt at the edge of the riverbank. "A mark like this?"

"Yeah, that's it," Traver agreed, peering at it. "At least, I'm pretty sure. It's been several years, like I said. Some of them I think had two lines through the swirly bits."

"The mark means Banished from the Plains. Two slashes means both the Shifting Plains and the Centa Plains. It's an automatic death sentence if they cross the border, if they have two." Kenyen frowned and pitched the twig into the river. "How did they cover it up?—No, I can't believe I'm actually asking this . . . You *can't* cover up a bluesteel scar. Once you've been marked, it's there for the rest of your life. Not even a Healer's best spells can remove it!"

"That's not true. If you had a . . ." Traver caught himself, flushed, and cleared his throat. He swallowed and gestured at his head. "They do this skin-flap thing with their foreheads. And they grow a fringe of hair along the edge, then comb it into the rest and tie it in a ponytail, or sometimes a braid. And they also wear headbands across their foreheads. There are some days when I wonder if every Corredai man with his hair pulled back or his forehead covered is secretly a shapeshifter in disguise."

The thought both disgusted and intrigued Kenyen. Wondering if it was even possible, he moved over to his saddlebags and dug until he found the hand-sized, polished steel mirror his father had given him at the onset of puberty so he could study himself more carefully while trying new shapes. The lightly scratched surface could have used repolishing, but it allowed him enough of a view to frown at himself and slowly bulge out a flap of skin. Growing hair along the edge was the tricky part. After the fourth try, he caught the Corredai youth staring in half-horrified fascination.

"That is . . . so . . . I'm sorry if this offends, milord, but that is just *disgusting*. Skin shouldn't *move* like that!" Traver swore, shaking his head.

"Little partial shapings like this are not looked upon with great favor, I'll admit," Kenyen said, smoothing out his brow. "We prefer to honor the animals created by Mother Earth and Father Sky by making ourselves look as natural as possible, indistinguishable from the real ones. It's . . . not *common* for us to pretend to shape ourselves like others, save for maybe in our earliest years—not to scare you, but I used to be somewhat good at making myself look like my friends. I haven't done it in years, though, and I only ever did it for a laugh. My mother made me stop after a few turns of Brother Moon."

Traver digested that. He nibbled on the remaining cheese in his hand. Finally, he shrugged. "Can you still do it?"

Kenyen blinked, bemused by the odd request. "I suppose I could *try*. I was only doing this to see if it could hide the scar in question," he added, gesturing at his forehead. "It looks like it might actually work."

"I already know it can cover the scars," Traver agreed, dismissing the subject. "What I want to know is, can you make yourself look like someone else?"

"The question is, why?" Kenyen countered back.

"Well, since I don't know who *is* a . . . a man-shifter, and who's the real person, then maybe the only way to find out is to get invited to one of those midnight bonfires and catch them all in one place," Traver offered, shrugging. "The best way to do that is to pretend to *be* one of them. Only I can't shift my shape. You can."

The idea was perverted: a true shifter didn't imitate another person. Animals, yes. People, no. Not once they learned to control their abilities. But Kenyen couldn't deny it also made sense to try.

Since he lacked any other candidate, Kenyen faced the other man, lifted his mirror, and carefully started shaping his face to match. Traver's forehead was a little broader, his chin a little more pointed, and he had a small tuft of not-quite-beard on his chin. The sort a young man would try to grow to make himself look older. His eyes were lighter brown, his nose thinner, if with a little bump from having been broken and reset, and there was a mole near the Corredai's left ear.

"Um . . . you put my mole on the wrong cheek," Traver told him, gesturing at the right side of Kenyen's head. "It's on the left, not the right?"

Flushing, Kenyen tried again. He got the face more or less right, but when he tried to smile, it looked awkward. Sighing, he relaxed his face. "Something like this would take practice. Same with the forehead-flap thing. And that's just the face; there's also the body. I'm a tiny bit taller, with narrower shoulders, and our muscles are bulked up differently. I might lose the sense of one of my other shapes if I tried to really grasp a total transformation."

"I have no idea what that means," Traver admitted, shrugging, "but like I said, it was just a thought. You said there were other Shifterai here in the mountains, in a town somewhere nearby? True Shifterai?"

"Yes, they're headed to Teshal to question someone," Kenyen said.

"Then I guess we should saddle up," Traver agreed. "One of them might be able to do it."

Kenyen bit back a retort on that, rephrasing his reply a little more politely. "It's not a matter of power; it's a matter of control. I might lose the sense of a less-familiar shape, but I can do it. I'd just need to practice for a bit. And we're not leaving for a few more minutes, to give the saddle and pad a little more time to dry. Your pony will also need to be walked for an hour or two, and her hocks checked for swelling. But we should be able to reach the village of Kethrin by nightfall.

"From there, I think it's just a couple days to Teshal, maybe less if she recovers tonight. When we do get there, Ashallan of Clan Cat, Family Lion, is in charge of our search," Kenyen told the young man. "She can hear what you have to say and decide what should be done about these man-shifters. If they really are banished ex-Shifterai, then part of your problem is in a way our fault." Kenyen checked both sets of tack. His was almost dry, but the pony's saddle was still a little damp. "You should take care of your mount a little better, you know."

"Well, I've been in kind of a hurry. It's bad enough I left the caravan in the middle of the night," the young Corredai man muttered. He grimaced and pressed a hand to his stomach. "Ugh, that was a bit too much cheese. I love eating it, but it doesn't always like me back—um, if you need me, I'll be in the bushes . . ."

Kenyen chuckled and flicked his hand, giving permission. He still had his shirt and pectoral necklace to pick up, plus a bit of food to eat and his waterskin to refill. "Take your time. Just don't take all day."

The other man nodded, grimaced, and hurried off into the undergrowth. Kenyen eyed his mirror in curiosity and tried folding the flap of skin from his hairline down this time. That seemed to work better than trying to haul it up from his eyebrows, while allowing him to keep the lead edge properly fringed with hair.

Forming and retracting it a few times, he ignored the noises in the distance, playing with the minor changes, then tried tracing a false scar on his forehead. After almost getting it right, he chuckled, relaxed his flesh, and reformed it so that it appeared *reversed* in the mirror, which meant it would display correctly on his brow for anyone who wanted to look at his face and read it. *Right versus left, yes . . . mirrors are great for looking at oneself, but even they don't show you how you look to others.* Sweeping the extra fringe into a partial braid atop his head, Kenyen checked his reflection, wanting to know if the seam could be easily seen.

A crash in the bushes and a startled yelp—which evolved into a scream and more thrashing—made him drop the polished scrap of steel. Launching forward through the bushes, he shifted stronger muscles and grew claws on his fingers and toes, giving him better traction across the forest floor. Foliage rustled with another yelp, followed by a thud. Bursting through the branches, Kenyen leaped and hit the figure that had pinned the Corredai man to the ground, sending the two of them tumbling.

Both males scrambled apart, whirling and facing each other on hands and toes. Kenyen's feral, feline hiss, teeth bared and body tensed to spring, was met by the other man's bared canines and wolfish growl. They stared at each other. A crackle of dried leaves and twigs distracted both of them. Traver froze, his trousers mostly pulled back into place, his fear-filled attention more on the stranger than on Kenyen.

The stranger, older than both of them by a few years, glanced between Kenyen and Traver, visibly torn between dealing with his original target and the newcomer. The unexpected shapeshifter. With instincts honed by nearly eight years' worth of experience following his brother into battle with the rest of the South Paw Warband, Kenyen struck.

"*My* prey," he growled. "Find your own!"

The stranger glanced briefly at the wide-eyed Traver, then looked back at Kenyen with a smirk. "Well, I do have a prior claim. I suggest we secure him, then discuss the matter in a civilized way. Did anyone send you here?"

"A former son of Dog. He didn't give me a lot of information," Kenyen hedged.

"What sort of information?" the other shifter asked, narrowing his eyes.

"Strangers have been sniffing around certain *caves*. He only told me enough to do *this*," Kenyen added, freeing one hand from the ground to tap his forehead, though he didn't actually reveal the fold of shapeshifted skin held upright in its braid. "Then he told me to head south, to Nespah. And to bring a gift."

Glancing pointedly at Traver, Kenyen studied the other shifter out of the corner of his eye. The man looked at Traver, too. While his attention was diverted, Kenyen shifted his face. When the man glanced back, he twitched and blinked. Kenyen knew the imitation wasn't perfect, but his nose was a lot more snub like Traver's and his brow a little higher, his cheekbones a little broader, and his chin a little softer with the signs of youth. He grinned, displaying feline-long teeth, then reshaped his face back to normal with a little shake.

The other shifter studied Kenyen a long moment, then pushed himself upright, glancing around the woods. "Right. I'm taking you and him to see the others. He had a pony he took with him . . ."

Kenyen smiled slightly. "I convinced him to stop riding and let the poor thing rest. I was just waiting for him to use the bushes before making my move, so I wouldn't have to deal with that later. I didn't expect anyone to stumble across us, let alone a fellow shifter."

The other shifter narrowed his eyes. "Why *him*, as a gift?"

Kenyen flushed. He hadn't considered being caught on that point, and his mind raced. *I can't tell him what Traver told me, but I have to seem evil enough to be acceptable. Father Sky, how can I show myself evil without having to prove it?* To kill time, he smiled at the other youth, doing his best to make it look slow and feral. Traver gulped and licked his lips under the weight of Kenyen's stare.

That gave him an idea. Shifting his gaze to the other shifter,

Kenyen shrugged. "Not *him*. His belongings. That's a nice pony he was riding. I take it you know him, so he's probably from the same area as you?"

The older man shot him a dark look. "He's been acting weird lately, and when he ran away from the tea caravan . . . well, we have orders about this one. Particularly given the latest rumor about why he fled. We won't have to kill him, don't worry. At least, not if he cooperates."

"But I was so looking forward to it," Kenyen pouted. He didn't want to lay it on too thickly, but he did want to try to establish that he fit in with the other criminals hidden in these mountains. "I like it when they scream." Eyeing Traver, he licked his lips. The Corredai youth shuddered. "So what's this rumor about him?"

"He ran away so he could try to tell someone about us—and you *can't* run, let alone hide," the other shifter added, glancing back at Traver, who had started to shift his weight. The subtle movement stopped. "When we get what we want, you'll be set free. Until then, you're our prisoner, boy. Cooperate and live; run and die. You *do* want to make it back to your pretty little betrothed, don't you?"

Kenyen didn't like the way the other man mocked the Corredai, nor the way Traver paled and swallowed at the older man's threat. He tried distracting the older shifter with a question. "What's your name?"

The other shifter glanced back at him. "You can call me Zellan Fin Don. Particularly if the others have a use for you in our area. Until they do . . . I'll just call you Catson. Our real names aren't meant to be discussed around outsiders."

"Then 'Catson' I am. For now. If you want *him* replaced," Kenyen pointed out, lifting his chin at Traver, "you probably can't afford to use one of the others. Given how long you've been doing this, there probably aren't many free bodies left. My arrival seems to be a bit of good timing for both of us, given the circumstances."

Zellan eyed Kenyen thoughtfully. "You're rather smart, for new blood."

Actually, it had been a wild stab in the dark, a guess at best, if something of an educated one. Kenyen accepted the compliment with a dip of his head. "I try. I have some rope in my saddlebags, Zellan. Why don't we drag this tasty little prize back to where I left our mounts?"

"A good idea. *Get up,*" Zellan snapped at Traver. "Remember, if you run, you die. And there is nowhere you can run that I cannot track you."

Swallowing, Traver did as he was ordered, rising slowly. He paused to finish tying the waistband of his trousers, then carefully picked his way back toward the small, grassy clearing where Kenyen's horse and his pony waited. As much as Kenyen wanted to reassure the Corredai, he couldn't, daren't say anything out loud.

It didn't take long to return to the two mounts, nor to bind Traver's hands behind his back. Flexing shapeshifted muscles once both steeds were saddled again, the two Shifterai put him on his pony. Kenyen mounted his mare and took the reins of the pony. The man named Zellan tucked his clothes into Kenyen's saddlebags and shifted shape into a large, rangy, gray-furred wolf. The short fur on his forehead looked mangy, however; Kenyen belatedly realized that was because the skin beneath it was scarred.

He's one of the ones Banished from the Plains, Kenyen realized.

"We go to de hiding plaze." Zellan stated the words carefully through his wolfish muzzle. "You, Catzon, follow me on de road. I am fazter den I look; you vill not be able to run from me, eider."

"I didn't have time to hear much before being sent on my way, but I did hear enough to know you have a sweet setup in these mountains," Kenyen retorted. "I'm not about to ruin it. Not when I have a chance at a piece of your little pie."

Huffing, Zellan trotted up the path. Knowing the hearing of a wolf—one of his own shapes—was quite good, Kenyen didn't try to reassure Traver. He did, however, slip the other man a quick wink when he glanced back, making sure the mountain pony was comfortable with following his larger mare. Some of the worry left Traver's gaze, but not all of it. Not when Kenyen gave him a sharp look.

I may not think things through as fast as my brother—I just know this is going to come back and bite me on the tail if these Mongrel shifters get a hold of Nollan Sil Quen and find out I didn't come from him—but it's not like I had enough time to think of anything better. Dissatisfied but unable to do anything about it for the moment, Kenyen urged both steeds up the semi-steep path, headed back to the road that mounted the slopes of the foothills flanking either side.

The wolf glanced back a few times, but continued upward, moving first on the path, then through the bushes at the side of the main road once they reached it. Kenyen followed dutifully, glad the pony wasn't fussing too much from the scent of the predator leading them. *If I didn't need to know the identities of these Mongrel types, I'd have rather fought this fellow in straightforward combat. I'm* good *at fighting. Father Sky . . . if You can hear me here in this foreign land, help me be good at disguising and dissembling, too. It's not just my life on the line but the life of this Traver fellow, too . . . and however many more may wind up duped, threatened, impersonated, and slaughtered by Family Mongrel.*

Gods, how am I going to get word of this mess back to the princess and the others? I don't dare leave Traver in this cur's hands. Until I can get him free in such a way that they wouldn't even think of tracking him . . . Kenyen had no clue how to manage that. The twists of Fate, distant Threefold God of another land, had put him in this awkward place.

Here's hoping that, whatever comes, I can act fast enough to save all our hides.

* * *

Cullerog Twil Ziff—if that was his name—rubbed his gray-stubbled chin, eyeing Kenyen in the fading light of dusk. The cabin behind him, not much more than a shepherd's croft at the edge of a high meadow, had taken the trio the rest of the day to reach. With the scent of smoke curling up from its stone chimney and the muffled baaing of sheep herded into their barn for the night, the scene was remarkably tranquil for such a tense moment.

"You say Nollan sent you?" Cullerog challenged.

"That's right. Though he'll probably deny it," Kenyen added. The long ride had given him time to think of several defenses for this moment. "There were rumors of Shifterai on his trail when I was kicked out. Something about some cur of a shifter female claiming some Family Mongrel was committing crimes up here. So he'll probably deny our meeting from fear of secretly being watched." He smirked. "Me, I'm just looking for work and a place to live . . . and the chance to keep doing what I love doing."

"And that is?" Zellan asked, stepping through the doorway of the cottage. He had taken Traver inside, supposedly to the root cellar, and now appeared alone in the doorway.

Reaching for the braid at the top of his head, which he had tied in place between saddling the mare and the pony, Kenyen carefully, subtly reshaped his forehead under the guise of working the locks free of their plait. A scrape of his palm dropped the fringe of hair and its flap of flesh, revealing the fake brand he had shaped, long enough for the elderly man to get a good look. Smoothing the false flap upward again, he rebraided his hair with a few flicks of his fingers. Cullerog grunted, watching him fasten the thong in place.

"What did you get that for? In specific, I mean," the older shifter ordered, lifting his chin.

"Well, first off, I killed a man," Kenyen stated plainly, keeping his expression impassive. Zellan snorted, and Cullerog did not look impressed. Keeping his tone matter-of-fact, Kenyen ad-libbed, "Then I took a bite in the heat of battle rage . . . and I liked it. So I kept eating him. I didn't kill the next one, though. I just started eating her."

Both men blinked, staring at him.

Kenyen shrugged. "That's when they caught me and cast me out. I should've gagged her first, or maybe killed her, though I liked the way she struggled."

Cullerog wrinkled his nose. "Well, don't do that *here*. Not on a whim—not without orders. We've worked hard to blend in. And what we're looking for in the Nespah Valley is too important to draw any further undue attention to ourselves."

Lifting his chin at the cabin, Kenyen said, "Zellan said I could eat him when you're done with this one. I can wait until then."

"—I didn't say *that*!" Zellan interjected firmly.

Kenyen ignored his protest. He kept his gaze on the older shifter. "Of course, if I'm going to be the one imitating him, I'm not exactly going to eat him right away, now am I? Besides, it's like honey. It's a special treat, the kind you don't eat every day—if I did, I'd wind up fatter than an outkingdom pig."

Cullerog snorted. "We'll see. For now, he's my 'special guest' . . . as are you. You'll stay here tonight, though we won't chain you up in the cellar. Zellan, go fetch three of the valley elders from your area. Tell them to be here by midnight, and don't show yourself to anyone else. As for you, 'Catson,' go stable those mounts, then come inside. You'll eat mutton tonight, not man."

"Whatever you say." Leading his mare and the pony toward the barn, Kenyen wondered when, or even if, he'd get a chance to talk privately with Traver. Improvisation would only carry them so far in this unexpected, increasingly convoluted charade.

THREE

Solyn was fairly confident her family was alone when they sat down to dinner. Her sister, Luelyn, fidgeted, eager to have the basket of biscuits passed her way, though her gaze was more on the dish of butter and the jar of honey waiting to be applied to them. Their mother, Reina, carefully poured out the steeped tea, a blend of freshly picked leaves for the aroma and partially fermented ones for the base. Her husband, Ysander, accepted the first cup. Sipping carefully at it, he nodded. Not that he was a tea planter by trade, being the local blacksmith, but it was his place as head of the household to approve of the first cup.

Solyn's older brother, Ysenk, lived in his own home with his wife and newborn son. Their cottage was placed a little higher up the slopes of the sprawling plantation, though not too far from the rest of the homes sheltering Reina's extended family. Rather than trying to divide up the family lands into smaller and smaller plots, some wise Corredai soul of ages before had formed a cooperative holding.

It had proven both profitable and popular. The hills and valleys of the Correda Mountains had been dotted with such holdings from a time long before the collapse of the old Aian Empire. It was that sense of community and communal property that had allowed them to survive despite the abrupt loss of their central government. Sometimes the Corredai pushed back the edges of the local forests to plant and tend more tea; other times they simply added more cropland to the local, terraced slopes, and shared the produce and the profits with all.

Despite the way the locals shared the land and its produce, most families still preferred to live in their own homes whenever possible, however large or small. As the resident Healer, Reina had inherited one of the largest houses in the holding. With her husband also being the valley blacksmith, they could have afforded to furnish it with fancy things, but it hosted the same sort of furniture as any other home, neatly carved, cushion-lined, and clean.

Tonight's dinner was a sauce-and-bread combination made from dove meat, a few vegetables, and the biscuits. It was simple fare, the sort most families ate at this time of year. Solyn poked at her food with her fork and wondered what exotic lowlands food Traver would get to eat. She also worried whether he would be safe, sneaking away from the others. He had no way to tell a shapeshifter from a real man.

"Oh, Solyn, some good news," her father stated, pausing before his first bite. "Your cousin Zanbar, from down in the Tequah Valley, found another magery book. Samdan, the tinker, dropped it off at my shop when he brought me the metal scraps he had traded for on his route uphill. I forgot to bring it home, though. We can go find it after supper."

Poking at her food, she nodded. "Another book would be nice, especially if it's one I don't have. What I *really* need . . ."

Reina reached over and touched her older daughter's forearm. "What you *really* need are lessons. You don't *have* to stay. No one has tried to find . . . it . . . for the last six months. At least, not that I could tell."

"It's a false lull before the storm," Solyn stated, shaking her head. "I *know* they're after it. I know they won't give up. And if there's any little thing I can do to stop them from hurting more people in their quest to find it . . ."

"We'll go get you the book," her father promised. "I could also ask Samdan to take word back down the mountain that you need an actual mage-tutor—we can pay in delicate mountain tea, if nothing else," he joked. He gave her a lopsided smile. "Or I could put up some barstock as payment. Not that I'm happy about how much Tunric has been charging his neighbors for what his miners have been digging out of the mountains, but you need actual lessons, not just book learning."

Luelyn snuck a bit of butter onto her plate, then stealthily reached for the honey pot. Reina deftly scooted it out of the way, pushing the bowl of meat and vegetables into her youngest child's reaching hands.

"No sweets until you've had your meats. You know the rule," she admonished the young girl.

"Yes, Mum," Luelyn mumbled. She halfheartedly buttered her split biscuits anyway. Solyn reached over and spooned a bit of the sauce over the biscuits for her.

"Good girl. Thank you for helping bring in the herbs the other day and digging up all those roots today," Reina praised her child. She gave Solyn a pointed look. "We need to make more cheese in the coming week. Greenvein cheese."

Luelyn wrinkled her nose. "I don't like it. It tastes funny."

Ysander smirked at his wife. "It's an acquired family taste. Did you want to bring some of the ripened stuff by the forge tomorrow, dear?"

"Not tomorrow. The older rounds aren't quite ripe enough, yet. Solyn, you will help me, yes?" Reina asked her daughter.

Solyn nodded. Greenvein cheese was very important to her family. Only a few others in the Nespah region liked it, but then most of the families in the valley tolerated Reina's experiments in food. She was the second-best Healer for three valleys around, ranked right behind Uncle Veston—not that he was actually related to anyone; that was just what everyone called the elderly man. There were other cheeses her mother had created and produced, too, more popular ones, but greenvein was special. Too special, in a way.

"Eat your sauce, Luelyn," Reina ordered her youngest. "Then you can have a biscuit with butter and honey. Both of you."

Sighing, Solyn dug into her own food. She had to firmly set aside her nerves over Traver's mission and think of more pleasant things in order to be able to swallow her food, but managed after a moment. It was important to set her sister a good example, after all, and doubly important to make sure the subtext behind her mother's words passed unnoticed.

If it hadn't been for Traver gasping out the name, Kenyen would not have known that the aging leader of the three summoned elders was the one who had been selected to imitate the now long-dead Tunric Tel Vem. The body in the cave had been too desiccated and insect-nibbled to know.

"Tunric" looked somewhat handsome for his age; his brow was fairly smooth but his jowls were starting to sag. Broad shoulders and muscular arms couldn't hide the curve of a paunch around his belly, but that didn't give Kenyen a clue, either. Most shifters who continued to travel, trade, and fight in the warbands kept themselves lean and fit, but some of the men who retired to tend the herds and help the Family in its spring through fall migrations did develop a little bit of a saddle-gut after a while, so that wasn't a hint as to his true identity, either.

For his own part, Kenyen held himself carefully still, face impassive but muscles ready to move in any direction if needed. He had kept most of his answers short during the interrogation by Tunric and two other middle-aged men. Yes, Nollan had sent him uphill. No, he didn't know much about what was going on. Yes, he knew the trick with the forehead flap.

Yes, he could shift a full seven shapes and hold himself in his best shapes for hours on end, as well as hold himself in partial versions of those shapes hour after hour. Yes, he had killed and eaten a man several turnings of Brother Moon ago, then bitten chunks out of a girl until her screams had summoned other shifters to come rescue her. No, he didn't know exactly what Tunric and the rest were looking for, though he did know they were taking over prominent villagers' identities and living lives of relative leisure, and wanted in on that aspect of things.

At least, a life leisurely enough to allow someone like Tunric to develop a saddle-gut problem. Kenyen wasn't foolish enough to state it that way, however. He wasn't too sure why Tunric, Zellan, and the others hadn't asked for his real name. Even Kenyen would've thought they'd want to know, to backtrack his story. *Then again, I suppose they don't want me asking about theirs, either; what a person doesn't know, he cannot be forced to give away. Not that I'd complain, since my story would fall apart rather fast.*

". . . What do you know about blacksmithing?" Tunric finally asked him.

The non sequitur puzzled Kenyen. "I . . . learned a little bit of it, back in the Family."

He hadn't claimed which Family he was from, yet. Tunric lifted his chin in a go-on gesture, so Kenyen elaborated.

"When I was young, back in one of the farming years when we

stayed by the capital, there was an interest in developing armor and weapons for the women and the non-shifters. We had a good supply of iron and coal for making steel, so between planting and weeding, a number of us got to spend time in the city forges, helping smelt the ore, pump the bellows . . . I even had a chance to hammer on the steel," he stated, shrugging. "I liked it, but I was more interested in being a shapeshifter. I can't remember which bordering kingdom was making everyone worried at the time, and it later came to nothing, so we didn't do much more than the one summer's worth of work."

"Do you still remember enough to make something small?" Tunric pressed. "Like, say, a knife?"

Kenyen frowned in thought. "I *might* be able to . . . but I'd have to watch a blacksmith working with metal for a bit before all of it came back to me."

Tunric looked at the other two elders. They exchanged a series of looks, eyebrows lifting and lowering, mouths twisting, then quirking. One of them finally gestured at Tunric, who sighed roughly.

"Fine." Turning back to Kenyen, he lifted his chin. "Imitate my face."

Unlike the blacksmith question, Kenyen had anticipated something like this. Actually, he had expected to be asked to imitate Traver's face, but no one had brought the youth up from the cellar, yet. Studying the older man's appearance for a moment, Kenyen reached for the saddlebags he had tucked under the stout table separating the sleeping half of the cottage from the eating half. Inside the left one was the steel mirror he had salvaged from the forest floor.

"*Without* looking in a reflective surface," Tunric ordered, guessing what Kenyen was doing.

Sighing, Kenyen sat up and acquiesced. It wasn't easy; he had to *feel* his face expand with the plumpness of age, feel the sagging of his cheeks and the graying of his hair. Unlike Cullerog, Tunric was clean-shaven, but his jowls did have hints of black and gray stubble.

His brows were also a bit bushier, his gray-salted, dark brown hair pulled back in a tight braid, and his nose had been broken twice. Kenyen almost swerved it to his left, before remembering the mirror rule; if he was supposed to imitate Tunric, it had to swerve to the right instead, pointing the opposite way from what Kenyen himself saw.

He only changed his head, however. To have fully imitated the older man, Kenyen would've stressed his skills as a shifter. Partial shifts were one thing, particularly brief ones. Full shifts, or repeated, lengthy shifts would have required a sacrifice in compensation.

Zellan and the two elders peered carefully between the two of them. They nodded slowly after several moments. "Not bad," the gray white–haired man admitted. Kenyen hadn't been introduced to him. "Not bad at all. He didn't quite get the eyelashes right."

Kenyen squinted. They were doing this in the light of the hearthfire and half a dozen oil-dipped reeds; their smoky flames fluttered and curled, making it somewhat difficult to see whenever a draft seeped through the one-room cottage. He made a few small changes to his eyes, and the elder nodded in approval.

"Not bad. He just might do."

"No, not bad. Most of the free men we have aren't the right age for this. It takes a young man to play a young man, but some are too old, and the remainder are too young," the other elder stated. His hair was more gray than black, but lacked the white of the first one, and his mouth shadowed by a mustache that ended in long points on either side of his chin.

"Tell me about the boy I'd be imitating," Kenyen offered, "and I'll tell you whether or not I can do it."

Tunric chuckled darkly. "How arrogant. Keep it in check, *boy*. We've been playing this for as long as you've been alive."

Kenyen knew that wasn't true; the words of his sister-in-law's mother hadn't hinted at anything remotely related to the theft of

Corredai identities, and he was older than his sister-in-law. He didn't argue, though.

"He's the son of a farmer. A dirt grubber and a cow milker. He's also best friends with the daughter of a certain blacksmith and his Healer wife . . . and apparently became her betrothed right before leaving the area," Tunric stated, mouth twisting.

"If he's a farmer, why do you need to know if I know blacksmithing? Shouldn't you be asking if I can fake farming like a Corredai?" Kenyen asked.

"You're fresh off the Plains. Unless you went out of your way to avoid it, you know how to tend animals and grow food," Zellan dismissed.

"We believe the blacksmith knows the secret for making a certain something which interests us," Tunric explained.

"It's not bluesteel, is it?" Kenyen asked, puzzled by the possibility. While it was true only a few blacksmiths on the Shifting Plains knew how to make the metal, which was the only metal capable of solidly wounding and permanently scarring a shapeshifter, he couldn't figure out why Banished criminals would want to get their hands on more of it.

"No. Not bluesteel—what it is, you don't need to know. Not at this point in time," Tunric dismissed. "But if you're going to imitate the betrothed of the blacksmith's daughter, then it's possible you'll have the opportunity to hang around his workshop without nearly as much suspicion hanging over your motives as anyone else would have."

"Do you want me to apprentice to him?" Kenyen asked, lifting a brow.

"Only if he offers," the white-haired elder countered. "Don't push. Things go badly when you push. As it is, you'll be walking into this role with the handicap of suffering from a blow to the head."

Kenyen twitched, taking a half step back in pure, instinctive defense. Tunric chuckled, eyeing his raised hands. "Relax, boy. We'll teach you how to *fake* a concussion. Though we might have to rough you up a bit to make it look believable. Your betrothed's mother is a Healer, after all—what do you think of females?"

The sudden change in subject threw Kenyen. He blinked, recalling belatedly the women-hating words written down in the book that had sent him and the others into this land. Aware that all four men were studying his reactions to his words, Kenyen answered the question. "Ah . . . nothing, really. They're important for cooking and tumbling and begetting sons, but . . . I guess you could say I really don't care, either way."

"Can you seduce a woman?" Zellan asked him. "You'll want to stay on the blacksmith's good side; you can't just take her and tumble her. Though she is an outkingdom woman, and therefore no different than any earth-whore from the Plains."

If he hadn't already read the accounts of the horrible ordeals suffered by his sister-in-law's mother, Kenyen might not have been able to keep his face calm. Calling an earth-priestess an earth-whore was a deep insult to the time-honored, culturally honorable task of giving physical comfort to unmarried men, back on the Plains. Women were to be respected, and maidens allowed to remain chaste, untouched.

After the Aian Empire had shattered, its capital literally turned into a crater during the Convocation of the Gods, the survivors in the area had been about as civilized as the deeds written about this Family Mongrel. That the Shifterai had pulled themselves out of such violent barbarism and had established a successful, peaceful society was something to be praised, not vilified. Earth-priestesses gave their efforts out of compassion, nor were all of their tasks sexual in nature.

So instead of flinching at the insult, he gave Zellan's words careful thought. "*Can* I seduce a woman? As in, ingratiate myself with this betrothed girl, to the point where she'll encourage her family to cozy up to me, or at least permit me to cozy up to them? It would help if she's attractive, of course, but . . . I think I can. If nothing else, as the daughter of a Healer and 'my' betrothed, I could play the part of the grateful invalid."

"Females are often quite gullible, if they think they're needed," Zellan agreed, smirking.

The dismissive insult turned Kenyen's stomach. It wasn't nearly difficult enough now to picture the abuse Atava's mother, Ellet, had suffered at the hands of these callous curs. *Yet this is only the tip of the claw. I suspect the wounds these beasts tear through their victims are the kind which dig painfully, permanently deep.*

"Alright. Light the globe and take him into the cellar. Get all the information you can out of the boy," Tunric ordered. "Imitate his whole body, too, though you're close enough to him in size—you might lose a shape. Run through your mind the ones you want to keep, and which one you're willing to forget."

Kenyen nodded. He didn't like the idea of losing a shape, but knew it would probably happen anyway. He hadn't been able to progress beyond seven pure forms for the last two years, so it wasn't likely he'd be able to add "Traver Ys Ten" as his eighth shape at this stage of his life.

I'll keep the tiger and the wolf; they're good fighting forms. The magpie for flight, or maybe the owl—I might have to fly about at night, so I'll keep both. That's four. I should probably keep the viper for the venom I've learned to replicate, and the horse form in case I need to carry Traver out of here myself. Which leaves my hunting cat shape, I guess. I like being a medium-sized cat . . . but of all the shapes I know, it's the least useful for this moment. And I know I can get it back. I lost the viper one when I tried being a duck for a while, then decided to go back to being a snake; that venom has been handy in the past, even if it gives me a stomachache if I swallow too much.

Zellan had pulled up the trapdoor to the root cellar. He slung a waterskin over his shoulder, picked up a milky white globe in a net, rapped it once sharply to make the enchanted glass glow with a bright, steady light, and descended carefully into the shadowed depths. Grabbing the steel mirror from his saddlebags, Kenyen followed the other man into the cellar, where Traver awaited them. Rather than being bound hand and foot, the youth had been hobbled at his feet and manacled to the stone-dug wall by a modest length of chain.

It hadn't been necessary to gag him; the shepherd's croft stood quite alone on this particular foothill, with no signs of neighbors or paths to other homes for the last two miles. Traver could have shouted himself hoarse and no one but the shapeshifters and sheep would have heard him. From the quiet but clear murmurs of the three elders' voices overhead, discussing some minor business related to the mine that Tunric apparently oversaw, Traver had probably heard every word of their earlier debate.

Kenyen dared a brief, subtle wink while Zellan's back was still turned, but his expression was calm, almost bored, when Zellan glanced back at him. With his features no longer copying Tunric's stubbled jowls, it wasn't difficult to look impassive.

Hanging the netted lightglobe from a hook overhead, Zellan lifted his chin at Kenyen, then looked at the Corredai male. "I know you've been listening to us, up above. I also know that *you* know he's going to copy your face and take your place. If you want that pretty little girl of yours to *survive* what he needs to do, you will tell him *everything* about yourself."

Kenyen slowly licked his lips, then gave Traver a feral grin. Zellan lifted his brows briefly at the younger shifter, then looked back at the chained man. Traver swallowed, touched the cuffs on his wrists with a soft clink of his chains, and nodded. "I . . . I'll do it. Just don't hurt her. And you *will* let me go, right?"

"As free as a bird, once the elders get what they want . . . and once I get paid in my cut of the prize," Kenyen agreed, doing his best to sound like a hardened, uncaring criminal. "Of course, the more I know about *you* and how to *be* you, the less I'll have to beguile her with a tumble. They smell so tasty when I tumble them, too . . ."

Zellan shot him a quelling look, then tossed the waterskin he had brought to the manacled youth. He lifted his chin at Traver. "Start talking, boy."

Traver looked between the two of them. "Um . . . what should I talk about?"

"Start with your family, follow it up with a typical day in your life, and work your way outward from there," Kenyen ordered, holding up the steel mirror so that he could start practicing not only Traver's face but his facial expressions as he spoke. "Things that you like, things that you don't like, childhood memories that you remember with fondness, things you remember with fear . . . but start with yourself and your family."

"And you won't hurt me?" Traver asked.

Kenyen leveled a firm look at the slightly younger man. "If you don't try my patience, no."

"Um . . . I'm Traver Ys Ten. Son of Ysal Trud Hen and Tenaria Tev Kee," he explained. "I have two older brothers, Belseth Ys Nar—their mother was Narian, she died before I was born—and Sellah Ys Nar. They both have their own farmholds farther down the Valley. My older sister is Namya Ys Ten, and my younger brother and sister are Tellik and Tinia Ys Ten; we all live at home with our parents—they all look like me, of course, brown eyes, wavy brown hair, not too stout but not too slender . . ."

Hours later, when Kenyen was tired and Traver was resting in silence, his voice rendered hoarse, unable to say much more, the Mongrel shifters finally left the two young men alone. Sort of alone. Hints of the gray light of dawn filtered down from the open trapdoor, mingling with the steady glow of the lightglobe and the flickering glow of the rush lights upstairs. Knowing that they didn't have much time, Kenyen shifted close enough to clasp Traver's hand.

The two of them exchanged worried looks, though the Shifterai tried to convey hope toward the Corredai. Traver breathed deep, gave the opening to the upstairs a wary look, then shifted his hands toward the waistband of his clothes. Frowning in confusion, Kenyen watched as the slightly younger man pulled at his laces and . . . bared himself? His disbelieving expression earned a pointed glare from the Corredai male. Traver pointed firmly at his manhood, then tugged on something hidden on the underside of his flesh.

A ring. A beaded one, which pierced his foreskin. Deeply disturbed—ears and noses were often pierced on the Plains, but never *that*—Kenyen watched Traver carefully remove it, trying his best not to make his chains clank. When the youth held it out to him, Kenyen recoiled a little. Rolling his eyes, Traver grasped his hand and dropped the ring in it, mouthing something. Unable to make sense of it, Kenyen gave up and leaned close.

"Solyn expects me to wear it," Traver breathed. "She'll know you're a shifter without it. You have to wear it."

Face hot with embarrassment, Kenyen reluctantly accepted the metal loop. *What kind of a maiden—outkingdom or otherwise—would demand her betrothed wear a ring on his . . . his . . . ? And I have to wear it, if I'm to be successful at pretending to be this man?*

Footsteps overhead warned both of them that the gray-haired elder was returning; hurrying, Traver relaced his trousers, hiding himself once more. Zellan had gone upstairs to sleep a few hours back, and the other man—still unnamed—had come down to take his turn in watching their "newest" member of Family Mongrel, leaving just long enough to make a trip to the refreshing hut outside. Shifting back slightly to hide his proximity to their prisoner, Kenyen clenched his fist around the ring and made a show of smothering a yawn.

"No rest for you," the aging shifter grunted, working his way down the rungs of the ladder. "You'll need to look exhausted and out of it, if you're to fake a concussion. Show me your game face."

Flexing his muscles, Kenyen shifted from his own heart-shaped face to the somewhat more oval visage of Traver Ys Ten. He also shifted his body, picking up more muscles in his arms and less in his legs. The whole transformation took less than three seconds.

As he had thought might happen, the memory of what it felt like to be a hunting cat, only slightly larger than a typical house cat, was already fading from his consciousness. Kenyen could still consciously remember how to shift into any of his other shapes, but looking like Traver Ys Ten, being Traver Ys Ten, took concentration. Memory. That robbed him of the room to be aware of at least one other shape.

"How do I sound?" he asked.

The stocky elder raised his brows. ". . . Remarkably like the boy. A little rough around the edges, though."

"Well, he's been speaking for hours." Kenyen glanced at Traver, narrowing his eyes slightly in a feigned show of wariness. "Maybe a little too helpful. I hope you haven't been lying to us."

"You said if I cooperated, you'd let me go. And that you'd leave the valley," Traver croaked, licking his lips. "That's what I want. I want all of you gone. So you go take whatever you're looking for and just go, and leave the rest of us alone. That's the deal, right?"

". . . Right. That's the deal." Kenyen didn't believe it for an instant. The other shapeshifters would not want to leave any witnesses alive, which meant Traver was a dead man. "Well, you just stay put, and be nice and cooperative. I'll be back for more information. Don't make me track you down."

The growled threat made Traver nod, then shake his head. Turning toward the ladder, Kenyen reached for the rungs. The other shifter cleared his throat. Glancing back, Kenyen lifted a brow in inquiry.

"You'll want his clothes. Take them now. Give him yours so he doesn't freeze at night," the elder added, holding out the keys to the manacles shackling the young man to the root cellar wall. "We're almost ready for you to make your debut. You'll need to *be* Traver Ys Ten from head to toe to pull this off."

Sighing, Kenyen accepted the keys and turned back to the other young man. Tucking the beaded ring into a fold of flesh in his palm, he started to unlock the manacles. A thought occurred to him while reaching for the ankle cuffs. Carefully shaping one finger into a stiff, tough claw, he in turn shaped that into an imitation of the next key.

Using his body to hide what he was doing, he tested it in the lock. It hurt a little, twisting his hand hard enough to move the metal pins inside the hole, but it did work. That wasn't the problem, however; the problem would be figuring out a way to get Traver away from these curs without them being able to track him by scent.

"Get your clothes off," Kenyen ordered gruffly. He took a few moments to subtly study the ends of the keys, doing his best to commit their angles to memory without being obvious. There was no guarantee he'd be able to get ahold of them later, and a high chance he'd be in a hurry to get Traver free.

Once Traver had stripped off everything but his underdrawers, Kenyen did the same, then donned the plain brown linen pants, lighter brown shirt, and darker brown tunic the youth had been wearing. The smell of the Corredai permeated his clothes. Kenyen was grateful most outkingdom residents didn't have the sensitive nostrils of a shifter; had they tried to attempt this on the Plains, those who knew the victim best would be able to smell through any such disguise.

The wool socks smelled even worse, full of sweat and fear and the need to be changed. Pulling them on with a flinch, Kenyen stuffed his feet into Traver's calf-length boots, grateful those at least were close enough in size to his own that he didn't have to keep his feet constantly reshaped. Rechecking the buttons along his shoulder and side, he wrapped Traver's leather belt around his hips. Traver in turn tugged on his gathered *breikas*, his linen *chamak*, and his boots. The Corredai wrinkled his nose at having to do so without the cushioning of socks but didn't complain openly.

The only things which they didn't trade were the tinder kit Kenyen carried, his money pouch, his eating knife, and his pectoral necklace. The beaded collar was too distinctively Shifterai, with its seven rows of animal forms carved on the small spheres of wire-linked wood, so he couldn't wear it. But neither could he leave it behind. For now, Kenyen stuffed it into his, or rather, Traver's pouch next to the metal tin containing his char cloth, flint, and steel knapper.

"Up you go," the elder shifter ordered Kenyen, taking the keys so he could restore their prisoner's bindings. "We'll be scraping your head and giving it a bloody bruise, which you will exaggerate rather than downplay. You'll also need to roll in the mud—if you can twist your ankle or sprain your wrist, even better. The plan is to have Zellan find you tumbled in a ravine, your pony gone, and your memory dazed."

"Let me guess. I ran off from the tea caravan because I forgot something back home, only my pony got spooked and abandoned me before I made it, correct?" Kenyen asked, face and voice and build still shaped to look like the young man they were holding.

"You can't remember why . . . but that's what Zellan proposed to the rest of the caravan when he offered to go looking for 'you,'" the unnamed elder agreed, huffing with age as he crawled up the ladder.

The man imitating Tunric had long since gone home, as had the eldest one, the white-haired shifter. Cullerog apparently lived here, but he wasn't in the cabin, no doubt gone to check on the sheep before turning them out to their stone-walled fold for the day. Zellan breathed softly where he lay sprawled on the bed, his body limp and his face slack in the way that only deep sleep could provide.

The gray-haired shifter picked up a stout length of wood almost as thick as his wrist, selecting it from the bin by the hearth. "Bend over, boy, so I can hit you on the head with this."

"In a Netherhell, you will," Kenyen growled. He held up his hand, his gaze firm. "I'll hit *myself*, thank you. I'm *not* going to bend over and let you hit me so hard, you splatter my brain across the floor—I don't want to find out this was just an elaborate setup staged by those bitches back home to get their revenge on me."

The older man snorted in derision, then chuckled. "Maybe you *are* one of us after all. Good choice, boy—but if you don't hit hard enough, I *will* clobber you enough to make it look real."

Kenyen concentrated, drawing up memories of his many injuries over the last five years, fighting with the members of his warband. He didn't even have to take the stick from the other shifter, let alone swing it. His left eye, still shaped like the Corredai's, blackened and grew puffy. His hair shifted, sporting not one, but two lumps. His right ankle twinged, shifting his weight to his left leg, and his left arm sagged from its socket. The elder blinked, brows lifting in surprise.

". . . Either you've pretended to be injured before, boy," he murmured, "or you've been injured a *lot*, to be able to re-create it so convincingly on a whim."

Kenyen almost pointed out that if he'd had only three more shapes, qualifying himself for the rank of *multerai*, shapeshifter-lord, he'd have been put into the rotation for his warband's leadership. A last-moment twinge of caution stayed his tongue. Instead, he merely said, "I've taken a lot of damage, yes, but I've also learned how to survive it."

"Good. You'll need to be tough. Just don't *show* it. That boy down there is a weakling," the unnamed man dismissed. "Pretend to be him, and you'll get close enough to the blacksmith to be trusted. The moment you are that trusted, we'll tell you what to look for." Crossing to the bed, he whacked the frame with the stick. "Wake up, Zellan Fin Don!"

Zellan, or rather the shifter playing him, woke with a snort. Twisting onto his side, he pushed halfway up on one elbow, blinking at the two of them. "Wha . . . ? Oh. It's time, already?"

"Yes, it's time, you lazy mutt. Go drag this son of a cur through the mud, then haul him back home to that Healer bitch and her little girl," the elder ordered.

"As for you, and Cullerog," Kenyen interjected, "keep the *real* Traver alive and unharmed. I know I didn't learn enough to imitate him flawlessly. That means I'll need more cooperation out of him."

Zellan snorted. "Are you *concerned* for him? I thought you ate people."

"Only when I'm in the mood." The words turned his stomach, but they had to be said. Kenyen didn't want to give these men any excuse to doubt that he was as much of a bastard cur as they were. "Besides, any herdsman will tell you that you always tend your flock carefully when raising them, even if the end result is an intent to slit their throats and hang them up to bleed dry."

"I'll go get that pony ready," Zellan stated, levering himself off the bed. "We can pretend it was lost when you fell, then recaptured shortly before finding you."

"What about my horse?" Kenyen asked. The elder snorted.

"That'll be your 'gift' to join us, of course. Traver wouldn't have the means to acquire such a fine steed," the stocky, older man dismissed. "He's just a farmer's boy. A dirt grubber."

"I'm expecting to get back four times what that mare is worth, off the Plains," Kenyen warned him. What he wanted to do was protest the mare's loss, period, but couldn't. That wasn't a part of the role he was supposed to play. "As it was, they barely let me keep her when they threw me out. So whatever it is you want, it had better be worth it."

"Oh, it is. If the rumors are true . . ." Grinning, the elderly shifter patted his flap-covered forehead with his fingers, then shooed Kenyen and Zellan out of the cottage. "Go on; you've a long ride to get back home, and a bit of a rough time dragging yourself around, making it look like you really did fall."

Nodding, Kenyen headed outside. Not to the barn, though that was his eventual goal. The first thing he had to do, however, was to clean off that . . . ring . . . hastily buried in the skin of his palm, and dredge up enough courage to apply it to the necessary spot. Being a Shifterai, he wouldn't have to actually pierce such delicate skin, but he would have to shift a small hole for it . . . and then remember to maintain it, so that he didn't accidentally lose said ring down one of his trouser legs later.

As dangerous as his situation was, Kenyen couldn't stop worrying over one particular thought in the back of his head. *What kind of woman, outlander or not, would* want *a man to pierce that part of himself?*

The slopes of the Nespah Valley, covered in the tea plantations and terraced gardens of the various holdings claiming the land, looked like a patchwork blanket sewn from a thousand shades of living green. Most of it was darker than the paler pastels of spring, but here and there, the stone hedges supporting each terrace had been strewn with wildflowers, sending streaks of bright colors across the hillsides. Fruit and nut trees lined the ridges and the vales, waves of wheat and oats rippled in sinewy streaks, and mossy-roofed, pale stone cottages dotted the landscape.

The scent of tea perfumed the air; not quite pungent, it played the dominant scent for all but the closest of those blooms. Still,

Kenyen breathed in a hundred different aromas, from the wild roses lining the hedge walls rising up on his right, to the scent of roasted beef wafting out of one of the larger homes lower down the hillside on his left. The rippling curves of the terraces and the mazelike paths between the tea hedges gave the landscape a scribbled texture; the shouting peals of children at play, racing from level to level with baskets bouncing on their arms and dogs chasing merrily at their heels, gave the sounds of the scene a happy level of chaos to match.

Not that he had control over where they were going. Zellan had picked up his own mountain pony at an inn just a couple of hours from the shepherd's cottage, hastily left behind in the need to track down the missing Traver with shifter tricks. Now he held the reins of Traver's pony, leading it and its swaying lump of Traver-shaped flesh, since Kenyen was trying to look too injured and dazed to have guided his own steed.

From the sudden quieting of the children and their wide-eyed stares as the two men passed, Kenyen wondered if he had gone a little overboard in dotting his face with scrapes and bruises. Nor did it help that Zellan had literally dragged Kenyen behind his mountain mare for several yards, scraping and muddying his borrowed clothes for verisimilitude.

Turning onto a path that rose a little bit higher, they made their way to a cluster of homes a little too big to be called cottages. This was a prosperous holding, for many of the buildings had been plastered and whitewashed beneath their slate-and-moss rooflines. It also boasted the large, stone-walled blacksmith's forge Traver had mentioned. The other buildings were surrounded by herb beds, vegetable patches, even chicken coops sitting in the middle of reed-fenced runs, but the smithy sat in the middle of a broad, flat, flagstone-lined patch. That, Kenyen guessed, was no doubt so that any fires accidentally sparked wouldn't be able to spread far enough to threaten the other structures.

As it was, the makeshift courtyard around the forge served as the gathering place for the locals. They drifted onto the flagstones, the men in gathered *breikas* similar to what the Shifterai wore on the plains, the women in gathered skirts instead of more sensible trousers. Then again, they weren't expected to pack up and ride every handful of days, following their herds nine months out of the year.

Men, women, and children alike peered in curiosity at the injuries Kenyen sported and muttered in worry when they recognized the bruised and bloodied features as those of the missing Traver. One of the older women abandoned the basket she was weaving on the stoop of her home. Bustling over to the second house from hers, she rapped on the door. "Reina! Solyn! We need a Healer out here! Traver and Zellan came back without the caravan!"

Within moments, two women emerged. They looked like before-and-after images of each other; both were slender with somewhat heart-shaped faces, both had hazel green eyes and brown hair pulled into braids, with curly little wisps that tried to escape here and there. Both were clad in faded blue skirts and matching *chamsa* tunics, their garments partially covered in stained beige aprons.

The elder one had dark, polished horn buttons holding her tunic together down her right side; the younger one had pale bone buttons. The elder had her hair braided and looped around her head; the younger wore her braid dangling down her back. Beyond that, the only difference between them was the twenty or thirty years that had weathered the elder's face.

Wiping her hands on her apron, Reina Lai Fa—wife of the blacksmith Ysander Mil Ben, according to Traver—flicked her fingers at a couple of the curious loiterers. "Well? Don't just stand there! Help the boy down, and get him into my sickroom. If he hurts half as bad as he looks, he could fall out of the saddle at any moment."

Kenyen remembered to blink and give her a dazed look, then winced and whimpered, moving stiffly as helping hands lifted him down from the saddle. His injuries were faked, far less painful than they technically looked, but he knew enough—and remembered enough, from injuries past—how to move slowly and awkwardly, as if they were much worse.

It didn't take long for him to be ushered, limping, into the home of the local Healer. The house was large enough; it had an entry hall with three doors. One led to the right, to what looked like the family gathering place; one led back to what looked like a kitchen, and the one on the left led to a smallish room with a pair of tables pushed against the walls, a couple of stools, a chair, a small hearth sheltering an equally small fire, and a cot. One of the tables was crowded with bowls, bottles, tools, and bandages in neatly but tightly spaced arrangements; the other was bare and clean, broad enough to have supported a man.

It was to the cot that he was led, not to the bare table or one of the stools. Female hands plucked at his clothes, unbuckling his belt, tugging off his boots and socks—he remembered to wince when the left one was removed from his mock-swollen ankle—and then Solyn shooed the other women out of the room, letting her mother unbutton Traver's brown tunic from Kenyen's reshaped chest. Zellan lingered in the room, the concern furrowing his brow no doubt as much from his worries over Kenyen's impending performance as from overt compassion for all those injuries.

"However did this happen, young man?" Reina asked, fussing over his wounds.

"Uh . . . I fell?" Kenyen muttered, matching Traver's rougher-sounding tones. He blinked and followed the Healer's movements as she hustled into the next room to the left, which reeked of the scents from a hundred herbs in various stages of preparation and preservation.

Zellan stepped into the breach. "He took off the first night out. We don't know why; we think he forgot something and wanted to come back and get it. I found his pony wandering loose, backtracked it to a ravine, and found him at the bottom of it, dehydrated. He'd lain down there all the next day, I think."

The young woman, Solyn, gave Kenyen—or rather, the man she thought was Traver—a worried look. ". . . Are you alright?"

Kenyen debated how to react. His own reaction would have either varied between brushing it off with humor—since he was a shapeshifter and could heal his own injuries quickly enough, given time and effort—or sarcasm. Traver, however, hadn't seemed the type to use either. He shrugged awkwardly, hissed, and supported his sagging left elbow. "I can't remember if I've had worse. My arm doesn't want to work."

Reina tutted as she came back from the herb-room, carrying a precious glass cup and a brown glazed vial. "I'm not surprised. Congratulations, it seems you've thoroughly dislocated it. We'll get these scrapes cleaned up, wrap some bandages and poultices on everything, then roll it back into its socket. But first, a pain posset. You'll need it." She poured a dose from the bottle to the cup, eyed him, and added a tiny bit more. "Drink this. Do you need me to hold it for you? No? Good."

Taking the cup, Kenyen sipped at it. The combination of herbs and spirits warned him it would be fairly potent. If he did drink all of it, without *real* pain to absorb the effects, the dose she wanted to give him would send him into a drugged daze and possibly be strong enough to lose his shape. Thinking fast, he drank about half of it, then made a face, took another sip, and held it out with a grimace.

"I . . . I can't . . . It's making me feel sick. I'm sorry," he mumbled.

Reina took back the glass, setting it on the table under the window. "If you want more, it'll be over here. If you need to vomit, there's a bucket under the bed, to the right of your legs. Solyn, start bathing that side of him. We'll also need to get his trousers and underthings off—no ogling or thoughts of twining, young lady," her mother added briskly. "He's in no shape for such things."

Solyn wasn't the only one to blush. So did Kenyen. He cleared his throat and stated carefully, "Uh . . . twining? I don't really . . . I'm sorry, but I don't know what you're talking about."

That made the younger woman glance up at him sharply. He gave her his best helpless look and shrugged his good shoulder.

"I don't remember a lot. I mean, you both look familiar, and I know a couple things when I look at you, but . . . My head really hurts," he finished lamely.

Zellan spoke up again from his spot near the entry door. "He couldn't even remember my name, though he did know me as a friend when I found him. He may have had a concussion while he lay in the ravine for all I know, but it seems to be gone, now. Along with bits of the boy's memory and wits."

Stooping, Reina pried open each one of Kenyen's reshaped eyes. She peered intensely, gaze flicking back and forth, then straightened and shrugged. "His pupils are reacting normally. It's rare to lose a lot of memory in a fall. Not unheard of, but rare. It should come back, though, particularly now that he's back on familiar ground.

"Still, a concussion can be serious. I'll probe you with my magics once we've tended to the more obvious wounds. I'd be more concerned if your eyes weren't dilating," she added, patting Kenyen on his uninjured shoulder. "As it is, let's make sure none of those scrapes get infected. Let's get you on your feet and drop your trousers."

Blushing, Kenyen obeyed, grunting in a show of pain as he stood. It didn't take long to remove the rest of his garments—technically Traver's clothes, not his—but when the Healer calmly unlaced and dropped his undertrousers as well, gesturing for her daughter to stoop and help him step out of the crumpled linen, it was all Kenyen could do to keep his altered shape. Particularly when he saw the younger woman's eyes widen, her head low enough to have a good view of his limp genitals.

Face red, Traver's betrothed quickly exchanged underdrawers for the cloth and bowl her mother passed her, accepting the ointment bottle Reina plucked from the crowded table. Pouring the contents into the bowl, she started bathing his legs. Kenyen wobbled, startled by the intimate touch. It was rare for a shifter to *need* tending by a Healer, once he or she grew into their powers.

He clung to his mental image of Traver Ys Ten, as much to keep himself unresponsive as to keep the appropriate shape. Knowing that this was another man's beloved made the intimacy level that much more awkward. Added on top was the instinctive urge to grow a protective, modesty-screening pelt, either of fur or feathers or scales, *something* to preserve his civilized dignity. But he couldn't, not when the real Traver certainly couldn't have done that.

It helped somewhat, in a bruise-stinging way, that her mother was doing the same thing up by his head and arms. His upper body bore the worse of his faked injuries, so it made sense for the Healer to tend those, and leave the rest to her daughter. The moment Solyn started patting near his upper thighs, however, Kenyen flinched involuntarily, shifting away from her and bumping his legs into the edge of the cot. His dignity was already in tatters; he did *not* need her gentle fingers tickling near *that* part of his anatomy, and he particularly didn't want her commenting on that ring the real Traver had insisted he wear.

"Enough—enough! Trust me, *that's* not injured."

Reina chuckled. "Clean off his backside, Daughter, then give him a blanket, help him to sit, and let him recover his dignity. I'll want to look at the swelling on his ankle, but it seems like that's the worst of the lower troubles—how many times did you hit your head, young man?" the Healer added in an exasperated voice, gingerly feeling her way across his shapeshifted locks. "Three times? Four?"

"I honestly don't remember. I'm sorry," he added, twitching a little as his purported betrothed scrubbed at his buttocks with her damp rag, then wrapped a strip of toweling cloth around his hips. Cheeks still flushed, she added a soft wool blanket from the foot of the cot, draping him from hips to feet in the lightweight wrap. Grateful, Kenyen sat back down.

The tension of the moment and his embarrassment kept him from reacting to her touches—she was quite attractive, in an understated way—but he was still grateful for the modesty shield. Nakedness on the Plains wasn't the same as nakedness anywhere else, something of which the warbands that headed outkingdom in search of mercenary work were well aware. Healers had to tend their patients' various needs, true, but that didn't mean casual nudity was acceptable, here.

The younger woman, Solyn, glanced up from time to time, her hazel eyes meeting his brown ones. A question lurked in her gaze, unspoken and unanswerable. As Zellan described the condition he had "found Traver in," she continued to work under her mother's direction, cleaning his scrapes, coating them with salve. Kenyen heard her hissing in sympathy when her mother had him stand, brace his dislocated shoulder against the wall, and push it back into its socket with a roll and a grunt. The grunt was manufactured; literally, a shifter couldn't dislocate anything for real unless they were very weak.

Healing was a matter of remembering how a body part should properly feel, and just shifting and reshifting until it felt whole and functioned right. The stronger the shifter, the faster they could heal. He wasn't his brother, who had more than a dozen shifts to his name, but Kenyen could have repaired a dislocated joint in just three or four shifts. Twenty or thirty would start to tire him, and up to fifty full shifts in a day would exhaust him, or twice as many minor shifts. However, the point wasn't to heal himself. The point was to fake his injuries enough that it would fool a Healer.

The moment Reina settled him back on the cot and laid her hands on his shoulders, pouring her magics into him in rhythmic, lyric murmurs . . . he sneezed. Repeatedly. Kenyen couldn't help it. Some shifters—himself, his brother, and his father included—could "feel" magic as if it were a tickle in the nose. Once he had reached puberty and his shifting abilities developed, he had rarely needed the spells of Family Tiger's Healer to fix his injuries, though he had accepted some of the herbal remedies for colds and such. Mages of any flavor just weren't common on the Plains.

"—*Achoo!*" He sneezed one last time, grateful that her spell had finally stopped.

Taking away her hands, Reina eyed him warily. "I don't *sense* a cold lurking in the energies of your body . . . but those energies feel rather unusual. A bit higher than they should. I can't detect a fever, either, which might've explained it . . . Normally I'd just send you on home since you don't seem to have a concussion anymore, Traver, but I'd like you to stay here overnight for observation, just in case I'm missing something."

Rubbing at his nose, Kenyen nodded.

Reina nodded and turned to the doorway, where curious onlookers had lingered. "Alright, you lot, out you go! Zellan, you, too—ah, there you are, Tenaria; thank you for bringing him a fresh change of clothes. You can fuss over your boy for a little bit, but then he'll need to rest. Spells don't heal bodies purely on their own, you know. As soon as I'm done whipping up a milder pain posset, he'll need to drink it and lie down for a while. Solyn, will you go get him something to eat, then come keep an eye on him? Go get some of the pottage from the hearth pot and thin it into a light soup, in case his concussion is still lingering."

"Yes, Mother," she agreed, shifting away from the cot.

Bodies shuffled through the doorways. Kenyen found himself engulfed in a gentle but thorough hug while "his" mother fussed over what she thought was one of her sons. Guilt coursed through him as he accepted her attentions and resurged when she fussed over him when he lied to her about his memory problems. Stuck in this awkward position, Kenyen did his best to pretend to be the real Traver Ys Ten, one with touches of amnesia to hide his ignorance. The real one's life hung in the balance, after all.

Somewhere outside the Healer's sickroom, the shapeshifter named Zellan would be lurking, waiting to catch the least little slipup from him.

FOUR

There was something different about Traver Ys Ten. Solyn wasn't sure what, but she knew there was something different. Something in the way he had slept on the cot last night, curling up to use his own arm as his pillow instead of the one provided, and something in the way he moved. It was just . . . different.

More graceful, she realized, walking with him down the path to his family's home. His other set of clothes had been cleaned and dried overnight, though they would need some mending. She carried them for him in a string bag slung over her shoulder, with the intent to show his mother what needed repairing. Traver couldn't ply needle and thread if his life depended on it, though he had plenty of other domestic skills.

Huh . . . yes, he's more graceful. He always stumbles a bit on those two steps, but he didn't this time. Having given herself the task of helping him regain his fuzzy memories—a convenient excuse to try to get alone with him to ask him what had really happened—she had plenty of time to observe him. In a series of holding farms like the ones in the Nespah Valley, it was difficult to be alone for very long. Still, when they were out of earshot on the path, her ring did twist on her finger, indicating they were alone.

Changed or not, this *was* her friend Traver. He had reassured her two years ago that he had hidden his ring in a very unlikely spot, somewhere that no one would think to look and probably wouldn't find in a search. Solyn originally had guessed he had hidden it inside his mouth somewhere, which was the only place she could think of for it, but its actual location was nowhere near his mouth, as she had seen for herself yesterday. Tapping his shoulder, she stopped him on the age-worn stones of the path.

"Alright, Traver, we're alone enough for the moment," she murmured. They might not have anyone near them for several hundred body-lengths, but that didn't mean she wanted to shout and have her words echo off the terraces. "What *really* happened with the caravan?"

Stopping and turning politely at her touch, Kenyen resisted the urge to glance around. Struggling against the urge to blush, he carefully kept his face Traver-like. "I told you. All I can remember is my mount bucking, and bits of me tumbling down the hill. Of lying in the mud for a long time. And . . . and I can't remember which house is mine. I just know it's down this path somewhere."

He flopped his hands uselessly, taking the time now to look around and make sure they were alone. Bodies young and old were weeding the sinuous ranks of gardens arrayed along the winding, green hills, so very different from the flat, rolling fields of the Plains. Thin, low clouds rendered the sky a bright shade of humid gray, and the shrieking laughter of children echoed in the distance. No one seemed close enough, but it was too soon.

If he revealed himself now, even to Traver's beloved, Zellan would race off to the others, to send shifters after Kenyen himself, and probably to that shepherd's hut, to ensure that the real Traver would die. All he could do was morph his own sense of frustration and helplessness into the role he was constrained to play and hope it worked.

Solyn eyed her friend, who looked helpless and frustrated and earnest, and relented. Patting him on the shoulder, she turned him back down the hill. "It's the second one on the right. Just . . . do me a favor?"

"Anything," he promised quickly.

Taking a deep mental breath, she trusted her friend, and the presence of that hidden ring on his body. This *was* the real Traver. It had to be. "If you should remember *anything* about heading down to the Shifting Plains, or having suspicions about the identities of certain folk, *don't* talk about it to anyone but me . . . and only if I myself bring up the topic."

Kenyen nodded. He did so more from comprehension than agreement, though he did agree. Her words fit in with what little Traver had told him before that other shifter had found the young man. "I won't. Just, be patient with me. I *hate* feeling this way. I've lost so much, and there's nothing I can do to recover it. Nothing but time."

"Well, just don't go hitting yourself on the head again," Solyn ordered him. "That never helps to restore the memory loss and would probably only addle your wits even further." Teasingly, she reached out and rumpled his hair, pushing his head a little.

Unsure how the real Traver would react to that, Kenyen turned and swatted her hand away, not sure if she was playing or harassing. She grinned and teased him further, trying to tickle him on the arms, the ribs, the scalp, anywhere she could reach. Giving in, he grinned and fought back just as lightly. Fingers slapping, hands fluttering, arms tangling, they ended up in a half-hugging embrace, swaying a little for balance on the uneven stones lining the path.

Kenyen stilled. She was warm, smelled sweet, and felt very feminine in his arms. Very nice. Aware of her curves, but not very sure of the local customs on such things, he just held her. *Back home, this would be bordering on scandalous. We haven't traveled much among the Corredai, but I don't* think *this is outright scandalous. Except I'm holding another man's betrothed, and it would be absolutely wrong to take advantage of this moment.*

Resting against him, Solyn could smell the liniment she and her mother had used on his bruises, a hint of male sweat, and something more. Something that made her breathe deeply. He felt warm and strong, and just a little . . . Frowning, she looked up at him. "Are you *taller*?"

Blushing, Kenyen quickly shook his head, then dipped his chin at the path. "No, I'm just standing on a higher bit of ground." Changing the subject before she could notice whether or not he actually was, he urged her along the now gently sloping path, shrinking his frame a tiny bit as he moved. "So, do I have to go back to doing chores right away, or do I get another couple of days to recuperate, first?"

"Mother said you aren't to do any heavy lifting for the next three days. But that doesn't mean you can get out of working," Solyn chided him. "Your brother was saying—Sellah, that is—that the leaves on the upper west terraces were in need of clipping tomorrow. I heard him through the kitchen window when I was getting your dinner last night. If you take it easy and make several trips with the net-cutters, that shouldn't be too heavy for you. The other choice is picking dark plums and red nanjeras, but you really shouldn't lift your left arm over your head for at least a few more days—you didn't hurt it just now, did you?"

"No," Kenyen dismissed. Then realized he should've gone for the sympathy angle. He faked a slight grimace and touched his shoulder. "Well, not really. It does hurt a lot in general, but . . . what?"

Solyn smirked, studying him. "You don't lie very well."

He blushed at that and retorted defensively, "Well, as my betrothed, aren't you supposed to offer to lovingly tend my wounds, however small they might be?"

She snorted and pushed him down the path. "As if! You know very well I only said that to Tunric's boy so he'd stop trying to pressure me into accepting him."

Kenyen stumbled a few steps before recovering. Her confession changed the whole scenario for him. He *wasn't* cheating by holding her, if she and Traver weren't . . . *And that's where I run into trouble again, because if I* do *take advantage of the situation, how is that any better? I've enjoyed the company of a few outkingdom women in the past, but this isn't the best situation to try for a casual romp!*

"Wait, that confuses you?" Solyn asked him, watching her childhood friend frown as he followed the path to the right. "I told you how we ended up betrothed just before you left. Don't you remember?"

"Well, I *don't* remember how we ended up betrothed, so *yes*," Kenyen defended himself. "I don't know a *lot* of things, at the moment. Forgive me for stumbling around."

"Okay, that one wasn't so much a lie," she conceded. He did sound lost and frustrated to her. "And I'm trying to keep that in mind. You just . . . there's *something* different about you, and I don't know what it is—and this conversation is at an end, because we've just come into hearing range of others," Solyn added in an undertone as they approached the first stone-and-plaster cottage. "But we *will* continue it soon."

"Second house, right?" he asked.

Solyn nodded. "This is your brother Bel—"

"—Belseth's place, yes. I remember that, now," the man at her side said, glancing first at it as they passed, then at the next home. "And my room is . . . in the loft. With my brother Tellik . . . yes?"

Solyn chuckled. "See? It'll all come back to you. We don't get many head injuries around here, more like broken bones from taking a tumble down the hillsides, but Mother did mention her uncle taking a dive the wrong way, back when she was my age. *He* remembered his bed was in the loft, except it hadn't been up in the loft since he was a child, and he was a full-grown man with a wife and two children."

Impulsively, Kenyen caught her hand and smiled. "Well, maybe that day isn't far off, when I'll have what he had as a man."

He said it for the benefit of the woman peering out through one of the cottage's windows, since from their too-brief discussion a few moments ago, this betrothal between her and the real Traver sounded like yet another layer of deception. But from the startled look in Solyn's eyes, she hadn't expected him to play along. For a moment, he debated dropping her hand, then kept hold of it, leading her to Traver's house. His house, temporarily.

Uncomfortable with the masquerade, he resolved to fly back that night to Cullerog's cottage. He did need to question Traver about a few things, but he was also worried for her betrothed's sake. Her friend's sake. Actually, her he-didn't-know-what's sake. *Not like I can ask either of them outright, "How do you really feel about each other, and how do you want me to play this role-within-a-role thing I'm stuck doing?"*

Given what she had said just now, Solyn was undoubtedly Traver's unnamed accomplice. That meant he *should* be able to tell her who he really was. Kenyen didn't have a chance, however. "His" little sister came running out of the second house on the right, arms lifted, her little legs making short work of the distance between them.

"Traver! Traver! Up up up!" she commanded, in the way of little girls everywhere. Clad in a pale blue skirt and side-buttoned tunic much like Solyn's brighter blue clothes, brown curls bouncing as she moved, she looked adorable.

"I'm afraid I can't, Tinia," he said, remembering her name. Kenyen touched his shoulder. "I hurt my arm and I have to wait until it heals."

"Uuuup!" the toddler whined, bouncing and tugging on his trouser leg.

A glance at Solyn showed her biting her lip in an unsuccessful attempt to stifle her grin. Apparently this was a common ritual for the real Traver to endure. Sighing, Kenyen stooped and scooped her up with his right arm, balancing her by her linen-skirted bottom. A subtle shift gave him a little extra muscle so that he could hold her easily.

The little girl immediately wrapped her arms around his neck and gave him a messy kiss on his cheek, then demanded, "Down down down!"

Solyn rolled her eyes. Catching sight of it, Kenyen made up his mind in an instant. "No."

Tinia reared back, staring at him. "Down? *Dowwn!* Down down down down!"

"No," he repeated. If she kept acting like this, and if everyone else kept giving in to her as she expected, Kenyen knew the little girl on his arm would grow up to be spoiled, expecting everyone to give in to her demands. *I've seen a few maidens down on the Plains acting this way, and they're never pleasant to be around, unless you do give in. She may not be my sister, but I got the feeling Traver isn't the type who would want her to grow up spoiled.*

"Whyyyy?" Tinia whined when her wiggling didn't get her set down. She fisted her little fingers in his tunic, tugging on the faded brown linen.

"Ask politely, and I will let you down," he explained. "Whine, and you won't get what you want. Now, say, 'Please put me down,' and I'll put you down."

"Dooowwwn!" she whined.

"Nope." Hefting Tinia a little higher, he winked at Solyn, who was struggling not to laugh out loud. Together, they walked toward Traver's house.

Tinia squirmed as they crossed the threshold. She gave up after a few moments but asked hesitantly, "Down?"

"Say please—hello, Mother," he added, catching sight of Tenaria. Unlike the Healer's home, this one had a front room with tables and chairs, leading into a partially visible kitchen at the back, behind the fireplace in the center of the house. Doors to the left led into what looked like bedrooms, and a steep staircase to the right of the hearth led up into the loft.

"Dooowwwwn!"

"Tinia, we do *not* speak in such tones," Tenaria admonished her child, peering around the stone-and-mortar corner of the fireplace.

"Say please," Kenyen added, grateful "his" mother agreed. Tenaria ducked back into the kitchen area.

Tinia pouted, lower lip sticking out. She finally mumbled, "Please, wan' down."

"Of course." Stooping again, Kenyen let her squirm free once she was low enough and let her totter off. The little girl headed straight for a trio of rag dolls piled near the unlit hearth, where she plopped down and started playing with one of them, bouncing it on the linen of her skirt and mumbling to herself.

"It's good to have you home, my boy, though I'm sorry you came home in such a fashion. Still, if you can lift up your sister . . ." Tenaria started to say, her voice slightly muffled by the fireplace between them.

"Actually, it was just my right arm. Anything with my left arm is forbidden for the next . . . four days?" Kenyen quickly stated.

"Three to five days," Solyn filled in for him. "Mother will take a look at him again in a few days. Traver should be fine for helping with some light chores, but nothing more heavy than a loaf of bread in that hand, if it can be avoided."

"And are you going to help him?" Tenaria asked the younger woman, coming fully into view. Her fingers were sticky with dough, which she picked at idly as she spoke. "Since he is your betrothed now? About time, if you ask me. You need to pull your head out of the clouds, young woman, and work on learning the *important* things in life."

He didn't know what the older woman meant by that, but from the set of Solyn's mouth, Kenyen guessed it was an old argument. Disapproval was disapproval, whether or not there were actual grounds for it. Impulsively, he put his right arm around the younger woman's shoulders. "Whatever Solyn chooses to do, so long as she harms no one by it—and I've no doubt she will choose to help people by it—well, I will support her in it. After all, *I* will be the one to live with whatever she chooses to do. Not you, Mother."

Taken aback, Tenaria blinked. She stopped cleaning the dough from her fingers for a moment, then drew in a breath and let it out with a shrug. Shaking her head, the plump, curly-haired woman returned to the kitchen without another word.

"Traver . . ." Solyn stared at him. Of all the things he could've said to his own mother's argument, well, she *knew* he was supportive of her attempts at learning magic, but not to the point of standing up to his own mother. *Whatever happened to him when he hit his head, he has* definitely *changed . . . and I think I like it.*

The name, barely breathed, made Kenyen realize such instincts were dangerous; he had spoken with the cultural drives of his own people and not the Corredai. Not that he knew much about the Corredai outlook for such things, but what was said could not be erased. Shrugging awkwardly, he whispered back, "What? Look, if we're in this thing together, we're in it together, right?"

"Shh," she admonished. "Not here." Raising her voice, she lifted her chin toward the stairs. "Let's get your things upstairs. You'll have to show your mother what needs stitching later, when she's not busy. *Or* finally learn to wield needle and thread like a *real* man."

"What, and deprive my beloved the chance to show how much

you care for me by doing it yourself?" he quipped back, startling Solyn with his quick wit. He grinned, looking rather cute and sure of himself. "I wouldn't dream of denying you the opportunity."

Eyeing him up and down, Solyn snorted. "You really *did* hit your head, didn't you?"

"What, you don't sew?" Kenyen asked, trying to keep his tone light. This wasn't one of those things he and the real Traver had discussed.

"Of course I do," she dismissed. "But I thought you were going to support me in anything I *wanted* to do."

Caught off guard, he laughed. "Oh, fine. If you'll show me what to do, I'll fumble through it on my own."

"And have you looking like a rag doll?" Tenaria quipped from around the corner. "Set it on the hearth table, and I'll look at it later. The two of you can go search for eggs in the hen yard. *That* I know you can do, young man, even with a wounded arm."

"Yes, Mother." Kenyen sighed. Tenaria looked nothing like his own mother, who was taller and had straight, dark brown hair, but the two women certainly sounded alike in some ways. "Hand me the basket, and we'll go look for eggs."

And maybe have a chance to talk quietly with each other, he hoped, though he wasn't going to hold his breath. Very little in any of this mess had gone quite right since finding that corpse in the cave. *If we can be alone long enough for me to reveal who I am* and *convince her I'm speaking the truth, maybe Solyn can help me when I'm acting too far out of character for her friend. I hate this hit-or-miss nonsense.*

Traver was definitely different. He moved with more grace, he spoke with more confidence, he acted with more sureness. Solyn knew she should be doubting his identity, awkwardly placed ring or not, but she couldn't quite bring herself to completely mistrust her friend. *Part of it's because he's just so . . . so* nice, she acknowledged silently, watching him barter with the spice trader for the things his mother wanted. *I can usually spot a fake Corredai simply by the little things he does. The subtle sneers, the covert condescensions, the dismissive demeanor. But Traver is still as nice as ever.*

Just . . . different. Nice, but different. He puzzled her. Two days had passed, and Solyn was still being his watchdog, as much to make sure he suffered no lasting harm from his injuries as from the need to try to find a moment alone with him, one long enough to discuss what had happened to their plans to send him north to the Plains.

Not that she had much else to do. Ostensibly, she was her mother's apprentice. In reality, her magics weren't quite the right kind for healing spells, though she could manage a few, and she knew how to craft most of the herbal remedies her mother used. Setting bones, stitching and binding wounds, those things she could do, but her powers flowed just a little too differently to help a body to heal.

What she needed was to be sent to a bigger city, where she could find real training in the arcane arts, not just whatever she could puzzle out from books and extrapolate from her mother's methods. What she had to do was stay to protect her mother, and her mother's greatest secret.

Fourteen years ago, when Solyn was just eight, Reina Lai Fa had been experimenting with variations on bluesteel, the specially crafted, blue-tinted metal which could permanently scar anyone, even a shapeshifter. Reina had discovered something astonishing. Something which turned out to be deadly.

Bluesteel had been created by accident; after making a huge cauldron of tea, an ancestor of the Nespah holdings had discovered the tea leaves had moldered, rendering the brew undrinkable. The stories varied. Some said it was a drought year, meaning they didn't dare waste the precious liquid; others said it was just the blacksmith's wife being disgusted with either her brew or her husband. Whatever the version, the moldered tea steepings had ended up in the smithy, being used repeatedly to quench the blacksmith's blades during their crafting.

The aquamarine-blue cast to the silvery metal had first been considered a novelty, then a curiosity when their scar-forming, shapeshift-quelling qualities were uncovered. After the Shattering of Aiar, they became a vital trade point with the shapeshifters to the north, helping turn the savage barbarians into civilized souls.

Solyn's mother, a curious, adventurous sort who dabbled in alchemy as well as Healing remedies, had decided to see what other qualities could be imparted to metal, depending on what was used to quench the heated material. Many plants had magic-enhancing effects, and some had actual magical qualities of their own. Her mother wanted to know if any new properties could be infused, despite the high temperatures involved, like bluesteel could.

So, with Ysander's help, she had experimented. Most of their efforts did nothing to change the metal. Only a jest on her husband's part had revealed a new possibility. Instead of dipping the heated blade in yet another herbal infusion, he had jokingly sliced a bit of cheese with one of his small, red-hot blades . . . imparting an unnatural, grass-green hue to the half-worked steel. The special molds in greenvein cheese altered the blade.

Solyn remembered watching her mother very carefully experimenting on herself, expecting the small cuts to scar as they healed. Instead, they had healed faster than expected. A careful experiment on her husband, cutting across one of the many small scars that had nicked his hands over the years, caused the sliced section of scar to heal seamlessly. Their astonishment had filled the young Solyn with wonder: Reina Lai Fa and Ysander Mil Ben had created the perfect tool for Healers everywhere, to help victims of burns and cuts, gouges and so forth to renew their bodies whole.

Excited by the prospects, Reina had loaned the finished green-steel blade to a fellow Healer two valleys over, a woman who also liked to experiment with alchemical properties. Reina had then turned back to working on crafting more of the odd, sharp cheese so that more of the helpful blades could be made. Somehow, word got out . . . and bad men had come, seeking the blade. No one knew quite what had happened, other than how the Healer and her family looked like they had been mauled to death by wild animals . . . and that the blade had been badly etched by acid.

The King's men had come to investigate, but they couldn't follow the tracks of the beasts, and no culprits had been found. Those few who knew the importance of that acid-ruined blade, frightened for Reina's and Ysander's sakes, had immediately agreed to keep their mouths shut on the source of the miraculous metal. At first, nothing seemed to come of the matter, but then the owner of the local mines, Tunric Tel Vem, went away on a long trading trip. He came back changed. Harder, crueler, more arrogant . . . and rather interested in the Healers and the blacksmiths of the region.

Other men changed as well. After Solyn's best friend stumbled across the strange bonfire, he had confided to her how eerie and surreal the whole thing had been. When she heard about that, Solyn had realized the mauling-by-animals and the face-melting men had the same source: evil shapeshifters.

The Shifterai did come south into the mountains, looking for trade and other forms of work, though they never quite came this far into the kingdom. Nespah wasn't on a major trade route, nor on a road that led to the capital. With the secret of bluesteel smithing long since passed into their hands, all the Shifterai needed from the Corredai tea farmers were properly moldered leaves, which were created carefully, deliberately, when the tea was *im*properly stored. In fact, the cave where that mold grew had been specially set aside specifically for making and moldering bluesteel tea leaves, at the top of the valley. But it was the Corredai who usually took that tea down to the Plains, and not the Shifterai who came in search of it.

Another cave held the source of the mold for making greenvein cheese. It was uncomfortably close to one of Tunric Tel Vem's mines, upriver at the wooded base of the valley, but the entire family had been using that cave for cheese-ripening for generations. Greenvein was sharp, tangy, and a touch on the pungent side; few people enjoyed eating it directly. But it preserved well, sliced neatly, and a little bit grated into a dish went a long way in flavoring various foods. She actually liked it a lot, herself.

Traver finished his bartering, measured out the silver scepterai and the copper thronai coins, and shook hands with the trader. The trader then helped him put his paper-wrapped purchases into the net bag slung over his good shoulder. Solyn realized belatedly that Traver had paid quite a bit less than she would have for an equal amount of the costly, imported spices. *When did he learn to barter so well? Okay, not that I know how well Traver barters for anything* other *than sweets. Every honey-nut-bun baker and sugar-curl crafter in the valley knows they can charge him an extra thronai or two for those sorts of treats, but I can't remember the last time I watched him buying spices and herbs.*

He turned to her with a smile that revealed his delight in his bargain. Solyn found herself smiling right back. *Odd, but . . . but maybe being hit on the head and forgetting a few things finally helped him to finish growing up?* That could be it. Traver had always struck her as a bit like a gangly lamb, or a spindly-legged colt, not quite fully grown. Not quite comfortable with his adult body and the strengths which came with maturity. *Until now, that is.*

"I still don't see what *you* think you see in that idiot."

Oh, great, Solyn thought, shutting her eyes for a moment. *Tarquin Tun Nev. What a beautiful day this is . . .* Opening them again, she glanced at the idiot. Tall and handsome with his sun-browned skin and dark brown curls, he made many a young maiden's heart skip a beat whenever he smiled their way. Except for hers.

For one, he was the son of Tunric Tel Vem, which meant anything she said to him would no doubt make its way back to a known shifter. For another, he, too, had changed several years ago, after his mother had divorced his personality-altered father and taken herself and her daughters to distant relatives. And for the third reason, Traver was certain he'd seen Tarquin alongside his father at that bonfire several years back. That was more than enough for her to distrust him.

Still, it paid to be polite. "Hello, Tarquin."

"Honestly, what do you see in him?" Tarquin dismissed, ignoring the puzzled frown Traver was giving the two of them. Cupping his hand around her arm, Tarquin stepped close enough that Solyn tried to sidle away. Unfortunately, that put her up against the cloth seller's wagon, leaving her no room to retreat. The wagon was narrow, well suited to be pulled along the winding paths that lined most of the mountains, but he had her trapped against the wheel.

"I see someone more polite than you. Stop pushing me into the wagon, Tarquin," she ordered, elbowing him. "It's not polite!"

He pressed closer, making her scowl. "I think you need a *real* man, someone who can take *charge* of you." He flashed her a grin. "Certainly, if you marry *that* pile of goat droppings, you'll eventually come looking for one. You need passion in your life, Solyn. And I—*yeeowch*!"

Tarquin jumped back, wincing and rubbing at his inner arm. Traver pulled back his hand, though he raised it in warning, thumb and forefinger ready to pinch the other young man's bicep again. "She has made her choice. Respect it."

"Some choice," Tarquin scoffed. He rubbed his arm one more time, giving Traver a wary look, then lifted his chin at Solyn. "She'll come to realize who the better man is. When given the choice of being mauled by your cow herder's hands or enjoying *my* touch . . . she'll come to *me* for her pleasures."

Embarrassed by such frank, arrogant, idiotic words, Solyn glanced around. More than one holding had sent family members to chat with the spice traders, and that meant more than one pair of eyes was watching this little interaction. More than one pair of ears, and more than one lifted set of brows.

"She'll have nothing to complain about in *my* arms," Traver stated flatly, once again displaying that odd new confidence.

Tarquin smirked. "That's because she doesn't know any different. Still, her 'choice' isn't irrevocable, is it? Let me help you make up your mind, my sweet."

Before she knew what he was up to, Tarquin had her face cupped in his hands and his mouth pressed to hers. His tongue probed at her lips, making her flinch back at the unexpected, unwelcome invasion. Disgusted by the attack, she groped for her magic, ready to fling him back with blunt power. Even as she did so, two things happened: Traver sneezed and flung Tarquin back himself.

Staggering, Tarquin regained his balance and rubbed at his shoulder. She hoped he was bruised by the rough handling. Traver glared at him, then turned to Solyn. He lifted his own hand to her cheek, but his touch was gentle, and his gaze the only thing that brushed her lips. "Are you alright?"

She nodded, then scrubbed at her mouth with the back of her wrist. "I'll be fine. I'd have hit him myself, if you hadn't pushed him away."

Nodding back, he slipped his arm around her waist, sheltering her at his side. Traver faced Tarquin. "As I said, she's made her choice. Respect it."

Solyn slipped her arm around his hips as well. It was her fault Traver was now her betrothed, but he was man enough to defend her choice, however impulsive and inadvertent. *And really, who else should*

I wed but a great friend? There might not be raging passion between us, but we'll still have something to talk about in old age.

Tarquin sneered. "Another man kisses your woman, and that's the best you can do?"

"That's because you're not worth fighting," Traver stated dismissively, sounding far, far more confident than Solyn had ever heard him speak before.

A strangely humorous look curled up the corner of Tarquin's mouth. ". . . You *can't* kiss her, can you?"

Solyn felt Traver stiffen at her side. The corner of his own mouth curled up, but it wasn't very amused-looking. Turning to her, he once again brushed her cheek with his fingers, then lowered his head. His lips dusted over hers, then alighted with gentle pressure, showing that he could indeed kiss her.

Those lips nibbled for a moment, then the tip of his tongue swept lightly over hers. Not to probe invasively, just to moisten. It tickled . . . and it intensified everything. The warmth of his arm holding her close, the nibble of his lips as they teased and tasted, the mingling scents of spices and male sweat. He didn't even smell the same anymore; before, there was always a lingering hint of farm animals and sourness to his scent. Now, Traver smelled more manly, with hints of musk and something else. She supposed it might've been the lack of barn-cleaning duties since his last bath, and the seasonings he had bought.

His mouth coaxed hers open, nipping here, licking there. Shivering under his slow assault, a corner of Solyn's mind wondered who her best friend had been kissing behind her back, to know how to do it this well. The rest of her mind . . . well, it melted, and took a good portion of her body along with it.

Sagging into him, she tightened her own grip on his waist, her other hand coming up to clutch at his shoulder. He cupped her closer, switching his right hand from her face to the back of her head, fingers twining in her curls. A soft, hungry sound escaped him, and her own throat released a sigh that hummed in tune with the rest of her nerves. The astonished, unmelted corner of her mind wondered, *Cora, Goddess of Hills and High Places . . . where in the world did all this* pleasure *come from?*

"That's enough, you two!" Aunt Hylin's voice dashed over them like a bucket of cold water. "No twining in public!"

Shuddering in shock, flushed with embarrassment, Solyn pulled back. Traver did as well, though he kept his left hand at the small of her back while turning to face her aunt. With his own cheeks distinctly red, he searched the crowd around the spice traders' caravan, no doubt looking for Tarquin.

He wasn't in sight; at some point during that slow but rather intense kiss, the other young man had slunk off. Clearing his throat, Traver nudged Solyn off to the side, away from the caravan. Aunty Hylin chuckled, waggled her finger with a mock-stern look, and turned back to her own spice hagglings, leaving them alone.

More or less alone, not counting the watchful eyes of a dozen men, women, and youths all visiting with the trading caravan. Frustrated with their lack of privacy, Solyn resolved to drag Traver down to the cheese caves. The only thing she could be grateful for was that the other holders waited until they were almost out of earshot before gossiping about the fact that Traver Ys Ten had kissed Solyn Ys Rei, and ". . . practically twined with her on the spot!"

Equally grateful to leave, and even more embarrassed, Kenyen escorted his false betrothed away from the gathering field located halfway down the valley. Tarquin was one of them, a member of Family Mongrel. Someone who had taken over the life of the real Tarquin Tun Nev, and no doubt allowed the real one to be murdered. To hear such a cur mocking true Shifterai ways had not sat well with him.

On the Plains, the sanctity of maidens was absolute. If a man wanted physical intimacy, he arranged to meet with an earth-priestess. As widows, they could have gone back into the maiden's *geome*, the communal dome-tent where all maidens lived until wed. Instead, some of them chose to take up the holy calling of tending to the pleasure needs of the men in a particular Family. Each young man learned how to please a woman properly, thanks to their teaching. And each man learned to respect the compassionate generosity of each duly ordained earth-priestess.

Outlander women, the kind when met while traveling outkingdom . . . some of them could be approached, but it was always best to be polite and avoid such things unless a Shifterai was sure about two things. One, that the local culture didn't forbid it, and two, that at least one of them had a contraceptive charm. Because of the peculiarities of their kind, it was thought best not to beget any shapeshifter sons, or even a rare shapeshifter daughter, on an unsuspecting woman.

To kiss a maiden is anathema, Kenyen acknowledged. *Maybe not an outkingdom maiden, but the hesitation and shame are still there. But to kiss someone else's betrothed is an outright betrayal. To enjoy it makes me depraved as well as a criminal. Except I had little choice. If I heard her right, if his name is Tarquin, then he's one of the shifters the real Traver warned me about. By now, he undoubtedly knows I'm a face-shifter, too.*

"Traver? . . . Traver!"

Pulling himself out of his guilty thoughts, Kenyen looked back at Solyn. "Yes? What?"

"You missed the path," she pointed out, literally pointing back at the right one.

Sighing, Kenyen moved back to join her. A glance all around showed they were more or less alone. Not very, since it was the start of the harvest season and anyone working the various terraces could have glanced their way, but as close as they would get to being alone. The guilt wouldn't go away though. She was a sweet young woman who didn't deserve to be treated like that. "I'm sorry if I offended you, kissing you like that."

Solyn blushed. *There* was the Traver she knew, awkward and uncomfortable with man-woman things around her. On these narrow, sloping paths, pony-drawn wagons didn't work so well, which was why the main road through the valley had fields and yards for traders to park their carts. A glance around showed how they *seemed* to be out of earshot, but her ring hadn't reacted. Apparently someone could still hear them, though she couldn't see who.

"*You* didn't offend," she pointed out, climbing the shallow stone steps to the next winding stretch. "Tarquin did that. Actually, I'm more wondering who you've kissed before, to kiss so well!"

He blushed. "I just . . . thought of a way to kiss you that matched you. Sweet and gentle, and, um . . ."

That made her laugh. "Since when have you ever thought of me as gentle? I can still arm wrestle with you, you know."

He smirked, clearly not believing her. Not that she believed it, either, not if she used just her muscles, but Solyn didn't mind augmenting her efforts with a little magic. To her surprise, he impulsively caught her fingers in his, lacing them together. It made walking on the narrow paths a little awkward, but the contact felt surprisingly nice. It also made her awkwardly aware of how much the effects of his kiss still lingered. Every nerve was now more aware of his presence, reminding her of the unexpected pleasure they had shared.

Zellan startled him. The older shifter rose into existence inside the goat barn, where Kenyen, still shaped to look like Traver, son of Ysal and Tenaria, was patiently grooming the family holding's milk goats. He jumped a little and the nanny goat bawled, startled by the scrape of the currying brush. Soothing her with a few pats, Kenyen eyed the other man warily. "Yes?"

"You're not doing a bad job," Zellan praised him quietly. "But you can do better. Tonight, when Brother Moon is two fists above the horizon—shortly before midnight—you will come out here and wait for me. You *can* fly at night, yes?"

"I can," Kenyen admitted, keeping himself calm by stroking the brush over the goat's surprisingly silky hide. "Why should I?"

"It's a gathering night. The others want to meet you and critique your progress."

"I was hoping to go see my 'brother' tonight," Kenyen countered, unsure if he was ready to meet a whole bunch of criminal shifters. "I have more questions to ask."

Thankfully, Zellan didn't object. "Then meet me here when Brother Moon rises. Make sure no one knows you're gone."

A ripple of flesh, and the shifter shrunk down, resuming the shape of one of the small hedge birds that flitted about the terraced hills, pecking at insects and seeds alike. Kenyen didn't know the local name for the kind, but he did study what he could of the shifted Zellan before he flew off. *I won't be able to assume I'm alone at* any *point, unless I can find a deep cave to hide in. With my luck, it'll be a cave stacked with yet more dead bodies.*

An unpleasant thought. It didn't give him nearly as much apprehension as the thought of this gathering thing Zellan mentioned. *Is it one of the bonfire nights that Traver recalled seeing? Or is it going to be my funeral, as they gather around me to tear me to pieces, having uncovered my true reason for being here?*

. . . No, they don't know. They might suspect, but they can't know for sure. Whatever they want, they're desperate enough to use a stranger to get it. Nudging that goat aside, he coaxed another one near with a bit of straw, then began grooming it as well. *I'd better think of several different ways I could react to anything they might throw at me. And think of a list of questions for Traver. I'll also want to figure out just how difficult it might be to break him free. Because if I can do that without getting caught*

or tracked, one of us could run to Teshal to tell the others what's really happening up here.

The alternative was him taking all night to fly out and try to find the town himself, but that risked not making it back in time to avoid his absence being discovered. *Not to mention being exhausted the next day. What a tangled mess this is . . .* A stray thought as he finished grooming the goat made Kenyen chuckle. *If only I could find a big enough currying comb to brush it all out.*

FIVE

Traver looked all right. A little dirtier, but he'd been given enough slack in the chains to use a chamberpot. A pair of waterskins and the remnants of food in the bowl he hugged to his chest proved he was at least being fed. With Cullerog and Zellan right there, Kenyen couldn't do much. He did crouch to examine the younger man's face in the light of the oil lamp illuminating the space and sighed roughly.

"He's starting to get pale," Kenyen pointed out. He did his best to sound gruff, almost disgusted, rather than concerned for Traver's condition. "He might even get sickly looking if he stays cooped up down here. I can't imitate someone who looks like they're wasting away, particularly when he's supposed to be a dirt grubber. Make sure you march him around outside in the sunlight for at least an hour a day."

"Are you giving *me* orders, boy?" Cullerog growled.

Zellan snorted. "You *should* be good enough to keep his face going, no matter what the real one looks like."

"I am. But a *good* shifter knows that a living shape isn't a static image. Living creatures grow and change, and that includes my fellow human, here." Rising, Kenyen faced the other two, his gaze shifting back and forth. "I'll also bet it took *you* a few days of studying your replacement targets before you could keep it up. I had only one night—emphasis on *night*. I didn't get as much of a chance to study him in daylight as I'd have liked, since I had to guide both mounts. Forgive me for trying to get it *right*."

Cullerog grunted. "I'll give it some thought. Ask your questions, boy, then be on your way."

Nodding, Kenyen turned back to Traver and crouched. He hadn't been able to bring a list, since he wore nothing more than a coat of fur from waist to knees, but he did have a few things memorized. With his back to the others, he risked a slight wink, then spoke. "I discovered today that you've never kissed your girl. What a shame. I had to do it in your place."

Traver glanced quickly at the others, then scowled at Kenyen. "You leave her alone!"

"I can't. She's expecting such things from her betrothed. *Wanting* them, even," Kenyen taunted. At least, his tone of voice was taunting. He rolled his eyes briefly and continued. "But she did say something that made me curious. She wanted to know who else 'I' have kissed, to be so *good* at it. So, who *have* you been kissing?"

Traver blushed. "A gentleman doesn't—"

"—It's going to come up," Kenyen countered. "She'll start asking around, and if you don't cooperate, and she finds out I'm not the real you . . . then *you* become expendable."

His flat warning made Traver swallow. "Uh . . . right. Killia Lis Pel. We kissed a little bit behind her holding's cattle barn a couple months ago—but she's now twining with Lunnor Bel Nath, from farther down the valley, about three holdings down."

"What does she look like?" Kenyen interrogated him.

Behind him, Cullerog grunted again and started climbing the ladder. Zellan sighed and settled against the shelves holding bags of grain and baskets of vegetables on the far wall. Kenyen wished Zellan would go away as well, but he didn't expect that much trust this early in the game. Paying attention, Kenyen focused on memorizing each of the answers Traver gave, as well as on the expressions Traver used and the way he sounded when he spoke.

The food was good. Most of it was wild game, caught and cleaned earlier, seasoned with local herbs and skewered onto planks that faced the fire. The way they treated the woman scuttling from plank to plank, tending it, wasn't good. They kicked her as she passed, made crude comments about her figure, and at least two of the fifteen or so members of Family Mongrel abused her in ways that made it hard for Kenyen to hide his blush.

Zellan had told him on their arrival that this was by no means all the shapeshifters in the Correda Mountains. Not everyone made it to every meeting, though many gathered in one of two locations. One was somewhere to the east, closer to the Morning River Valley and the land of the Mornai who lived along its banks. The other took place in this cave-sheltered clearing, hidden in a steep ravine a modest distance from the Nespah Valley. The high, shallow arch of the cave concentrated the light and reflected the heat of the chest-high flames in the bonfire pit, providing a warm, well-lit venue for this gathering.

Most of the shifters had left their clothes at home. The few men attending the gathering who did bother with modesty shifts used scales instead of feathers or fur; Kenyen was one of them. Traver's covert handing of the ring to him suggested it was something he didn't want anyone to know about. Until Kenyen could get Solyn alone—truly alone, with no chance of eavesdropping by Zellan or another shifter—he couldn't say for sure. Prudence told him to hide its existence beneath reptile-style modesty.

One discrepancy was noticeable. Whenever the shifters around him relaxed into what Kenyen presumed was their natural, normal shapes, all of the older ones displayed Banished brands on their foreheads. But only a couple of the dozen or so younger ones—around Kenyen's age but not younger—bore the burn scars. That meant the younger ones were sons born to the Mongrels after their Banishment from the Plains. Kenyen's sister-in-law hadn't been the only child in the Mongrel's camp, just as her mother Ellet hadn't been the only woman being held captive back then. He tried not to think of the implications of that.

Someone had brought a keg of plum wine, and someone else produced a couple skins of fermented mare's milk. Kenyen sipped a little bit from the skins simply to blend in as they were passed around, but it wasn't as good as the kind made back home on the Plains. Aware of the scrutiny of the others, he mirrored the actions of the others for the most part, eating the meat, drinking the beverages, laughing at the crude jokes.

The only thing he didn't do was touch the woman, who was simply called "bitch," a nickname accompanied by barking noises and crude laughter. He tried not to think about that, either, so that his disgust wouldn't be seen. As much as he wanted to stop all of this, the important thing was blending in, gathering information, and not getting caught.

The white-haired shifter from earlier, whom the others called Ankah, finally stood and raised his hands. The others quieted down, giving him a modicum of respect. Dipping his head slightly in acknowledgment, he spoke.

"As you know, we have a new, tentative member of Family Mongrel. He has taken the place of that whelp, Traver Ys Ten. Zellan, what's your opinion of the new Traver's performance?" Ankah asked.

Zellan swallowed whatever he was eating and stood. Scraps of cloth and animal hides had been scattered on the ground or draped over sections of log for seats, though the latter seemed to be reserved for the older shifters. Zellan, like Kenyen, was seated on the ground. Hiding his apprehension, Kenyen listened to the middle-aged shifter.

"He's not bad. Quick-witted. And he's been playing up the mix of memory and memory loss fairly well," Zellan stated, relieving Kenyen. "However . . . he's too confident. Too careful. You need to bumble things a bit more. Traver Ys Ten is still a hatchling, someone who hasn't matured."

Kenyen dipped his head in acknowledgment. His face was his own at the moment—and his body ached from holding the other shape for so long—but his forehead bore a Banished scar similar to the ones marking the others. "I'll try harder. Though it's difficult to play a fool. It's not my style."

"Play better," Tunric growled. "And work your way faster into that family. After looking at two score possibilities, we've narrowed it down to this one. The Healer bitch liked to experiment, particularly years ago, and she's married to a blacksmith. It all fits."

"If I *knew* what I was looking for, I'd be able to look for it faster," Kenyen retorted.

The thick-jowled shifter smiled, his teeth visibly sharpening. "Are you sassing your elders, *boy*?"

"Just stating a fact." He dared a brief smile. "I like how things are set up around here. I'm not about to set the grass on fire."

"If you knew, you'd push too hard," Tunric countered. "Just

ingratiate yourself into that Gods-be-damned family. Seduce the girl. Marry her if you have to. Get into their good graces fast."

Tarquin laughed and waved the half-eaten duck leg in his hand. He was one of the youths who lacked a scar. "I've already helped him with that."

"You mean you almost ruined it," Zellan countered, moving over to smack the younger shifter on the back of his head. Tarquin dodged most of it, but not all; his hair swayed under the glancing blow.

"Hey, now; if it were up to the *real* Traver Ys Ten, he'd never have that bitch in heat." Tarquin shot Kenyen a feral grin. "Besides, I was testing to see how much of the Plains was still shackling our new boy, here."

Ankah grunted. "All that Gods-be-damned *respect* they show for women." The elderly shifter spat toward the woman scuttling to turn the latest pieces of meat. She didn't look up, didn't react. He smirked. "We get enough of *our* kind into the village and holding elders, we can change things in the lives of these mountain sheep so that they're the *right* way. *Our* way of thinking."

Kenyen smiled along with the rest. Tarquin got up and crossed the distance between them, settling next to Kenyen on the scrap of canvas covering the ground. He elbowed the Shifterai. "You're not upset I did that, are you?"

"No, I figured it out." He hadn't been happy about the challenge to his cultural beliefs, but knowing in advance that Tarquin was a Mongrel shifter, Kenyen had figured his actions were being watched and measured. "I don't care either way about women. They're nothing special, no matter what they tried to claim back on the Plains. I just didn't want to get smacked by the locals, because I didn't know how much was allowed."

Tarquin smirked, tearing off another piece of duck meat. He chewed it and said, "Just about anything . . . provided you don't get 'em pregnant, you don't do it in public, and you make sure they don't complain to anyone. Get caught, though, and they'll force you to wed—that's an idea, by the way," he added. "Ysander's traditional enough, so long as it's out of sight, it's out of mind . . . but you get caught twining with his precious little girl, he'll have you strapped either to his anvil for a beating or to the nearest altar for a wedding."

"Well, she's passably pretty," Kenyen allowed, "but I'm not sure I'd want to be tied down to her."

Tarquin coughed, choking on a laugh. Clearing his throat, he rasped, "You don't have to be! Bitches are for breeding shifter sons, nothing more." He grabbed the cup he had brought over and drank some of the plum wine it contained, then gestured at the middle-aged, scuttling woman in their midst. "In the meantime, you can go plow that one."

Kenyen wrinkled his nose. He couldn't help it and didn't stop it. Putting disdain into his tone, he said, "No, thank you."

"No?" Tarquin challenged, eyeing him as he plucked off the last bits of meat from the bone in his hand.

Kenyen wrinkled his nose. "I prefer my meat fresh." Leaning closer to the other young man, he asked under his breath. "Do you know what I'm supposed to be looking for? I don't like working blind. I even went back to re-interrogate that little pup whose face I took over, to make sure I'm doing the job right . . . but I don't even know *what* the job is, yet."

Tarquin shook his head. "What the alphas want, the alphas get. If they don't want you to know . . . well, they probably don't trust you enough, yet. You'll have to prove yourself before they'll tell you anything. And I wouldn't go against them, if I were you. They're *multerai*. They'll change their shape faster than a blink and tear your throat out. They'll tell you when they think you're ready to know, when they trust you."

Kenyen grunted. Someone nudged him with a nearly empty skin of mare's milk. He took it and pretended to drink more than the few sips he actually did. *At least they're not going to kill me tonight. They're still dangerous men, but they're not deadly. As for that threat about one of the elders getting the jump on me . . .*

He slid his gaze around the bonfire-lit gathering. A few moved like hunters, like warriors, but the rest didn't have the right edge, the right mix of competence and confidence. *If these Mongrels have fought more than each other and a few frightened Corredai holders, I'd be surprised.* He started to smirk at that thought, then checked himself. *Careful, Kenyen,* don't *get overconfident. You have several lives at stake. Yours and Traver's foremost, followed by Solyn's, and so forth.*

Assume these men are cold-blooded killers who can take on a warband and survive. Lay your own plans accordingly . . . what little you do plan, he acknowledged wryly, *and then you'll be ready. Maybe.*

A heavy hand came down on his shoulder. It belonged to the shifter impersonating Tunric Tel Vem. "Make sure you ingratiate yourself, boy. Do it quickly, but don't make any mistakes." His meaty, callused hand tightened to the point of pain for Kenyen, proving the older man was shifter enough to strengthen his grip. "You may be a murdering cannibal back on the Plains, but here, you're one of the lowest members in this pack. Mess up any of this, and *I'll* eat you alive."

"I'll keep that in mind," Kenyen grunted, hiding his pain. Once Tunric let go of him, he subtly shifted his shoulder, healing the damaged tissues before they could leave darkened fingerprints on his bare skin.

Solyn muttered to herself all the way down the path to Traver's home. Not out loud, not very often, but in her head. *He's too different. He's too changed. He's too . . . manly. He's not the real Traver Ys Ten. He's too graceful, too confident, too handsome . . . handsome?*

She almost stopped on the path, wrinkling her nose, before

resuming her steady strides. The gathered folds of her light blue skirt swished against her calves. *Traver is Traver, and he's always* been *Traver! He's always looked like that, and I've never found him attractive before now. Cute, yes. Good-looking, that's undeniable. But attraction?*

On reflection, it wasn't really his looks. It was more the way he held her, muscular and strong, warm and male. The way he touched her, without awkwardness and without hesitation. *The way he kissed me . . .* Shaking it off, she firmed her thoughts. *He's not the real Traver, and he's trying to muddle my mind with . . . with seduction—Goddess! I can hardly even* think *the word* seduction *in the same breath as Traver . . . but he's not the real Traver. Surely that means he knows what happened to Traver, and that means I'm going to get this version alone today.*

And thanks to this morning's hard work by Mother, Aunt Hylin, and me, I have the perfect excuse to get him alone with me . . . Waving absently to his sister-in-law as she passed the older woman, Solyn reached the door of Traver's home. The sound of his laugh—even *that* sounded slightly off—caught her attention before she could knock on the open door.

Detouring to the goat barn, she stopped at the entryway and peered into the shadowy depths of the large building. Clumps of hay fell from above, pitched by Traver and his younger brother Tellik. They looked like they were in the last stages of tidying the barn for the morning, for the straw on the ground was clean, and the stalks they were shoveling from the loft were landing in the mangers. Mostly in the mangers. Flapping her hand at a stray wisp that floated her way, Solyn waited patiently for them to notice her.

"Oh, hello, Solyn! Hey, Traver, it's your *betroooothed*," Tellik teased. He did it with a friendly wave to her, at least.

"Keep your mind on your work," Traver returned calmly, though he did give her a smile. "Hello, Solyn. We're almost done here."

He's acting like he's gained four or five years, Solyn decided, hands going to her hips. She had to consciously remind herself not to seem belligerent, and relaxed her arms again. "Well, that's good. Mother wants to see you for your checkup, since you're *not* supposed to be doing heavy work until today, and then you need to . . . I mean, I would *like* your help in transporting the cheeses, if she clears your shoulder for heavy lifting and carrying. Which she should, if you're mucking stalls and pitching hay."

"Goddess, not even married yet, and already she's giving you orders." Tellik snorted.

Traver narrowed his eyes. "Just for that, *you* can finish pitching the hay and filling the water buckets. Mind you pour out the old on the garden herbs, and don't just dump in fresh."

"I *know*," Tellik complained, rolling his eyes.

Traver jumped down into one of the larger mounds of straw. Solyn held her breath, since that was an uneven surface, but he *thumped* in an easy crouch, picked his way out of the straw, and hung his pitchfork from one of the pegs on the wall, making sure the metal tines faced the wall. "Let me tell Father; he's turning the compost piles behind the hen yard, then I'll be free to go."

Nodding, Solyn waited in the shade of the goat barn. Tellik finished his chores, jumped down, and hung his pitchfork on the wall next to his brother's. Catching sight of it after a few moments, she tsked and turned it around. Metal tines were more sturdy than wooden ones, but they were also more dangerous. A scratch carried the risk of infection, and a puncture carried a risk to one's life. A good Healer—even if she was only so-so at the magical side of things—made sure her charges took the appropriate steps to prevent injury.

He took his time in coming back to her. She saw why when whoever it was pretending to be Traver returned. Face, arms, and chest had been scrubbed clean, and he was shrugging into an equally clean tunic. At her look, he smiled. "Father wants a round of your mother's hyssop cheese in exchange for my labor, and my mother would kill me if I ruined whatever batch Reina's making, so I took the time to clean up a bit."

Fastening the short-sleeved garment from throat to waist, he smiled and nodded. "Lead the way."

Doubt once more crept into her mind. *He can't be an impostor. One and all, their personalities went downhill. Ruder, more arrogant, crueler, dismissive of women and children, argumentative . . . but this fellow is . . . is . . . nice. But he's not the same as Traver. So I cannot be wrong . . . can I? None of the others would've thought of the need to be clean first.*

Dithering silently, she escorted him up to her mother, where he sneezed three times. Each time, Solyn noted, was a moment when her mother used actual magic to examine him. *How odd. He's never reacted like that before. Not like magic was . . . was like weed pollen to him.*

Her mother pronounced him perfectly healed and ready for work. "With that in mind," Reina stated briskly, clearing away the materials she had used to make him one last posset for his health, "I want you to help Solyn haul the cheeses we made this morning to the caves. Flavor them with the greenvein mold, set them in the presses overnight, and help her wrap them for the next two weeks, or until they stop beading with whey."

"Solyn told me she wanted my help," he agreed, "and I'm ready and willing."

Reina eyed the two of them, brows quirked in suspicion, then sighed. ". . . Wait here."

She ducked into the herb-room. Traver glanced at Solyn, visibly puzzled. She shrugged in return, muttering under her breath. "Don't look at me. The cheeses are still in the draining cloths, which are in the kitchen, not the herb-room. I don't know what she's doing in there."

"What I'm doing," her mother's voice drifted through the herb-room door, "is what I should've done when the two of you finally made up your minds about each other. Ah, there they are . . ." A cupboard door snapped shut. Moments later, Reina emerged, two braided leather thongs in her hands. Strung onto the braids were rune-carved beads.

Belatedly, Solyn realized what they were. Face flushing red, she protested, "*—Mother!*"

"If you're old enough to be betrothed, then you're old enough to think about twining all the way with each other." Pushing one into her daughter's hands, she held out the other to Traver. "You *will* start wearing these contraceptive amulets, both of you. And you in specific, young man, *will not* get my daughter pregnant outside of marriage. Is that clear?"

Traver blushed as well. Taking the anklet from her, he mumbled a polite, if awkward, "Yes, Healer Reina. No, Healer, Reina. Um . . . thank you?"

"Mother!" Solyn huffed. "As if I'd . . . ugh! We're going to be wrapping and waxing *cheese*, Mother, not making babies!" Clutching the amulet, she grabbed Traver by the wrist and hauled him out of the healing room. "Come on—I've parked a barrow cart by the kitchen door. We made sixty pounds of cheese this morning. Or at least it feels like it," she muttered, hauling him through the front entry and back to the kitchen. "Everyone contributed buckets of milk last night. You start loading them into the cart, and I'll grab the cloths Aunt Hylin boiled for us yesterday."

It didn't take long for them to load up the narrow, two-wheeled cart, nor did it take much effort for Traver to heft the handles up and start guiding it around the house and down the sloping, shallow-stepped paths. The hard part was making sure the cart didn't get away from either of them; the return trip, burdened with fewer cheeses, would be much easier to make.

"You'll have to direct me," he grunted, braking the cart by leaning back as it bumped and rattled down a set of uneven stone steps.

"Some things are coming back, but my memory's still unreliable. Sometimes I recognize a location, and other times I'm all turned around. I'd rather just have you lead the way."

"Right." Since they weren't alone—it seemed like they were never alone—Solyn bit back what she wanted to say. Instead, she gestured at the trees lining the bottom of the valley. "It's a lengthy walk. We're going up-valley this time, to a cave near Tunric's mine shafts. I brought some bread and water and a few plums to eat. You're pretty much stuck with me for the rest of the afternoon; less time, if you can at least remember how to press and wrap cheese."

Personally, she doubted it. The real Traver knew how; they'd been making cheese runs together for ages. His mother, Tenaria, was the woman who specialized in goat's milk cheese, just as her own mother was known for ones made from cow's milk. An impostor might know a bit about farming or pick it up easily, but cheesemaking was an art; any lack of knowledge would show.

"Ah," he murmured. "No wonder your mother thought we, um . . . needed . . ." He trailed off on a cough.

That, too, was an oddity. *Most of the ones I think are shapeshifted men, they're awfully randy*, Solyn thought, puzzling over the differences. *They'll leer, they'll smirk, and like Tarquin, they'll even try to steal a kiss. But this one—if he is one—is, well, uncomfortable about it. Except he really knows how to kiss, and something like that surely takes practice*?

Thoughts circling uselessly, Solyn gave up on them. Nothing could be settled until they had privacy, and they wouldn't have privacy until they reached the cheese caves. She searched for an innocuous topic. "So . . . any thoughts about the Early Harvest Faire?"

"I . . . think I'd enjoy it?" he offered. She couldn't tell if he shrugged, since his shoulders were straining to brake the cart over a steep spot. He continued after the barrow reached a more level section. "I really can't remember my last Faire. Most of what I remember is working hard—which doesn't seem fair, you know."

"Oh?" she asked, wondering if she should offer to take the cart on some of the more level stretches. "Why not?"

"Why should I remember the boring bits after being knocked silly, when the exciting and fun and lovely bits are so much more interesting?" Traver asked her, flashing her a grin.

Rolling her eyes, she didn't dignify that with a response.

Finally, her ring twisted on her finger. She almost missed it, washing the whey from her hands in the basin provided near the cave entrance. Thankfully, her father had crafted it with a set of rounded notches along each edge. The bumping sensation was distinct. *About time. Who in the Gods' names could've been so close as to have heard us, yet not be noticed by either of us?*

Drying her hands on the scrap of linen hanging from the iron washstand, she hurried back into the lantern-lit depths of the cave. Once upon a time, the place had been a mining tunnel, but the vein of silver had long since run out. Now it was used to store cheeses and other goods which needed to be kept cool.

As she hurried deeper into the mine, the tangy, pungent smell of greenvein mold and wooden racks mingled with the scents of salt-rubbed cheeses in various stages of aging. The place reeked of age-old family secrets to her senses, but at least it was a familiar smell. The way her best friend was acting, on the other hand, stunk of much fresher ones. ". . . Traver? Where are you? Traver?"

He had washed his hands before her. Solyn knew that much. He had moved back, and she had stepped up to the basin to wash her own, and . . . and he had vanished. The man walked too softly; that was another point against him being the real Traver. Making her way back to the front of the cave, she called his name again as she moved.

"I'm here. I stepped out to use the bushes." His voice came from ahead, out by the entrance. She hurried back in time to see him rinsing his hands at the basin. He gave her a lopsided smile. "So. The cheeses are in the presses, having the last of the whey squeezed out overnight. Which means we come back tomorrow for salting and wrapping, right?"

"Right," she agreed. Then planted her hands on her hips. "But we're not leaving just yet. I want to have a few words with you, first."

He glanced at the cave mouth, then lifted a damp finger to his lips. Wiping off his fingers, he shooed her deeper into the cave. "Not up front. I'm tired of people constantly hovering near—within eyesight, if not always earshot."

She blushed at the implications. "Traver Ys Ten, if you think for one moment I brought you back here for *twining* . . . Well, you're *obviously* not acting like yourself."

He flashed her a grin, tucking her behind a row of shelves. "Maybe I'm just looking at you with fresh eyes."

That made her roll her eyes. "Ugh. Just stop it, please? I *know* we're finally alone. You don't have to act around me . . . because I *know* you're not the real Traver Ys Ten. If you were . . . I think the sunsets are particularly orange at this time of year. What do you think?"

He gave her a blank look.

Her hopes fell. "You're *not* the real Traver. And that means I'm going to have to do something about you. Don't even bother lying."

Kenyen lost his smile. He glanced nervously at the passage back to the cave entrance. "Hush . . ."

Seeing his worried look, she held up her hand, displaying the silver ring on her middle finger. "What, the real one didn't tell you about this? Or our code phrases?"

Looking back at her, he blinked. "I . . . don't remember?"

Solyn poked him in the chest, emphasizing each point. "You. Are not. Traver. You are too confident. Too self-assured. Too graceful. Too . . . *manly*. Too strong—and too *tall* . . . I think." She frowned a little in thought, then shook it off. "But that doesn't matter. I'd swear you were one of *them*, but you're also . . . too *nice*!"

His brows lifted. "Well, as far as accusations go, that last one isn't too bad."

Again, she rolled her eyes. "Traver! Or whoever you are. Ugh . . . sometimes I think you *are* still him, and others . . . Well, there's only one way to be *sure*-sure."

She reached for his forehead. Kenyen flinched. He hadn't formed the skin-flap to hide his fake Banished brand because he hadn't needed to form it, save for at the bonfire gathering last night. His hair was pulled back in a braid, to hide the fact that he couldn't quite get the curl right, but she wasn't after his hairline. She was after one of the short, wispy hairs that had escaped his plait.

"*Ow!* Why'd you pull that out?" he demanded as quietly as he could. Kenyen scowled at her, rubbing the stinging spot just above his left temple. "What was that for?"

"*Kuzon-ghiff!*"

The odd words triggered a sneeze from him. It also writhed the finger-length wisp of hair in her grip, twisting it into a loose knot. Kenyen frowned, confused. "What . . . ?"

"It's the one truth-sensing spell I know. If it tightens the knot," she explained to him, her chin lifted belligerently, "then you're telling the truth. But if it *loosens*—and especially if it straightens—then I'll know it's a lie. And I want the *truth* from you. Who are you, really?"

He studied her for a long moment, then looked back at the entrance. "That's a dangerous question, if we're not truly alone."

"You *will* answer me," she ordered. "I'll not let you leave until you do. Don't think you can get past me."

"Shhh." Eyeing her slender frame, Kenyen didn't believe she could stop him. Not a warband-trained shifter. But he didn't contradict her statement. Lowering his voice, Kenyen murmured. "I will answer, *if* you speak softly." Waiting for her to nod, Kenyen sighed when she remained stubbornly silent. "Fine. Please, just *listen* to me. All the way through, before you go running and screaming."

Solyn watched the loosely knotted hair. It squeezed tighter, sliding on the side of the truth. She nodded. "Alright. Speak."

"You're right, I'm not the real Traver Ys Ten. My name is Kenyen Sin Siin, and I am from the Shifting Plains—but *not* as a Banished criminal," he stated quickly, cutting her off before she could do more than open her mouth. "I actually came here with a group of fellow Shifterai to look for a group of Banished criminals, who we feared were committing further crimes along our borders.

"We split up to cover more ground after we found some disturbing evidence of their activities in these mountains, and that's when I ran across the real Traver on the way here," Kenyen confessed. Her gaze darted between his face and the knotted strand of his hair, which had tightened. "I heard his story about shapeshifters taking over the faces of local townsfolk, and it matched with some of the things we'd found . . . but before I could help him get back to the others, he was ambushed by the man you call Zellan Fin Don."

Solyn sucked in a breath, startled by that news. The hair was still closely knotted. Licking her lips, she asked. "Is he . . . is he all right?"

"For now. I saw him last night," Kenyen added. "He's being fed and watered, but they're holding him captive somewhere—I couldn't tell you what roads to take from here, since I don't know the area well enough, but it's in the root cellar of some isolated shepherd's hut. They've told him that once they get whatever it is they want, he'll be let go . . . but I'm pretty sure they're lying."

That made her wince. "Mother . . ." she breathed. Solyn checked the wisp of dark brown hair in her grip—still knotted tightly—and met his confused look. "They're after something my mother made. You don't need to know what."

Kenyen shook his head. "I think I do. Because they want me—in the guise of Traver—to worm my way into your family's graces and get it. They won't tell me what it is just yet, since they don't quite trust me enough. Probably to make sure I won't run off with whatever it is myself. But whatever it is, they are willing to kill for it . . . and that means the real Traver's life is on the line."

She mulled that over, nibbling on her bottom lip. Occasionally Solyn glanced at the hair. Now that he wasn't speaking, it slowly relaxed into its neutral, half-knotted state. "I'm not sure . . ."

Not sure what she was thinking, Kenyen offered, "Maybe if I knew what to *avoid* telling them, I wouldn't accidentally let the wrong thing slip. Have you considered that? My goals right now are to get Traver, you, your family, and myself out of this mess alive, then to get word to the other Shifterai about what's been going on in these mountains, and finally to find *some* way of stopping these shifters, of bringing them to justice."

The hair knotted itself tightly, and stayed knotted for several seconds after he finished speaking. It finally relaxed as the silence stretched between them. He was telling her the truth. Solyn sighed. She wasn't the best mage out there, lacking as she did anything resembling real training, but this was one of the spells she had mastered. With the real Traver's help, no less. "Alright. I believe you. I just . . . you're *not* him, and yet . . ."

She blushed. The pink tint to her cheeks, visible in the light from the oil lamps hung around the cave, intrigued Kenyen. "And yet . . . ?"

Her cheeks warmed further. Solyn tried to dismiss it, turning away from him. "It's nothing."

Catching her hands, Kenyen gently held her still. "Oh, no, you don't. You're the one person I have available to help me pretend to be Traver well enough to fool these curs. What is it?"

"*Nothing.*" She tried tugging her hands away but couldn't shake his grip. Not without losing the enspelled hair. The moment she released it, the truth-telling magic would fade and she would have to pluck a fresh hair and start all over again. Sighing, she gave up trying. "You're just . . . I wasn't attracted to Traver the entire time I knew him, until . . . well, obviously I'm still not attracted to *him*. But don't let that go to your head, shifter! You've stolen his face. I don't like that."

Flushing at the compliment, Kenyen cleared his throat. "Actually, it was his idea." She looked up at him, and he nodded at the strand of his hair, still pinched between her thumb and forefinger. The knot had tightened. "Neither of us wanted to be in this situation, but we are. He's been smart about it, playing along. So have I. As much as we'd wish differently, this is what we've had to do.

"Now, *you* tell me the truth, Solyn," he ordered her, watching her carefully. "Is my kissing you breaking any oaths you gave to my counterpart? And is it making you uncomfortable? Because I'm being pressured to court you fast, to seduce you into bringing me into your family and win their trust before you or they can ask any questions about my differences. These Mongrel curs are *expecting* me to kiss you. If I don't at least act like I'm willing to comply, they'll suspect *I'm* not what I'm pretending to be. Toward them, I mean."

That made her blush harder. Reluctantly, she muttered, "No, we haven't broken any promises. I just, well, panicked when Tarquin the Pushy kept trying to kiss me, and I blurted out that Traver had already asked me to marry him. He didn't really believe me, but Traver—the real one—was willing to play along. But then he had to go with the caravan, and . . . He was *supposed* to head down to the Morning River Valley, then cut north and head for the Plains, but he did manage the formal visit to my parents before he left. Or was supposed to leave."

"Only things didn't work out that way," Kenyen agreed under his breath. "Well. If I'm not breaking any vows between you, that does make me slightly less uncomfortable, at least."

The way he phrased it made Solyn eye him warily. She didn't know whether to be offended by that statement or not. "What do you mean, slightly *less* uncomfortable? You didn't exactly kiss me like you were uncomfortable with it!"

That made him wrinkle his nose. "On the Plains . . . maidens aren't to be kissed. At all. That's reserved for marriage. You're not a Shifterai, and the rules for outkingdom women are a bit less restrictive—mostly it's making sure you fully agree and aren't coerced, and that it doesn't go against local customs. But you didn't know who I was at the time, which is why I didn't want to kiss you without . . . Unfortunately, Tarquin is one of them, and he was testing me, to see how much 'loyalty' I retain to the Plains."

"Loyalty?" Solyn asked, relieved he wasn't offended at the thought of kissing *her*. And slightly annoyed with herself that such a thing should even matter. Another thought crossed her mind. "Wait—if maidens aren't to be kissed at all, how can you possibly be so good at it?"

He blinked at the question. Solyn blushed, realizing how blunt that statement was. Before she could retract her curiosity, he cleared his throat and spoke.

"We have a special rank of priestesses whose duty is to instruct young men on how to . . . kiss women, and so forth . . . so they'll be good husbands. They also tend to the physical needs of the men who aren't married. *And* the earth-priestesses instruct our maidens on what to expect and how to . . . so on and so forth . . . so that it's enjoyable for both parties," Kenyen stated, hedging around the direct words for such things.

Tugging her left hand free, Solyn fanned herself. "Goodness," she mumbled. "That's a bit more . . . um . . . organized than the Corredai way."

He released her other wrist. "It's our way of showing respect. Which is why these *curs* who are impersonating people are trying to press me to show disrespect by seducing you. They have a long history of *not* respecting women."

Solyn considered that. "Didn't you also say that there are a different set of rules for dealing with outkingdom women?"

"The woman has to be mature enough to handle a frank discussion, as well as fully grown and not still developing physically," Kenyen told her. "She cannot be married to anyone else. She has to be fully aware and consenting . . . and it's strongly discouraged from, um, I believe you call it 'twining completely' unless one or both parties is wearing . . . well, something like this."

He pulled the amulet from the pocket of his gathered trousers, displaying it for a moment, then tucked it away again. Face warm, he cleared his throat. Solyn, equally uncomfortable, sought for something else to discuss. She recalled her earlier question.

"What was that you mentioned about loyalty, to the Plains?" she asked. He started to shrug, looking like Traver but not moving like him; the difference, knowing that he *wasn't* the real Traver Ys Ten, disturbed her. Solyn interrupted him. "—Wait, could you show me what you *really* look like? Your face is Traver's, but you just don't *move* like him, and it's bothering me."

Nodding, Kenyen relaxed his shifted features. It felt good, like stretching and relaxing a muscle that had been clenched for too long. His clothes didn't change and his hair remained braided, but it darkened and turned straight. His face shifted from oval to more heart-shaped, he gained a thumb-length in height, and the proportions of his muscles shifted, filling out more evenly over his body, rather than concentrating in his shoulders, calves, and thighs.

He spread his arms. "This is the real me. Take a good look. I won't be able to stay this way until after the real Traver is free and these members of the so-called Family Mongrel have been dealt with."

Solyn glanced quickly at the hair still clutched in her hand. It was firmly knotted, proving this was the shifter's true form. She nodded and studied him. He was actually kind of handsome. Most of it, she could still sense lay in the confident way he stood in front of her, neither hunching his shoulders nor ducking his head. Solyn nodded again when she had his face and figure committed to memory. "Thank you."

"Thank *you* for believing me," he murmured. Reluctantly, Kenyen shifted back. The process of turning himself into Traver Ys Ten took three times as long as returning to himself, particularly as he had no mirror to consult. Once he felt confident in his shape, he spoke again. "I'm sorry; I'd stay in my true shape, but it takes concentration to put on another man's face, and I can't risk anyone wandering in here and finding us together like this—as it is, I'm thoroughly nervous that one of those damned shifters is still outside, watching us."

Solyn gave him a puzzled look. "Wait . . . didn't Traver tell you anything when he gave you the ring? I know he gave it to you. I saw it . . . and *why* did you put it *there*, of all places?"

He blushed at the mention of it. "Uh, no. He didn't. He just handed it to me as covertly as he could—and I wore it *there* because *he* was wearing it there. We weren't in a position to exchange more than a word or two—he did tell me you expected me to wear it, but that was all he had the time to say, so I couldn't exactly ask him *why* it was being worn there. In fact, I thought *you* knew I was supposed to wear it there."

"Well, I had no clue where he'd put it!" Solyn retorted, embarrassed by mention of the ring's location on the underside of his manhood. "I thought he put it inside his mouth or something."

Kenyen wrinkled his nose at that. "Wouldn't that bang it against his teeth, maybe chip them, or at the least make noise whenever he chewed or talked? At least where it is now, it's not interfering with anything. Um, yet," he added, blushing with the thought of it possibly getting in the way for certain activities. He diverted the conversation away from that train of thought, though. "Is there something special about his ring? Or yours?"

"Of course it's special," she told him, covering the band with her other hand. "It's an enchanted pair of rings. So long as we stay within common speaking distance of each other, if anyone lurks within hearing range of us, my ring will warn me of it. It also tells me when they're *not* there . . . and right now, nobody is there. Which means we're free to speak. It won't last, since we do have to go back, but we're free to speak. For now. You can . . . you know, look like yourself for a while."

Debating the risks, Kenyen relaxed his features again. Under her curious gaze, he did what he had been longing to do since morning: rub his face until the muscles stopped trying to spasm.

Solyn watched. "Does that hurt when you do that? Change your shape?"

He shook his head. "No. Well, not normally. You can stretch and squish, pull and twist, and if you do it right, it doesn't hurt. It just feels . . . stretchy."

"Stretchy?" she repeated, dubious.

"You'd have to be a shapeshifter to understand it," he said, dismissing her confusion. "Here's another question. What made you think it was *wise* of you to confront a possible shapeshifter on your own? I *could* have been a member of Family Mongrel. These are dangerous men, and from what I've read, they wouldn't think twice about hurting you."

"Pliss." A bubble of fire appeared above her upturned palm, burning without visible fuel source. It cast gold-hot light on both of them for the few seconds she held it there. Dismissing it, she lifted her brows in silent emphasis.

Kenyen sneezed. "Ah, right," he muttered, pinching his nose.

"You're a mage. Well, I hope you'd be fast enough with a counter-spell, but I'd feel a lot better if you didn't let yourself be cornered by any of them."

He was definitely not Traver. Frowning, Solyn studied him. "How odd, that you sneeze every time someone does magic around you. None of my books mentioned that as a side effect of magic."

Sniffing to clear his sinuses, Kenyen shrugged. "I'd say one in ten or twelve shifters gets this way around mages. Most don't always sneeze, though our nose tickles like it wants to. But then mages are pretty rare on the Plains. Most of our magics seemed to have soaked into our flesh, making us shifters."

"Hm. Well, maybe an allergy posset might help," she offered, mulling over the possibilities. "It's not well known that I'm a mage—other than just enough to be my mother's apprentice. Everyone knows that Healing magics are a bit different from other magics, focused toward nurturing life and health rather than altering other aspects of reality. They all think I take after my mother, and I've encouraged that view, but aside from a few spells and of course all the herb-based remedies, I actually can't do most of what she does. Nor can she do most of what I can do."

Nose no longer itching, Kenyen lifted his chin. "You know, if you ever came to the Plains, my people would pay you well for your spells."

That made her roll her eyes. "You really *aren't* Traver. I do know a *few* things. I can defend myself, certainly. But what I've learned is only what I've puzzled out of books. What I *need* is to head to one of the cities, maybe even the capital, and learn from a real mage. I've heard there's a mage academy there. My father's offered several times to send me, but . . ."

"But, what?" Kenyen asked. There was a stool at the back of the racks, used to reach the top shelves. He pulled it over and sat on it, tired of standing. "Why don't you go? What are these Mongrel curs after, that you feel you have to stay and help protect it?"

Solyn bit her lip, indecisive. She looked at the hair in her hand. "You won't tell them?"

"My word of honor as a son of Family Tiger, I will not tell them," he promised. The knotted hair tightened.

Solyn lifted her gaze to the wheels of cheese around them. "They're after this. Well, sort of."

SIX

Confused, Kenyen peered at the waxed rounds on the shelves around them, then peered at her. He looked between the two of them again, confused. ". . . They're after moldy cheese?"

"Do you know how bluesteel is made?" Solyn asked him. "Your people craft it all the time."

"I know there's a special process which turns regular steel into bluesteel," Kenyen admitted. "It's some sort of liquid in which they quench the hot blades during the forging process. And that we trade with the people of this kingdom for the special ingredients to make that liquid. Beyond that, I don't know. Most people don't, unless they apprentice themselves to the blacksmiths in the Shifting City."

"It's moldy tea," Solyn stated flatly. That made him blink. She gestured at the cave around them. "Specifically, moldy tea that's been improperly preserved and stored in a cave not much different from this one. You can't drink the stuff; it'll turn your insides inside out for a couple of hours if you do. But quench a blade in the brew every time you heat and cool the metal, two dozen or more times, and it picks up something from the tea that makes permanent scars."

"Quench it fifty or more times, and it makes it impossible for a shifter to shift shape when being touched by it, too," Kenyen muttered. That much, he knew. "It also starts to interfere with magic, though not to as great an extent. But what does moldy tea have to do with moldy cheese? Is this the same kind of mold?"

She shook her head quickly, her braid bouncing across her back. "No, this is greenvein cheese. Unlike the bluesteel tea, it's quite edible. Even those who have trouble digesting cheese, such as the real Traver, find this one less likely to upset their stomach. But it's an acquired taste. Very tangy and sharp. Not everyone likes it."

Kenyen still didn't know what cheese, moldy or otherwise, had to do with bluesteel. "Why would the Mongrel shifters want to get their hands on a special kind of cheese? Didn't you say anyone could store cheese in this cave, if they wanted to flavor it this way? And, by extension, come in here and pick up a wheel if they really wanted to? There aren't any doors on this place."

"By itself the cheese does nothing. But quench a blade in it, repeatedly, and . . ." She shrugged. "My mother was curious to know if anything else might alter the properties of steel, besides the bluesteel mold. She tried this and that, all manner of steeps and brews, and for love of her, my father indulged her. Nothing made any changes other than the moldy tea, for a long time.

"But one day, while crafting a small knife, my father jokingly cut a slice of greenvein cheese with the red-hot blade, 'pre-melting it' as he called it. He did this a few times for a snack, then realized when the blade had cooled that it had changed color slightly. It became greensteel."

"*Green*steel?" Kenyen asked, amused by the name. "Why not redsteel, or yellowsteel?"

Solyn rolled her eyes. "Because that's the color it turned? It had a greenish cast to it, so they named it greensteel. He finished forging the blade that way, deepening the color, then my mother claimed the knife so she could do some experiments with it. When she did . . . she discovered that anything cut by it, the cut would heal whole and well. Even if she scored a new cut across an old scar, the section that was injured by the knife would reknit itself whole."

"Gods, that has to be the *best* Healer's . . ." He trailed off as the implications hit him. Kenyen paled. "Oh, no. That could be enough magic to *remove* a bluesteel scar. Or rather, a bluesteel *brand*," he muttered, one hand lifting to rub his own unmarked brow. "*That's* what they're after. The book said they repeatedly swore they'd find a way to get back onto the Plains and take revenge against the women who Banished them, but so long as they bore their permanent scars . . ."

". . . Book? What book?" Solyn asked as he trailed off, confused. She leaned against the nearest shelf as she asked the question; standing for so long after the hard work of flavoring and pressing all that new cheese was tiring. She flexed each knee under her skirt, making sure her circulation was still good.

Seeing her restless movements, the Shifterai held out his hand. She gave it a bemused look, until he patted his knee. Blushing, she hesitated, then accepted the proffered seat, sneaking him a wary, curious look. Kenyen didn't take advantage of her closeness. Instead, he answered her question.

"Most of what I do is travel as a member of one of the warbands from Family Tiger, Clan Cat. Last year, we rescued a maiden from potential abuse by a group of Mornai villagers. She and my elder brother, Akodan, fell in love. It wasn't easy, because she didn't trust us at first," Kenyen told Solyn. "Her village was kind of isolated, and all she knew about the Shifterai was what her mother had told to the village scribe. He recorded her mother Ellet's words in a book, which my sister-in-law brought onto the Plains with her.

"In that book . . . it detailed the horrible abuses Ellet had suffered at the hands of a group of Banished shifters who called themselves members of Family Mongrel—that *isn't* an official Shifterai Family—which is sort of like one of your valley holding groups, only bigger—nor is it affiliated with any Shifterai Clan, which is like a holding of a holding," he told her. "In truth, we didn't even know that Banished criminals had banded together, nor that they were skirting the southern edges of the Plains.

"Winters on the north side of these mountains are much worse than on the south side, so your people don't have very many settlements that close to the Shifting Plains. Our people are usually busy tending their herds down on the Plains themselves, and thus we don't go up into the foothills all that often . . . so for years, nobody knew they were there," Kenyen explained.

Solyn nodded slowly. "I can see how that could come to be, when you put it that way."

"Well, that's what we were doing when I stumbled across Traver. I came with a group of fellow shifters into the mountains, led by a trio of Princesses of the People, to officially track them down and make sure they weren't tormenting women, still," he explained. "In a cave which appeared to have been used by shapeshifters, we found a long-dead body and a hidden message claiming that he—the body—was the real Tunric Tel Vem, but we weren't sure of the location, so we split up to try and find the right place."

She nodded in comprehension. The shift in her weight on his thigh made Kenyen put his arm around her back, steadying her. Solyn didn't object to the support, so he left it there. This much, he knew was allowable in both of their cultures.

Seated on his knee as she was, Solyn found herself once more drawn to the shapeshifter in Traver's clothes. More so, despite knowing he was an impostor. He *wasn't* Traver, which meant she wasn't abruptly, puzzlingly attracted to someone she'd never been attracted to before. She was drawn to someone new. Having him look like himself helped clarify the difference in her mind . . . and looking as handsome as he did didn't hurt. Technically Tarquin was the better-looking man, but she suspected that was as much from shifting himself near-perfect features.

But tentative thoughts of twining with this near-stranger weren't helping their situation. She redirected her attention back to the past, to the cause of their current mess. "Mother loaned her knife to a fellow Healer a few valleys away, while she and Father worked on crafting more. The Healer and her family were slaughtered by what looked like wild animals, but there was no sign of animals having forced their way inside.

"The knife was found next to their bodies, badly damaged; Mother suspected a combination of magic and something acidic, because the other Healer was an alchemist and had jars of acidic and alkaline solutions in her herb-room. The investigators could just make out my father's maker's mark, which is how we heard about it. The damage had also ruined the blade's properties, so they didn't know the real significance of the knife, just that it had been found at the scene.

"*We* knew why the knife was there, and what it used to be. Mother figured the other Healer must have realized what her attackers were after and had done something to destroy it. Everyone who knew about the greensteel knife in all the valleys around us kept silent after that, for fear my family would be next," Solyn told him. "I'm trusting you a *lot* in telling you this. I want you to *swear* to me on this hair that you won't . . . oh. Perfect."

The hand she lifted was empty. Somewhere in their discussion, she had forgotten to keep hold on his enchanted hair. Disgusted with herself, Solyn lowered her arm back to her lap.

Kenyen covered her fingers with his own. "I swear to you, I will not tell them. You know I'm still telling you the truth. I have no reason to lie, and every reason to be honest with you. As great as this greensteel thing is for helping wounds to heal whole and sound, Ellet's book spoke of the curs who tormented her, of how they boasted they would find a way to sneak back onto the Plains and 'put women in their place.' Given the horrible things they did to my sister-in-law's mother . . . and given what I saw last night when they invited me to one of their shapeshifting bonfires . . . that is something I will *not* help them to do. No true Shifterai would, knowing what I know about these curs."

Solyn studied him, taking in his sober gaze. His real face wasn't as familiar to her as Traver's face, but she could still read his expression: he was telling the truth. She nodded. "Alright. I'll accept your oath. *Don't* break it. I'm a lot meaner than I look."

He snorted at that. "Not from what Traver's told me."

As much as his words implied a compliment, it was still a backhanded compliment when he used it to dismiss her threat like that. Determined to be taken seriously by this near-stranger, Solyn pinched him through his tunic. He yelped and batted her hand away, twisting on the stool. She pinched him again, or tried to; he blocked more successfully. It didn't take long for their squirming little fight to end with him wrapping his arms around hers, pinning her hands in place with his greater strength. He didn't hurt her, nor use his muscles to crush her, but he did hold her still. Solyn didn't struggle to get free. Being held like this felt surprisingly good.

Chuckling, Kenyen rested his chin on her head, taking advantage of their positions to cuddle her. She was sweet, pretty, smart, and in his arms for the moment. "You do know I wouldn't have impersonated him if the circumstances hadn't kicked both of us between the legs . . . but I find myself wishing I *was* him, just a little, so I could've grown up knowing you better."

"I doubt Traver could've handled himself so well, had your positions been reversed." She sighed, admitting the truth to herself.

"He's a good man, but he's still young. And he's not quite, um . . . well, he doesn't keep up with me, sometimes. He's content to be a farmer for the rest of his life. That's good and all, but I want more. I *need* more. I want to explore more than just the local valleys, and I need to master my magics, and go forth and do great things.

"Traver is meant to live in the Nespah Valley. I'm meant for something else. And you?" She sighed. "Well, you're not Traver. You're a lot more confident. A lot more . . . worldly, I suppose."

"Mm," Kenyen murmured, relaxing his grip enough so that he could cuddle her more comfortably. She shifted closer, leaning into his shoulder. That pleased him. They were in this situation together, so it was good she was willing to trust him. "Traveling can be fun. I've enjoyed going out with the warbands, exploring new lands, meeting new people.

"I had plans to enjoy this summer's warband expedition, before things got turned upside down." At her questioning look, Kenyen elaborated. "My brother stayed home with his wife, since she's now pregnant, so our friend Deian was going to lead the next warband expedition outkingdom, looking for trade or work. For the first time in a long time, I'd have been completely out from under his shadow.

"I don't always like being compared to my brother—near constantly, because he's a very strong *multerai*, a shifter-lord with fifteen shapes while I have only seven to my name—but I do like being useful. But my brother asked me to go on this trip instead, along with our friend Manolo, to be representatives of both his interests as Lord of Family Tiger and Atava's interests as the daughter of one of their victims. So his name keeps coming up every once in a while."

Solyn nodded. This Kenyen fellow didn't hold her like the real Traver would have, but the differences were an improvement. Part of it came from the scent of him: musky, warm male mingled with whey, salt, and the curing tang of the cheeses stacked around them. Part of it came from the way the arm around her back held her comfortably close, similar to the way he had held her during that kiss. Traver would've held her tentatively, or awkwardly, or loosely, or . . . or brotherly.

Solyn was well aware this wasn't her brotherly best friend holding her, and she suspected he was aware of it, too. Which did bring up another question. "So . . . what are we going to do?"

"Figure out a way to get Traver out of this mess alive. That's the first priority, since he's in the greatest, most immediate danger," Kenyen murmured, content to hold her. There was nothing untoward in his cuddling a maiden on his knee, especially an outkingdom one, but he admitted to himself it was a treat. The last time he had done anything like this had been almost half a year ago. It felt good, but thankfully wasn't too much a distraction to prevent him from thinking. "The second priority is to keep them from getting their hands on your family's secret.

"Third is keeping the rest of us alive, and fourth—but not least—is stopping these men and punishing them for the crimes they have committed since leaving the Plains." He smiled wryly at her. "It may make me sneeze, but that hair-knotting trick of yours is quite clever. Not quite as easily visible to everyone as a Truth Stone would be, but clever all the same."

"I don't know how to make a Truth Stone," Solyn admitted. "I know there are a couple of different ways, but I don't know the actual steps involved."

"Well, the people I came here with have one, so between the two of you, it's a start on helping us uncover the truth," Kenyen said. He shook his head. "I'm just not sure how to *tell* them what's been happening here. I'm constantly watched by the other shifters, and if *you* went anywhere outside your normal routine, I'm sure they'd think that was suspicious, the same way they thought Traver's leaving the caravan was suspicious. Particularly since I'm supposed to be seducing you."

That lifted her head from his shoulder. "Well, I don't *have* to leave the valley to send a message, you know."

"They might be watching for any messages being sent with another person, just like they were watching for someone like Traver to leave," Kenyen reminded her. He loosened his grip a little as she shook her head and sat up again.

"No, no, I mean if I or someone I'm working with *personally* knows someone else, I can send a spell-based message to that person. We couldn't do that because neither of us actually knew anyone from the Shifting Plains, so that's why he tried to go in person. I don't know why he left the caravan early, though," Solyn added. "Maybe something about one of the others frightened him?"

"Probably Zellan," Kenyen muttered grimly. "Traver hasn't been in a position to say in detail what made him break away early, nor can I ask him." He eyed Solyn. "This spell of yours, if *I* know the person, you can get the message to them? How does that work?"

"Well, first I enchant the paper, then you write the message you want while keeping a solid image of the person in your thoughts—I do some further chanting while you do that—and then I fold the paper into a bird shape. You write the person's name on each of its wings, and you should have a general idea of where the bird is . . . er, I mean, the person," she corrected herself, blushing at the gaff. "Well, that is, presuming you can write."

"I can," Kenyen confirmed. "Every Shifterai child is expected to learn how to read and write. We may be nomadic spring through fall, but we are civilized."

Solyn nodded, relieved. "Good. Not everyone bothers to teach their children, here in the mountains, but my parents insisted my siblings and I learn. Which turned out to be a good thing, when I discovered I had magic to spare. Anyway, once you've labeled its wings, I write the final rune on its head, and the paper bird flies off. Barring heavy rain or winds, it should reach its target about as fast as a regular bird can fly, only it doesn't have to stop to rest. But you have to know within an hour's travel of where the person will be, or the paper bird gets lost."

Kenyen didn't like the sound of that. He was fairly sure there would be enough shifters hanging around the town of Teshal, but weather was unpredictable. Particularly in the mountains, when it couldn't be seen approaching, as it could down on the Plains. Predicting the movements of his fellow shifters was slightly more certain than whether or not it would rain. He gave it a moment of thought, then offered, ". . . What about writing several letters? And sending them to several different people? That way at least one of them has a chance of getting through."

She nodded quickly. "That's a very good idea. We can write half a dozen letters without exhausting me, I think. But I don't have paper down here. Well, not the right kind. There's the paper in the ledger for keeping track of the cheeses," Solyn admitted, lifting her chin at an alcove farther back along the winding tunnel, "but it's too thick for easy folding."

"Then we'll just have to do it when we have the materials and the time," Kenyen reassured her. "Being able to send messages to the others is a big relief, but we don't dare let down our guard in the meantime. I need to keep pretending to be Traver Ys Ten, and you need to *treat* me like I'm Traver Ys Ten—after all, if you believe I'm the real one, your parents will believe it. His family is still giving me the occasional odd look for my differences, but the Mongrels don't care about Traver's family. The important thing is to make your family believe."

"I know. I also need to treat you like you're truly my betrothed. We still have the problem of Tarquin to overcome," Solyn reminded him. "You said they wanted you to worm your way into my family's trust. That means acting like a betrothed . . . except Traver and I have never really felt that way about each other."

"True, but we're expected to put on a show—or rather, I'm expected," Kenyen amended. He sighed again, rubbing his forehead with the hand not hooked around her waist. "My brother is better at laying long-term plans than I am, I'll admit . . . I tend to react with the flow of things, go with my instincts instead of my thoughts in the thick of battle. I do more of the thinking afterward, which isn't always the best time for it." Lowering his hand, he looked at Solyn, giving her a lopsided smile. "But *this* time, we can lay our plans in advance, right?"

Solyn nodded in sympathy. "I have trouble under pressure, too. That's how I ended up 'betrothed' to Traver in the first place. I wasn't expecting Tarquin to be so heavy-handed in approaching me like that." She snorted at the thought. "Ha! As *if* I'd be interested in him . . . He flirts with anything in a skirt, but doesn't actually care for any of the girls in the valley. Some of us are smart enough to realize it, but the rest just see his handsome face and think of his father being one of the wealthiest men in the Nespah Valley. They think about him inheriting the wealth of Tunric's silver and copper mines, and that's all they care to know or see."

"Well, then we'll just have to put on a show of you discovering just what a great lover Traver is. So to speak," Kenyen amended, clearing his throat. "I mean, I don't want to push you into anything you're not comfortable with, and I am a near-stranger . . . but it'll have to be done where the other shifters can see it happening, so they think that progress is being made while we wait for those paper birds to fly to their targets."

"Yes, it does have to be done in public for it to be convincing," Solyn agreed. Blushing a little, she added in warning, "But if we go *too* far in the act of pretending that you're seducing me, Father will have a fit and insist that you marry me."

"*Your* father? *My* father would insist on it, and he's not even here!" Kenyen snorted. "What's done in private with an outlander woman is something strictly between the two in question. Only they and the Gods will ever know. But what's done in public is an entirely different matter. The problem is, we *are* strangers. I don't feel comfortable courting you when I hardly know you. I do like everything I've learned so far, but . . ."

He trailed off. Solyn nodded in understanding. A stray thought curled up the corner of her mouth. "I'll bet you like everything but the sneezing part."

That made him chuckle. Squeezing her with his left arm, Kenyen rested his head against hers. "You'd be right, though it's tolerable enough, I suppose. I also like your sense of humor."

Her cheeks turned pink at the compliment. "Thank you. I like yours, too."

"Thank you," he murmured. A stray thought crossed his mind. "Solyn . . ."

"What?" she asked, tilting her head enough to glance at him.

"What if, instead of trying to court you like Traver would—relying on past memories and such, which I can't fake accurately enough to fool everyone around us—what if instead," he offered, "we just courted in the moment? Speaking nothing of the past, but instead talk about everything right now, and thinking about things for the future? *That* I can do easily enough, and still pretend to be Traver. The future isn't set in stone, and a man can always change his mind about his wishes and dreams."

She nodded slowly, thoughtfully. "That could work . . . Particularly if I let it slip that you've decided either your past memories will come back or they won't, so you're just going to get on with your life instead of trying to wait for them."

"I think we should also lay contingency plans for a reason to cover our tracks, should we have to run away," he offered. "Like say how disappointed I am that I didn't actually get to go with the caravan, and how excited I was to be traveling, and how much I'd like to give it a second try, only this time with you. Maybe you could say something similar, too—like how you'd want to go to the capital to get more training as a Healer than what your mother alone can provide."

"That could work. It's close enough to the truth—mage magics instead of healing magics—that I wouldn't have to pretend so much," she returned. Then chuckled. "I suppose I could also say I'd like to go along with you to make sure you don't fall off your mount and hit your head again. Traver and I have been pulling each other out of trouble ever since we were little, you know."

He grinned. "And I'll bet you were pulling each other *into* just as much trouble, too."

Solyn grinned back. "More, actually. We just pulled each other out whenever we were in danger of getting caught!"

They both laughed at that. When their laughter died down, Solyn found herself drawn to him. Before she could chicken out, she dared herself to press her lips to his, wanting another taste of his kiss. He pulled back for a moment, blinked, then relaxed and leaned in again, kissing her back.

She's not a Shifterai maiden, and she clearly wants this. She started it, Kenyen reminded his startled instincts, brushing his mouth against hers. *You've done this before with a couple of other outlander women. If she's willing, it's perfectly alright . . . mmm, and she tastes so good, too . . .*

To Solyn's delight, he was still a good kisser. A single day hadn't changed that fact. Nor had the sight of his true face; if anything, it added to the spice, since she didn't have to fight that voice in the back of her head crying, *But this is Traver! I've* never *felt that way about him!* Instead, the voice murmured, *This is definitely* not *Traver . . . and I like it!*

The thought made her giggle. She parted her lips, maybe to comment, maybe just to breathe. He took advantage of her offering, running his tongue along her upper lip before tilting his head and delving in for a deeper, more sensual kiss. Shivering in pleasure, Solyn clung to shoulders that were a little narrower, but definitely more muscular. All she could think of was how good this felt, sitting here with Kenyen's arms around her, his body warming her in the cool depths of the cheese cave, his mouth teaching hers that there was more to kissing than a few quick pecks or a bit of pressure.

This was wrong, yet right; Kenyen kept feeling like he was doing something naughty, since he wanted to respect Solyn like any maiden of the Plains. But she wasn't, and this by her own customs was alright. With her permission to kiss her, deeply and thoroughly, he was free to enjoy it while still respecting her by her own ways. Yet it still felt wicked. Thrilling. Arousing, even.

She shifted closer on his thigh, making him very aware of her curves. She smelled sweet and lovely, distinct among all the other odors in the cave. Womanly. Willing. Kenyen let his instincts take over, immersing himself in the taste and the touch and the scent of her. Only when her shudders turned to a stiffened sort of shock did he realize his free hand was gently kneading her breast through her tunic. Blushing, he pulled back.

"Um . . . sorry. For getting carried away," he apologized gruffly, embarrassed at his forwardness.

Solyn found herself blushing. "N-no, that's . . . um . . . I liked it. I just wasn't expecting it. To like it so much." Her blush deepened, and she covered her face with her left hand. "Oh, Goddess, I sound like Traver would . . . not that he's a total idiot, it's just . . . I'm babbling, aren't I?"

Chuckling, Kenyen hugged her with his left arm. "Actually, I'm surprised *I'm* not babbling, in the face of all this."

"It helps that you're not a murderous shapeshifter out to destroy my family," she muttered. One of the nearby lanterns hissed and guttered, sending shadows flicking all over the shelf-lined tunnel.

Solyn straightened, relieved that he let her sit up. "It's getting late. We need to get the cart back up to the house."

"Right. I have chores first thing in the morning, and then I'm supposed to come back here with you. Up you go." Letting her stand, Kenyen remained seated on the stool. Digging out the mirror from his pouch, he studied his face in the dancing glow of the lanterns. He was fairly confident he could shape Traver's face well enough without it, but he wanted to get it right. Stretching his body, he shrank some things, enlarged others, and altered his hair so that the color was a lighter shade of brown and the bits not caught up in the braid at the top were curly rather than straight.

Fascinated, if disturbed, Solyn watched him transform once more. She pointed at one of his eyebrows. "That brow is a little off. It's supposed to be a little thinner right there in the middle of that one, and the hairs are a little more scattered toward the end . . . There, that's close enough."

"Thanks." Clearing his throat, Kenyen shifted that, too. He offered her a sheepish smile, and spoke with Traver's lighter voice. "I think I feel uncomfortable now, wearing this when I know you know otherwise."

She smirked. "Good. Use it to act awkward. Or at least less graceful. Come on, let's finish cleaning up and readying things for tomorrow."

Kenyen took the hand she offered. Once he was on his feet, he pulled her into a hug, doing his best to make it brotherly and awkward, then grinned at the roll of her eyes. It felt too good to have another ally on his side to mind her reaction.

"So, did you twine with her yet?"

Kenyen slanted a look at Tarquin Tun Nev. Having finished his morning chores early, Traver's father had sent him on the task of gathering deadfall from the semi-wild woods at the bottom of the valley. A quick check showed they were more or less alone, but Kenyen didn't take any chances. *His* ring didn't let him know about such things. Which was a good thing in retrospect; he couldn't imagine it squeezing or sliding on his . . .

"Well? Is she any good?" Tarquin asked again, smirking.

"She let slip how many times she's turned you down," Kenyen countered calmly, stooping to pick up more twigs and toss them in the barrow cart. "She also implied how she wouldn't touch you even if you offered her your weight in gold." A glance showed the other man reddening. "So does it really matter how good she is?"

For a moment, Tarquin looked angry. Then a sly expression crept onto his face. He rubbed his chin thoughtfully. "You know . . . if I shifted shape to some stranger's face . . . I *could* find out. And then you could have fun 'comforting' the leftovers."

Bits of twigs flung out and down. Before most of them could hit the ground, Tarquin's back thumped into the nearest tree, thrust there by Kenyen. He choked and grabbed at the hand pressing his throat into the bark. Pressing, but not crushing. Kenyen kept most of his weight braced on the palm he had slammed into the trunk beside the other man's head.

Leaning in close, he growled in the other shifter's ear. "*My* prey. You don't steal honey from a bear, you don't take a kill from a tiger, and you don't touch *my prey*." He paused, mind racing, then added quietly. ". . . Not unless you offer me something much, much better. Like *you*."

Shifting his tongue broader and longer than normal, Kenyen slowly licked the other young man from chin to temple. Tarquin squirmed, gagging in disgust. Letting him go, Kenyen reshaped his tongue back to normal and licked his lips. He kept his gaze flat but quirked up the corner of his mouth in what he hoped was an unsettling half smile.

"Gods! You're *sick*!" Tarquin scrubbed at his cheek with the edge of his short sleeve.

"And *you're* an idiot. Which is more important, you forcing yourself on a single woman—when there are a hundred in this valley for you to choose from—or you *ruining* what your own elders have specifically ordered me to do?"

Tarquin wrinkled his nose. "You're acting like you couldn't use the old 'comforting the victim' routine to worm your way deeper into the family!"

Kenyen thumped the pad of his forefinger against the other shifter's head, right where Tarquin's Banished scar would be located, had he been an exiled criminal like his so-called father. Tarquin staggered back and scowled. Kenyen didn't let him speak.

"*Think*, you spawning defect," he ordered roughly, finger-thumping again until the other young man dodged the third time. "If you do *that*, her family will focus on it, and they won't let down their guard! They'll be worried your attack is somehow linked to whatever precious secret the others want, and they'll clamp up tighter than a dog guarding its first fresh meal in weeks! The best way to worm the secret out of them is to get them to *relax*, and that means letting me do my work. Preferably unfettered by any idiocy on your part.

"Besides, if *you* could do it, you've have wedded and bedded the girl, and dug up the secret by now," he added, giving Tarquin a dismissive, scornful look. "But you're so wrapped up in pursuing your own pleasures, you've hobbled yourself with shortsightedness. You don't have the discipline to go after bigger game. *You* can go after all the rabbits and sheep you want. *I'm* after a fat cow."

He meant it purely in hunting terms, but Tarquin threw back his head and laughed at Kenyen's word choice. "Ha! And you say *I'm* the spawning defect? Make sure you do succeed. Should you fail, when I go to comfort her, I'm telling her *you* called her a fat cow!" Still chuckling, he headed off through the woods, the tension between them thoroughly spoiled. "Good luck, 'Traver.' With seductive skills *that* smooth, you'll *need* it."

Aware that his time was shrinking, Kenyen returned to gathering fallen wood and tossing it in the cart. Rice and wheat stalks would be used later in the year to heat the homes of these Corredai folk, twisted into makeshift logs in styles similar to what the Shifterai did with dried grass from the Plains. The fallen limbs were still needed though, along with whatever else could be scavenged in the time he had left before he was supposed to meet Solyn.

When I do meet her, I'm warning her about Tarquin's suggestion the moment I can. And I'm going to ask her to tell me all the fighting spells she does know, so I know she'll have good ones ready if she ever has to defend herself.

Kenyen wrinkled his nose. Not from the pungency of the cheeses around them, but from the list of choices she had given. "That's not a lot of offensive spells. Plenty of defensive, but . . . well, some of them, I don't know why you even bothered to list them."

Solyn shook her head. "It isn't always about scorching, or . . . or zapping. The sticky spell, I could use that to glue someone's foot to the ground. Or their arm to their side. It's all in thinking up new ways to apply what you know."

"Except these are shifters," he reminded her, dipping his brush back into the lamp-heated pot of wax between them. The newly pressed cheeses had been wrapped in clean cloths to wick away the last of the whey as it escaped. These were some of the rounds from an earlier pressing, ones ready for protective waxing. "I'm not sure how well that spell would continue to stick in the face of our abilities. Most of what we do in the warbands is go up against feral livestock, bandits, or locals rebelling against the law, and mostly only in the neighboring kingdoms. We almost never go up against an evil mage, and the three times we did where I was along, either we knocked them out fast and wrapped them in bluesteel, or we killed them equally fast."

"Most of the surrounding kingdoms don't have that many mages, compared to the edges of the continent," she agreed, painting her own cheese with the green-dyed wax. "You'd think that after almost two hundred years, the ways of magic would have settled back down, but the birthrates have stayed low in Correda, and from what I hear, in Zantha and Morna as well."

Kenyen shrugged. His brother was more the type to think about such things, but he offered an idea of his own. "Maybe the explosion that destroyed the capital was a curse? Magic can be pretty potent when hurled with enough emotion behind it. Even we Shifterai know that much."

She snorted and dipped her own brush, coating the last bit of unwaxed cheese exposed on the round braced in her lap. "Even an ungifted farmer can hurl a curse and make it stick, if they really, *really* mean it. It won't be as strong a curse as a real mage's efforts, but . . . Well, whatever happened at that last Convocation of the Gods, they had plenty of mages in attendance, so any one of them could've been at fault. Or even a dozen of them."

"Whatever happened, it destroyed the Empire. Lucky us, we get to live in the shattered remnants of whatever was left." Kenyen chuckled wryly. "Literally, in the case of Shifting City."

They both reached for the maker's stamp at the same time, with his hand covering hers. He smiled at her and squeezed briefly, then withdrew his touch with a flick of his fingers, indicating she should go first. Nodding, Solyn picked up the stamp from the low table and pressed it firmly into three different spots on the soft wax. Setting the stamp back on the table, she twisted to put the cheese on the nearest shelf. The act of stretching forced a grunt out of her.

"Umff . . . I'm getting stiff and sore, sitting in one spot for too long," she grumbled. "We're about halfway done. How about we do something different for a bit?"

"Like what?" Kenyen asked, stamping his cheese before handing it to her. Setting aside the thick linen drop cloth that caught the excess wax, she stood to place it on the shelves. That meant Solyn had to bend over to rearrange the cheeses, and that in turn meant he found himself admiring her rump as it wiggled and swayed with each movement. There was nothing wrong, culturally, in enjoying the view, and it was a rather nice view in his opinion.

"Oh, I don't know. Stand and stretch, talk for a bit . . ." Glancing over her shoulder, Solyn caught him staring at her backside. She blushed and finished moving the newly waxed cheeses as she spoke. "This section is almost full. We should just go ahead and move to the next alcove, since we still have another twenty cheeses to do, and there's only room for three or four here."

He set aside his own drop cloth. "That'll help with the stretching, I suppose."

Mindful of the flames in the heating lamp, Kenyen picked up the hot pot of wax and set it on the table, then carefully moved the combination of brass stand and three-wick lamp. Once it was positioned, he came back for the pot of beeswax. Solyn, writing down the tally numbers for the current set of cheeses, joined him in moving the little worktable, picking up the cloths and brushes, the writing brush, inkstone and stick, and the thick-paged, age-stained ledger.

That reminded her of the papers she had snuck into her dinner bag. Setting everything on the table once he had it positioned, Solyn diverted to the oilcloth sack. "I brought some folding paper. It's not much; I had to cut it down small and pack it carefully so it wouldn't get bent prematurely on the trip down here. But I do have six sheets, and the ledger ink will do. Why don't we write out those messages?"

"Are you sure about that?" Kenyen teased mock-solemnly. "It *does* involve more sitting."

The dirty look she shot him was worth it. Chuckling, he set up their workspace for waxing, then followed her to the alcove where the ledger was normally kept. Kenyen picked at the bits of beeswax on his hands. The stuff clung, even when mixed with plant-based waxes to modify it better for food preservation.

"Here—*manumundic*," Solyn chanted, covering his fingers with her own. He sneezed as the magic cleaned both of their skin, quickly turning his head into his shoulder. She patted his pink-scoured flesh and released him. "Our hands need to be clean before I unwrap this paper—wait, didn't you bring the ink?" she asked, peering at his empty palms, then past his shoulder. "Go on, fetch it! The ledger table has a clean brush pen we can use."

Kenyen obediently followed her command, fetching the bottle in question. Unsure of how long this letter-writing would take, he paused to blow out the three flames flickering under the beeswax. It wouldn't do for the ceramic pot to get hot enough to crack and leak, permitting the wax to catch on fire without their being close enough to notice right away. There didn't seem like much to catch on fire down here, since the tunnel had literally been carved out of rock, but between the wax-covered wheels and the wooden racks supporting them, he didn't want to take that chance.

"What did you . . . oh, you blew out the wax lamp?" Solyn asked, turning away from the folded packet of papers. At his confirming nod, she smiled at him. "Thank you. It won't take that long to reheat it. Now . . . oh, bother." Her ring squeezed on her finger. Dropping her voice, she hissed, "Someone's coming—quick, your face!"

Not sure how quickly whoever it was might approach, Kenyen pulled Solyn close. Putting his back to the rest of the tunnel, he kissed her as he shifted his body. Lightening his dark brown locks, he kinked them into soft curls, then broadened his shoulders. Only then did he start altering the rest, shaping his flesh to match the image held in his mind. He was getting better at holding the shape of Traver Ys Ten, enough that he could no longer remember how to shape himself as small and mottled as a hunting cat, but better wasn't yet perfect. Better wasn't as fast as the shape of a stripe-cat, his oldest and most familiar shape.

Not a lot of his attention was going into the kiss; most of it focused on rounding and lengthening his face, altering his nose and his brow, his cheeks and his chin. Solyn didn't seem to mind, however. She wrapped her arms around his waist and leaned into his frame, tilting her head with a sigh of what he hoped was enjoyment. She was the one who nibbled on his lips even as he flattened out the natural bow on the upper one, making it smoother, more like Traver's.

". . . Oh!"

Finally confident of his face, Kenyen broke off their kiss. He peered over his shoulder, trying what he hoped was an awkward, embarrassed expression. He blushed at the sight of Reina—a real blush, not a faked one—and reluctantly let her daughter go. "Uhh . . . hello."

Solyn greeted her with equal awkwardness. "Um . . . Mother. Hello."

Reina eyed both of them, empty basket handle clutched in her hands. "Well. You *are* wearing those amulets, I trust?"

"Mother!" Solyn exclaimed, blushing.

"Alone down here together, for hours on end?" Reina asked, arching one brow. "As far as euphemisms go, 'waxing the cheese' isn't one that *normally* comes to mind for such—"

"Please!" Kenyen interjected firmly, as Solyn's face headed toward purple. He gave the older woman a quelling look. "We *haven't* been doing that."

"It was just a kiss, Mother!" Solyn added, recovering some of her composure. She felt flustered, but it truly had only been a kiss. "We're taking a short break—to *stretch*," she asserted firmly as her mother lifted one brow again, "—and then we'll go back to work. Cora's Truth!"

Reina eyed both of them, then shrugged. "Whatever you see fit to do, you may do . . . so long as you wear those amulets. And so long as you realize Ysander isn't going to wait forever for the two of you to make your twinings the *married* sort." She shrugged blithely, turning away. "But what do I know? I'm just a mother, here to pick up a couple of cheeses . . ."

Loading three rounds into her basket, Reina strolled back out of the winding tunnel, leaving them alone once more. Embarrassed, Solyn covered her face. She stayed that way until the ring spun on her finger, reassuring her they were alone. Slumping, she dropped her hands, then fanned her overheated face. "*That* was awkward."

"We're alone again?" Kenyen asked her. Solyn nodded, turning back to the table. He nodded as well. "Right. Let's get those messages written and sent."

Taking his hands in hers, Solyn muttered the spell her mother's approach had interrupted. "*Manumundic!*"

Kenyen hastily turned his head into his shoulder, muffling his sneeze. He gave Solyn a sheepish look. "I'll have to get better at suppressing the urge to do that."

Contrite, Solyn wrinkled her nose. "I should've remembered an allergy potion, myself. You'll just have to suffer until I can make one, I guess. Okay . . . let me prepare the first paper . . ."

His nose itched. From her first murmur, his nose stung and itched. Kenyen tried rubbing it discreetly, then pinched it openly. As her power rose, so did the sting deep in his nostrils, like smelling something acrid, though not unpleasant. He sneezed twice more, then the itching subsided. When she beckoned him over, Kenyen sniffed hard to clear his nose as he picked up the pen.

"Who is the first person you want to write to?" Solyn asked him. "Hold that person's name, face, mannerisms, and all of who they *are*, firmly in your mind."

"Ashallan," he stated, holding the image of the foremost of the three princesses in his mind. He had given a lot of thought to who he would contact and what he would say. Picking up the pen, he dangled it over the ink jar. "Do I start writing now?"

Solyn nodded, shifting a little farther away. She watched as he frowned in concentration for several moments, dipped and tapped the pen, and stroked small, neat lettering onto the prepared sheet. It didn't take him long, but then the sheet wasn't very large.

Ashallan Nur Am, Cat, Lion;

Nespah Valley the correct one. Multiple curs in area, twenty-plus. They want something dangerous. Trapped into imitating endangered local; being watched but have ally. Need help rescuing local. Be discreet; ask for greenvein cheese.

Sin Siin, Cat, Tiger

Lifting his hand from the page, mind still focused on thoughts of Ashallan, with her middle-aged features, her long, dark brown hair, Kenyen nodded at the message. "That's it. What now?"

She nodded. "Give it a few moments to dry. You might want to step back and get ready to sneeze again."

Stepping back, he gave her room. She peered at the inked sheet, counted quietly under her breath, and finally nodded. As Kenyen watched, she picked up the sheet and started folding it diagonally, then crosswise. To his surprise, she sang as she worked. The words and the power behind them made his nose itch once more, but the tune was nothing more and nothing less than a children's melody, the kind he himself had sung back on the Plains. Different words entirely, but the same rhythmic, happy tune.

He almost sang along. Catching himself, Kenyen kept silent while she worked. The paper folding was fascinating, each bend simple enough on its own, but when put together, complex. By the time she finished, the square of paper vaguely resembled a sharp-beaked bird with its wings upraised, and no legs.

Solyn stopped singing. She eyed her creation critically, turning it over to check all sides. Running her fingers along each leading wing edge, she made them curve, then held the bird by its folded paper breastbone and pulled on the tail. The wings moved, flapping down and up with each tug.

Startled, Kenyen blinked, then tentatively touched his nose. "I didn't sneeze?"

Solyn smiled. "No, you didn't, because the movement isn't magical. If you fold it right, the pressure on the paper makes the wings flap. That's what makes the flying spell possible. They do have a limited range, but Teshal isn't even half that—I've successfully sent bird-notes to tea caravans stopping in cities on the far side of the Morna River. I can even show you how to fold a non-magical one afterward, if you like. Here, hold firmly in your mind the memory of the person this message is for, and paint their name on each wing."

She had folded the bird so that the writing was on the inside. Kenyen had plenty of room to write *Ashallan Nur Am* on each wing. When he finished, he asked, "How will she know this is a message that needs to be opened up and read?"

"It'll flutter around her hand until she tries to catch it. The moment she does, it'll unfold on its own and she'll be able to read the message inside. Anyone else would have to tear it open, and they'd be fighting the power of the spell to do so. It's not *quite* a reliable means of secret communication, but it does resist casual spying," she told him. Instead of reaching for the paper bird or the pen, Solyn plucked the next sheet from the pile. "We'll do all of them up to the part where you paint the name on the wings, then I'll bind the flying enchantments in place all at once. Let me get the next one started . . ."

Kenyen realized he was hungry. Getting up, he returned to the alcove with the bag of food she had brought. Inside were a couple rounds of flatbread, bits of cold roasted beef, thinly sliced onion, leafy greens of some sort, and a jar of pickle sauce. The sauce was an acquired Corredai taste in Kenyen's opinion, alien and a bit strange, but it wasn't too bad. Uncorking the jar, he sniffed at the paste inside, wondering if he wanted any on his flatbread. *Huh . . . the smell goes with the scent of the greenvein cheese around us. I wonder if they taste good together?*

". . . Kenyen? Where did you go?"

"To fetch the food," he called back. "It's past noon." He recorked the jar and tucked it back into the bag. Picking up it and the waterskin, he carried both back to the ledger alcove. "As soon as we're done writing and folding, I figure we can eat. And since you're busy chanting and folding, I might as well set it up, right?"

That earned him another smile. She was passably pretty under most circumstances, but Solyn's beauty truly blossomed when she smiled, in his opinion. Even the amused half smile she gave him, twisting up one corner of her mouth in teasing. "I'll have to keep cleaning your hands, though."

"I'll suffer the sneezing," he promised mock-solemnly. Grinning with her, he settled the bag on the table, sneezed as promised when she cleaned his hands, and picked up the pen. "Ready for me to write?"

"Remember, keep firmly in your mind who this new person is. Everything about them, their mannerisms, their nature, their voice and their face and their name, everything that makes them who they are, and the person you know," she instructed. "I'll go get one of the cut rounds so we can have some greenvein with our meal—you might as well have a taste of what we're trying to protect."

Kenyen nodded absently. The next person he knew he wanted to contact was Manolo. The older shifter wasn't high-ranked in their expedition, but he was levelheaded and the one person whom Kenyen knew for absolute sure. The first letter had to go to Ashallan as the head of their little mock warband, but this letter was the one Kenyen was sure would get through. The message was the same; now that he had composed it to fit on the small square, it didn't take long to write.

Once she started humming and folding, Kenyen picked up one of the slices she had cut from the mold-mottled round of greenvein cheese. Eyeing the streaks of green warily, he braced himself and tried a nibble. And sneezed. Not just any sneeze, but a really *good* sneeze, the kind that wasn't too hard or too stingy. The kind that cleared his nose in just two deep breaths post-sneeze, allowing him to smell everything a lot better than before.

I guess her magic literally made me allergic, he thought in wonder, listening to her chant away. Even more oddly, his nose didn't sting anymore, though she was still singing as she folded. Bemused, Kenyen nibbled again at the cheese. It had a good flavor, tangy and tasty. He liked it. *Heh . . . I don't know much about magic, but if this stuff stops me from sneezing, I know many a husband down on the Plains, married to mage-wives, who would pay dearly for rounds of this. Being married to a mage is a rare treat, and we'll endure it for our lady's sake, but the chance to* not *sneeze would make a most profitable trade arrangement.*

Dutifully, he let her clean his hands so he could paint Manolo's name on the wings of the second bird. Then went back to nibbling more of the cheese while she started on the next page. The actual act of spell-cleaning his skin made his nose sting, though not enough to sneeze. But with the first bite of green-mottled cheese, the tangy-sharp flavor cleared away the itch. *It* must *be the cheese. Definitely a point of trade to consider . . .*

Curiosity drove him to use the small spoon provided, dabbing a bit of pickle-sauce on the remainder of his cheese slice. The combination was sharper than expected, but very, very tasty. Catching sight of his actions, Solyn quirked a brow. He grinned back at her.

"You know the drill. Hold in your mind an image of the person *this* message will reach . . ."

SEVEN

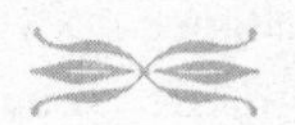

They made two more messages, one to Asellah, the princess from Family Mustang, Clan Horse, and one to Narquen Vil Shem, the male who had headed for the holdings of the Mespak Valley to the southeast. Kenyen knew both of them well enough from their travels. The group had been together since setting out at midspring, after all. But he didn't know them quite as well as he knew Manolo.

When the fourth bird was properly painted and the lot carried to the cave mouth, inked, and released to flap their way high into the sky, Kenyen was ready for a real meal. Accompanying Solyn to the back of the cave, they sat down on the stools at the table and set about slathering sauce on the rounds of flatbread, layering it with greenvein cheese, vegetables, greens, and meat, then folded each roughly in half.

Eating the food Corredai-style put a crick in his neck, since it required holding the folded flatbread upright in both hands and tilting the head to one side, but Kenyen couldn't deny the combination was worth the effort. Though perhaps not the embarrassment. Solyn giggled at him when he dropped a chunk of cheese on his lap.

"Now *that* is more like the real Traver," she snickered. "He *definitely* isn't the most graceful when eating flat-folds."

He rolled his eyes, chewed, and swallowed. ". . . Laugh all you want. It's delicious. And the sauce goes with the cheese."

She smiled at the compliment. "Thank you. I made it myself."

"Speaking of cheese . . ." Kenyen muttered, plucking the sauce-smeared scrap off his lap and tossing it in his mouth. She wrinkled her nose at him, but didn't comment. Kenyen lifted his chin at the sliced round sitting patiently on the table. "When I ate that stuff, I stopped sneezing. It even quelled the itching deep in my nose, practically from the first taste. If that thing *does* quell the magic-itch plaguing a tenth of my people, you'll have a brand-new market for it as soon as we can get a couple rounds back home. A huge market."

She blinked at that. "Really? It stopped your sneezing? And your people would *want* to eat it, enough to import it in a high quantity?"

"Not just the shifters married to our few mages," Kenyen told her, "but the warband shifters as well. We've had a number of sticky moments going up against renegade mages. A sneeze or three at the wrong moment has put several lives in danger over the years."

"Huh." Solyn considered the possibilities. "I suppose it makes some sense. I never really considered the other potential properties of greenvein mold, nor do I think has my mother . . ." Shrugging, she lifted her flatbread fold. "Well, here's to your good health!"

Grinning, he took another bite . . . and dropped a bit of meat on his lap this time. Wrinkling his nose at the spill, he ignored her snickers and kept eating. When they finished, Solyn pulled over the last two pieces of paper and showed him how to fold the square sheets back and forth, this way and that, until a paper bird emerged.

His bird was lopsided, one wing sticking up high and the other angling off low, but it was still recognizably a paper bird. The wings even flapped . . . sort of . . . when he pulled on the tail. More on one side than the other, but both of them flapped, which Solyn kindly pointed out, though her mouth did curl up on one side a bit too much.

Peeking at him as they cleaned up the remains of their lunch, Solyn kept doing a double take. He was wearing Traver's face, and practicing some of Traver's mannerisms, but most of him was, well, Kenyen of the Shifting Plains. She sighed. "You know, we *are* alone. You don't have to wear his face all the time around me."

"I know. I just . . . keep expecting your mother to come back." He shrugged and turned it into a ripple of flesh. "I hope you don't mind how I hid my face, earlier."

She blushed. "Well, I kind of mind that it wasn't the best kiss ever, but . . . I didn't mind that it *was* a kiss."

He flushed as well, feeling awkward. Part of him didn't like her pointing out it *was* a kiss, but part of him wanted to prove he could do better. "It's . . . awkward. We only kiss the earth-priestesses, back home. Or our wives. So it's sort of . . . forbidden. The lure of the taboo. Except it's not forbidden with willing outlanders. But I want to respect you, to show you the same level of respect I'd show a maiden of the Plains, and yet . . ."

Smiling, Solyn stopped his babbling with a finger on his lips. "It's not forbidden in Cora's Mountains. It's just a matter of discretion, and, um . . . wearing the right amulet. It's not encouraged to twine fully with someone unless there is an intent to wed, but it does happen."

He liked the touch of her hand on his mouth. Kenyen puckered his lips in a kiss, then pulled back. "Well, if I ever do anything you don't like, tell me and I'll stop."

She blushed again. "I'll keep that in mind. In the meantime, we still have more cheese rounds to protect. I'll go light the tripod to remelt the wax. Having magic is useful for that."

That reminded him of her mother's quip. He chuckled, picking up the ledger, ink jar, and pen. "I still can't believe she said that. 'Waxing the cheese,' indeed. I have *never* heard it put that way, before. And we make plenty of cheese on the Plains. Most of it fresh or soft cheeses, though. We don't have nice, cool tunnels like these for ripening and storage."

"You make it sound like you've led a very different life from mine," Solyn offered, heading for the shelf-lined alcove where he had left the wax.

"In some ways, yes," he agreed, raising his voice so she could hear. He lingered at the table, cutting off another slice of the wax-wrapped product of their efforts in this cave. "But, we still have pesky siblings, and nosy mothers, and all the little details that are the same. And a fondness for greenvein cheese. I think it's growing on me."

Chuckling, she quipped back, "Just so long as it doesn't turn *you* mottled green."

Impulsively, Kenyen shifted the color of his skin. He poked his head around the shelving, and grinned at her startled shriek.

"*Ack!*—Ohhhh . . . *you!*" Flapping her hand at him, she ordered, "Turn back this instant! You almost looked like a corpse, just now, and corpses do *not* get up and walk around."

He complied, shaking off the webwork of greenish veins. "I think that would be a very strange sight. Alarming, even. Thank the Gods such things don't actually happen."

As he set the ledger and writing implements on the low table, she murmured a word, sparking the wicks back to life. Another word softened the skin of hardened wax that had formed inside the pot. Solyn gave him a rueful look. "I have to be careful with that spell, so it doesn't set the wax on fire. Not that it'd burn all that well without a wick, but one can never be too careful. It's the same one I use to heat bathwater, too—and the bedsheets on cold winter nights."

"I'm sure it's useful in many ways. And I'm still not sneezing," Kenyen added, giving her a smile. Fetching the stools, he positioned them around the pot, then gestured for her to take her pick. Settling onto the other one, he accepted the drop cloth she passed to him, then stretched for the nearest dry-wrapped cheese on the shelf behind him. "Here you go . . . and one for me . . . Is the beeswax ready?"

She stirred the pot with her brush and nodded. "I think so. Ready to wax the cheese with me?"

The absurdity of her mother's comment caught up with him. A wheezing snort escaped Kenyen, his face scrunching with laughter. "Waxing the cheese! *Ha!* Ahahaha . . ."

His mirth was infectious. It *was* absurd. Biting her lip to stifle a giggle, Solyn unwrapped her round and dipped her brush in the green-dyed beeswax. The moment she stroked the goop over the cheese in her lap, however, she burst out laughing. The first splotch looked like a pair of puckered lips to her, and it was too much. Snorting, she finally gave up and dropped cheese and brush on the table beside her, laughing heartily.

Grinning, Kenyen wiggled his eyebrows at her. "Hey . . . wanna *wax the cheese* with me?"

Flopping the back of one hand over her forehead, draping the palm of the other over her heart, Solyn quipped right back. "Oh! Oh! Such eloquent words, such passionate words! How can a maiden resist!"

"But you *cannot* resist! This is *greenvein* cheese!" he retorted, snickering at their overblown dramatics.

"Oh, Goddess, yes—greenvein cheese, and green wax!" she shot back, arms flinging wide. Rising from the stool, she mock-stumbled to his knee. Collapsing across his lap—still giggling, she clung to his shoulders. "Wax me, my dearest darling! Wax me now!"

Her husky, fervent exclamation suited the over-the-top moment. He wrapped his arms around her quickly, catching her before she could overbalance from the giggles spasming through her curves, and growled back, mock-leering at her. "My dearest darling, I'll not only wax you, I'll *ripen* you, too!"

Solyn laughed so hard, she cried, kicking her feet and squeezing him close as she writhed. He laughed hard, too, wheezing for breath. They clung to each other, rendered so breathless from mirth that it was a wonder he didn't drop her or fall off the stool. Eventually, they wound up with their foreheads touching, brown eyes gazing into hazel, noses brushing lightly together.

Kenyen grinned at her. Solyn grinned back.

The mood shifted. Solyn felt her smile fading, replaced by wonder. This wasn't Traver, yet there was a definite feeling of being comfortable in his arms. At ease, but with an underlying tension. Excitement. This *wasn't* Traver, and that made all the difference. Taking a deep breath, she seized her courage and kissed him, this near-stranger holding her on his lap.

Her kiss wasn't unexpected. A pleasure, that she gave it so quickly, but a part of him did anticipate it. Thrilled at it, since it still felt semi-illicit, for all that she initiated it. This was a woman he respected, someone he was coming to care about. How deeply, he couldn't yet say, but he did care. Still, he didn't resist when the tip of her tongue tasted his bottom lip, coaxing it open. Nor did he resist the urge to deepen it.

Wrapped in the warmth of his arms, Solyn shivered. The old mining tunnel was cool, this deep into the hill, but it wasn't the temperature that made her shudder. It was the slow way he suckled her lower lip, the slanting of his mouth against hers. Even his scent, male, confident, ensnared her senses. It was the taste of cheese on his tongue that made her laugh again. Pulling back a little, she rested her forehead against his once more.

"You even taste like greenvein," she murmured, sharing the reason for her mirth.

"At least I don't taste like wax," he quipped, smiling back. The mood between them shifted a little. Kenyen cleared his throat. "Do you, ah, actually want to wax the cheese now? Or . . . ?"

"I don't know," Solyn whispered, though she smiled as she said it. "I do know I'm enjoying this twining thing with you, right now. And you *are* supposed to be seducing me, right?"

"Not for their sake," Kenyen quickly denied. He flushed a little at the revealing words but didn't deny them. Licking his lips, he confessed, "I'd rather court you for *your* sake. They just . . . they caused me to stumble across you, like an unexpected detour that led me to a treasure hidden in the grass. They don't have anything to do with how I'm feeling about you."

The smile she gave him was a shy one. For a moment, Kenyen thought her friend Traver was a fool, then realized the other man actually wasn't. This was just how all their lives were playing out. What he chose to do from this moment on would define their future directions.

What he chose to do was taken from him. Instead, Solyn kissed him again. Disinclined to argue the point with a beautiful, confident outlander woman, he kissed her back. With his right arm tucked behind her back, supporting her on his lap, he used the fingers of his other hand to caress the soft skin of her cheek. They brushed back the fine, curling wisps that had escaped her braid, and cupped the curve of her neck, supporting her head.

In response, Solyn slid her own hand from his shoulder to his chest, feeling the warmth of his chest through the linen of his tunic. She wanted to feel the real warmth behind the fabric, but refrained. At least, for the first moments. As their kiss grew more heated, her fingertips played with the buttons holding his *chamak* in place down the side of his chest. His hand tilted her chin up, giving his mouth access to her throat. The shivers returned with each caress of his lips.

Her fingers worked at his buttons, pulling down the upper corner of the panel. A twist of her head let her return each nip on her neck with a taste of his own. Now it was his turn to shudder, his turn for his breath to flow unsteady and fast. Smirking, glad she could make this confident man tremble, Solyn daringly licked the side of his throat.

"Ohh . . . Mother Earth!" An earth-priestess might do that, wise and experienced, but a maiden? He shuddered again when she suckled on the base of his throat. The cool air of the tunnel wasn't the only cause of the shivers prickling at his skin. With the side of her thigh brushing against his groin, Kenyen was aware that it had been too long since his last intimate encounter. Catching her fingers before she could unbutton more of his tunic, he whispered, "That . . . should be enough. For now. Or this will go a lot farther than just . . . aheh . . . waxing the cheese."

The humor banished some of her disappointment. Smiling, Solyn snuggled closer to him. He shifted on the stool, adjusting their positions, but held her close. It took her a few moments to realize why he had shifted, and what, exactly, that lump at her thigh meant. Blushing, she sought for a safer topic, though she didn't leave his lap. "Sooo . . . our last topic was what sort of horse we'd want to ride. How about . . . oh, what sort of pet we'd want in the house?"

"Not a dog," Kenyen murmured. There were two at Traver's home, and both of them had growled at him, rightfully acting wary of his not-Traver scent. It had taken him some care and patience to get them to grudgingly accept him. "They don't always get along with shifters. I'd rather have a cat."

"Well, I like cats, but I wouldn't mind a pet fish," she admitted.

Craning his neck, Kenyen peered at her. "A pet fish?"

She nodded, temple resting lightly on his shoulder. "My father's mother—Bennia Del Non—had a beautiful blown-glass bowl filled with sand, and little plants, and tiny little stream fish with little red and silver streaks down their sides. She'd feed them bits of biscuit and of course the plants. They were fascinating to watch, as a child. She lived two valleys over. She was an herb-Healer, and I remember her telling me watching the fish helped calm her patients while they were waiting for her to fix up an herbal posset. They moved so slowly, yet swiftly, and it's such a different environment from our own . . ."

"You have a lot of Healers in your family," Kenyen observed.

She shrugged. "Mostly herbal, a few magical. You?"

"My mother's a good cook, and knows a few common remedies, but that's about it. Magic is very rare on the Plains," he reminded her. "Non-shifting magic, that is."

Solyn smiled and tickled the patch of skin bared by his half-opened tunic. "I meant, would you mind having a pet fish?"

"Life on the Plains is life on the move, three seasons of the year. Carting around a fish-filled bowl every dozen days would be hazardous to the glass," he told her.

That wasn't a pleasant reminder. Sighing, Solyn asked wistfully, "Do you *have* to go back to the Plains?"

"Well, we always . . ." Kenyen broke off, considering her question. "I mean, no one . . . Shifters are Shifterai. It's awkward growing up a shapeshifter when you don't have that kind of support. My sister-in-law didn't have it. Her mother escaped from the curs now plaguing these mountains and gave birth to Atava in a remote Mornai village. Atava managed to figure things out on her own—she's very smart—but it's easier growing up a shifter among your own kind. We even get cross-kin from the Centarai, since they birth the odd shapeshifter now and again, and we trade them non-shifter sons in return."

"Yes, but you make it sound like your kinswoman didn't have any other shifters in her life, just herself. You're fully grown, and I'll presume fully taught. Surely you'd be around to teach your own children?" she pointed out.

"I'd hope to be," Kenyen allowed. He hadn't seriously considered finding a mate and settling down before now, but her words stirred his thoughts. "I suppose, if I lived *near* the Plains, it wouldn't be so bad . . . Being able to visit would make things bearable. What about you? Could you consider coming to live among us?"

"I suppose . . ." Solyn admitted. It was only fair of him to ask her that, since she'd asked her own version. "Except I really do need to go learn how to be a better mage. And I'd like to travel. I suppose that could extend to visiting the Plains. But living in a tent three seasons out of the year doesn't seem quite as nice as living in a house for all four."

He shrugged. "It's not as bad as you might be thinking. Our *geomes* are soundly built, and we make them as pleasant as possible inside. Our homes in the winter are communal, everyone sharing a building, with each couple having their own sleeping rooms. If we *could* safely transport a bowl filled with fish, it wouldn't be a bad idea. Or stay constantly in the city year-round. But mostly we have hunting cats for pets. They get along with shifters better than dogs do."

As much as she wanted to stay on his lap, Solyn was aware of their surroundings. Sighing, she straightened on his lap. "I think we really should get back to waxing the cheeses. Actual waxing, that is."

Smiling ruefully, he let her rise. "Your mother has completely ruined that phrase for me, you realize."

"You're not the only one," Solyn muttered, settling onto her own stool. She draped the wax-spattered cloth back over her lap, then smiled. "But while we'll only have enough cheeses to wax today . . . we still have to come back for a few hours tomorrow, and the day after that, and a dozen more after *that*, to rewrap the fresh rounds in clean cloths. And then we'll have to wax *those* cheeses, too, once they finally stop seeping out the last of the whey."

His mouth quirked higher on one side. Kenyen reached for his own supplies, copying her movements. "Well, then, we'll have plenty of time for more twining as well as for cheese-binding, won't we?"

She blushed, but she still smiled. Picking up her fat-bristled brush, Solyn stirred the wax and started painting it onto the round sitting in her lap once again. Kenyen followed suit.

"You really are different, you know?"

The comment from Traver's younger brother, Tellik, snapped Kenyen's eyes open. No longer sleepy, he worried over what the boy meant. The candles had long since been blown out, leaving their attic room dimly lit at best from the glow of the hearthfire embers down below. Mentally checking his disguise, he asked in Traver's voice, "Uhh . . . how so?"

"Liking Solyn so much. Not complaining about your chores. And *cheese*-making."

The disgust in Tellik's voice amused Kenyen, relaxing him a little. This wasn't quite as serious an accusation as he'd feared.

"Maybe I'm growing up," Kenyen offered softly. Navigating the hazards of living another man's life was a difficult task. He didn't *want* to lie, but the real Traver's life depended upon it. He also didn't want to leave awkward questions behind, if he could escape with his deception undiscovered. And if it was . . .

Silence stretched between them. Kenyen felt the pull of sleep again, only to be awakened by another question.

"Traver?"

"Yes?"

"How do you get a girl to like you?" Tellik asked.

That question took him back a dozen years, back to when he was barely fourteen and his brother Kodan was a more worldly sixteen, almost seventeen, old enough to visit the earth-priestesses and start the courting rituals of the Plains. Only Kenyen's question had ended, "*. . . to like you, when you only have a few shapes?*"

Many shapes were favored over fewer, since that was how a man displayed his strength down on the Plains. Constantly being in his brother's shadow, able to shape half the number that Akodan now could . . . At the age of sixteen, Kodan hadn't yet proven he could shape and hold ten pure forms, the requirement for a *multerai*, so his advice from back then had been less confident in such things, but more practical in other directions. Kenyen tried to shape his older brother's advice for Tellik now, since the real Traver wasn't here to play the part of the older and presumably wiser man.

"Women . . . girls young and old . . . want to be respected," he stated slowly, dredging up the right words. He didn't want to sound too Shifterai-ish, but there were certain things that surely applied to all cultures. "When you give a girl your attention, listening to what she has to say and respecting her ideas and beliefs, this is very flattering—it's like how you feel when someone gives *you* that same kind of respect."

Tellik snorted, shifting on his pallet. "I'd *like* to have more respect. I'm still just a kid in everyone's eyes—and that's another thing where you're different. *You* don't treat me like a little pest anymore."

Kenyen chuckled. "You still are, but if you think about it, whatever you expect of a person, they'll live up to it. Or down to it. If I treat you like a pest, you'll act like one. If I treat you like a young man, you'll try to act like one, too. Girls aren't that much different. They *do* think differently. More caring, more cooperative. But still human in the end. Um . . ." He wracked his mind, trying to think of other pieces of advice. "Don't be interested just in a girl's looks. She may look pretty, but her figure and her face will change as she ages. The thing that stays constant is her mind.

"Oh, and find a girl that makes you laugh," Kenyen added,

remembering the waxing joke. The memory curved his lips in a smile. He shifted onto his back, staring up at the darkness of the low-raftered ceiling. "And if you can make *her* laugh, that's even better."

"I don't get it," Tellik muttered. "You say a girl's mind stays constant, but girls are always changing their minds about stuff."

"Ah, yes. That's the difference between their opinions and their intellect. A girl who is smart will always *be* smart, even if she can't decide whether to wear a yellow skirt or a red one on any particular day," Kenyen told him. "A girl who is interested in traveling will always want to travel. At least, until she's tried it and decided whether or not once is enough. If she still likes it, then you'll have to accept it as a part of her. Just as she has to accept the things that you prefer.

"Sometimes you can even discover something new, together. Or she teaches you something you didn't know before," he added, thinking of folding those paper birds. "Or you can show her something. Show you're interested in a girl—don't push too hard, but let her know you enjoy her company. Smile at her whenever you see her."

"Tarquin teases the girls a lot," Tellik offered. "I've heard him say to Mari that Juna is prettier, but that he'd rather be with Mari because her hands know how to touch a man. And then he'll say to Juna that her figure is great, but Pelonna makes him laugh. And then Juna tries to make him laugh, too, and Mari gets her hands all over him, and . . . well, he has a lot of girls fighting over him."

"Tarquin isn't the best role model on how to treat girls," Kenyen stated. "What Tarquin wants from them is only a small part of what women really are."

"So what *does* he want from them?" Tellik asked innocently.

Kenyen cleared his throat, face warming. Grateful for the dark, he replied honestly, "He wants to twine with as many as possible, but doesn't actually *care* about any of them. They're just, um . . . things for him to twine with."

". . . Oh. Ohhh!" Tellik exclaimed softly. "So it's like he only cares for their pretty faces, but doesn't care about their minds, like what you said, right?"

Relieved, Kenyen nodded in the dark. "Exactly. You're very smart for figuring that out."

"Solyn doesn't like him, does she?" Tellik asked next. "He's rich and has a nice house, but she never has time for him."

That made him chuckle. "That's because she's smart enough to realize he only wants one thing from her, and she deserves to have *all* her different bits appreciated. Body, mind, heart, interests, and abilities."

Tellik stayed silent for several moments, then asked, "Do you think I might find a girl like that?"

"You might. She might live here in one of the local holdings, or she might be in the next one over . . . or you may have to go looking for her in a place that's farther away than you thought," Kenyen murmured, thinking of the distance between this valley and his homeland. "You can look locally first. And you should take your time making up your mind, if you have the chance. But . . ."

". . . But?" Traver's little brother asked.

Kenyen thought of Solyn, with her bright hazel eyes, infectious laughter, and sneeze-inducing abilities. "But sometimes you just have to seize the moment and go with your instincts. Sometimes you just know. Or think you know. And then it becomes easier. Not always easy, but easier. Your heart and your mind will prompt you to do little things for her, help her with her chores, give her little gifts . . . You'll want to spend time with her, whatever you're doing. Or just holding her hand makes you feel warm all over. And when she says nice things about you, it might make you feel twice as tall as you already are . . . or *she* might feel these things when you share them with her."

Tellik mulled that over. Finally, he sighed. "Twining stuff is complicated, isn't it?"

"Yes, it is," Kenyen chuckled. "Take your time, Tellik. You don't have to rush out and find yourself a bride tomorrow . . . but you *do* have to be rested enough to do your chores tomorrow. Now, go to sleep," he ordered. "I have both chores and cheese-making to manage, myself, so I need my sleep, too."

"Do you twine with Solyn?" Tellik asked. "Like Tarquin says he does? He says there's a lot more to it than holding hands and hugging and kissing, but he only laughs at me and doesn't say what the rest of it is. It isn't like what the goats do with each other, right? 'Cause that doesn't look like it's all that fun, just noisy and weird, and I've never heard anyone human making those sorts of noises before . . ."

"Go. To. Sleep," Kenyen ordered. He was more amused than offended by the boy's curiosity, but made sure his tone stayed firm, with no room for argument.

Silence descended between them. Kenyen relaxed. Just as he started to drift off once more, Tellik spoke again.

"D'you think Ysander would take me on as an apprentice? I really like watching him work in the forge whenever I can, and Tarquin says he needs an apprentice," the youth added, interrupting the quiet of the night once more.

"Good night, Tellik!"

". . . G'night."

Between the time he had left the cavern to go use the bushes and the time he had returned, hands freshly washed at the basin by the entrance, Solyn had set up a small but sturdy, kettle-style teapot on the three-flame heating stand. Steam roiled out of its spout, proving she must have used a spell to heat the water so quickly.

She had also laid a pair of clean linen cloths over the low table that served as their workstation when rewrapping the fresh cheeses, but the cheeses were not on it. Instead, she had placed a soup bowl, a small bowl, a glass vial full of green powder, an odd little spoon with a lump on the end of the handle, forming a sort of stand that permitted it to sit level on the table, and a strange, fringed wooden whisk. As he watched, she carefully uncorked the little glass jar.

"What are you doing?" Kenyen asked, curious. He debated releasing his altered face back to its natural form, but decided to refrain when she didn't respond, in case it meant they were being watched.

Solyn heard the question, but her focus was elsewhere. Gently tapping the vial, she measured out just enough powdered tea to fit into the bowl of the little spoon. Recorking it, she placed the powder in the larger bowl with a murmur and a pulse of magic. Predictably, he sneezed. Trying not to smile too much, she used another scrap of cloth to pick up the steaming teapot and poured some of its contents into the whisking bowl.

Another murmur of spellwords, focusing and shaping her powers, lifted the whisk and dipped it into the bowl. A final trio of syllables set the spell in motion. Free to relax, she watched as the whisk whipped the mix of water and powdered tea into a frothy foam.

"I'm making tea," she said, finally answering his question. A glance at his face provoked a wry smile. "We're still alone. You can look like yourself, again."

"Thank you." He relaxed his features with a smile, then peered at her concoction. "That doesn't look like any tea *I've* ever had," Kenyen confessed, eyeing the mint green mix in the cup.

"It's a special kind of tea, mostly used in important religious ceremonies," she told him. "It is also the best kind of tea to use for weather divinations, particularly when prepared this way."

"Weather divination?" Kenyen asked her. She quickly hushed him as the whisk lifted itself back out again under the direction of her spell, settling once more on the butt of its handle. Subsiding, Kenyen watched.

Her gaze never left the larger bowl. The thick foam swirled around and around, gradually slowing. It then contracted abruptly. She heard a soft gasp from the Shifterai at her side but kept her gaze on the foam, which had formed an anvil shape very similar to a thunderhead cloud. It still moved slowly about the center of the cup, and was very close to that center. After a moment, it collapsed, turning soft and frothy, once more merely the foam found on top of properly whisked tea.

Sighing, Solyn nodded. "Two, three days at most, given the distance from the center, and from the size . . . two or three days of steady rain. We usually get one bad storm before the driest, hottest days of the high harvest season, but with the hills and mountains blocking full view of the horizon, a storm often rolls over us before we actually know. It's important to avoid harvesting the grain early; if it gets soaked in a heavy rain while it lies on the ground, instead of drying properly in the sun, the grain has to be abandoned. It cannot be stored."

"And so you use a special spell," Kenyen observed. He lifted his chin at the bowl. "What do you do with the leftover tea?"

She smiled. "We drink it, of course. Mascha tea is *never* wasted. It is picked from the youngest buds that have been carefully sheltered from direct sunlight, the buds gently harvested by hand, not by clipper. The leaves are dried flat in the shade, guarded against insects and animals until dry. Then the veins are carefully removed when they are crumbled, and the crumbles ground and sifted, thrice to honor Brother Moon for the main kind most people drink, and once more for Sister Moon, for the finest powdering which is used by the priesthood.

"This is Brother's Tea," she added, nodding at the vial of powder.

"An expert maschen, a tea maker wise with many years of practice, can whip the froth without a spell and get a suggestion of the coming weather for the next few days. I don't have nearly that much practice at normal tea reading, but then I don't need to. *I* can use a divination spell and get more accurate results, making predictions up to a week in advance. It still takes practice to divine the *timing* of a coming storm, and its size, but then I've been doing it this way for a good five years now, more or less once a week."

"A handy trait. Most of the time we send fliers up into the sky every hour or so. You can see a very long ways on the Plains, and the weather rarely deviates from its course," he told her. "Every Family has shifters with bird shapes for reading the weather and sending messages to other places, even if they're not a part of Clan Bird. And those stuck on the ground learn to read the coming weather as well."

"Flying sounds like it would be rather handy for such things," she agreed. Since the foam was no longer remotely cloud-shaped, she poured half the tea from the larger bowl into the smaller bowl. Lifting it to her lips, she bowed her head for a moment in silent prayer, then drank the stimulating, bittersweet brew. Draining it to foam, she set the smaller bowl down and picked up the larger, pouring in the second half.

"My turn?" Kenyen asked, reaching for the bowl.

Shocked, Solyn quickly covered the drinking bowl with her fingers, shaking her head. "Oh, no, you mustn't!"

He gave her a puzzled look. "Why not? You said *we* drink it. Doesn't that both mean you and I?"

"Well, yes, but *not* from the same bowl," Solyn asserted, blushing. At his confused look, she blushed harder. "That's part of the marriage ceremony. And, well, I wasn't thinking, and only brought the one bowl."

Kenyen almost pointed out that he could easily use the larger bowl, but refrained. It was probably some custom thing unique to the Corredai, and it had been drummed over and over into his head as a warband member to always respect the customs of outkingdom peoples even if he didn't understand them.

"Alright, I won't drink it this time . . . but would it be acceptable for me to try it another time?" he asked her. "I do enjoy tea when I can get it, and I've obviously never tried maschen. I'll admit I'm curious to see what that tastes like. I can bring my own cup, next time."

"There's nothing wrong with curiosity," she agreed, smiling. "I'll bring a spare bowl tomorrow." Lifting the smaller bowl to her lips, she paused and added, "Maschen is never drunk from a cup, because a cup implies enough wealth to own several types of dishes."

"Oh?" Kenyen asked, curious. "Why is that?"

She nodded. "The ceremony is meant to be available to all who live in the mountains, from the king and queen themselves, who live in a rich castle surrounded by all manner of fine things, all the way down through to the poorest laborer, who lives communally in a hut with several others and only owns a single porridge bowl for eating—it is said that Cora Herself drinks the maschen of the Gods from a simple porridge bowl when She is alone, and only uses a golden one on Her holiest days."

She saluted him with the tea and drank. Kenyen nodded his head in return, silently thanking her for the lesson. He was in Correda, which meant respecting the local Goddess, but he did want to share a little bit of his own culture with her.

"Our own Gods, Father Sky and Mother Earth, have no special way of eating. But They do share Their bounty of rain and grain, milk and meat, with the highest and the lowest alike," he told her. "When we have a feast in the Family, everyone contributes something, even if all a person can afford is to haul a bucket of water from the nearest cistern, or help stoke the brazier fires for making tea—steeped tea leaves, not this whisked powder of yours."

Solyn nodded, draining the last of the tea. The stimulants from the first bowlful were already being felt, heightening her senses, sharpening her mind, and tingling through her blood. "Mm, steeped tea is very different from whisked tea. This is *much* stronger than steeping, and the flavor is different. The best maschen tea leaves are grown several valleys away—the kind preferred for Sister's Tea—but we do pick and process our own for Brother's Tea, locally. We don't *worship* the Moon Gods," she added. "The names just refer to the level of fineness in the grinding and sifting process, taking their numbers from the times each moon circles the world in a single season."

"We don't worship Them, either," he agreed. "But we do honor Them, as the visible children of Father Sky and Mother Earth."

"So what do you do for your own marriage customs?" Solyn asked him, curious.

"Well, just as you never drink from the same bowl as someone else," Kenyen lightly teased, "a maiden of the Plains is taught never to hold out her hand to a man on the opposite side of a fire, whether it's in the ground or in a brazier. Not even when requesting something. She holds it off to the side, or she walks around the fire to meet him, but she doesn't hold out her hand casually."

"You don't?" Solyn asked. "Er, I mean, she doesn't?"

"It's an invitation for the man to leap over the fire and catch her hand. That is how we marry, on the Plains," Kenyen explained. "In front of witnesses, of course."

Solyn gave him a puzzled look. "How odd . . . Ah, no offense meant."

"None taken," he allowed. He shrugged. "It's simply a different way. All systems are valid in the eyes of the Gods."

"It's just . . . so simple. There isn't a priest involved?" Solyn asked. He shook his head. She blinked and absorbed that, then shook her own. "Marriage maschen is prepared by a priest, here in the mountains, in front of a gathering of family, friends, members of the local holdings, everyone who can come. The groom provides the bowl and the bride provides the tea—the nicer the bowl, the better, for it proves how well he will be able to take care of her. There is also some symbolism in the colors, words, or images painted on the tea bowl, if any, and of course the material it is made out of has meaning as well.

"The bride usually provides Sister's Tea which she has made herself, or which a trusted female relative or friend has made—I had to learn how to make both kinds as part of my Healing lessons, since we use similar methods to refine other substances," she added. "It takes a lot of time and the finest of sifting cloths, usually silk, to make the highest grade of powder. The attention a woman gives to Sister's Tea indicates the attention she will give to the needs of her family. There is a lot of meaning behind the ceremony, and a lot of effort."

"I can see that. There is meaning behind our own ceremony as well, if not as much effort," he admitted. "As men are most often the shifters, we are said to rule everything in the air, the water, and the earth via the various animal shapes we can take. But women are the traditional keepers of the hearthfire, representing the fourth element. So a man must be courageous enough to brave the flames of the fourth element when leaping to his lady's side."

She smiled. "I like that. In our ceremony, fire is simply used for heating the water, though it also represents the magical element of fire. *We* don't go leaping over it," she teased, provoking a smile from him. "In the wealthiest families, special scented woods can be burned, and in winter, incense perfumes the air. In spring or summer, even the poorest family showers the couple with fragrant flower petals to invoke the scented blessings of the mountain winds. Earth is obviously represented by the cup, whether it's made from pottery, glass, or gold, and of course the tea represents water."

"So then what happens?" Kenyen asked her, curious. "The priest prepares the tea, the flame boils the water, the tea is whisked, and the air is perfumed . . . and . . . They just drink it?"

"They just drink it," she confirmed, grinning. "From the same bowl in which it is prepared, rather than a separate whisking bowl." She checked herself, amending, "Well, they also say, 'With this tea, I drink you into my life as my beloved groom.' Or 'my beloved bride' in your case as a man. The groom speaks and drinks first, one quarter of the tea. Then the bride speaks and drinks one third of what is left. The groom drinks half of the remainder, this time without words, and the bride drains the whole of what's left in the bowl."

"And then they are married?" he asked.

"The foam is first checked for augury by the priest—the priest usually keeps silent and speaks privately to the bride and groom later if anything needs mentioning. Silence doesn't have to mean something bad, just something private, so everyone assumes all tea-reading results are a good thing. The priest then blesses them, the witnesses cheer, and a feast is usually served," Solyn explained. "At the end of the feast, everyone helps one half of the newly married couple move their belongings into the other half's home.

"Often it's the bride moving into the groom's home, but sometimes it's the groom moving into the bride's, if her home is larger. Sometimes they stay with one or the other set of parents, particularly if that family needs the help, or they don't have the land or the wealth available to build their own home just yet," she said.

Kenyen rubbed his chin, absorbing her words. "So the one moves in with the other, which isn't so different from a maiden moving in with her mate. On the Plains, a man doesn't leap to a woman's side until he is wealthy enough to afford his own *geome*."

"*Geome?*" Solyn asked, curious.

"It's the special kind of domed, lattice-walled tents that we use," he explained. "The maiden saves up her own wealth so she can afford a brazier at the very least, though a portable cookstove is preferred. And when we retire to the Shifting City each winter, the newly married couple usually get their own room in the tenements set aside for each Family. But that doesn't apply here. It's not at all the same. Traver doesn't have a *geome*, let alone a house to call his own."

"Well, Traver's family isn't as wealthy as my own," Solyn admitted, giving it some thought. "Technically, since I have my own bedchamber and Traver sleeps in an attic with his little brother, it would be expected for my family to accept him into our house, while we built up the funds to buy or build our own. As far as everyone is concerned, I'm still the Healer's daughter, which means I would inherit the house with its herb-room and such, so I would be expected to stay with my family, and my husband would stay with me.

"In fact, the night before the caravan left, Traver came and discussed such an arrangement with my parents, since I would need to stay near all the Healing supplies. At least until my training as a Healer is complete, then I'd be expected to find and settle somewhere that needs a Healer, unless the local one is very old. Which Mother isn't."

He could hear a hedge lurking in her tone and voiced it as a question. "However . . . ?"

"However, I'm a mage. My magics aren't the kind that are very good at healing things, so I really *should* be sent to a city where I can learn from other mages," she reminded him. "A half-trained mage is a danger to herself and those around her. Particularly if I tried to experiment with the more complex spells without understanding the principles behind whatever magic I'm trying to effect—the more complex the spell, the more I have to understand it. Anyone can brew a pot of willow-bark tea for simple pain relief, but you don't want to try to mix up a truly complex posset for some ailment, the kind containing several different ingredients, without the right sort of training."

"True," he agreed. "What about moving to a city? Where would you and your husband stay while you trained?"

"If I did get to travel to, say, the capital, either I'd be given quarters at the Mage School as an apprentice—provided they'd let my husband room with me—or I'd rent rooms from someone. Or Traver could stay here and continue to farm while I studied for a few years in the city, since there wouldn't be anything for him to do while I was training."

"Nothing at all?" Kenyen asked. "What about . . . what about representing his family or holding's trade interests in the city?"

"Traver, a merchant?" Solyn snorted with laughter. "Not likely. You'd make a far better agent, given what I've seen of your bartering prowess. No, he wouldn't be interested. Unless, of course, the local holdings got together and appointed him as a representative of the Nespah Valley," she allowed. "Then he would be able to present our concerns at the various trade and craft meetings, and perhaps even help give counsel to the King and his advisors on the needs of this region. *That*, he could do. Managing a shrewd bargain isn't his strong suit, but he is honorable and does have a good mind for what people need. Actually, in some ways, it'd be easiest if he was an apprentice instead of a farmer. He could learn a trade skill in the city. Smithing, pottery, tanning, woodwrighting, weaving, glass-blowing . . ."

Kenyen nodded slowly. "The Mongrels wanted to know if I knew anything of blacksmithing. Specifically, enough to forge a knife. They also wanted to know if I could work my way so deeply into your family, your father would take me on as an apprentice. I know a few things, since it's encouraged for all of us to try different trades until we find something we're good at, but I was better at the tasks of hunting, fighting, and trading, so I found my place in a warband."

Solyn wrinkled her nose, amused at that. "Traver, as a blacksmith apprentice? He tried, once. After one week of burns, cuts, and bruises, of sore arms from pumping the bellows and an aching back from lifting the ore and hauling the ingots, he went right back to the family goats and terrace fields and swore we couldn't pay him enough to labor like that again. He's very much a farmer at heart."

"Tellik says I'm not complaining about my chores like 'I' should," Kenyen murmured.

That earned him a chuckle. "I didn't say he didn't *complain* about being a farmer," she quipped. "He just doesn't complain like he did when he tried being a blacksmith. If he hadn't quit when he did, my mother was about ready to scrub his tongue with soap, his language was so awful."

He grinned at that. "Now there's something else I don't know. How *do* Corredai swear?"

Blushing at the topic, Solyn started packing up her tea-making things. "Well, I'm not *supposed* to swear, since my family does have some high standing in the valley . . . but since Traver was the one who originally taught *me* how to do it, you should probably know."

She looked very pretty when she blushed like that. Following his impulse, Kenyen leaned down and kissed her cheek. Solyn blinked and looked up at him, then smiled and rose. Wrapping her arms around his neck, she pulled him into a proper kiss.

Raised to be polite regardless of location or culture, Kenyen kindly obliged her in her silent demand for more. It didn't take long for passion to rise between them; when he finally ended their kiss, separating their bodies, the ache of wanting her, warring with his cultural instincts to respect this bright, talented young woman, made him very inclined to swear.

From the heartfelt words she muttered, giving him his first lesson in Corredai vulgarity, it was obvious she felt the same way.

EIGHT

Solyn sent her younger sister to him the next day, an hour or so before he was expecting her to arrive for their next trip to the cheese cavern. Luelyn found him in the root garden, digging fresh vegetables for Traver's mother. Looking particularly sober, even a little scared, Luelyn informed Kenyen that Solyn and their mother were busy with someone who'd had a woodcutting accident, and that there was ". . . blood *all* over the place!"

As concerned as he was for Solyn and her patient, Kenyen knew the young girl needed a distraction. So he asked her if she'd help him pick out the prettiest onions and carrots, and then had her help him pick out the best greens for the midday meal. Tellik huffed at the table when she sat down to eat with them, but Traver's parents gave Kenyen subtle but proud looks for so carefully distracting the girl from the things she had just seen.

Receiving such looks felt like a sham. It was a sham; they thought Kenyen was Traver, and that it was their son being this thoughtful, not a stranger who wore his face. When Traver's mother, Tenaria, pressed a bag of freshly boiled and dried wrapping cloths into his arms, then offered to teach Luelyn the secrets of baking her favorite sweet biscuits to further distract her, Kenyen gratefully escaped.

Now that he'd had some practice in the task, Corredai style—and wasn't being distracted by rambling, fun conversations with Solyn—he made short work of lighting the lanterns with his flint and knife, then spent several minutes checking the freshest rounds for dampness and rewrapping them with the clean cloths. It didn't take that much longer than it had with two sets of hands, since he wasn't talking, laughing, or kissing the very pretty outlander.

Since there were no more dried rounds in need of being waxed, he debated returning to the east wall of the valley to help Traver's family some more. Impulse turned him instead toward the very back of the tunnel. Stripping off his clothes, he folded them neatly and placed them in the darkest corner, then headed back up the tunnel, ears enhanced to pick up any sounds.

No one was near. Blowing out each lamp as he came to it, he shifted shape as soon as he could see daylight from the entrance. A moment later, a magpie fluttered out of the cave mouth, winging its way by memory back toward a certain mountaintop in the distance. The biggest danger in flying came from the sky. Wary of hawks and eagles, he flew as fast as he dared, zigging and zagging to thwart any predators.

He spotted the sheep first, grazing along a meadow farther down the slope. After a few moments, he saw Cullerog with them and his herding dog. At least, he thought it was the older shifter; the man had a woven hat on his head and a shawl draped over his shoulders. Here on the west side of most of the mountains, the wind was beginning to pick up intensity, though the skies were still clear. Fluttering closer, he caught a glimpse of Cullerog's nose and chin, recognizing the man. Satisfied of his whereabouts, Kenyen headed for the cottage.

Within minutes, he reached the cabin and circled it as well. The shutters on the windows were open; the hut had two of them, but no glass. If no one was inside, there was a possibility that he could get Traver free and far enough away that when Cullerog returned, the trail would be cold. Landing on one sill, he could see inside . . . and see the large dog dozing on the hearth. Not the one Cullerog used to help him herd sheep, either.

Now Kenyen wished he hadn't given up his hunting cat shape in exchange for copying Traver's face. That had been one of his quietest forms. His sharp bird sight did pick out a hole in the floorboards, a body length or so from the dog and a little small, but possibly enough for his snake form to slide through. Fluttering quietly to the floor, he hopped close to the knothole, one eye on the dog.

The canine slept quietly, side heaving up and down in steady rhythm. Shifting shape, stretching his body into a sinewy line, Kenyen flicked his tongue at the air, tasting the scent of the beast. The sting of man sweat exuded from it, a smell different than Cullerog's. Vaguely familiar. This, then, was a shapeshifter.

So much for my half-formed idea of getting Traver out of here, right now, he thought, disappointed. *Though when that storm Solyn predicted hits, if it's a heavy rain, that'd go a long way in washing away any possible scent trails. But then where would we take him? I don't know if those paper birds have reached their targets yet or not.*

Dog-shifter or not, he still wanted to check up on the other young man. Slithering quietly forward, he peered down into the hole. It was dark down there, but the heat-sensing dimples on his nose gave Kenyen a view of sorts. A cool bucket of water, a slightly warmer bucket of slops, and a distinctly warm body. Traver stirred restlessly, a blob of heat that shifted a leg.

Guilt speared through him. *I've been living a soft life—hard work on a farm, yes, but soft compared to his. I need to let him know he hasn't been forgotten. Because I haven't.*

The easiest way to drop was feet first. Or the equivalent, on a snake. Returning his attention to the not-dog sleeping on top of the trapdoor, Kenyen eased his tail into the knothole. It was a tight fit, as suspected, but even with only half his brother's shapes, Kenyen wasn't a weak shifter. Dangling his body into the room below, he almost hit his serpentine head when the weight of what was below overbalanced the mass still on the cottage floor.

Shifting fast as he fell, he fluttered owl-soft wings, catching himself on the stone-carved floor with only the slightest of thumps. As soon as he landed, he held everything still but for his ears. Those, he elongated into something horse-sized, magnifying his ability to hear. Two creatures breathed nearby. One was the quick, startled breaths of Traver Ys Ten. The other was the slow, steady breaths of the shifter-dog sleeping over their heads.

The tiny bit of light that did come through the cracks and the hole in the boards over their head, coupled with Kenyen's owl-keen vision, proved more than enough light. It showed Traver Ys Ten gaping at him. Unfurling his body into its natural shape—but keeping the ears—Kenyen carefully shifted forward. Crouching next to the man whose body he had learned to shift, Kenyen brought his head as close as he dared.

"*Are you all right?*" He barely breathed the words, never mind whispered them. Traver rolled his eyes and looked around the room. Kenyen nodded. The Corredai didn't seem injured, so he breathed next, "*I'm working on a way to get you free.*"

Traver nodded. He breathed back a single word. ". . . *And?*"

". . . *I'm still working on it.*" Kenyen returned, lifting his head and his gaze to the trapdoor, where the not-dog slept.

"*Ask Solyn,*" Traver offered. "*She has good ideas. Usually.*"

Kenyen could guess what he meant. The startled, flustered claim of a betrothal, which Solyn had already explained had been a spur of the moment thing and not her wisest choice in retrospect. At least, where the real Traver was concerned. More guilt surfaced at that thought. In a way, Kenyen was taking advantage of the situation. With a willing outlander woman, since there was no doubt in his mind that Solyn enjoyed their semi-intimate twinings so far, but it was still . . . illicit, he supposed was the word for it, and on several levels.

"*Be ready for us,*" Kenyen told him. "*When the rains . . .*"

He froze, ears twitching. The dog's breathing had changed. Depending on the skill of the shifter up there, that canine nose could be quite sensitive indeed. Enough to maybe detect Kenyen's smell. Growing a covering of feathers—the best way to trap his personal scent close to his body—Kenyen looked back at Traver.

The younger man bravely lifted his chin, shaping the words, "*Go. I'll be ready.*"

He lifted his chin, not toward the knothole in the ceiling, but toward a dim patch of light to one side, near a spot where the support beams holding up the cottage floor disappeared into the stones mortared in place on the downhill side. Moving slowly, cushioning each step with a bit of fur, Kenyen headed toward the promised bit of light. *If that's a hole over there, and it's at least as big as the knothole, I can get out without being . . .*

The dog moved. Floorboards creaking slightly, it heaved up onto its paws. The patterns of shadow and light shifted as the dog snuffled around the edges of the trapdoor. Yawning with that faint but typical canine whine, he padded toward the cottage door. Indecision held Kenyen still. If the dog knew of the hole, if the cur was headed outside to check it out—the four-legged shadow shifted shape. A moment later, something scraped on the floor. A hiss of liquid filling a pot told him what the Mongrel watchdog was doing.

Using the cover of the noise over their heads, Kenyen quickly moved to the indicated corner. The opening was small, and longish, reminiscent of the tunnel under the rocks in that cave to the north.

It also bore tiny mouse tracks. Relieved, Kenyen tucked his fingers into the hole and flowed his body up into it, pulling himself onto the tiny ledge in a very ugly, un-pure fashion. *Where a mouse can go . . . so can a serpent, thank the Gods.*

His body had to be shifted longer and thinner than normal for a viper, since he needed enough room to push off of the crumbled mortar, but it was the best way to escape. For him. *But not for Traver. If only he had his own magics—of course! Some mages can shift their shapes via magic. Maybe Solyn knows a spell?*

Pausing at the exit, he flicked his tongue out, tasting the air. The floorboards creaked behind him. As yet, there were no scents indicating anyone else was right outside. Slithering into the sun, he worked his way through the tufts of grass growing outside the cottage. The sheep were no doubt allowed to nibble on it from time to time, but from the length of the stalks, they hadn't been this close to the cottage in a handful of days.

A shift and a flutter launched him back into the sky. Mindful of predators, Kenyen hurried down the valley, flying at an angle to the Nespah Valley in case the dog-shifter was looking for anything suspicious outside. Magpies weren't long-distance fliers, but they were agile enough that he could duck into the trees whenever he passed a bit of forest or an orchard. Detouring back toward the valley, he mulled over the choices as he flew.

The best time to effect a rescue would be during a heavy rain, since that would wash away smells, he knew. *The best time would also be right after lulling the Mongrels into complacency, disarming them with the scent of success. So I should start hanging around the smithy. I'll go see Ysander after I get back, then. I can pretend it's a roundabout way to check up on Solyn without disturbing her and her mother's healing work—oh, I should check up on little Luelyn, too.*

He did care for Solyn's family. They were as nice as Solyn herself, so it was easy to like them. It was a tiny bit harder with Traver's family, but not through any fault of theirs; guilt kept overshadowing his experiences with them. *But if I can extract Traver and get him to safety, then that guilt will ease. Which begs the question,* where *would be a place of safety?*

Ideally, that would be in the arms of shifters he trusted. Men and women who wouldn't be taken by surprise in a shapeshift-enhanced attack. People who could literally smell friend from foe. *But I have no idea how far those paper birds can fly, or even if they've found their targets by now.*

Hopefully that'll be before that storm she predicted hits—I can tell it's coming when I fly high, because the upper winds are so strong and cold, but I still can't see any sign of clouds—why didn't I learn to shape myself like an eagle, with an eagle's eyesight?

"Is he alright?" Solyn asked quietly, reaching up to pluck another dried herb off the lines overhead. She swayed on her toes and missed.

Kenyen—in Traver's body—steadied her, pressing one palm to her waist, and gently lifted the brittle spray of greenery from the string with his other hand. "For now, I think so. But well guarded. We need a rainstorm and a diversion. And enough time to get him far enough away for the rain to disperse his scent. Do you think the birds have arrived by now?"

"They should have. But we can release more of them after the storm rolls through." For a moment, she thought her ring had squeezed. She peered at the doorway. In the sickroom beyond, one of the holding laborers from down near the bottom of the valley was resting, heavily sedated by painkilling possets. Barely whispering, she continued, "You say you want the scent to dissipate, but . . . um . . . what if his scent wasn't on the ground?"

Removing more of the herbs from the upper line, Kenyen laid them in the large basket on the preparation table. He took his cue from her, asking in a whisper, "Where else would it be? He can't exactly fly, you know."

Stepping away, Solyn ducked under the far end of the table and pulled out a gathering basket. Unlike the round, high-sided one with the dried herbs in it, this one was designed for gathering items with long stems. The handle was a large loop, and the basket itself was nothing more than a broad oval woven in a shallow curve, without even a lip. Both had been woven from willow withes and reed strips, but were two vastly different implements.

She presented it to him. "With this, he could." Kenyen gave her a skeptical look. She started to say more, to explain the spell she had in mind, but her ring squeezed. Quickly bringing her finger to her lips, she returned the basket to its spot under the table. "Thank you again for rewrapping the cheeses without me, today. And for being willing to help me with my chores in here."

Kenyen accepted the change in topic. "I do enjoy being with you. Despite not having all my old memories back, I'm very much enjoying the woman you are. I enjoy the memories I *do* still have of you . . . and I'm enjoying the new memories I'm making with you."

She smiled at his words. There was plenty of sincerity behind them, particularly the ones generic enough, he could speak them from the heart, rather than as the deception of being Traver Ys Ten. "As you said, you're seeing me through fresh eyes? Is that it?"

He pulled her close, murmuring in Traver's voice and with Traver's face the words that came from his own heart. "Face-to-face, mind to mind . . . every day I spend with you, I keep finding new things to appreciate about you, Solyn Ys Rei."

The words, she knew, came from the real man. Not wanting to see them spoken with her best friend's face, she rested her cheek on his chest, listening to him speak.

"If that's not with fresh eyes, I don't know what would be. If that's not a deepening of my . . . my love for you, I don't know what could be." The words were half truth, half deliberate seduction. Kenyen hated the latter half, but knew their unseen audience needed to hear them, just in case they were the sort to gossip and let word get back to the shifting ears of Family Mongrel.

A masculine voice, deep and firm, interrupted them. "If you don't get yourselves to the priest soon, I *do* know what *will* be. And *no* twining in your mother's herb-room, young lady. Behave yourself, young man."

Blushing, Solyn pulled back from Kenyen's embrace. He let her go with a soft clearing of his throat. Politely facing her father, Kenyen dipped his head. "Milord."

"So formal," Ysander mocked lightly, looking large, tanned, and imposing with his skepticism pinching his dark brows. "Particularly when you had my unwed daughter in your arms a moment ago, in my own house—I do thank you for your help in the smithy, earlier. But that's not your normal thing. What do you *really* want from my family?"

Both of them stilled. Solyn bit back a protest. Whatever she said, she knew her father would interpret it through the clouded thoughts of a woman in love, not the clearheaded one she actually was. She looked at Kenyen, who subtly squared his shoulders.

"To protect your family. To share with you and provide for you. To work with you and work beside you," he stated. "To continue to . . . to play with and work with and learn with and . . . and love with your daughter. If you have a problem with that," Kenyen stated quietly, taking Solyn's hand in his, "well, I suggest you learn to live with it. As much as she has been your daughter for most of her life, she is a woman grown and has her own life to live. The decision of what I will *get* from this family therefore rests entirely with *her*."

"Tellik is right," Ysander muttered, eyeing the younger man. "You *have* changed. Matured, in some ways."

"Sometimes a man does," Kenyen agreed. "I spent a full day at the bottom of that ravine, barely able to remember my own name. I had plenty of time to try to remember all the things that *are* important."

Solyn's father grunted softly. He lifted his chin at the basket. "Get those herbs sorted and sealed in a jar. Your mother wants you to check on and change Maullin's bandages."

"Yes, Father," Solyn agreed, releasing Kenyen's hand so she could turn back to the table.

"Are you staying for supper?" the blacksmith asked Kenyen, not looking entirely friendly.

"I would like to," Kenyen replied calmly. "But if you do not wish it, I can return home."

Ysander grunted. Solyn sighed and turned back just enough to roll her eyes at him. "Father . . ."

He grunted again. "You can stay. But no twining in here. You aren't married yet."

"No, milord," Kenyen murmured, feeling a twinge of guilt for the kisses they had shared already, even if they had taken place elsewhere under full, mutual consent.

The rains came when they were over halfway to the old mining cave. At first it was a light sprinkle, but by the time they reached the trees sheltering the entrance, the clouds were pouring down. Soaked to the skin even under the canopy of leaves, Kenyen and Solyn ran the last hundred lengths. Once inside, they dripped and shivered, for even the wind dug at the mouth of the cave, stirring the air.

Kenyen peered out at the pounding the leaves were taking. "This is awful! It's going to flatten the wheat in the fields!"

Solyn gave him a puzzled look, then chuckled. "If we were using a lowland grain, yes. But we bred a short, stiff-stalked variety generations ago. It's better suited for terrace farming, for withstanding the winds that whip around the hills, and the heavy rains of the last midsummer storms that strike the mountains. We're more in danger of the root vegetables rotting in the ground, if the terraces aren't set to drain just right."

Her mentioning that made him acutely aware they were near the very bottom of the ravine-like slope. "What about flooding? Are we safe in here?"

She rolled her eyes. Her ring had spun in the middle of the sprint for cover, so she used his true name. "Kenyen, we're at the *upper* end of the valley? Even in the worst of storms, the water will never flood this high. Down by the copper mines, yes, it's always a big concern. But they have bags of clay down there and Callan Tre Fin is a good owner; I already spread word the storm was coming, so his workers are all out by now and the entrances have been blocked up to keep the mines dry."

Hearing his real name, Kenyen took it as the cue to relax his features. "Well, at least no one else would be idiotic enough to come this far in a storm this bad, so we should be safe for a while."

"Safe, but soaking wet." She wrinkled her nose. "And we can't light a fire. Greenvein cheese tastes terrible when it's been smoked."

"If we move back into the depths, we'll be out of the wind," he offered.

"True, and we can strip off our wet clothes and wring them out." She held up the oilcloth sack slung over her shoulder. It was fuller than her usual collection of luncheon food alone would imply. "I came prepared with a blanket and some extra food, in case the storm trapped us here." She paused, the implications hitting her. A blush warmed her cheeks. "Um . . . there's only the *one* blanket, so . . . I suppose you could borrow it first, until your clothing dries."

Kenyen chuckled. "I'm a gentleman as well as a shifter. *You* may use the blanket. Go on back and get wrapped up in it. Let me know when it's safe to come back there."

Nodding, she lit the first lamp near the entrance with a whisper of power. Kenyen sneezed. Solyn grinned. "I'll cut a few slices of greenvein while I'm at it."

He followed her a short distance back, far enough that the wind no longer chilled him, then stopped and waited. As soon as she was out of sight—and two sneezes later—he stripped off Traver's wet clothes. Coating his body from waist to knees in black magpie feathers for modesty, he wrung out the garments as best he could and waited.

Finally, her voice echoed up the tunnel. ". . . I'm decent! Well, sort of decent. It's a good thing we're supposedly betrothed!"

Grinning, he padded deeper into the tunnel, sandals in one hand and clothes slung over the other shoulder. He found her draped in a creamy, soft-spun blanket that she'd knotted over one shoulder and belted around the waist for modesty. It barely reached her knees, though.

Her calves were magnificent, muscular and curvaceous thanks to the constant uphill-downhill travel of life here in the mountains. Around one lovely ankle, she had fastened the braided bit of leather, with its rune-carved beads meant to prevent unwanted conceptions. As he watched, she stretched up, spreading out her skirt a bit more on a section of storage shelves covered in wax-preserved rounds, then turned.

Her mouth dropped open, and her hand clapped over it. Slightly self-conscious, but only slightly, Kenyen spread his clothes—Traver's clothes—along another set of empty shelves, and waited for her to get used to the sight of him in his shifter-style modesty.

"Are . . . are those *feathers*?" she finally asked, lowering her palm. Her gaze remained fastened on his hips.

"Of course. This is what the Shifterai do—well, mostly the men," he amended, explaining. "We can't shapechange our clothing or our gear when we change our bodies, so when we strip, we shift what's called a modesty pelt. The princesses—the female shifters—cover themselves from chest to knee, but this is what the men do. It's one of the first controlled shapeshifts we learn, beyond our initial shape."

The matter-of-fact way he treated his near-nakedness helped. Getting over most of her shock, Solyn nodded. ". . . I've heard there are spells which simulate the same thing, but I haven't found any books describing how that works. Not yet. What . . . what does that *feel* like?"

Turning sideways, Kenyen offered her his hip. Her curiosity was like anyone who had never seen a Shifterai shapeshift feathers before. "Touch it for yourself."

"I meant to *make* the feathers," Solyn retorted, blushing. She started to say more, but curiosity pulled her closer. Hesitantly, she lifted her hand. At his nod, she touched his hip, then stroked the feathers coating his flanks. "Ohhh, that *is* soft. The only birds I've touched are chickens meant to be plucked for cooking—most of my books have stressed that mages aren't supposed to take lives, in case we're ever tempted to take the life energy released at death. I never have been," she admitted, still petting him gently. "The most I'll do is crack open an egg, but then I'm careful about avoiding temptation."

Her choice of words, coupled with the stroking of her fingers along his buttock and upper thigh, made him blush. He twitched when she carefully parted a few of the tufts, trying to see the skin beneath. "Careful, or you'll find another temptation to avoid."

"What? Oh." Reluctantly, Solyn removed her hand. She couldn't help asking in curiosity, "Are feathers the only thing you do?"

"We also do scales and fur. Most everyone does fur, but feathers are warm and shed water more easily." The loss of her touch made him offer, "Would you like to see?"

Fascinated, she nodded. "Please?"

The feathers retracted. Within three or four heartbeats, they had shrunk down and altered themselves into matte blue-black scales, cupping his backside. Kenyen turned with the shift, hiding the front of his body. She was a Healer's apprentice and had literally seen him naked before, albeit in the shape of her captured friend, but he had shaped a reptilian pouch up front. The lack of obvious genitals would no doubt disturb her, so he presented his backside instead.

Again, she hesitated, then touched him, fingers gliding lightly over his rump. Solyn raised her brows, enjoying the feel. The surface was cool, slick but dry, and subtly textured. Much like any garden-variety snake, in fact, though there were no reassuring vertical stripes on his darkened hide. Curious, Solyn asked, "Can you take on a snake or lizard shape?"

"I can form a Plains viper . . . and yes, I can re-create the venom as well," he added, glancing at her over his shoulder. Solyn lifted her head at that. Kenyen nodded. "It wasn't easy, but I was determined to learn."

"How would someone learn something like that?" she asked, frowning.

"By being bitten. Repeatedly. My older brother helped me," he added as her eyes widened. "He's a *multerai*, a shifter who can make more than ten pure shapes. They can sort of *push* their power into a fellow Shifterai, lending us energy. He helped me survive the venom by pushing it out of my system, taking a little bit longer each time while my body was learning the feel of it. It both builds up an immunity and gives a shifter time to figure out how to re-create it within themselves."

"That must have been rather painful," Solyn muttered. "We have a couple kinds of mildly poisonous snakes around here, but the very name of 'viper' suggests something quite deadly. You were that willing to risk your life?"

He rubbed his chin and chuckled. "I wouldn't say it was a case of risking my life so much as it was my brother and I risking our mother's wrath. I wanted to do it to prove I was ready for inclusion in the warbands. Every young man has the right to join them for at least one season. I'm rather good at bargaining, and figured if nothing else, I could be one of the more trade-inclined members if it turned out I couldn't handle much of the fighting. Though we all fight when there is need."

Aware her hand was still caressing his rump, Solyn blushed and pulled it away. "And can you fight?"

"Almost as well as my brother, though I don't quite have his battle stamina, since I only have half the shapes," Kenyen admitted. Raking his hands through his damp locks, he sighed, staring at the far wall. "I love my brother, but I like being *away* from him. Like a plant finally allowed to grow in the sun, instead of his shade."

"At least you're allowed to be away," Solyn muttered. He twisted to look at her and she gave him a wry half smile. "Until I can run away and learn to be a mage, I'll only be a semi-lousy Healer's apprentice, hardly much better than an herbalist."

Kenyen smirked and tipped his head in teasing invitation. "Maybe we should run away together?"

She laughed at that. "Oh, don't tempt me." Patting his backside—his very nice, shapely backside, she ordered, "Shift me some fur, shapechanger. Make it something pretty!"

Grinning back, he played a trick on her, one he had played on his Shifterai teachers ages ago. The sinuous scales simulating his skin shifted and reshaped, sprouting fur. But not just any fur. Bright, *sky-blue* fur. With lilac-purple tiger stripes. Her shriek of surprise, followed by palm-muffled laughter, was worth it. Laughing as well, he twisted around, showing her all sides as he proudly displayed the silly sight.

Extending her hand to touch his hip and feel the unnatural-hued fur for herself, Solyn froze when her fingers instead brushed across his groin. He stilled as well. That left her fingertips half buried in the thick, plush fur providing a modesty screen.

For a moment, she didn't know what to do. Just as she made up her mind, he drew in a breath. Kenyen choked on it a moment later when she gently petted his nether-pelt.

"It's very soft," she murmured, stroking her fingers through the long guard hairs. She knew what she was touching; being a Healer's apprentice had given her a thorough education in not only anatomy but its proper, healthy function. She couldn't quite bring herself to look at him—not with her face so red—but she asked, "Are your natural nether-hairs this soft?"

He choked again, coughed, cleared his throat, and attempted to speak. "I, uh . . . you . . ." Kenyen twitched his hips away, turning his back on her to hide the inevitable reaction to her touch. He lost control of the color of his fur with the move, letting his modesty pelt return to its most familiar color, the same dark brown as his hair. "You *shouldn't* do that. I'm, ah . . . *trying* to be respectful, here."

"I appreciate it," Solyn murmured, returning her hand to his rump. She squeezed lightly, making him jump. Smirking, she met his startled gaze over his shoulder. "But right now, you and I are about as close to truly alone as we're probably going to get, and will be alone for quite some time. This storm will take several hours to weaken . . . and I, for one, find *you* attractive enough to take advantage of this opportunity. Um . . . if you don't *mind* the thought of . . . ?"

"I'm torn." The words escaped him. Once they were out, he couldn't take them back. Shrugging, Kenyen admitted the truth. "I honestly care about you. I think you're funny, and smart, and charming . . . and I'd consider courting you if we weren't stuck in this situation. And *that* has me torn. When a man of the Plains courts a mate, he treats her properly. Respectfully. He makes sure they are compatible mentally and emotionally. Physical needs are for the earth-priestesses to handle, until a man is wed."

"But what about all the times you're not near one of these . . . earth-priestesses?" Solyn asked. "Like when you're away from the Plains, doing warband things? For that matter, you did mention something about earth-priestesses, but I'm still not completely sure how they came to be, or what they do. Um, in full."

The conversation had deflated some of his interest. Turning back to her, Kenyen gave her the truth. "It's simple. Earth-priestesses are widows who . . . well, no, actually it isn't, because you don't know the underlying parts. Let me back up," he corrected himself, looking around for a seat. The stools they had used before were in the next alcove, so he brought them over, speaking as he moved. "It's a long explanation, and we might as well be comfortable for it."

Setting the stools down, he gestured for her to take one and settled on the other. Solyn, absorbing that, sank slowly onto the wooden surface. "Alright. Tell me about them."

"The background part first. When a young girl physically matures, we celebrate her status as a maiden," Kenyen began. "She then moves from her parents' *geome* to the maiden's *geome*, where she spends the next several years learning how to manage all the womanly things she needs to know. How to keep her tent-home clean, how to cook and manage finances, how to honor Father Sky and Mother Earth; they finish their education with the hearth-priests and -priestesses in things like writing and numbers . . . and the earth-priestesses teach her how to find pleasure in her own body and what to do when they finally join with a man."

"So . . . earth-priestesses *are* priestesses. How do they become one?" she asked.

"When a maiden is married, she becomes a wife and moves into her husband's *geome*," he told her. "If she becomes a widow, or should she divorce him—which is rare but does happen—she goes back into the maiden's *geome* for a full year, so that she can grieve, recover, and get her heart and mind set straight. At the end of that time, if she so chooses, she can enter the priesthood as an earth-priestess, where her duties are twofold.

"First, she is to train the young men as well as the new maidens in all the ways of women and men. And second, she is to make herself available to the unmarried men of her Family so that—no, no, no!" Kenyen quickly corrected, the moment her eyes widened. He had already encountered this same look of disbelieving confusion on the faces of other outlanders in years past. "Remember, on the Plains, a Family is a *group* of many extended kin-families, not all of whom are related to each other . . . much like the Nespah Valley is a group of many holdings filled with several extended kin-families as well as laborers from other regions, but not everyone is related to each other. Your valley is similar to our Family, except our Families travel, and your valley is defined by a single location, not by its inhabitants."

Solyn nodded hesitantly, somewhat relieved though still puzzled. "Alright. Go on . . ."

"Family Tiger, the one I come from, has over eight hundred people, and of actual parents, siblings, aunts, uncles, nieces, nephews, and first cousins . . . I probably am only related to about sixty or seventy people at most, almost all of them in the South Paw. There are eight segments in our Family, with names like South Paw, Tailtip, and so forth," he reassured her. "If I were a widow and chose to become an earth-priestess after my full year in the maiden's *geome*, I would not serve any of the men in the South Paw segment of Family Tiger, because of the lineages involved.

"I probably would serve in Tailtip, which has no close or immediate relationship to my bloodline. *Or* I could ask to serve in another Family within Clan Cat, such as Family Lion . . . or even cross-serve in another Clan entirely. *Now* do you get it?" he asked.

She nodded more firmly this time. "It would be like me going to . . . to Tallat Valley, which is a couple days' ride from here. I'm not related to anyone there."

"Exactly. Or to Mespak instead of Nespah," he agreed, pleased she had grasped the analogy. "Since we all meet in the wintertime at Shifting City, there are plenty of opportunities for earth-priestesses to be swapped around between Clans and Families. Or for maidens to meet and court with men. If they're from a different Clan or Family, the woman usually goes to the man's Family. The only exception being princesses, women who are born with the ability to shift their shape. They're rare, so usually a Family prefers to keep their female shifters," Kenyen finished.

"I see." She mulled that over for a few moments, then shook her head. "Back to the original topic. When you're not on the Plains, and you have . . . needs . . . what do you do?" She blushed on the word *needs.*

Kenyen blushed as well. He rubbed at the back of his neck. "We find the local equivalent of an earth-priestess, if there is one . . . and we treat her with the same respect. Except earth-priestesses on the Plains are supported as a member of the priesthood, which means they receive a stipend from the Family as a whole each turning of Brother Moon, whereas outlander variants, um, expect their payment to be a bit more direct. If it's not that sort, but the woman is willing, mature, and understands it is merely a dalliance . . . well, we treat her the same way. With the respect we would approach an earth-priestess."

"I see." Again, she paused to consider that. "So . . . basically . . . what's tearing you apart is the urge to treat me like a *maiden* of the Plains, instead of a willing, mature, understanding outlander equivalent of an earth-priestess?"

His blush deepened. He gave her a sheepish smile. "Yeah. That's pretty much it. I *like* you, and part of me wants to court you properly. It's being held back by the circumstances we're caught up in, but there it is."

How sweet, Solyn thought, warmed by his interest in her. She was also cooled by the reminder that their situation *was* awkward. *However . . . I think there might be a way around that . . .*

"I have a question," she said. "What happens if an earth-priestess doesn't want to be an earth-priestess anymore? Say, they've served as one for three or four years, and want a break, or maybe even wants a chance to be courted like a regular woman. Is that allowed? Or must they be an earth-priestess forevermore?"

"Well, of course it's allowed!" Kenyen scoffed. "It's her time, her effort, her body. Only she can make that choice, and she has the right to change her mind at any time. Or change it back again. A number of women who do sign up to be an earth-priestess often drop out within the first year, for a variety of reasons. That's why there's a year of training involved, of supervision under the assistance of a more experienced priestess, and of course lessons from the rest of the priesthood to absorb, since it's often easier for a man to confess his troubles and seek counsel when he's been physically relaxed.

"But if she wants to go back to being a maiden and have the chance to be courted, then yes, she can do so at any time. It is a requirement that she waits for one full turning of Sister Moon before she can wed anyone, though," he added. "That's just in case her contraceptive charms might have failed. We don't have a lot of mages who can craft new ones, and Healer-mages are rare, so most women want to know if they've conceived from their time as an earth-priestess before they wed—children created during an earth-priestess' service are considered as legitimate as any other, because in a sense the earth-priestess is wedded to her duties."

"Ah. Well, that makes sense," Solyn murmured, pleased. She felt a bit daring, but the storm guaranteeing their privacy for a while gave her the chance to be bold. To seize what she wanted. "Well, I was thinking just now, what if you treated me *first* like an earth-priestess . . . and then, once we've untangled ourselves from this mess, when we've rescued Traver and gotten rid of the Mongrels plaguing the valley . . . what if you then treated me like a maiden afterward?"

He stared at her, absorbing the implication behind her words, until a chuckle escaped him. A rueful one. "Traver implied you were quite clever. Now I see just *how* clever."

Rising from her stool, she moved over to his and slipped onto his lap. Her blanket rode high enough that she could feel some of the fur on his thighs brushing against the backs of her own. It wasn't blue and purple anymore, just plain dark brown, but it was still as soft as cat fur. Kenyen blushed when she settled on his lap, but didn't push her away. Looping her arms around his neck, Solyn smiled at him.

"Do you like the fact that I'm clever?" she asked.

He cleared his throat. The position of her arms threatened to make the side gap of her makeshift blanket dress show more than it rightfully should. "Yes . . . yes, I do."

"Then how would you approach me as an earth-priestess?" she asked, smiling.

Opening his mouth to reply, Kenyen stopped, thought, and finally asked, "*Do* you have any experience in coupling with a man?"

She blushed at the blunt question and shrugged. "I know all the facts regarding the *theory* of it. I *am* a Healer's apprentice, and it all falls under the heading of midwifery skills."

"But you have no practical knowledge?" Kenyen asked, feeling awkward once more.

"I've kissed and touched," she confessed. It was her turn to clear her throat. "And, erm . . . fondled . . . a bit. It was with a young caravan merchant last summer. Nothing really came of it, because it's difficult to find time alone *because* I'm an apprentice to my mother. *Everyone* comes to me when they have a minor scratch in need of an ointment, or a cough in need of a posset."

Kenyen wrapped his arms around her, cuddling her close in

sympathy. "I've heard similar complaints from our own Healer priests. Were you to come back to the Family with me, you'd have . . . well, actually, I'm not entirely sure you'd have Priest Yemii to spell you, because you would be asked to serve more as a mage than as a Healer, herbal or spell. Though you'd be highly welcome if you chose to do both. But whether or not you'd even be posted to Family Tiger would be up to the Council of Mages, at the capital. Every Family should have at least one, and we already have Priestess Soulet."

"Well, first I'd have to go to *our* capital city, to *be* trained as a mage," Solyn countered. "Something like that would take me a couple of years, if not longer. So before we even got to the Plains, if we went back to them, we'd have to decide if there *was* going to be a 'we,'" she pointed out. "Would you be willing to wait for me to complete my training?"

Kenyen considered that. "Is there a . . . a law in this land against Corredai mage apprentices being married?"

"Well, no. Not that I'm aware of," she admitted. "So long as the person is seventeen or older, and judged mature enough to handle the responsibilities of marriage—and for the record, I am twenty-two—then anyone can marry who they please. Divorce is difficult, since it requires counseling with the priesthood to see if the marriage can be salvaged, and then swearing upon a Truth Stone or a Truth Wand that the love cannot be revived, and listing the reasons in front of both families and any friends, and . . . Well, we try not to do it lightly, as it's a big hassle."

"It's more or less the same on the Plains," Kenyen agreed. "My brother did marry my sister-in-law quickly, but they knew their minds and their hearts were quite compatible. They're both bookish, thoughtful, responsible . . . They bring out the best in each other. As much as I dislike being in his shadow, if I can make half as good a choice in my mate, I'll be well-off . . . and yes, I consider you to be a potential candidate from the better side of that halfway point."

As far as compliments went, it was a little awkward, but she knew it was heartfelt. Warmed by it, she kissed him on the cheek. "Thank you. The more I get to know you, the more I like you a lot, too. Enough to consider courting you as well. But as you said, we do have this tangled mess wrapped around us," she muttered, sighing. "On the bright side, you *are* supposed to be seducing me, and it *is* acceptable for us to twine fully . . . so long as we don't do it in public and provided my father never finds out." She wrinkled her nose, smiling ruefully. "He wants to keep me his little girl forever."

"Most fathers are that way, in all the lands I've visited," Kenyen agreed. Now that she was on his lap, and her logic had been considered, he could see her point. There was still a twinge of conscience in him, one that made him ask, "Are you *sure* you want to do this?"

Solyn nodded. "Quite sure. Whatever we're both comfortable with, however far we both want."

Her reassurance on that last part relieved him of some of his tension, some of his lingering resistance. However, getting from the discussion of what they were about to do, to actually *doing* it, felt awkward.

"So . . . should we just start kissing?" Solyn asked him. "Or should we just jump straight to waxing the cheese?"

That broke him up with laughter. Hugging her, Kenyen shook his head. "No, kissing is fine. *But* we really should do what we came here to do, first, which is to rewrap all the damp rounds."

"Ugh," she muttered, rising from his lap. "*Everything* is going to be damp, in this storm. Let me get the cloths I brought."

"By the way, you owe Traver's mother a stack of clean cheese cloths. She sent some down here with me yesterday, so I wouldn't interrupt your healing efforts. Speaking of which," he added. "How is the patient?"

"Recovering. Once the pain-posset put him to sleep, Mother scored the inner edges of his thigh wound so it'll heal as scarlessly as possible, inside. A limp really curtails your ability to walk far, here in the mountains." Extracting the pouch with the fresh strips of fabric, she handed him half the stack.

"So your mother has one of the blades?" Kenyen asked. "Given the risks of Family Mongrel's ongoing search for it, isn't that dangerous?"

"It is, but she's a Healer, and greensteel is still a very valuable healing tool," Solyn reminded him, moving off to find the first of the fresh rounds. "It was the inside she scored, very lightly. It's utterly contrary to the usual healing practices, and disturbing to watch, but the wound will heal more neatly for it. She did not, however, cut the flesh up at the skin. He'll heal with a slight but visible scar, which is what those—what did you call them, curs?"

"Curs," he agreed, finding his own set of rounds on the shelf opposite hers. "A scar is what they'd expect to see, yes."

"Yes. Mother's healing spells will heal most of his wounds well, but the blow was deep, and . . . well, best left unmentioned," Solyn dismissed. She changed the subject. "What exactly *is* a cur, anyway?"

"A baseless brute with no civility, no compassion, no mercy. No honor," Kenyen explained, his tone grim. "Basically what my offensive ancestors were before our women tamed us a few decades after the year the Empire shattered. They acted with even more brutality than these Mongrel curs, though without nearly as much cunning. Then again, they had the liberty to act openly in their criminal ways, for there was no law on the land but the strongest shift of muscle and claw. They forced themselves on any female they could find, and subjugated the few non-shifter men as well."

"Ah. So that's why your men decided to sequester your women, to keep them safe," Solyn murmured.

"What? No," Kenyen chuckled. "No, that was the *women's* decision. We honor women because we wish to remember that women may not be as physically strong as men, and most of them may not be shapeshifters, but they are smart and wise, compassionate and strong-willed. We honor the fact that these are traits all civilized people should value.

"Conflict is something men excel at, because our size and build can handle it, and sometimes it is needed. When a feral bull gets loose, when bandits try to raid, these are things we can prevent. Cooperation is something women excel at, whether it's getting children to mind their manners or relatives to share their resources. We try to strike balance in our lives, and—"

Light flashed, blue white and bright, visible all the way from the mouth of the tunnel; not even half a startled heartbeat later, thunder *kra-koommmed*, rattling the very air. Near-simultaneously, Solyn yelped and Kenyen swore, jumping and spinning to face the distant opening. The pattern hiss of rain turned into a rush from the droplets shaken out of the sky.

Steadying her nerves, with several deep, shaky breaths, Solyn raised her voice slightly, wanting to be heard. "I am *very* glad we got in here before *that* struck!"

More lightning flashed and more thunder boomed. He managed a smile and a nod, still shaken by the sudden, near strike. "As am I."

NINE

Morbid curiosity sent both of them to the cave mouth once they were done with their task. They peered out at the storm through the wind-lashed trees, watching the dark gray clouds swirl and flicker with light. Kenyen was able to expand his fur to the rest of his limbs, protecting him against the chilly gusts, but Solyn only had her blanket.

After a few minutes of fascinated storm watching, the shivering got to her. A good storm was more enjoyable when she not only had shelter but had more layers to wear. ". . . I'm going back inside. I'm a little too cold out here."

"I'll come with you," he murmured.

She chuckled as they reached the back section of the old mining tunnel. At his inquiring look, Solyn explained what was on her mind. "Oh, I was just thinking of Jelinna. Heh . . . she always said she liked a hairy man, but I wonder if she'd like one *this* hairy."

Her hazel eyes flicked to his fur-covered figure. Kenyen chuckled and blushed. Retracting most of it, he spread his arms. "How's this?"

"Still a little strange," she admitted, smiling. "But I think I envy you for it."

"You wouldn't be the first, but you have an advantage that *my* people would envy, and that is the ability to do real magic." Taking her hand, Kenyen tugged her close. Kissing her brow, he smiled and said, "Even though you make me sneeze by it, I wouldn't trade your spells for any princess' ability to shapeshift."

Warmed by his open regard for her abilities, Solyn wrapped her arms around Kenyen in an impulsive hug. Tucking her cheek against his shoulder, she inhaled his distinct scent, male, musky, and a hint of something animal-like. The scent of fur, she realized. It clung to his smooth skin even though he had retracted everything above his waist. Impulse moved her head, turning it enough to taste his skin.

Kenyen stilled at the touch of her lips. Warm and willing, he fought back the conflict of *maiden* versus outlander, and reminded himself to treat her with the honor due to—*oh, dear Gods . . .* The feel of her tongue licking the skin just below his collarbone made him tremble. *Let her make the first moves . . . let her . . . ohhh . . .*

His head tipped back as she kissed higher, giving her access to his throat. Her soft growl startled him. She followed it with a giggle, squeezing her arms around his chest and nipping at the base of his neck. "You're not the only one with an animal inside. Rrrawrrr."

Chuckling at her silliness, he brought his head down and his hand up. Tilting her face toward his, he captured her mouth in a slow, succulent kiss. Her hand explored his back, first feeling each muscle, rubbing and kneading them, then sliding down to his rump. From the way she hummed and scratched her fingernails lightly through the fur covering him, she apparently liked the feel of it. So did he; the light scrapes sent shivers of pleasure up his back.

Solyn felt his body stir against hers. Not wanting him to back away this time, she pulled on his hips, keeping him close. Only a few young men had stirred her feminine interest in the past. Of them, only this man stirred it enough to want to twine fully with him. What she did know of such things, she applied to him by alternately scratching Kenyen's skin lightly with her nails and soothing the marks with her palms. In nibbling licks and nips, she returned each taste in their kiss.

Not sure how far he wanted to take this, Kenyen only knew that it would end in pleasure for her, at the very least. He would respect her willingness to make love, as he would respect an earth-priestess' willingness, but he was also aware of her inexperience. *So I will be a sort of earth-priest for her*, he decided. *This is her first time, and I will treat her like her . . . like her husband would.*

The thought was forbidden, because they weren't mated. Illicit.

It took him only a moment to decide they would not go that far. No intercourse. But, warm and willing, soft and sweet, she felt right in his arms. She excited him despite the illicit thrill, not just because of it. This was Solyn Ys Rei, a wonderful, sweet, funny outlander woman. There was still much they could do that would share pleasure, and Kenyen made up his mind to show her the many things he knew.

The first thing he did, aside from continuing to kiss her, was stroke her soft, tanned skin. At first, he kept his touches firm, soothing, then shifted to tickling, featherlight touches. When she shivered, when he felt the goose-prickles on her arms, he kissed her chin, then her throat. Clothing was not an impediment; the only things she wore were the blanket and her belt, and the belt was easily discarded.

Solyn didn't notice him unfastening it. Her attention was on holding on to his shoulders, with her head tipped back to give him willing access. When his fingers slipped beneath the soft wool, cupping her breast, she shuddered again, breathing deep to press her flesh into his palm. His thumb brushed over her nipple, circling the desire-tight nub.

"Mmm, that feels good," she murmured.

At that, he lifted his lips from her throat. A smile curved his mouth. Nipping at her bottom lip, Kenyen smiled and murmured, "Let me make the rest of you feel that good."

A swirl of his thumb accompanied his promise, as did an answering shiver of pleasure from her. Solyn knew he meant it; Kenyen's confidence was one of the things she really liked about him. That, and the competence underlying it. One of his hands stroked her body through the blanket, caressing her left side. He followed it with the hand touching the bare skin of her right side. The feelings through the blanket were soothing, gentle. The ones generated by his palm on her flesh were arousing, sensual.

Solyn squirmed. Her right side kept growing more sensitive, but her left side was beginning to feel dissatisfied. Needy. *Hungry, and quite possibly jealous*, she decided, watching him as he let his gaze follow his hands. *At least I can take care of that, myself.* Pulling the knotted blanket over her head, she tossed it on the ground and waited to see how he would react to her boldness.

Light flickered from the mouth of the tunnel, followed by another nearby crack and rumble of thunder. Kenyen blinked and looked at what she offered so willingly, then smiled at her. Solyn held her breath. Brown eyes gleaming with masculine interest, he returned his gaze to her breasts but didn't touch them. Instead, he teased her ribs with the backs of his fingers. She squirmed, not quite stifling a giggle.

Changing tactics, he smoothed his palms around her waist, sending them down to cup the curves of her backside. That pulled them together, allowing her to feel the growing lump of his erection despite the soft, dark fur shielding it from immediate view. The feel of that fur made her quirk one brow. "This isn't fair. Here I am, all naked, but you're still, um . . . Wait, *does* your fur count as being clothed?"

He grinned. "It does." A ripple of flesh left nothing but skin and the natural curls of their nether-hairs pressed together. "Is that better? Of course, you've already seen me naked."

She blushed at the memory, but not for the fact he was naked. "For one, that was Traver's body you were wearing, not your own, and for another . . . I *still* can't believe you put the ring down there!"

"Blame him for its location! Besides, most of what you saw *was* me," Kenyen countered. "It wasn't as if he was unusually large or small, or deformed, or . . . or had *two* of them."

That thought first horrified, then fascinated her. "*Two* of them?"

It was his turn to blush. "It, um . . . there was a group of young men at the City this last winter who had experimented with, ah, shaping *two*, and . . . well, I personally didn't try it with a lover, but it, um . . ." He cleared his throat. "It sounded like those who did try it had fun."

Solyn blinked. "*Two* . . . but . . . where would the second one go?"

Face heating further, Kenyen reached a little lower, sliding down her nether-cheeks enough to glide a fingertip between them.

"*Oh!*" She jumped a little when his finger hit the suggested second spot. It wasn't unknown to her; as part of her Healer's training, Solyn had learned that particular location was the cheapest form of contraception, since not everyone had access to a Healer who had enough magic to craft the sort of amulets her own mother could make. But the thought of *two* . . . Flushed, she shook her head. "I don't think I can. I mean, not the *first* time, and um . . . not . . ."

Kenyen rescued her. Shaking his head, he kissed her forehead. "Relax. We're not going to do any of that."

Solyn mumbled, "Well, I've heard it can be pleasant, and I'm not, um, objecting to a *future* possibility . . . distant future . . ."

He chuckled and hugged her, moving his hands back up to her

waist. "Pleasure on the Plains is all about what *both* people want in a particular moment. Right now, we're not going to do that."

She hugged him back, grateful the discussion was being shelved. When he just stood there, hugging her, she finally asked, "So, what *are* we going to do?"

Kenyen released her. Smiling, he stooped and picked up her makeshift toga. It didn't take long to unknot the blanket, nor to flip it out so that it lay flat on the floor. Kneeling on the soft, felted wool, he held up his hands, inviting her to step on the makeshift bed. More thunder rumbled as she moved, though the flash wasn't as apparent. He waited for it to pass, then spoke. "We will do whatever we both find pleasurable."

With that, he leaned forward and licked her stomach, circling his tongue around her navel. Solyn sucked in a breath, startled by his choice. It was both ticklish and sensual at the same time, nerve-racking in the best sense. When he dipped the tip of his tongue into her belly button, she could feel it down in her loins and up in her breasts.

She shivered, moaning softly. He licked again, this time working his way toward the underside of her breasts. Stroking her fingers through his hair, Solyn found and freed the tie holding his braid in place. Her hands weren't all that steady, thanks to the way he licked the sensitive underside, but she loosened the plait, enjoying the silky-soft, mostly straight texture, so different from Traver's curls. The strands did have a slight kink to them, thanks to the braiding, but most of it was different from her own.

The man also had a slight kink in him. Rather than going straight for her nipples, tight with desire, he licked the line of her sternum, rising up on his knees. Hands coming up on either side of her breasts, he cupped them together against his cheeks, humming happily. That made her laugh. The play of his thumbs against her peaks made her bite her lip, stifling a moan.

Glancing up, Kenyen noticed her restraint. Licking one soft curve, he admonished, "Don't hold back. I want to know it whenever I please you. I want to hear it . . . I want to *taste* it."

He lapped at the tip of one breast, matching actions to words. Solyn let herself moan. They were alone, deep in a cave devoted to the boring task of storing cheese, isolated by a summer storm. Not that she hadn't heard the sounds of passion before from other couples, but this was the one place where she felt free, uninhibited by eavesdroppers, Mongrel cur or otherwise.

So when he switched breasts, flicking her other nipple with the tip of his tongue, she sucked in a sharp breath and let it out on a loud moan. "Ohh, *yesss* . . ."

Encouraged, Kenyen smoothed his fingers over her skin, caressing her curves. Her breasts were a little on the small side, but delightfully sensitive when he brushed his fingers over them, judging from the way she gasped and squirmed, pressing them into his touch. Her hips were full and shapely, the kind he liked to hold. And her smell . . . he buried his face against her abdomen, nipping and inhaling, enjoying her womanly scent, augmented by some sort of herbal soap and hints of sweat.

Licking his way back to her navel, he teased it some more. The hands playing with his hair clenched at his more ticklish touches. A twist of his neck to either side let him lick her inner wrists as soon as her body relaxed. Her fingers brushed his cheek. Rubbed along his jaw. Kenyen caught the first two of her digits with his lips. His tongue danced over them, tasting and suckling hungrily.

His right hand, still on her hip, felt her flesh tremble under his touch. Abandoning her fingers, he ducked his head and kissed her hip bone instead. Both hands held her in place when she instinctively tried to twitch away. With his head so close, he could smell her most intimate scents, the kind which no perfume could match. Inhaling deeply, hungrily, he licked a path to her inner thigh.

Tickled and unnerved, Solyn pulled out of his grasp, stumbling back two steps. He let her go, but dropped to his hands and knees, his gaze still on the apex of her legs. She stared at him. *He looks rather . . . predatory, doesn't he? Male and predatory.*

That thought made her nervous. Yet at the same time, the Shifterai crouched before her didn't move, didn't chase after her. He did, however, lick his lips slowly, his gaze firmly fixed on the focal point of his attention. That sparked a thrill behind her unease, charging her indecision with instincts as old as femininity. *I trust him. I know Kenyen would never hurt me. Thrill me, tease me . . . but not harm me.*

Mind made up, she centered herself on the blanket. Lowering her body to the ground, she leaned back on her elbows—and lifted a foot, planting it on his shoulder when he swayed forward. A slow smile of her own teased him, tested him to see what he would do. He didn't disappoint her. Turning his head, Kenyen kissed her ankle. Saluted it in a slow, sensual suckling that made her thigh muscles quiver.

Nipping, licking, even rubbing his cheek sensually against her calf, he worked his way up her leg, lowering his shoulder so that her heel slipped upward. With her leg supported by his back, Kenyen slowly advanced on his goal. Shivers kept rippling over her skin. Solyn knew they weren't from the cool air of the old mining tunnel; no, she ached with the heat he stirred in her blood.

Her breath caught in anticipation when he paused mid-thigh. He liked the sound of that; it meant she was growing ready for him. Not wanting her to relax just yet, Kenyen traced lazy circles with the tip of his nose, followed by the tip of his tongue. A lightning-fast lap—accompanied by a distant rumble of thunder, amusingly enough—tickled her other leg, making her gasp and lift it a little. That opened the way for the flesh he did want to taste.

Crawling closer, Kenyen dipped his head. A slow, deep inhale infused his senses with the scent of her. A long, equally slow lap made her gasp. It wasn't salty, it wasn't sweet, but it was exactly the flavor he wanted. Exploring each fold with lips and tongue, swirling and flicking over her peak, he did his best to coax forth more of her dew. Each little sound she made drove him to lap and nip and suckle more at her flesh.

A corner of Solyn's mind wanted to move to the Plains. If this was how all Shifterai men were taught to pleasure their women, she *really* wanted to move there after this whole mess with the evil face-shifter invasion was over. The rest of her was busy melting and tensing, gasping for air. That thing he did with his tongue, circling and flicking rapidly, stole most of the breath from her lungs. And when he probed gently at the same time . . .

Wait . . . what? Struggling to think through the pleasure his caresses invoked, she asked. "Wait, you . . . Ohhhh . . . *Two* tongues?"

His chuckle did its own naughty thing as it vibrated against her flesh, connecting her loins to her ears and back, detouring through her breasts. Kenyen pulled back long enough to murmur a simple explanation. "Forked tongue, actually." He dove back in with a groan. "Mmmm, *delicious* . . ."

That did it. Bucking in her climax, Solyn clutched at his hair. Spasms of pleasure washed through her, followed by trembling bliss. Thankfully, he eased his attack on her now-sensitive flesh. Switching instead to gentle kisses and stroking her stomach with one hand, he soothed her into a gentle afterglow.

"More?" Kenyen offered when her heavy breathing had calmed.

Blinking sleepily at the tunnel ceiling, fingers stroking through the locks she had tugged on moments ago, Solyn quirked one brow. ". . . More?" It took her a moment to realize what he meant. *Oh, right. Now it's his turn for pleasure.* She found enough strength for a smile. "Mm, yes, more."

He licked her just as she started to sit up. It was not what she had expected. Apparently he had meant more pleasure for *her.* Unsure if she could, since normally once was quite enough, Solyn lay back on the blanket, tensing a little. She expected him to work more on her still-sensitive nub, which would not have had the desired result. Thankfully, he instead licked up and down the sides of her nether-seam, then kissed his way to her inner thigh.

Once there, he teased her with a soft growl and a gentle, scraping bite. Pushing up onto one elbow, Solyn's uncertainty was met by the mischievous grin he aimed up the length of her torso. Strokes of his fingers soothed and stimulated her nerves, coaxing her into lying back down. Closing her eyes, she gave herself to the mix of gentle caresses, exploring licks, and teasing nips.

Exploring her body, Kenyen discovered her toes weren't particularly sensitive to pleasure, unlike some women, but the backs of her knees decidedly were. Squeaking, she jerked her leg up away from his tongue, and giggled when he caught her thigh and pulled her back.

She squirmed when he flicked his tongue, and moaned when he sucked gently on the delicate hollow. Nipping his way back to her loins, he lapped at the fresh dew seeping from her flesh, before making his way to her other knee. By the time he returned to her center, she was panting unsteadily again, rearoused.

This time, she didn't question the dual use of his tongue but instead strained into each probing, flicking, swirling taste. This time, she moaned loudly with each thrust and suckle, and cried out hoarsely when she climaxed again, tugging once more on his hair, though only with one hand, this time.

His own arousal was quite strong. It took effort, bathed in the scent of her dew, to refrain from crawling up the length of her body and claiming the depths he had so thoroughly pleased. He did move upward, but shifted so that he settled on his side next to her.

As her panting eased, awareness seeped back into her bliss-filled senses. Specifically, awareness of the hot shaft pressing against her hip. Breathing deeply to regain some energy, Solyn twisted onto her side as well. Licking her lips, she looked at Kenyen. He was studying her with a very male smile.

She couldn't help but return it. "Pleased with yourself, are you?"

"I should think so," he quipped in a murmur, teasing her. With his right hand propping up his head, he used his left hand to caress and cup her breast. "The real question is, did I please you?"

Solyn rolled her eyes, blushing. "I *know* you were paying attention just now." Daringly, she touched his shaft, curling her fingers around his erection. "At least, *this* tells me you were."

He grunted softly, closing his eyes against the urge to thrust against her palm. The gentle, explorative way she caressed him didn't help. Opening his eyes, he caught her wrist, stilling her movements. At her questioning look, he managed a smile. "I'm going to let you rest for a little while, then pleasure you again."

"You don't want to twine fully?" she asked, puzzled. In a flash, it occurred to her that, as an outlander, he might not actually know what that meant. "As in, share intercourse? The act of copulation, procreation, only of course I'm wearing an amul—"

His fingers covered her lips, stopping her explanation. Kenyen managed another smile. "We're not going that far." At her disappointed frown, he explained. "My sense of honor will only let me take this so far and no further."

Pulling her head back, Solyn asked, "But don't *you* want some pleasure? It's not fair for me to have all the fun while you have none."

"Intercourse should be saved for when you marry your future husband," Kenyen countered quietly. "Whoever that is. Whether that's me, or the real Traver, or . . ." He broke off and chuckled at the wrinkling of her nose. Kissing the tip of it, he looked into her hazel eyes. "Or *whoever* it ends up being. That is an intimacy you should share with your mate alone. I will not spoil such closeness for you."

On the one hand, Solyn thought that was a very sweet and generous thing for him to give up, particularly in the light of his obvious need. On the other hand, she wanted to smack the back of his head for being so stupidly selfless, just as she would have smacked Traver for making some equally pointless, if noble, self-sacrifice.

Rather than argue the point, she shifted position, curling over him so that she could lick his stomach, much as he had licked hers at the start of all this. The spasm of his muscles and the sharp intake of his breath pleased her. So did the way he relaxed onto his back, giving her the chance to play with him as he had with her.

Not quite sure where to start, Solyn nipped gently at his stomach. Or tried to; his natural form was lean and muscular, with little flesh to spare. She scraped her lips and teeth a bit, licked the faint marks her mock-attacks made, then sucked on his flesh. The latter moves made him moan, so she did them again, licking and suckling on various spots. He sucked in the sharpest breaths, she noted, the closer she got to his nipples, but he squirmed more the closer she came to his hip bones . . . and he did both when she brushed her cheek against the shaft jutting up from his groin.

Grinning, she teased him a bit, nuzzling his flesh with her face, then moved to his thighs to give his legs some of the treatment he had given her. Unlike her, the backs of Kenyen's knees weren't ticklish, but his ankles definitely were. In fact, he swatted her rump lightly when she followed his squirming legs relentlessly. Chuckling, she kissed her way back up to his hips, where he squirmed even more. She teased his shaft, brushing it as she kissed and licked her way around his pelvis, until he threaded his fingers into her braid, and pulled her mouth away from his skin, breathing heavily.

"Either put me out of my misery," he mock-growled, "or find something *else* to explore."

Solyn debated for a long moment, then dipped and licked the side of his ribs. Kenyen choked and squirmed away, hunching protectively. Grinning madly at her discovery, she feinted toward his ribs again. He tussled with her, defending himself at first. After a few moments, he gave up and rolled on top of her, catching her wrists and pinning her bodily to the hard, blanket-covered ground.

That wedged his manhood between them, making her very aware of just how aroused he still was. Lifting her head, she nipped at his chin, coaxing him into kissing range. With a groan, he kissed her back, deep, heated, full kisses, the kind which played their tongues together in a simulation of full twining. His hips flexed against hers, simulating it as well. Hers lifted as well, thighs parting in sheer instinct.

After only a few moments, he groaned and rolled free again, releasing her wrists in favor of covering his face . . . honoring his promise not to go that far with her. She pushed up onto one elbow and looked down at him. As she did so, Solyn realized with a profound simplicity that she was in love with him.

Bending down, she pressed a kiss to his navel. He twitched and groaned. Smiling, she shifted to her right and put him out of his misery. Or perhaps tortured him even more, given the deep groan that escaped his throat the moment her tongue circled around the tip of his engorged shaft. The taste wasn't bad, but the texture was what drew her to explore it more.

Solyn couldn't remember ever feeling such soft skin before now. The closest she had ever come was bathing this part of him while tending to his injuries, back when she had thought he was merely Traver. But this wasn't her longtime friend, and she wasn't touching him with a damp rag between her flesh and his. This was Kenyen Sin Siin of the Shifting Plains, and she had fallen in love with him. Not with her childhood companion.

She wanted to show him some of that love, so she licked him from tip to base with her tongue and lips. Mindful of how delicate the contents were, she explored the sac at the root of his erection, tonguing his flesh through the thin dusting of hairs guarding his bollocks. Each careful touch made him groan and clench his stomach muscles. In turn, that made his shaft bob and sway, until she rose up, took the tip between her lips, and licked.

The ring got in her way. Pulling back, she examined it carefully. Seeing no signs of raw flesh, just whole, healed skin, she debated removing it. *But if we lose track of it, I'd have to enchant two new rings . . .* Giving up the idea, she pulled his foreskin down and licked the exposed flesh, avoiding the question of his enchanted piercing for now.

One of his hands blindly left his face, his fingers burrowing into her braided hair. Wincing a little as the act tugged uncomfortably on some of the strands, Solyn impatiently pulled the tie of her own braid from the end, and worked the plait loose with her free hand. The other was required to brace her weight, holding her head over his loins so that she could continue to give the tip of him little tasting licks. After a moment, his fingers joined hers, loosening her long curls. Once it was fully loose, she resumed her explorations.

Kenyen stroked her hair, overwhelmed by his mounting pleasure. He tried to use the feel of the silky-soft strands to ground himself while she explored his flesh, but it didn't help. When she started sliding her lips up and down, bobbing her head slowly, all he could do was grasp the blanket instead of her curls. But when she rubbed with her tongue on that one spot on the underside, he couldn't stop the urge to thrust; all he could do was confine it to little movements so as not to startle or choke her.

Solyn wasn't ignorant. Inexperienced, but not ignorant; her mother had been quite frank about the bodily functions of both men and women when healthy as well as when ill. Healers had to know both ends of the wellness spectrum, after all. Not sure she wanted him to climax inside her mouth—and curious to know what it might look like—she pulled back and stroked his shaft, increasing pressure and speed.

He whimpered and flexed his hips harder. She had to lick him a couple times to keep her fingers gliding smoothly, particularly over the small, bead-clenched ring. On the third time, when her tongue paused to play with that funny little ridge at the top, he choked.

"G-Goddess! I'm going to . . . I'm going—!"

Fascinated, Solyn watched as he climaxed, careful to keep her pace and pressure steady for the first few spurts. Mindful of her mother's warnings that men could be very sensitive afterward, she gentled her touch until she was just holding him, squeezing occasionally. Finally one of his hands shifted from the blanket to hers. She took that as the sign to release him from her touch. Her fingers were a little messy, but he held and squeezed them, struggling to calm his heavy breathing.

"Where . . ." He had to pause and lick his lips for moisture, for composure. "Where did you learn to do that? You were as . . . as good as an earth-priestess."

Knowing what she did now about what an earth-priestess was, what one did, and why they did it, Solyn smiled at his compliment. "Healing lectures. Mother was school-trained, and they covered the proper functioning of healthy bodies as well as what happens when someone gets ill, so she passed it on to me. I don't have the best flavor of magics to be a spell-Healer, but I am trained in most other methods."

Groaning at her words, he covered his face with his other hand, chuckling ruefully. "I really didn't need the image of your mother in my head at this moment. Although . . ."

"Although, what?" Solyn asked. She knew he needed to be cleaned up, since her lessons had included the fact that this stuff was sticky, messy, and dried uncomfortably, but lingered at his side, curious.

"Although she is a lovely looking woman, and very much like you. You'll be beautiful—still be beautiful," he amended, still struggling to scrape his wits back together, "—when you reach her age. You look a lot like her."

She smiled at the new compliment. "I think she's pretty, too. What about your father? Do you look like him?"

"A bit. My brother looks more like him. I take more after our mother's father in the nose and chin . . . and I need to go clean this off," he muttered, looking down at their twined hands. "And I could use something to drink—how about you?"

"Oh!" she said, remembering something. Pushing to her feet, Solyn helped him up as she explained. "I brought tea, and two bowls. I was going to share maschen with you yesterday, but then that accident happened . . ."

"I'd love to try some," Kenyen agreed, distracting her from what were no doubt unpleasant memories of yesterday's healing efforts.

Holding her hand, he walked with her out to the tunnel entrance. He shifted shape as he walked, making himself look like a naked version of Traver just in case someone was determined enough to brave the storm in order to spy on them. When they reached the mouth of the cave, the rain was coming down in a hissing mix of droplets and ice pellets, chilling both of them with the drop in temperature.

Kenyen let Solyn clean up first, peering warily at the hail. "That cannot be good for the crops."

"It will flatten some," Solyn agreed, washing quickly. "But the rest will recover. This isn't even pea-sized hail. One day, I hope to know enough about magic to shield the valley from nut-sized hailstones. But that requires getting rid of our infestation of face-changers."

Once her fingers were rinsed off, she tossed the dirty water outside. There was a broad-mouthed water barrel near the entrance, placed so that it would catch a fair amount of rain. She shivered, getting wet as she dipped the ceramic bowl into it. Half-melted pellets floated on the water as she carried it back. Kenyen—still looking like Traver—met her halfway, taking the bowl from her.

"You should've let me do that," he admonished, taking it from her and carrying it back himself. The heavy bowl threatened to slosh as he walked, making him admire her hidden strength and grace at having carried it so easily. Shifting his muscles slightly for balance, he smoothed out his walk, and poured a little water into the washing basin before putting the rinsing one back into its metal hoop on the stand. "It's easier for me to keep warm than you, you know."

Rolling her eyes, Solyn muttered a word. The rainwater soaking her body started to steam, evaporated by her warming spell. It also triggered an explosive sneeze from her shapeshifted lover. Biting back a giggle, Solyn took pity on him. "I'll go start the water boiling for maschen . . . and I'll be nice and cut you a couple of slices of greenvein, too."

"Thank you," Kenyen muttered, rubbing at his nose with his clean hand. "Remind me to keep some of that cheese on me at all times."

"Even when you're naked?" Solyn teased. He flicked water droplets at her for her impertinence before reaching for the softsoap pot. She squeaked in mock-fear and fled, giggling.

Several minutes later, both of them were still naked as they waited for their clothes to dry. Solyn, kneeling by the low table and the heating stand, finished whisking the maschen to an enchanted, mint-green froth. She studied the way it swirled and formed in the largest of the three tea bowls she had brought. All three were works of art, smooth conical curves fashioned from thin, green-glazed porcelain, all three from a tea bowl set gifted to her by one of the valley holding families in thanks for her modest but needed healing abilities.

Kenyen, assembling a makeshift meal of meat-filled pasties and slices of greenvein cheese on the scrap of cloth that had contained the pasties, didn't sneeze. He had already feasted on one slice, and its anti-allergen effects were already giving his sinuses respite.

"Well?" he finally prompted her.

"The clouds will be gone by this time tomorrow, then we'll have not quite a quarter turning of Brother Moon filled with bright, clear skies. After that . . . overcast, I think, but only lightly," Solyn judged, studying the mound in the center of the bowl and the thin rim of foamy bubbles clinging to the rim, before pouring it into the smaller bowls. "Enough to keep things relatively cool when the grain is ready to harvest. At least, for a day or two. Beyond that, I cannot see."

"At least you can see that far," he reminded her. Turning his own thoughts to the next few days, Kenyen shook his head. "I wish I knew whether or not those paper birds reached their targets. A heavy rain would be ideal for spiriting Traver away from those curs holding him. And days of clear skies means that 'Traver' will be expected to help with the harvest. No more accompanying you to the cheese caves, no more excuses for being alone . . ."

She smiled wryly. "Then we should make the most of it." Picking up one of the two smaller bowls, she offered it to him. "Here—for your first time, it's considered polite to lift the cup to Cora and thank Her for the maschen you are about to drink. Children aren't allowed to drink it, save on the holiest of occasions, but you're an adult. That won't offend you, will it? Being an outlander?"

"When in Correda, a Shifterai is expected to worship as the Corredai do," Kenyen countered politely. He lifted the bowl in both hands, since that was the way she had drunk from it the other day, and murmured, "My thanks to the Goddess Cora for this drink; may it honor Her when I partake in the ways of Her people."

"Well spoken," Solyn praised. She sipped from her own bowl at the same time he drank from his. The startled expression on his face at the first mouthful made her raise her brows.

Swallowing the drink, Kenyen eyed the remaining liquid. "I

know you didn't sweeten this—I didn't *see* you sweeten this . . ." He sipped again, more cautiously. "It also isn't nearly as sweet as sugar or honey, but it doesn't taste quite like the tea I do know."

"It is both bitter, because it is tea and therefore naturally astringent," she enlightened him, "and sweet, because of the care in which the tender, young tea leaves are prepared." She drank more of her tea, then added, "We consider tea the metaphor for life. You get more out of your life when you're submerged in hot water and stirred, rather than if you just let everything steep in tepidness. And life itself can be quite bitter, but it also has many hidden moments of sweetness. It requires careful tending in order to grow and properly be used . . . and it can be quite stimulating."

"Stimulating?" he asked, draining the last of his maschen. She hadn't made a lot, but that was alright. "I know tea can make a man feel more alert."

"Maschen is tea refined. It stimulates the mind, the senses . . . the body," Solyn murmured, slanting a warm look at his bared flesh. "It gives one clarity to see what needs to be done, and the energy to go forth and seize it."

He didn't miss her innuendo. Chuckling, Kenyen set down his empty bowl and picked up one of the pasties in exchange. "You went forth and seized it without any tea. I wonder what drinking it will spur you to do."

She grinned. "Maybe you'll find out. And in greater detail, next time."

"And maybe my sense of honor says I *won't*," he countered mock-firmly. "What we did do was more than enough to qualify as stimulating."

Her good mood fell a little. "You don't want to do it again?"

Face heating, Kenyen gave her a pointed look. "I didn't say *that*. I just meant it won't go beyond that point." At the resumption of her grin, he added, "You look rather pleased by that thought."

"Well, it does imply we get to do it ag—*aaah!*" The bright white flash and ear-aching crack of another lightning strike lit up the cave tunnel, startling her mid-speech. Hands flinging up to cover her ears, she didn't realize what she had done until after the delicate bowl hit the hard stone floor with a matching, if quieter crack. She stared at the shattered pieces, heartbroken. "Ohhh . . . oh, no . . ."

Startled twice, once by the sudden attack of the storm and again by the loss of her teacup, Kenyen flinched at a second flare and rumble of too-close lightning. When the noise faded enough to hear, he set down his unbitten pastie and touched her elbow. "Are you all right?"

She nodded her head, then shook it slowly. "I just . . . That was the *first* gift I received as a Healer. A gift specifically for *me*, and not just something my mother passed to me." She flinched at a third flash and again at the accompanying thunder, but the timing between light and sound proved that part of the storm was moving away. Shifting forward, she started picking up the pieces, putting them on the low table. "I still have four more bowls at home, and I know five should be more than enough for my needs, but . . ."

"But it's a very lovely set, and it hurts to lose part of it," Kenyen agreed, shifting to help her. Their fingers met over one of the larger pieces. He lifted her hand to his lips. "I'm sorry it broke, Solyn."

His sympathy soothed some of her upset nerves. The fact that he cared she was upset meant a lot to her. Leaning into him, she kissed his cheek. "Thank you, Kenyen."

Together, they picked up the pieces. Kenyen hunted down even the smallest shards, since while he could toughen the skin of his soles and quickly heal cuts, her feet weren't so gifted. Settled into a little pile on the table, they still made her sad. On impulse, he tugged the scrap of linen over them, dragging the half-dozen pasties and bits of cheese.

"There. It's all safely hidden," he quipped, rearranging the baked dough to hide the lumps of broken pottery. "You can now forget about it. At least for a while."

The light, teasing words made her smile ruefully. "It's still there, I know it, but . . . yes, getting it out of my immediate sight does help, thank you."

A thought made him frown in worry. "Um . . . a broken tea bowl isn't going to offend your Goddess, is it?"

She chuckled. "No, it won't. Spilling the mascha might upset Her a little," Solyn teased, "but I drank it—*ack!* . . . Gods!" she swore as the next crack of lightning flashed down the winding length of the tunnel. The blue white flare was a stark contrast, even at this distance, to the yellow glow cast by the oil lamps around them. "Cora! When is this storm going to end?"

Somehow, that struck him as funny. Shoulders shaking, Kenyen tried to bite back his laughter. At her wary glare, he blurted out, "You just predicted when it would!"

Watching him quake with mirth, Solyn rolled her eyes. That made him laugh even harder, wheezing for breath. Blushing, she shoved at his shoulder, knocking him over, then followed him down. Her fingers dove for his ribs, intending to give him a *real* reason to giggle. Choking, he squirmed and fought back, seeking out her own sensitive spots. It didn't take long at all for the broken cup to be fully forgotten. Or the pasties, or the cheese, or even the storm still rumbling and raining away outside.

TEN

Something woke her. It wasn't the cool air chilling her backside, nor the soft drone of not-quite snores from the man she had snuggled up against for warmth. Despite the deep darkness surrounding her, Solyn knew she was still in the greenvein cave with Kenyen; she could smell him, male and compelling, along with faint hints of the things they had done to drop them into such sated slumber. As she stared, propped up on one elbow, she realized he must have swapped bodies at some point, for he wore Traver's broader shoulders, rounder face, and wavy hair.

I . . . can see him? Blinking, she realized in the next moment the light was not only growing stronger, it was bobbing and swaying, brought in the form of a lantern. *My ring must have moved!* Whapping Kenyen, she hissed at him. "*Wake up! Someone's coming!*"

Disoriented from the sudden jolt back to awareness, Kenyen took a moment to realize where he was, what he had been doing here, and why he was in a shifted body. He had barely enough time to do a mental pat down, making sure his body was in the proper Corredai shape before the source of the light came into view.

It was an oil lamp, crafted in the same glass-chimneyed style as all the others, and it was being carried through the subtle curves of the shelf-lined tunnel by none other than Ysander Mil Ben, the local blacksmith. Solyn's father.

Solyn squeaked, also recognizing the bearer of the lamp. Mortified, she buried herself against Kenyen's side and tried to twitch a fold of the blanket over her exposed rump. Her father raised his arm at the noise, then widened his eyes in shock, recognizing them as well. Or rather, the condition they were in. "Solyn! *Traver!*"

There wasn't time or cloth to spare to cover his own pelvic exposure, and he didn't dare shift fur. Clearing his throat, Kenyen lifted a hand slightly in acknowledgment and tried his best to be polite, despite the circumstances. "Milord Ysander."

He received a paternal glare for his efforts. "So your little brother Tellik was right about this. You've been . . . been . . . *waxing the cheese*, my best hammers! If that's what you've been calling it, you'd better find another euphemism—and with my little girl!"

"Father!" It wasn't easy for her to snap the admonishment when she was doing her physical best to hide in the crack between the floor and Kenyen's side, but Solyn tried. "I'm a fully grown woman of twenty and two years. I can *wax the cheese* with whomever I like—and we *haven't* been, except for today. Tonight. Whenever it is."

"It's late evening, and your mother—and *his* kin—were worried when you didn't come back after the storm eased," Ysander growled. "I offered to come all the way down here, only to find you . . . *naked*!"

"Well, if you'll turn *around*, we'll get dressed," Solyn snapped back defensively, upset by the intrusion. "Our clothing was soaked by the storm just before we got here."

"Oh, I'm sure it was, and you just *had* to keep warm by huddling together while it dried," he muttered sarcastically. "I'm not stupid. I know what the two of you have been doing to *keep warm*."

Solyn blushed with mortification at the accusation, but before she could argue the point further, her father did turn his back on them, giving them a few moments of privacy. Scrambling to her feet, she snatched Traver's clothes off the shelves, tossing them at her shapeshifted lover, then grabbed her own. He struggled into the loose trousers favored by Corredai men, not bothering to don the undershorts first in his haste to get dressed. She did the same with her skirt.

The blacksmith, restless and impatient, glanced over at the low table containing the remnants of their meal. At some point in their twinings, the pair had eaten most of the pasties, all of the cheese, and shared water from the remaining, rinsed-out tea bowl, but it wasn't the relatively clean cup that Ysander focused on. It was the slightly larger bowl, with its wooden whisk and the half-empty vial of maschen powder, that caught his eye. Blatantly caught it, for he crossed to the table in two strides, snatched up the vial for a squint at the contents in the light of his lamp, and whirled to face the shapechanged young man.

"You—!" Ysander spluttered, face purpling. He thumped the lantern onto the table and snatched at Kenyen's ear, pinching it hard. "*Taking tea* with my daughter, without a priest present!"

"What?" Solyn, shrugging into her *chamsa* top, hastily pulled it over her breasts and whirled to face her father. "Father, no! It *wasn't* like that!"

"*Wasn't* like that?" he demanded, shaking the ear, and thus the head, caught in his callused grip. "One whisking bowl, *one drinking bowl?*"

Kenyen bit back a yelp at the painful tugging. He'd been in too many battles not to realize this was Solyn's fight to win. He did fumble the ties of his pants together. He could toughen the cartilage of his ear and shift away some of the nerve endings, but he couldn't do anything to escape the enraged blacksmith's grip. Not without harming, startling, or making the older man suspicious about his true identity. *In fact, the only thing that has gone right in this mess was my paranoid fear that someone from Family Mongrel might stumble across us. At least Ysander didn't catch his daughter sleeping in what would seem to be the arms of a complete stranger.*

"There were two bowls, but I broke one!" Fumbling one of the buttons through its hole, she hurried over to the table, skirting past Kenyen. Once on the other side of the low furnishing, she stooped and twitched back the fold of linen, revealing the mound of broken shards. "See? After that happened, we *only* drank water, Father. Now, let go of him!"

Ysander shook him by the ear again, evoking a muffled grunt. "Oh, *no*. No, I'm not letting him—or you—go that easily! This farce has gone on long enough. The two of you have known each other for *years*. You've finally settled down and agreed to wed . . . and now you think you can *twine* without the sacrament of marriage? *No* one gets more than the smallest sampling of tea for free in *my* family. *You*, young man, are going to buy the whole bush!"

He pushed the younger man away with that statement, thankfully releasing rather than ripping off the flesh caught in his grip. Kenyen recovered his footing, resisting the urge to rub at his smarting ear. Everything was going wrong—everything *had* gone wrong, from the moment he had stumbled across the real Traver Ys Ten. Somewhere up in the Heavens, Father Sky and Mother Earth were surely sharing both tea and laughter with Cora of the Mountains over this very moment. *Possibly with the distant Threefold God of Fate for company.*

It did not, however, change the fact that he, Kenyen Sin Siin, was *not* the man Solyn's father assumed him to be. "I will *not* have her forced into marrying me. It is *her* decision as to when and where we shall wed, *not* yours!"

"Oh, you *will* w—"

"—Father, enough!" Solyn snapped, cutting him off. Her sharp, mature tone was one she had never used on him before, and her father blinked from it. "He's right," she stated bluntly. "*I* am the only one who can make that choice. *Not* you."

"I will not have you disgrace our holding by dishonoring the sanctity of marriage!" her father shot back. "Either the two of you wed now—*tomorrow*," he corrected himself impatiently, "—or the two of you part ways and never twine again!"

For a moment, they were at an impasse. Solyn knew well that part of Kenyen's reluctance stemmed only partly from his cultural background. That it was not only about how the maiden was the one who was supposed to hold out her hand to the male in such matters, but that the situation they were embroiled in—with Traver's life and identity at stake—would complicate things beyond measure if the two of them did go through with this. Nor could she discuss the matter in advance, not with her father being as stubborn and unbudging as one of his own anvils.

It was his insistence that *she* be the one to choose that made up her mind. Meeting Kenyen's shapeshifted gaze, she held out her hand to him. Over the lamp her father had dropped on the table.

Kenyen frowned slightly at her, not quite grasping her silent invitation. Only when she glanced down, giving the oil lamp and its burning flame a pointed look, did his eyes widen in comprehension. She was offering her hand to him in the Shifterai fashion, over a burning flame. Deliberately inviting him to marry her as *himself*, under the customs of his own people, not just as the face-shifted Traver her father assumed him to be.

She wanted *him* in her life, despite the tangles of their present straits. And he . . . he wanted her in his life. As she was here in the valley, as she could be in some mage school, and as he hoped she would someday be, as the hearth keeper of his home and his life. As his wife in truth, however difficult it would be to get from here to there.

He couldn't leap over the table and its lamp. Not without inviting far too much confusion and curiosity in the blacksmith. But he did stretch his arm over the column of heat rising from the glass chimney and took her offered hand. "Then we will be wed."

"We will be," Solyn agreed, smiling at him. "By my choice."

"*Good*," her father grunted. "Now, finish getting dressed and gather up your things. You'll have no more chance to twine until you're both properly wed."

"Could we at least have a few moments alone, first?" Solyn asked tartly. When her father opened his mouth to argue, she glared and pointed up the tunnel.

Giving them both a narrow-eyed look, part suspicion, part warning, he grunted, "Fine. A *few* moments. Don't waste them on twining."

Grabbing one of the lanterns from its spike in the wall, he moved to light it, only to discover the oil well was empty. While the two young lovers hurried to finish dressing, he impatiently refilled it from a small flask he dug from the pouch slung on his belt, then took the refreshed, relit lamp up the corridor. Solyn quickly crossed to Kenyen's side, touching his wrist.

"I really am doing this of my own free will," she whispered, choosing her words carefully in case her father was straining to listen. "Besides, this way we'll have reason to be alone together, even after it stops raining. No one is going to expect a newlywed couple to have their minds solely on the upcoming grain harvest."

The Gods take away with one hand, and give with the other, Kenyen thought, still feeling as if the deities of both their kingdoms were having a good laugh at their expense. He nodded. "That's a reasonable expectation—you do realize we only have three choices of residence?"

"Three?" she asked, confused.

He gave her a lopsided smile. "Three. In your parents' home, under the same roof as your understandably upset father. In my home, in the attic I share with my little brother," he added, knowing she knew he meant Traver's little brother. Then looked at the tunnel surrounding them. "Or down here, among the cheeses."

The absurdity of the suggestion made her snicker. "We are *not* moving down here, K . . . Traver—and to be honest, I'm getting tired of this cave. Don't worry; it'll be fine. Father will calm down once we are properly wed. Besides, you're *supposed* to move in with me, remember?"

The reminder of their situation didn't have to be any more pointed than that. Nodding, Kenyen crouched to start packing up the shards of pottery and crumbs from their earlier meal. She crouched as well, to pack up the two remaining tea bowls. The teapot would stay here where it belonged, along with the blanket in case they or someone else needed it again.

The feel of the bowls, the meaning in them, made her look up at him. Barely breathing, she asked, "*Do* you know if T . . . if *you* had a tea bowl picked out for the wedding ceremony?"

He blinked for a moment, thrown by the question. The subject had never come up. Shaking his head, he said out loud, "You go on ahead with your father. Go back home. I'll clean up down here, then make my way back up the hill. I *will* see you tomorrow . . . at, what, noon?"

"Noon," she agreed aloud.

Under his breath, he added, "In case I *didn't* have a decent bowl picked out, where would I find one?"

"Uhh . . . down-valley, go left—sorry, right at the fork in the river, and take the left branch of the road which goes up over the hill," she told him equally quietly. "It leads straight to the town of Kallak, which has a good deposit of fine clay and a small holding of artisan potters. If you rode, or even just walked, you could get there in a few hours at most, and be back by noon. But as for the *money* to buy a tea bowl . . ."

"I have some coins on me, don't worry," Kenyen reassured her. He still had his money pouch, hidden carefully in the eaves of Traver's family home, though his favorite riding horse was long gone, stolen by the Mongrels whose face-shifting tricks had entangled him in this mess.

"Your few moments are almost up!" Ysander called out in stern warning.

Solyn rolled her eyes at that. Leaning over the lamp still between them, Kenyen kissed her, making her blush. Lifting his chin, he ordered her silently to move along. She paused long enough for a quick return kiss, then tucked the tea bowls into her satchel, slipped into her sandals, and hurried to catch up with her father.

"I'm coming, hold your hammers! Traver will tidy up and blow out the lamps behind us, so you can just . . ." she added, her voice fading as she headed for the exit.

Left alone in the tunnel, Kenyen stayed on his knees and rubbed at his face. *Yes, the Gods are laughing at us. I'm quite sure of it.*

It didn't take long to tidy the messes they had made, mostly because they had tidied up as they had gone along. Nor did it take long to strip back off the clothes he had donned and tuck them into the depths of the cave. The pottery shards, he took outside and buried in the wet soil off to one side. Once that was taken care of and his fingers were rinsed clean, he launched into the air in owl form, eyes wide with the right kind of vision to fly through the night.

Flying through the steady rain that pattered down from overhead wasn't his idea of fun, but at least that rain was no longer pounding down with lightning and ice pellets for accompaniment. As it was, he kept having to land every so often to shed the rain and reshape his feathers as dry as he could manage.

With every wing flap, Kenyen practiced in his mind what he would do, what he would say. It helped to clear his mind and steady his nerves. By the time he landed on the trampled dirt and grass in front of the cottage, he was almost ready. All he required was a shapeshift and a quick mental reassurance. *I can do this. I can do this. I am Catson, mean son of a cur, Banished from the Plains for the dual sins of attacking women and eating people . . . and enjoying it. Ugh. No—I* am *a mean cur. I can do this . . .*

Lifting his fist to the panel, he pounded on it, loud and forceful. There was no need to fear anyone else overhearing. He knew Cullerog had no nearby neighbors to be awoken by the noisy banging, and thumped hard again. Before he could hit the wood a third time, the panel swung open. A faint glimmer from the dying fire on the hearth barely lit the interior, but neither man needed it. Whether Cullerog used the eyes of a cat or the eyes of an owl to see his visitor, it didn't matter. He scowled in instant recognition.

"You're risking my wrath with this visit, boy! What do you want?"

"Why, to interrogate the prisoner, of course." Pushing past the older man, Kenyen headed for the sheepskin laid over the trapdoor. "And I'll risk anything I want. I'm here on *your* business, after all."

"Just because you're working for us—"

"—Two words, old man," Kenyen countered brashly, swaggering a little bit as he reached the sheepskin. Kicking it aside, he swung to face the shepherd and grinned. "I'm *in*."

"You're what?" Cullerog grunted, frowning in confusion.

Stooping, he grabbed the ring and hauled up on the trapdoor. "I'm in. As in, I'm in the family. Or I will be as of midday tomorrow, when I will be officially wed to the lovely Solyn Ys Rei, daughter of the Healer and her blacksmith mate."

"That was fast," Cullerog observed.

"Knowing the blacksmith's protective reputation, I arranged to have him catch the two of us twining," Kenyen half-lied. "The girl is enthusiastic for me, so obviously I'm doing something right. Now that I *am* 'in' . . . I'll need to know what to look for. However, I still have to navigate the marriage ceremony, and I have no Gods-be-damned *clue* what the blacksmith meant by a suitable tea bowl. Thus, I am here to interrogate my alternate face. I'm sure you won't object to *that*, will you?"

Not waiting for an answer, he jumped into the hole, landing with a thud that caused the real Traver to jerk, rattling his chains. Whether or not the Corredai male had been awakened by his pounding and his prattle didn't matter. Kenyen wasn't here to reassure the other young man; he was here to play out the role of a face-stealing, information-needing cur. So, though it was too dark to see much of Traver, he started by crouching and shaking the younger man's calf.

"Tell me about this tea bowl thing!" he snapped, making Traver jump. "What does a bowl of tea have to do with your Corredai marriage ceremonies, and what sort of bowl are *you* supposed to bring?" Hating himself, hating their situation, Kenyen listened as the sleepy-sounding Traver stammered out a reply.

Surreptitiously, under the cover of the deep darkness of the root cellar, he sketched the Aian words for *She is safe*, *Escape soon*, *Magic*, and *Fly* on Traver's leg. He didn't know if it worked, if Traver got the message—it wasn't as if Traver could do or say anything to acknowledge it—but the Corredai man did twitch his legs a few times under his touch. If the weather really was going to clear up soon, the Mongrels might hold another one of their bonfire meetings, and at that meeting, Kenyen knew he had better be prepared to "help" them find the greensteel they sought. That meant he had to be prepared to rescue Traver, and that meant preparing the youth.

I will get you free, he swore silently, though out loud, he berated the captive Traver for the stammering slowness of his answers. *I will get you free and take down our mutual enemies. And . . . apologize for stealing away part of your life . . . though I'm reluctant to give up Solyn.*

He didn't dwell too long or too hard on why he didn't want to give her up. His feelings could wait for a later examination. Faking this ugly compliance with Mongrel interests had to take precedence for now.

Seen from afar, the tea bowl Kenyen had chosen looked deceptively simple. It was a somewhat deep, green-and-blue bowl glazed in the popular crackled style, neither cheap nor overly expensive. That glaze could be applied to stoneware as well as porcelain, though the thin lip and light weight suggested it was porcelain. By the look of it, it wasn't a bad choice for a younger son of a farmer's holding.

The first clue Solyn had that Kenyen—in his guise of her friend and betrothed, Traver—hadn't simply selected the first tea bowl that looked vaguely acceptable was in the way the elderly priest's brows rose sharply the moment he removed it from the folds of its carrying bag. The Honorable Hennen Vel Guan didn't say a word, though, just picked up the bottle of Sister's Tea she had prepared ages ago, and began his prayers for serenity, prosperity, and fertility as he carefully measured, poured, and whisked the brew on his portable altar table.

She didn't see just how unusual it was, however, until after she had murmured her acceptance of the man at her side, drinking him symbolically into her life with the first sip. On the second sip, when the opaque green liquid in the cup had tipped far enough to reveal the bottom . . . her own brows rose sharply as well.

Below the finger-width rim, glazed in deep blue, the interior revealed the radiant double-whorl petals of a tea blossom carved into the porcelain. In the very bottom of the cup, beneath the clear glaze revealing the purity of the white clay, the maker had embedded a crownai, the small but economically potent gold coin of the Aian continent.

Placed at the heart of those petals, it represented the pistils and stamens of the flower. Symbolically, something like this was meant to represent the wealth of an eldest son being brought to a marriage—the wealth of a plantation holder's son, at that. Or, if not in land, then in some valued trade skill. Her own father had gifted her mother with one of these bowls, but then Ysander had already completed his journeying years as a young blacksmith before courting the young Reina. He had established his forge and had an income worthy of such a bowl.

The value of the tea bowl, coin and artistry combined, represented at least half a year's wages for a mere farmer. More than that, for a farmer's fourthborn child. It was an extravagance which should have been beyond easy reach, yet this Kenyen of the Shifterai had managed to pay for it anyway. She didn't know how much he may have hesitated or flinched, but she was sure he was honorable enough to have bought it.

Draining the last drop of the wedding maschen, she handed the tea bowl to the priest for the traditional reading. The Honorable Hennen had less magic than she did, but many more years of experience in tea readings. The fact that she saw the corner of his mouth quirk up slightly, as well as the eyebrow on that side of his weathered face, reassured her. Whatever he saw, it either pleased or amused him.

Of course, he said nothing aloud, since Traver's family, hers, and many of the holders who could be spared from up and down the valley had gathered for this impromptu wedding. Instead, he gestured for the two of them to turn and face the gathered witnesses. Held on the trader's yard, several of those holdings had brought large tent awnings, setting them up to shelter the crowd against the misting rain that had followed in the storm's wake.

"Unto Cora and the Corredai," the priest stated in a firm voice, "I present to you Traver and Solyn, bound as a new family in the bonds of holy marriage, and whose children shall be known as the Tra Sol. May the Goddess bless them and their progeny for many generations to come!"

Most of the crowd applauded. A few more cheered, calling out blessings, and a few smirked. Notably Tunric, Tarquin, and Zellan, the three shifters Solyn knew about. Not that she could do anything about their smug looks. Behind her, the priest cleaned the tea bowl. In front of her, members of the Nespah Valley lined up to congratulate her and "Traver" on their marriage. She did her best to smile and murmur her thanks, though she flinched inside every time they said the wrong name.

Eventually the congratulations faded, leaving people hungry for the food placed on tables under some of the awnings. It wasn't a particularly fancy feast, just whatever could be thrown together in a single morning. There was, however, plenty of it. Dumplings both fried and steamed, pasties filled with meat and cheese, grain porridge, fresh vegetables and fruits, a couple of fruit-filled pies, and even some fresh-caught mountain trout. Seated at one of the tables, her shapeshifted husband at her side—that was a thought that would require some getting used to—Solyn tried her best to enjoy the meal.

The Honorable Hennen came over. With a nod and a smile, he set the marriage bowl on the table between them, with its plain, crackle-glazed outside and fancy, tea blossom and coin inside. It was a tradition to display the marriage tea bowl, so that everyone could see the appropriateness of the groom's choice.

Hylin, Solyn's aunt, was the first to notice it. Eyes wide, she craned her neck for a better look and exclaimed, "Where in Cora's Peaks did you get *that* thing, boy?"

"From the potters in Kallak," Kenyen replied calmly between bites of fish.

"No, I mean, where did you get the *money* for this thing?" Hylin asked as others moved closer, drawn by their curiosity at her words. "That bowl is way beyond your means!"

Kenyen, mindful of who he was supposed to be, confined his reply to a blithe shrug. "Actually, I've been saving money for a long time, now. A thronai here, a thronai there . . . even an occasional scepterai. All that copper and silver does eventually add up. I consider it proof that I'll always be careful to spend wisely and give my wife the best I can afford."

"So I take it you'll be buying your own house soon, then?" The question came from Tunric, mine owner and face-stealer.

Solyn saved Kenyen from answering. "Oh, we're not moving just yet! Traver knows I still have several more things to learn from Mother before I could be considered a Healer in my own right. He'll be moving in with me, for now."

Covering her hand, Kenyen smiled and added, "It gives me more time to make sure I can afford the best home for my wife. In the meantime, I will respect and honor the generosity of her family in offering a place in their home to me."

Tunric tightened his mouth for a moment, then leveled a pointed look at the newly wedded groom. "Make sure you *do* fulfill your obligations, regarding your wife and her family."

"I consider it my highest priority," Kenyen countered calmly. "Thank you for your kind wishes for us in our marriage."

Grunting, Tunric turned away without actually giving them any such wishes. Kenyen didn't expect anything else. From what he saw, the men of Mongrel didn't believe in the sanctity and happiness found in marriage, just in the using of women for their own selfish needs. Others moved forward to take his place, thankfully, and the impromptu feast continued.

The only other sour note came from the red-eyed glares aimed at the couple by Killia Lis Pel. Kenyen could guess why, if she was the young woman the real Traver had been kissing. He gave her an awkward, apologetic smile, which only served to make her run off. *I thought Traver said she was now twining with someone else . . . but it seems she still has feelings for him. Yet another thing I'll have to try to fix, when this is all over . . .*

Finally alone, with Traver's modest belongings moved into her bedchamber and their supper consumed, Solyn flopped onto her bed. Rubbing her hands over her face, she sighed. "What a fantastically awkward day . . . Not exactly the wedding day I'd pictured."

"I'll make it up to you," Kenyen promised. "I'm not sure how, but I will."

She wrinkled her nose. "I'm not sure how, either—if you keep your voice as quiet as possible, we do have enough privacy to speak freely," she added, giving him a wry smile. "Not that I think my parents or my sister are going to eavesdrop, but you never know."

He knew what she really meant. Most of his attention was on hanging a toweling cloth over the small, shuttered window that peeked out from the eaves of her family home. There were six rooms upstairs, two bedrooms on either side of the house, a storage room at the front, and a refreshing room at the back. With the refreshing room between Solyn's and her parents' chambers, and with her sister sleeping on the parental side of the hall, they were as private as they could possibly get. Except the house was a Corredai house, with the upper floor extending into the hillside on which it was built. That meant her bedroom window, while technically on an upper floor, was also technically at ground level.

With it carefully draped on nails embedded around the frame, the cloth should block out anyone peeking in through the gaps in the shutters. As soon as he was sure they had privacy, Kenyen released the feel of Traver's face and frame. It felt good to be himself. The only thing he didn't change was the voice, lighter and younger-sounding. That was in case someone in Solyn's family came close enough to overhear, though the others had also retired for the night. Joining Solyn on the bed, he flopped onto his back as well.

"I'm beginning to wonder if I should've chosen a different career," he muttered.

"Oh?" Solyn asked, curious. "Which one?"

He grunted. "Acting. I visited you-know-who last night, and his host believed me."

"Everyone else has been believing you, more or less," she whispered, thinking about his performances as Traver, son of Ysal and Tenaria. That led her back to thoughts of her friend. "How is he doing?"

Kenyen knew who she meant. "Thinner . . . paler . . . He needs to be freed. I don't think we can wait for the paper birds—we're in so deep now, it's going to be beyond awkward, untangling the aftermath."

"Awkward, yes," Solyn murmured in agreement. She slipped her hand over his, clasping it. Relief trickled through her when he turned his fingers so they could twine with hers. "But we don't have to untangle *some* parts of it . . . if we don't want to."

He could guess what she meant. Feeling the urge to do more than just smile in response, he started to roll toward her. Then stopped himself. *Stop and think, Kenyen Sin Siin . . . Pleasure is brief, but trouble is lasting. You don't have your brother around to make long-term plans for you, so* you *had better make them . . . which means we have to do a few slightly more important things first.*

Squeezing her fingers, he sat up again, keeping his voice barely above a whisper. "We should make more birds, just in case the storm dampened the previous ones. And then you should tell me how this . . . this basket spell of yours will get him free. I think I can remember the shape of the key to his manacles, so I can unlock them, but without a storm to wash away scent . . ."

Getting up as well, Solyn followed him to her desk. Her bedchamber wasn't large, and the wall over the writing table was covered in shelves scattered with books on magic. With Traver's things in trunks and baskets taking up half the floor space, she knew she'd need more shelves to store it all. Except it wouldn't be stored here for long. Looking at it, Solyn sighed unhappily.

"What are we going to do about this?" she asked, gesturing at the baskets and chests.

Kenyen followed her gaze. He'd already considered this part while packing up the tangible parts of Traver's life. "We'll come clean after they've been caught. Most of them. I'm afraid I don't know every face-stealer in these mountains, yet—what I *should* do is pick one of them and practice imitating his face, too, to maximize confusion and infiltration. And find out a way to get that girl, Killia, calmed down. And avoid being attacked by your father for all of this, *and* prove I'm still a worthy enough husband."

"Where did you get the money for that tea bowl?" Solyn asked, at the mention of his worthiness. She glanced up at the shelf which held the glazed object, then looked at him.

"I had it on me," he answered, shrugging. "It didn't even cost a tenth of the money I brought. I did buy it with my own face, though, not Traver's. That way I could safely ask questions about the meaning of the various designs, as a foreigner. I didn't know if anyone in that town already knew him. I just . . . I want him out, and safe. And all of this over and done with, though it's such a mess, with so many secrets . . ."

Solyn cupped her hand on his shoulder. "We'll get him out. As for the basket trick, it's a clever levitation enchantment. You tug on the handle to lift or lower whatever the basket can carry. Originally, it was meant for just levitating normal contents, vegetables, flowers, clothing, and even rocks, but the variations in the spellbook I have includes uses for lifting a small human."

That made him frown. "You have baskets strong enough to carry an adult? He is *not* a small man. I should know."

She rolled her eyes. "I'll also apply a spell to reinforce the weavings. I've done it before. Trust me, I *know* they can carry me." Solyn grinned mischievously. "I tried it out myself a few years back. And for the record, he did, too, though he hadn't finished filling out with muscles at the time. It was one of those things where we, um," she confessed, chuckling quietly, "well, we almost got caught doing something we weren't supposed to."

"Oh?" Kenyen asked, wondering what amused her so.

"We were picking plums from the tops of someone's orchard trees."

She was rather cute when she blushed like that, embarrassed by her confession but also not fully repentant about it. Leaning close, Kenyen kissed her forehead . . . and realized that, for the first time, he *could* kiss her without restraint. It took a great deal of willpower to turn away from her instead of take advantage of their new, perfectly legal relationship. Rumpling his hands through his hair, he impatiently pulled his locks out of their braid.

"Right. Letters and spells. Work before play—what other spells do you have?" he asked her. "I've heard tales of mages putting people to sleep. Can you do that?"

"Umm . . . one person per spell, not several all at once, but yes," Solyn told him. "The ones I know are all standard Healing spells. I'm so familiar with two of them, using them on Mother's patients, I even can cast them without needing the focal words. Sleeping spells are more like regular magic, so they're easier for me to create."

"You may need to do that. I don't think they ever leave him completely alone. I visited in the daytime, and they had a shifter-dog sleeping over the trapdoor," Kenyen confessed.

"How did you get past it?" she asked him. "Or him, whatever?"

"By shifting into a snake. The holes I used were too tiny for an adult to stick their hand through, though," he added. "You wouldn't be able to get in or out the same way I did."

"Oh." She pondered that for a moment, then shook her head, her braid sliding over her shoulders. "No, I have a few spells for shrinking things, animals, even people but . . . I'm not very good at inanimate objects, and that's all I've tried so far. I wouldn't want to try it on a living being. My previous results were . . . uneven."

Her ring squeezed just as a door hinge squeaked in the hall. A moment later, a floorboard creaked. Solyn waited for the next board to make a noise, the one closer to the refreshing room door. Rolling her eyes, she flipped a hand at Kenyen, who caught on and shifted back into Traver-shape. That allowed her to reach for the lever and pull her door swiftly open. Luelyn blinked, mouth gaping visibly in the light from the lamp illuminating her older sister's room.

"*No* eavesdropping," Solyn ordered her sibling. She pointed back at her sister's bedchamber.

"I was just on my way to the refresher!" the young girl whined, pouting.

Solyn obligingly pointed at that door instead, her stern expression brooking no argument. Heaving a sigh, Luelyn marched off to the correct door. She banged the door shut behind her. That caused another bedroom door to open moments later. Reina poked her head out, more of a silhouette from the lamp in the room beyond than an actual, visible figure. She withdrew and shut the door after a moment, not saying a word.

Patiently, Solyn waited for her sister to finish; when Luelyn emerged, she found herself pointed across the hall, directed back to her own room. Only when the door had shut did Solyn retreat into her room once more. When she did, she found Kenyen arranging paper and ink on her desk, still looking like the wrong man.

A quick check proved he had selected the right weight for folding from among the different sheets stacked on her shelves. "You remembered the kind of paper needed," she noted, smiling. "Not many would know the difference."

"You did point it out back in the cave," he reminded her. "I may not be a mage, but I am curious about magic."

"Who do you want the first one to go to?" Solyn asked, pleased that he had taken an interest in her work.

"Manolo. He's the one I know best, and I want to send at least three to him—make it four," Kenyen corrected. "I'll picture points along the road here as I'm writing the letter. Hopefully the birds will find him at one of those spots. Then one again to the princess leading our group, and one to the fellow who went to the Mespak region." Pausing in thought, he wrinkled his nose and added, "And one to my brother on the Plains. It's a long flight, but someone outside this kingdom should know, and he is both Lord of Family Tiger, and mated to the woman who warned us about Family Mongrel's existence."

"You don't want to send word to your brother?" Solyn asked him, noticing the face he made.

"No, I do," Kenyen corrected quickly. He stared at the paper on her desk, trying to put his feeling into words. "I just . . . He's always been better, smarter, stronger, faster. Now that I'm trying to do something important on my own feels, it feels like a failure."

She touched his shoulder again, drawing his attention. "I don't see how writing to him is a failure. You're merely informing him of what's been happening all the way out here. *We're* the ones who can actually do something about this mess. We just need to figure out when and exactly how. We already have some ideas."

"Yes, we do," he agreed, lifting his brows at the reminder.

Moving back from the desk, he let her step up in his place and begin her preliminary enchantments. Then quickly moved to the stoneware jar on the shelf near the bed, where she had placed several slices of greenvein for his needs. Two sneezes escaped before he could swallow the first bite, but the itch in his nose did ease quickly.

The notes to Manolo, Ashallan, and Narquen were variations on the previous one. The letter to his brother, which required tiny, careful writing on a much larger square of paper, listed in some detail what Kenyen had learned and experienced so far, and a list of his goals in resolving the whole Mongrel matter. Shifting the curtain aside, he unlatched the shutters for her as she made the last magic-infused mark on each of the birds. With a rustling sound, they flapped their paper wings and swooped through the opening, disappearing into the starry night.

Resecuring the window, Kenyen relaxed his features once they were safe from any spies, his mind already turning back to the problem at hand. "I think the best time to attack would be at night. Preferably while they were distracted by a bonfire meeting. If it's night, they won't be able to see you fly away—though I do want to see that spell, first. If you cannot fly very fast, then it might not be a good choice, even at night," he warned her. "Shifters who can mold the right shape can fly as fast as a real bird."

She shrugged. "It's about as fast as a small bird, I think. I agree that night would be better than day, to help evade any pursuit. I'm not as sure about helping Traver to escape during a bonfire meeting. For one, we don't know when they'll hold the next one. For another, that might be a long wait. And for the third, I'd have to rescue him on my own, since they'd expect you to be there."

Wrapping his arms around her, Kenyen shook his head. "No, you're right. As convenient as it would be to have many of them all in one place, giving us a greater chance to slip away undetected, I'll not leave you to face them alone. Sleep-inducing spells or not, you shouldn't face them alone. I'm nervous enough doing that myself, and I'm just pretending to go along with their plans, not trying to double-cross them."

She hugged him back. "I'm just glad you've said they aren't hurting him. That gives us more time to figure out what to do. He shouldn't be left there, but there are only a few people I *know* aren't shifters. Untrustworthy ones, I mean. I know my parents aren't, because it's too difficult to fake being either a fully trained Healer or a blacksmith, but I don't want to involve them, either, in case the . . . the *curs* get their hands on them."

It felt good to hold her and be held. Kenyen mulled over her words, considering the possibilities. "What if we went tonight?"

Solyn lifted her head from his shoulder. "Tonight? Right now?"

"In an hour or so, when it's more likely the others are asleep," he murmured. "We *are* newly married, after all. Everyone would expect us to stay in bed, tonight."

"But I thought we *were* going to twine fully," she whispered, disappointed at the prospect otherwise. Her complaint earned her a kiss on her brow.

"We will. *After* he is safe. And after he knows that we are indeed wed," Kenyen added. "Although we really shouldn't, since it was done in *his* name, not mine."

"Husband," Solyn growled under her breath, poking the Shifterai

in the chest, "I married *you*. Not him. He has no say in who I twine with, other than maybe asking me not to do it in front of him. Which I wouldn't, anyway."

His delightful new wife had a rather sharp finger, for all her nails were trimmed and thus blunt. Suppressing a grunt at the poke, he caught her hand and lifted it to his lips, kissing her knuckles. "Then go find your spells and study them while we wait for things to settle down. We'll free him and then . . ."

"And then?" she prodded.

For a moment, Kenyen drew a blank. His gaze fell on the tea bowl, recalling her questioning his ability to pay for it. That gave him an idea.

"Then we'll find an inn and settle him at it with some of my coins. Somewhere far enough away, it'd be unlikely that he'd encounter anyone who knows his face. As soon as he's safe, you and I will return here, and I'll continue to pretend to be him while we wait for reinforcements," he said. "If they come after us in force . . . it'll be ugly. Shapeshifters who know how to fight are worse than feral livestock. All the horns, the claws, the teeth, and the ferocity, but with the full cunning of a human being directing the fight."

Solyn mulled it over in her mind. His logic was sound. "I think your plan could work. We know that bluesteel can prevent a shifter from changing shape, so I'll see what my father has in stock. Or maybe even find a way to convince him to make more of it. Or maybe there's a spell I can adapt that could force a shifter to stay un-shifted. I did get a new book the other day, and I haven't read all of it yet."

As much as he wanted to keep holding her, Kenyen released Solyn so that she could find the book in question. "You sound a little bit like my brother and sister-in-law. They're both mad for books."

That made her snort. Glancing over her shoulder, she shook her head. "I'm much more of a see-and-do kind of learner." Plucking the right book from the shelf, she turned and gestured with it. "Mother was able to teach me some of the basics, but mostly only what pertains to her branch of magic. Coaxing flesh to knit itself whole. Bolstering the body's defenses to thwart infections. Setting a broken bone so that it'll heal right. None of which have anything to do with . . . with controlling fire, or making paper birds fly, or . . . or scrying with a mirror.

"Which I *still* don't know how to do," she added in an aside. "Mainly because I can't make heads or tails of some of the terminology they use, though it's also because the best scryings are done with a glass mirror, and all I have is a small scrap of polished steel," she told him, lifting her chin at the framed piece of metal over the small washstand by the door. "There's enough of it different from what Mother does, it keeps tripping me up when I try certain things."

"Uh, is it *safe* for you to try some sort of containment spell on a shapeshifter, if you're that uncertain of the results?" Kenyen asked. He barely remembered to keep his voice low.

"Well, I wouldn't try it on *you*," she countered tartly, struggling to keep her own retort quiet. "I wouldn't try it at all unless it was an emergency . . . and only on the evil shifters. If something did go wrong, I'd feel less guilty if it hurt *them*. They'd deserve it." Subsiding, she shook her head. "I wouldn't think shaping flesh would be all that easy, but I'd still think it easier than shaping magic."

"I wouldn't know," Kenyen returned dryly. Backing up to the bed, he sat on its edge. "I can't shape magic. Let's see that book. I'm not the scholar my brother is, but maybe two heads can make more sense than one?"

Nodding, she sat down next to him and opened the book. Flipping through the pages, she found the ribbon marking the spot where she had last finished. "This is a grimoire, a personal spellbook. Some of the things in here are very simple, while others are complex. There are notes on the purpose of each spell and possible variations, of course, but most were written to make sense to the mage who originally wrote them. Others are from those who've used this book for their own studies in the years since, but all of them were from trained mages, so naturally I haven't had much luck in deciphering them . . ."

ELEVEN

The basket spell, Kenyen decided, was both terrifying and exhilarating. He supposed it might've been less perilous to have flown in the daylight, where the trees and hills weren't shades of gray to his owl-shaped eyes. It was always easier to see things in full color than with night sight. It might also, he acknowledged privately, have been *more* alarming to be flying about in the daylight, because then he'd be that much more aware of how flimsy the flower basket was and how far off the ground it carried him.

It was exhilarating because it *worked* . . . and it wasn't the power of his own wings that lofted him into the air, but rather a simple tugging pull on the broad loop of the wicker handle. Flying like this was unnatural. Undeniably, indisputably unnatural, and remarkably fun.

To rise up, he simply pulled straight up. To fly forward, he first lifted up, then pushed the handle forward. To slow down, he pulled it back, toward his chest. A turn involved a combination of twist and tilt toward the necessary direction, and sometimes he swooped a little too fast, but it wasn't difficult to stop.

The only drawback to this mode of locomotion was that Solyn couldn't reshape her eyes to see in the dark, and hadn't the first clue how to cast a spell to give herself the magical equivalent of owl-vision. She could craft little glowing balls of light, which she somehow fixed onto the back end of his basket, allowing her to follow him. That meant he was responsible for her safety as well as his own, but because she was following him, he couldn't *see* where she was in relation to him.

Some shifters could literally grow eyes in the backs of their heads, but Kenyen wasn't one of them. Twisting to look behind him made his basket fly oddly, so he couldn't do that, either. When they came near the high meadow where Cullerog and his sheep lived, he maneuvered carefully between the trees flanking the fields, picking a path down to the ground with plenty of room.

Once the basket was on the ground, with his legs stretched out in front of him, getting the spell to stop was as easy as grasping it firmly with both hands. The soft noise of her landing in the grass behind him was a relief, and a glance showed her faintly illuminated in the blue glow of the three tiny mage-lights she had created.

Getting out of the basket required an awkward wiggle. He heard her trying to smother a giggle and shushed her quietly. They both worked themselves free and stood. Clad as she was in baggy spare clothes of Traver's, hair pinned tight to her head and reeking of lanolin grease applied to the soles of her sandals and the palms of her gloves, she grinned at him. Then again, he wasn't much better, with his hair bound up and his gloves and sandals coated in sheep grease as well, though at least Traver's clothes did fit him better.

The trick of clothes and grease were needed to minimize their own scent as much as possible, hiding it behind the familiar smell of the real Traver and the much stronger smell of sheep. With Cullerog being a shepherd, that meant he was surrounded by the woolly beasts, and the scent would already be everywhere in the cabin. It was Kenyen's idea to dress in the spare sets of clothes, partly for the smell but also to ensure he would have fresh changes while staying elsewhere. It was Solyn's idea to use a lanolin-heavy ointment she had fetched from the herb-room, along with thin wool gloves that could be discarded quickly.

Each of them had an oilcloth sack. The one Solyn carried was filled with a change of clothes for her and a pot of softsoap, so they could wash the ointment from their sandals and hands. The other, slung over Kenyen's head and shoulder, contained bread and fruit filched from the kitchen for Traver to eat and several slices of green-vein cheese.

"Ready?" he whispered.

Nodding, she picked up her basket with one hand and gestured with the other. A single murmur extinguished the lights. His nose itched, warning him that the effects of the cheese were starting to wear off. Removing one glove, he dug into the bag, broke off a chunk of cheese, and stuffed it in his mouth; sneezing from her magics could get them in serious trouble if it happened at the wrong moment.

He tugged the garment back on and picked up the basket. Overhead, stars twinkled through the treetops. Neither the large white form of Brother Moon nor the smaller orb of Sister were visible at the moment; the larger celestial orb of Brother Moon had already set for the night, being close to the new, and the smaller one of Sister Moon wouldn't rise for another hour or so. That didn't leave a lot of light for the normal, non-shifter eyes of his wife, but it did help reduce their chances of being spotted by any Mongrels in the shepherd's home.

"Can you see anything?" he asked, concerned about her safety.

"Well enough," she returned, keeping her voice low. Though he had explained to her he would be using an owl's sight to see a dozen times better than any human could, Solyn didn't think her own night vision was bad. "If we stay out of the heaviest cover and move slowly, I should be fine."

"We'll head uphill, and approach from near the ridge, where there aren't windows to look out from," he told her. "Crouch low, keep the basket on the far side of you from the cottage, and use your hands if you need to. Try to move like a sheep."

Though he was little more than a silhouette with a hint of details thanks to the starlight, Solyn smirked at him. "Is that something you do often? Imitate sheep?"

"No, but I have moved like an animal—as an animal—when sneaking up on bandit holds. This is no different. Be ready with your spells," he warned her. "If I gesture for you to stop, get low to the ground and hold still. When we're close, I'll scout the cabin and see how many are in there and whether they're asleep or awake."

Nodding, she moved slowly and carefully. Noise was his biggest concern; he had learned in the warbands how to move through a forest at night, but she didn't move too badly, testing each footstep for noisy dry twigs before trusting her weight to the ground. It took a while to move up through the woods at that pace, and it took time to move slowly out across the upper meadow, pausing now and then to lower their heads, as if cropping at the grass.

No one charged out of the cabin. Nothing slithered out of the grass or flew down out of the sky. Insects chirped, night birds twittered, the wind occasionally whistled along the ridgeline off to their right, and the stars slowly moved by overhead. When they were within just a few lengths of the moss-dotted slates of the cottage roof, he gestured for her to stop and wait. Obediently, she hunkered down.

Shaping horselike ears, Kenyen listened. Night sounds from all directions but the cabin. Someone in the cottage was talking; from the muffled low level, he thought it might be coming from the basement. Creeping forward, he enlarged his ears and tested the wind with his nose, since its direction was in his favor, blowing from the cabin to him.

Sheep, of course, and smoke from the hearthfire. Cullerog the shepherd, the shifter who was the dog . . . and two familiar smells, one feminine, the other masculine. He couldn't place it immediately, but someone was visiting the small structure. Easing closer, he set his basket under the eaves and listened intently, creeping an inch at a time toward the hole he had used to escape, earlier.

". . . And how do you like *that*?" a male voice murmured. It was followed by a grunt of pain and a faint clank of metal. "I wonder if he can rut on her as many times in a single night as *I* can?"

The boastful tone, the smell, and the voice clicked together. *Tarquin is in there?*

"Lick harder, bitch; he's getting soft again. We can't have poor Traver rutless on his *wedding night*."

At that taunting, an ugly suspicion rose in Kenyen's mind. He found the right hole by the gleam of light coming from within and squeezed his upper body into the shape of a snake. The partial shift was difficult to maintain, but it allowed him to extend his serpentine head into the hole far enough to have his guess confirmed.

It wasn't easy for one man to violate another without doing so personally, but Tarquin had found a way. The same middle-aged woman from the bonfire meeting now crouched over Traver, who had his—Kenyen's—gathered trousers pulled down to his ankles. Her tangle of messy dark hair hid exactly what she was doing at his groin, but that much was obvious. It was the bruises covering Traver's legs that concerned Kenyen. Several of them looked like they were days old, while others were fresher.

He hadn't checked Traver's body visually past that first night, just the face and general build. Guilt rose up in Kenyen at that neglect, guilt prodded further by the memory of how Traver had flinched when he had drawn letters on that unknowingly mottled leg. *Of course he couldn't have told me about it; if he had, I would've had to fake an equal level of ruthlessness . . . and this does lend weight to the thought that they're just going to kill him as soon as they have what they want.*

Tarquin moved into view. The curly-haired shifter was naked and blatantly ready to do some rutting. He knelt behind the woman, and Kenyen quickly retreated, drawing his upper body back through the hole. He shifted awkwardly in position, rearing up to peek through a crack in the shutters. Cullerog was awake, along with an equally age-grizzled shifter. They were playing some sort of grid-and-counter game. Kenyen had seen a similar board in Traver's home, but didn't know how it was played.

This time, the grunting from below was feminine. The exclamation, rough and coarse, was masculine. ". . . See this? *This* is how a real man ruts!"

It was accompanied by worse sounds and a mock-howl. Moving one of his pieces, the gray-haired, gray-bearded shifter asked, "You gonna rut on 'er, later?"

"Thinking about it," Cullerog muttered, moving one of his pieces. "If my sap'll rise."

His companion chuckled. "That boy's got 'nough sap for both of us."

Seeing no one else in the building, Kenyen reshaped his head and chest. Easing back, he turned and gestured. The brownish lump on the hillside moved, creeping down the slope toward him. By the time Solyn reached his side, a few clouds had drifted into view from the east. They were lighter around the edges than they should have been, suggesting the rise of Sister Moon wasn't that far off.

The sounds coming from the root cellar, a mix of grunts, slapping flesh, and crude observations, were obvious enough that Solyn blushed. Focusing firmly on Kenyen's gestures, she watched him point at the window and hold up two fingers, then point down below and hold up three. He folded down one of those. She guessed that meant one of the three was Traver, leaving two other targets for her.

Nodding, she set her basket not far from his and rose up on her knees. Putting her eye to the crack between the two shutters, she peered into the cabin. Two elderly men sat at a table not far from the hearth. Between the crackling of the fire and the flickering of two oil lamps, she could see their faces easily enough.

I can't put either of them to sleep suddenly. If I did it to the first one, that would alarm the other one, not to mention the sound of either man falling out of his chair would put the idiot down in the cellar on his guard . . . assuming he'd notice it over the noises he's *making*, she acknowledged. *So the gentle dreams spell will have to be the first choice. That way, they'll lie down of their own accord.* Then, *I put them out firmly with the anesthetic spell.*

Focusing on the one with the beard, she reached for him with the part of her senses, her mind, that could sense his living energy. *Dormanuuu*, she thought, shaping the meaning behind the word, the sense of exhaustion and the need for slumber. The other man's nose twitched. He finished his move in the game and rubbed at his nostrils, pinching them briefly. The bearded one started to reach for his piece . . . and yawned.

Yes!

"Ugh," he muttered, rubbing at his eyes. "I think all th' noise that brat's making is pulling th' sap outta me . . . Let's finish this tomorrow."

Rising from his seat, he removed his shirt and stepped out of his trousers, shifting shape into an old sheepherding dog. Curling up in front of the fire, the shifter wiggled a few times to get comfortable, then settled his head on his paws. Solyn turned her attention to her other target.

This time, the use of her spell made him sneeze openly, twice, before a yawn split his mouth wide. Getting up, he picked up the iron tongs leaning against the stone-built hearth. Pushing and piling all the cinders together, along with enough ashes to bank the fire so that it would stay burning through the night, he finally set the tongs back down.

Another yawn was followed by a third sneeze, then he moved off toward what she presumed was his bed . . . which was out of her line of sight. Quickly, Solyn kept his face firmly in her mind, and pushed her magics into the shape for the anesthetic spell. The moment she heard the bed frame creak, then go silent, she released the spell. The bed creaked again, but he didn't sneeze.

Hoping her spell had worked, she returned her attention to the dog-man. The noises from below had ceased. Unsure what *that* meant, she quickly regathered her inner energies. Just as she released them, the trapdoor shoved up. Startled, Solyn almost lost control of the spell.

"Hey, Cullerog!" Tarquin called out, pushing the panel the rest of the way up. His tousled head appeared, sporting a grin. "I got 'er all wet, just the way you like. Dirt grubber, down there, can't keep it up long enough to plow the bitch, so it's your turn!"

Frowning at the lack of response, he climbed out of the cellar and padded toward the bed. That was when Solyn hit him with her gentle sleep spell, too. He paused and yawned, swaying.

"I don't . . . Tired," he muttered. Turning to look at the shape-shifted dog, he scratched his head, yawned again, then looked the other way. Toward the shuttered window. His eyes widened.

Afraid he had seen her, Solyn panicked and flung her other spell at him. His eyes rolled up and he sagged to the floor with a thud. The dog-man didn't move, though the flames of the lamps on the table danced from the impact.

Unable to see what was happening, Kenyen flinched at the noise.

He glanced at Solyn, whose eyes were wide, one of them lit in a thin vertical line of the light shining from the cabin interior. She relaxed after a moment, relieving him.

They both stiffened at the sound of a voice, light and hesitant.

". . . M-master?"

Solyn swayed closer to the crack in the shutter. An unkempt head appeared in the trapdoor opening. Wide brown eyes stared at the fallen body of the shifter named Tarquin Tun Nev, then darted around the room. They didn't even glance at the shuttered window where Solyn watched, holding her breath.

With an animal-like scramble, the woman climbed out of the hole. Hesitantly, she touched Tarquin, shoved a little on his shoulder. Then shook him hard. He stayed asleep. Crouching, the woman covered her mouth with her hand, then glanced at the bed. Scrambling in the same direction as Solyn's second target, she disappeared from view.

The sounds of the bed squeaking and cloth rustling suggested she was trying to wake him as well, then she came back into sight and poked at the dog. Shook the dog. Rose up to stand straight, both hands over her mouth and a wild, wild look in her eyes. Whirling, she faced the shelving to the right of the fireplace, where the kitchen supplies used by the shepherd were stored.

For a long moment, the woman stood there, thinking whatever thoughts might be tumbling through her head. Then she dashed forward, snatched the largest knife off the shelf, and ran back to the dog. Solyn flinched back from the window the moment she saw the older woman fling the blade high.

Concerned by her flinch, Kenyen was even more alarmed by the meaty thud and faint whine of a dog in pain. It changed to the groan of a man with a second thump, followed by a wheeze. Pushing Solyn out of his way, he took her place at the crack in the shutters, peering inside just in time to see the blade descend again. That third slicing stab spilled blood across the floor. The dog was no longer a dog, but instead a naked elderly man, bloodied and unmoving, indicating he was dead.

The woman scrambled for Tarquin's body next. Kenyen opened his mouth to protest, to do something, but she was too fast. This time her aim was more true; her slumbering victim—her victimizer—made no sound, dying with only two jabs of the blade. His face melted and changed, restoring it to the real one in the limpness of his death. She slashed at him a couple more times, her movements frantic with the release of her fears and her rage, though she fought them with nothing louder than panicked gasps.

Yanking the blade out one last time, she rushed for the bed. Fear coursed through Kenyen. Not for the old shepherd; this was merely a form of delayed justice at the hands of one of his own victims, given Tarquin's last words. He feared instead for Traver, chained up and nearly helpless in the cellar. Thrusting away from the window, he bolted for the door.

By the time he flung it open, the naked woman was half covered in blood, but she was still on the bed. Whipping to face him, she snarled in fear and rage and launched herself at him. This, Kenyen knew how to handle. Moving forward to meet her charge, he side-stepped her thrust, grabbed her arm, twisted it, and flipped her over his hip, using her own momentum against her. It wasn't always necessary to shift into an animal shape to fight.

He didn't try to remove the blade from her grasp, but he did plant his foot on her ribs, pinning her to the floor. Snarling, she writhed, trying to wriggle free with surprising strength. Grunting with the effort of containing her struggles, Kenyen called out, "Solyn, help me! Calm her down!"

Unnerved by the violence, knowing from her Healer's training just how deadly those wounds were, Solyn gathered her courage and hurried inside. Focusing her gaze firmly on the older woman and not on the liquids staining the floor, she held out her hand and hummed a lullaby, using the sound to shape her power into a net around the woman.

The combination of magic and song soothed the woman's struggles, dulling some of the fear and rage in her gaze. Nose itching, Kenyen loosened his grip, waiting to see what she would do. The woman clung to the blade, but did nothing more than watch them warily. Carefully, he released her arm, stepping back from her body. She rolled into a crouch, gaze darting from him to Solyn.

"We're not going to hurt you," Solyn stated. "We're only here to free our friend, the one in the root cellar."

Chains rattled down below, proving Traver was still alive, though he didn't call up to them. Like a feral beast, the woman stayed in her crouch, her expression disbelieving. She finally settled her gaze on Kenyen and spat defiantly at his feet, then looked up warily, knife clutched at the ready.

He didn't take offense. "Solyn, give her what you're wearing. And some of the money, too."

She caught his meaning. "And one of the baskets—she's in even more danger than we are," Solyn added at Kenyen's sharp look. "She needs to run as far and as fast as that spell can fly. I'll find something else to levitate for my own use."

"Alright," he agreed. Solyn nodded and began unfastening her oversized, borrowed tunic. Now was not the time for modesty, but rather expediency and compassion.

"You . . . you *help* me?" the woman asked, glancing between them, though she gave more of her confused attention to Kenyen, whose Traver-like face she had seen before. "You're . . . you're *one* of them!"

"No," he corrected her, shaking his head. "I am Shifterai. A *real* one, not one of these *curs*."

"Liar!" she spat. "Bonfire! I saw you!"

"I only pretended to be one of them to save *his* life," Kenyen countered, pointing at the open trapdoor.

"He's telling you the truth!" Traver called out in a semi-strong voice. More metal clanked as he shifted, his voice echoing up from the cellar. "I told him to pretend to be me, in case I was captured!"

Shaking her head, the woman looked like she was more in bewilderment than in denial. Solyn, slipping out of the loose trousers, caught her attention. When the younger woman held out the clothes, the older one snatched them with one hand, clutching them to her damp chest. She looked warily at Kenyen, who held up his hands.

"So long as you don't attack us, I won't touch you," he murmured. She watched him warily for a long moment, then started climbing into the trousers.

Solyn ducked out through the door, making the older woman freeze. Kenyen didn't move. The half-naked woman glanced between him and the door, then continued struggling into the garments.

"Why?" she finally asked, all but spitting the word.

"Twenty-three or more years ago," Kenyen told her, "these curs kidnapped a Zanthai woman. Ellet Sou Tred." She froze at the name. Gently, he asked. "Did you know her?"

She shrugged stiffly, not answering.

"She was treated much like you for a couple years. Then there was a grass fire. She escaped through it and fled to the Mornai. She gave birth to a little girl, then died . . . but before she died, a scribe wrote down what happened to her. Last year, her daughter ended up on the Plains, among the real Shifterai. When we learned what these Mongrels had done, what her mother had told to the scribe who raised her little girl, we decided to hunt them down. I was the first to stumble across them. Literally," Kenyen added wryly.

He didn't look at the bodies on the floor. "We *are* going to stop them."

Her shoulders shook. Fingers fumbling over the tunic, one hand still clutching the bloodied knife, she finally shoved the horn buttons through their holes. And sniffed, letting Kenyen know she was crying. Solyn stepped back into the cabin; the younger woman had taken the time to don her own clothes and had a shallow, oval, loop-handled basket in each hand.

"I have enchanted these baskets so that they will fly. The spell will last *only* until sundown tomorrow," she explained carefully, holding up one of them. "But this one should keep its spell long enough to get you far, far away."

"En . . . enchanted?" the woman asked.

"Yes. I am a mage. Something of a mage," Solyn amended. She quickly explained how to start, stop, and steer the enchanted item, and coaxed her pupil into repeating them. The older woman mumbled her way through the instructions, her gaze fixed firmly on Solyn and the basket. The younger one repeated them again, coaxing her to get them right.

Confident the woman wasn't going to attack either of them, Kenyen quietly climbed down into the cellar. Traver had shifted position, not only to pull up his borrowed trousers but also to avoid the blood trickling down from overhead. The smell of blood was thicker down here, mixing uneasily with the musty smell of damp earth, rutting, and the contents of the slops bucket.

"I take it that basket thing she talked about is going to get me out of here, too?" Traver muttered, and relaxed at Kenyen's nod. He lifted his wrists, changing the subject. "Where's the key?"

Kenyen shaped the tip of one finger into a claw. "I'm not sure. I didn't exactly have a chance to interrogate them."

Concentrating, he dredged up his memory of the original key and shaped his claw to match it. Poking it into the hole, he twisted his wrist. For a moment, the lock remained stubborn, then the inner parts gave way with a dull click. Traver sighed in relief, shaking off the cuff. Kenyen poked at the second one. It, too, was stiff, but it, too, released the latch. He *oof*-ed, caught in a hug from the other man.

"Cora bless you," Traver muttered, hugging him hard. "I got your message . . . most of it . . . the last visit."

"I'm sorry about the bruises." Kenyen returned the embrace. "If I'd known . . ."

"It wasn't bad," Traver dismissed, letting go. "It was only for a few days, and I knew you'd come back for me. They threatened me with a lot worse, but mostly they just demanded that I tell them everything I knew about Ysander and Reina, and kicked, or slapped, or pinched when I didn't know. Or didn't respond fast enough.

"They said you still needed to hear things from me, so they weren't going to do worse if I cooperated. They wanted to know about Reina's Healer experiments, and whatever I could tell them about all the things the blacksmith has made through the years. I didn't tell them anything useful. I made sure of that," he added darkly, looking down at his cloth-covered legs. "I won't trade saving my life for ruining someone else's."

He pushed to get to his feet. Kenyen quickly wrapped his arm around the Corredai's ribs, helping him up. "I take it tonight was the worst of it?"

Traver shuddered. "Don't . . . don't tell Solyn. She didn't see, did she?"

"No, she didn't see anything," Kenyen promised, helping him toward the ladder. "But she did *hear* everything."

"Wonderful," Traver muttered, flushing. "Well, I'll presume her flying basket trick will help us to escape, but where are we going?"

"You're going to fly as far away as you can. You'll take the clothes off my back, some food and some coins, and you'll find an inn. You'll stay there until we come for you, when enough of these *curs* have been caught that I don't have to pretend to *be* you anymore. Solyn said you'd know where the city of Hemplan is located, and that it's far enough away, no one should be able to recognize your face."

"No." Traver shook his head, reaching for the rungs. "I'll do what I *should* have done. I'll fly right to the capital, and find a Magister, and tell him or her my entire story."

"A what?" Kenyen asked, unfamiliar with the term. "Is that a kind of mage?"

"A judicial mage," Traver explained. His arms and legs shook a little as he started to climb. Kenyen planted a hand on his rump, lifting with a stretch of his body to help support the younger man in his climb. "Thank you. I haven't exercised in too long. I feel as weak as a newborn lamb."

"What will a Magister be able to do?" Kenyen asked, boosting him into the main cabin. He moved to blow out the lamps hanging from hooks in the root cellar's ceiling as Traver replied.

"Well, for a start, he or she can authorize whatever you need to do, in tracking down the rest of these face-stealers. We don't have one in the valley," Traver told him, "but then we normally don't have major criminals running loose."

Solyn added her voice to the explanation. "Magisters are exceptionally strong mages pledged to support the just laws of the kingdom. They're only found in the big towns and cities, but they have all sorts of spells to determine if someone is telling the truth *and* the legal backing of the King to take care of matters if a severe bit of lawbreaking is brought to their attention. They don't usually handle the petty crimes, like minor theft or being drunk in public. That's either for the city guards, the King's Guard who hunt down bandits and the like, or for the elders of a particular holding to handle—you, what's your name?"

Climbing up out of the now-dark cellar, Kenyen emerged in time to see the woman blinking in thought. "I . . . Parma. My name was Parma," she finally admitted. "Parma . . . Nol Vyth. But they called me Bitch. I . . . I haven't been called *my* name in . . . in . . ."

Solyn touched her arm, giving her silent sympathy.

"Hello, Parma. It's very nice to meet you, now that we're both free," Traver told her gently. He offered her his hand.

Parma stared at it. She didn't flinch from it, but it took her a long moment before she finally shifted the knife to her other hand and clasped his fingers. "N-Nice to meet you. Traver. It's . . . *very* nice to know you won't die. Like the . . . the others."

Her words made all of them think of the many men the curs of Family Mongrel had no doubt replaced over the years. For a moment, they remained silent in grim, somber respect. Finally, Traver breathed deeply.

"Will *you* fly with me to the capital, Parma?" he asked her. "Will you help me find a Magister, and will you be brave enough, *strong* enough, to tell them everything you know? Or almost everything?" he added, glancing at the bodies. "We don't have to mention how you helped free both of us just now. Not until they know just how necessary it was."

Kenyen looked at the young farmer with respect. Greater respect, since Traver's quick thinking and bravery had already proven themselves in this mess.

"I think that's a brilliant idea." The others glanced at him, so he explained. "One witness, however much he may *believe* his words are the truth, is one thing. Particularly with a tale as wild as rogue shapeshifters stealing the faces and the identities and the lives of innocent Corredai. I wouldn't have believed it so quickly myself, if I hadn't been confronted with all the evidence I've seen. But two witnesses, *both* of them swearing to the same story on a Truth Stone? That will be hard to dismiss."

"Yes, they'll *have* to listen to both of you, if both of you go," Solyn agreed quickly.

"I promise you will be safe with me," Traver added, still holding the older woman's hand.

She hesitated, then nodded, a single jerky movement of her head. "You . . . I will trust. You were . . . You *didn't*, down there. *You*," she added, looking at Kenyen, "I will not."

Again, he held up his hands. "I do understand, and I'm not offended. I'm just glad you're free."

"Speaking of which, we should get moving," Solyn urged them. She glanced briefly at the bodies, shuddered, and lifted her chin at the door. "The sooner we get out of here, the less scent we'll leave behind. If nothing else, when he doesn't show up in the morning, Tunric will come looking for Tarquin. Even if they technically aren't the original father and son, he'll have to come looking."

"He's . . . evil," Parma muttered, shivering. Her fingers gripped the hilt of her knife until they were visibly white. "Evil."

"All the more reason to make sure he gets taken down," Kenyen promised her. "These Mongrels, these *curs*, are like rabid animals. You don't let them live. You just kill them, quickly and cleanly, so their infection cannot spread. *You* did that, and I'll make sure this Magister knows it, if he or she questions you about it. But first, we have to get you to that Magister, and that means leaving this place."

Solyn moved first, heading out the door. Parma followed, with Traver behind her. Kenyen took a moment to check for signs of footprints. The only ones were the few smudges left by the older woman's bare toes. For all her kills had been bloody, they weren't overly messy, thanks to the cracks between the floorboards. There were no other signs that anyone else had been here tonight.

Tempted as he was to knock over the lamps and burn everything to the ground, to ruin even those few traces that might remain, Kenyen refrained. Eventually, the Magister would want to know what happened here. A part of him also wanted the other face-stealing Mongrels to know that something could hunt and kill *them.* That their days were numbered.

He did take one thing from the former owners. A scrap of toweling cloth from the kitchen area, one large enough to knot in a loop, since there were no baskets with large enough handles in the hut. Other than that, there was nothing he wanted from the place. Blowing out the lamps and leaving the banked coals on the hearth to dwindle and die on their own, he left the cottage, letting the door swing shut behind him.

Sister Moon had finally risen in the east, bathing the meadow in faint, silvery blue light. It was enough to see by even with normal eyesight, so Kenyen didn't bother shifting his eyes. Traver and the woman, Parma, had already squirmed their bodies between the oval curves and arching handles of the baskets. Each had an oilcloth bag slung over their heads, and Solyn was repeating the directions one last time for them.

Quickly stripping out of his borrowed clothes, Kenyen rubbed the last of the lanolin-rich ointment on his gloves into his soles before letting each foot touch the ground. Bundling up the spare clothes, he moved to Traver's side and stuffed them into the bag.

"I'll hold on to the rest of your things and treat them well," he promised under his breath, eyeing the younger man. "Keep the two of yourselves safe, until you can reclaim them."

Traver nodded. He hesitated, one hand holding the basket at his waist. ". . . Did you really marry her today?"

"I did. By *her* choice," Kenyen added.

"If she doesn't want you, you'll let her go?" he asked.

Kenyen nodded. "We don't hold our women prisoner on the

Plains. Not the *true* Shifterai. When the truth comes out . . . it'll be a mess, trying to untangle all of this, but she knew who I was within the first few days of my taking your face. She knew when she married me."

Solyn chuckled at those words. Finished with her instructions and reassurances for the older woman, she retorted quietly, "I'm sorry to say that he may have perfected your face, but he is *not* you, Traver Ys Ten. I'm very much glad I didn't drink Sister's Tea with the brother of my heart, earlier today. My choice may have been hastily made . . . but I think it'll be a good one."

"Well, if he doesn't treat you right, you come tell me," Traver ordered her, before looking at Kenyen. "I don't know how, since I'm not a shifter and I'm not a warrior, but I *will* find a way to beat you worse than they beat me, if you do anything to her she doesn't like."

"I don't have a problem with that," Kenyen agreed. "Fly carefully, you two."

"You have no baskets," Parma said, looking at Solyn. She glanced briefly at Kenyen, but only briefly, considering he was now naked. "How . . . how will you leave?"

"He'll shift into a bird shape, and I'll find something else to enchant," Solyn told them. "Go. Fly. Make good use of the moonlight. We're somewhere west of the Nespah Valley, maybe slightly north by a couple hills. The capital is somewhere to the south of here—if nothing else, you'll see the lights of the people who live in whatever big towns lie in that direction."

"And if it's big enough to be lit at night, it's probably big enough to have a Magister on hand," Traver agreed. Glancing at Parma, he lifted his chin. "Ready?"

"Ready." Squatting, she gripped the handle with both hands—and *oof*-ed in surprise as the basket, still at a bit of an angle, started forward without warning. She bounced across the grass, feet quickly lifted out of the way. Skidding, she finally lifted up into the air. Not quite as awkwardly, Traver gripped the handle as well, though he lifted to counteract the forward thrust of the tilted wicker loop. It had been years since his last try at the strange method of travel, but he caught the hang of it quickly enough.

Solyn bit her lip, smothering a snicker. The unlikely pair lifted up higher, getting the hang of the swooping, unnatural form of flight. As soon as she was sure they could handle basket-flying, she turned to Kenyen. "Well, shall I go find a basket?"

"Cullerog didn't have anything suitable. Can you enchant this instead?" Kenyen offered, holding up the loop of cloth salvaged from the shepherd's hut.

Taking it, Solyn studied the linen, thinking. She finally nodded and slipped it over her head. Spreading the middle of the material so that it cupped her bottom, she crouched a little, tugged experimentally, and finally said, ". . . I *think* it'll work. It won't be quite as stable in flight, but I can adjust it with magic as I go." It didn't take her long to mutter the right spell words. "Are you ready?"

"Almost," he said, rubbing absently at his nose. It didn't actually itch, but he was lost in thought. The other two had flown past the barn as they left, and that had reminded Kenyen of the sheep cooped up inside for the night.

Moving over to the door, he unlatched it and swung it open. A couple of the animals inside baaed at the noise he made, but they didn't leave the shelter of the building. Satisfied they would be able to get out and graze in the morning, he returned to Solyn's side. At her curious look, he explained his actions.

"They don't deserve to die of thirst or starvation, in case it takes a couple of days for someone to come by," he said.

Solyn smiled at him. "You're a good man, Kenyen Sin Siin. Alright . . . ready to fly?"

Shifting shape, he shrunk himself into the familiar feathers of his owl form. She gripped the cloth strap in both hands—and squeaked, shooting forward awkwardly. With stumbling, running steps, she hauled up and swung herself into the sky. Hooting in amusement, Kenyen launched himself after her, more than ready to return to their temporary home.

TWELVE

Sneaking back in again was as easy as sneaking out. The worst part came when she used a clever little spell to unlatch the shutters of her bedroom window. That made him sneeze. Kenyen hadn't known owls could sneeze, but he did.

Hopping in first, he fluttered to the bed and landed on it, reshaping his ears and cocking his head to listen for any sounds that might indicate their return had been noted. Hearing nothing but the faint sounds of a household deep in sleep, and the *oof*-ing of his wife as she slithered through the narrow opening on her belly, Kenyen reshaped himself into his natural form.

He was now short two changes of clothes, leaving him with just two to wear, and missing more than half his original travel funds. Crawling off the bed, he crouched by the chests containing his, or rather, Traver's things. *I'll have to see what sort of replacements I can afford. And when Manolo gets here—when, not if,* I know *he'll come soon—I'll see if he can loan me a few more coins. At least until we get back to Family Tiger and I can repay him . . .*

The lamp on the bedside table lit with a single muttered word. That startled him into standing. A moment later, arms wrapped around him from behind, preventing him from completing his turn. Warm feminine fingers slid down his abdomen and into the nest of modesty feathers habit had made him retain around his groin.

Solyn pressed herself closer to the warmth of his back. Not that the summer night was cool, but the wind of their flight had chilled her a little. As had the things they had done. The things *she* had done, giving that other woman a chance to murder—*No, not murder,* she corrected herself firmly, caressing Kenyen through his feathers absently. *Justice. That poor woman, all those years she suffered. He's right. They're rabid dogs, and you just kill a rabid dog. Swift and clean. That's what we did . . . but I want to forget. And we did win, didn't we? At least, this fight?*

"I think we should do something else now. Don't you?" she asked.

Kenyen recognized some of the way she trembled and the slight hitch in her voice. *Her first brush with real violence, is my guess. They deserved it, and it was more merciful an end than the curs had earned, but I don't think Solyn is that far off from being a true Healer herself. Healers mend; they don't end. Which means my wife needs a distraction . . . just as we all once did, in the warband.*

It was his turn to play the earth-priestess, the comforter, the distraction needed. Turning around in her arms, he lifted her chin with one finger and dusted kisses over her brow, cheeks, and nose. Words from his own counseling came back to him. They applied to her, as they had applied to his younger self. "You were very brave today."

"But I didn't do much," she pointed out.

"You were willing to, and that's what matters," he reminded her.

For a moment, he debated just breaking them. A wicked thought changed his mind. Kissing his way up her cloth-covered thigh, he pressed his lips to her mound and patiently picked at the strings. A kiss, and a tug. A lick, and a pluck.

Frustration made her growl. Batting away his fingers, Solyn focused on unknotting the string herself. She succeeded on her third attempt, but only barely; the dampness along her gusset wasn't just from the teasing of his tongue. It was her turn to squirm free, giving her the room to kick off the garment. For a moment, they faced each other, both of them on their knees. Then he shifted forward, rubbing his cheek against her arm and purring very much like an overgrown cat.

Lifting her hand, she stroked her fingers through his long, soft hair. His head twisted under her touch, and a moment later his tongue flicked around the tip of her breast. Caught off guard, Solyn shuddered. He did it again, and again, before nuzzling his way down her belly to her thighs, where he nipped just enough to sting.

Her thigh jerked up and out reflexively. That was all the room Kenyen needed to twist onto his back. Hands reaching for her backside, he pulled her down, onto his mouth. She moaned, knees parting wider, sinking deeper into his nether-kiss. Teasing, flicking, suckling, he coaxed more of her personal honey from her depths until she shuddered in bliss.

Curling low, trembling with pleasure, Solyn didn't realize how close she was to his own groin until his shaft brushed her hair. He kept licking her folds, prolonging her desire. Determined to repay him, she cupped the turgid flesh, coaxed into bending close enough for a hungry kiss. He grunted and licked harder, tongue swirling and dipping in parody of the next step.

Parody wasn't enough. The hunger inside her needed to be filled. He clutched at her hips when she tried to pull away, growling and lapping harder, patently hungry for more. She stayed in place, his shaft half forgotten, until a second set of spasms rippled through her nerves. In thanks, Solyn swirled her tongue around his manhood, dampening the skin and encouraging it to stiffen further.

It wasn't easy, focusing through his own continuing attack, but she persevered until his head dropped back onto the bed, lungs heaving for air. Faint whimpers escaped him with each pant. Satisfied he wouldn't resist, Solyn crawled off him and turned around. His hands did reach for her, but when she came back, they helped her to straddle him.

That one-sided smile was back. Grasping his shaft, he teased her slick folds with rubbing strokes of the tip. Solyn rocked her hips, at first trying to find the right spot to seat him, to finally twine fully with him. The feelings evoked from his flesh rubbing against her pleasure nub made her rock her hips harder, until both sides of his mouth curled up in masculine smugness. She didn't care. It wasn't like his mouth, but it did feel good, and she wanted more.

Kenyen brought his other hand into play. Twisting his wrist, he teased her with his fingers, coating them. One slipped into her depths, following the rocking motion of her hips. A second soon followed, gently fluttering as they worked. There was only so much he could do in the height of passion to change the size of his shaft; it wasn't a matter of skill so much as focus, so he wanted her body as ready for him as possible. He was definitely ready for her.

She shivered and bit her lip, hips slowing, then shifting direction. Now it was his fingers she stroked. It was his thumb that rubbed her little peak. His touch that guided her passion. His fingers, which weren't enough. Pulling his hand free, Solyn grasped his shaft. Together, they guided it to the right spot, but the act of sinking onto it was all hers.

It was a tight fit, and it stung just getting the head inside. Both of them drew in a sharp breath at their joining. After a moment, Solyn sank a little lower. That stung as well. His thumb brushed lightly against her peak, distracting her. With teasing little touches, he coaxed her hips into circling. Into sliding up, then down. Each circle lengthened the depth of her strokes, until he grabbed her hips and thrust, impaling her fully.

Solyn gasped. His move was a dual shock of stinging pain and sweet fullness. The former faded after a few moments, letting her know that the latter was what her body craved. It helped that he held her tightly in place, letting her get used to the feeling, until she rocked her hips, rolling them a little.

Pleased she was no longer so tense, Kenyen resumed his teasing thumb strokes. She was hot, wet, and tight, the perfect sheath for his flesh. The trick now was to hold on to the reins of his own pleasure while giving her lead to rediscover hers. Moving his other hand up to her belly, he splayed his fingers over her skin, rubbing a little. Her stomach muscles trembled. They shuddered when he tickled his way up to the undersides of her breasts, and tightened when he rubbed one nipple.

The combination of circling strokes, identical in speed but opposite in location, brought her pleasure back in a rush. Biting her lip, Solyn moaned low and long. Her hips moved again. His thumbs stroked harder, faster, until she just had to move. This time, the stinging was negligible, enough to ignore.

Instinct made her thighs flex, made her rise and fall. Slowly at first, then with increasing speed, she found herself restrained only by the hand that shifted from her breast to her hip, keeping her from rising too far. Wanting more, she dropped harder with each stroke, wresting faint grunts from her lover. Her husband.

He couldn't take much more. Whether or not she had learned of this in her Healing lessons, Kenyen would have sworn on a Truth Stone that Solyn was an absolute natural. Her pace was the perfect tease, deep and strong, the kind that had him whimpering, but not fast enough.

Giving up some of his control, he grabbed her hips and braced his heels, thrusting up into her as soon as he had enough purchase to move hard and fast. It was her turn to whimper, her turn to brace herself with one hand on his chest, her turn to rub his nipple with her thumb. Her other hand slipped between her thighs, playing with herself.

The sight, the sound, the feel, and the smell of their lovemaking made his senses reel. Even the taste of her lingered in his mouth, driving him harder. She cried out, a wordless keen of pleasure that tensed every muscle before they released with a quiver. He let himself go as well, stroking into her heat.

No sooner had she slumped to his chest, slick with sweat and limp with pleasure, than he groaned in his own climax. A few final thrusts were all he needed to complete his pleasure. Relaxing into the bedding, he struggled for air. Not because she was heavy, though she wasn't a feather on his chest, but because he just needed to breathe.

After a while, she started to rouse. Kenyen shifted his arms, wrapping them around her body. Holding her close, he kept her on top of him. She mumbled something into his shoulder, then tried speaking again after a moment.

"Mmm . . . too heavy?" Solyn managed to ask coherently.

"No. Perfect," he replied.

She sighed and relaxed against him for a while, then shifted again. "Cold. Want blanket. And you."

Chuckling, he kissed her, then released her. When she slid off of him, he dredged up enough strength to pull down the covers and help her under them. He climbed in as well, pulling them up to his waist. She snuggled up against his side, pulling the covers a little higher up her back, and yawned. Then kissed his chest.

"So . . . since you have all the experience in these things," she murmured, peeking up at him. "How soon will we have enough energy to try that again?"

He grinned at the ceiling, glad she had enjoyed lovemaking enough to want more of it. "Oh, one or two times a day for me. More often for you."

"More often for me, but not for you?" she asked, pushing up onto an elbow. "Are you trying to hold back on me?"

"Only if you want me to spend all my sap at once and thus have me wither away from overuse," he retorted, amused by the turn of their conversation. "I'd have thought your Healing lessons included the fact that men can only climax so many times a day before it becomes painful."

"Well, I suppose Mother did mention something about that." She mock-sighed. "Whatever shall I do for twining, if I let you wither away? I suppose I'll have to ration it out . . . though it might help if I keep you well watered with my dew, since you seem to like it so much. *If* you give me a good reason to water you."

He tickled her for her impertinence, fingers drifting over her ribs. Squeaking, she tickled him back, finding his own sensitive spots. Sheer self-preservation had him pinning her to the bed with his greater strength, though she weakened him when she twined her legs around his hips.

"Plow me, farmer boy," Solyn whispered, teasing him about his pretend role as her best friend. "Plow me, and I'll water you all you want."

Half laughing, half groaning, Kenyen kissed her, giving in to her demands.

"My, but you two slept in rather late," Reina observed late the next morning, chopping fresh herbs for some posset decoction. "Even for the newly wedded."

Solyn blushed. Reaching for the gathering baskets, she barely refrained from smacking her forehead when she didn't find them.

They weren't under the table because they were somewhere to the south, smelling of lanolin and having carried two newly liberated bottoms on the hunt for a Magister who would listen to them. *I'll have to dig some of my thronai out from under my bed and go buy a couple more*, she realized. *Megra, down-valley, weaves that style a lot. She usually has a few spare ones for sale . . .*

"I trust the two of you won't be getting up that late as a habit?" her mother asked her.

"No, Mother. Um . . . not as a habit." She blushed harder, remembering just what had kept the two of them up so late. Not the rescuing of Traver and that woman, Parma, but the celebrating Solyn and Kenyen had done after their return home. "But we *are* newly wedded."

"Then I trust he pleased you? Or does the boy need a lecture on how to properly twine with a woman?" Reina asked, scooping the herbs on the flat of her blade into the broad funnel placed over one of her jars. "He won't be the first husband some new bride has sent my way."

Solyn feared her face would burst into flames. Struggling with her embarrassment, she finally managed to blurt, "He's just fine! He twines very well. And what little he didn't know, I . . . well, I showed him what *I* like. And he showed me. A lot. And he's a *man*, not a little boy." A hint of rebelliousness, pushing back her mortification, made her add tartly, "And *if* we sleep in late tomorrow morning, we'll have just and good cause for it—the same good cause that made *you* sleep in late when you married Father, I'm quite sure."

Her mother chuckled, taking no offense at her words. "Good . . . good . . . Do you know what happened to my gathering baskets? The flat oval ones with the big handles?"

"I couldn't say," she hedged, silently promising herself again to go buy her mother new ones. "Maybe I left them in the greenvein cave? I could go look, if you like."

"With your husband?" Reina asked, amusement coloring her tone. She gentled it after a moment, adding, "I thought you were done waxing the cheese with him."

This is not *the conversation I wanted to have, this morning*, Solyn thought, embarrassed once more. Breathing deeply, she mastered her mortification and took her mother's words at face value. Firmly at face value. "We still have to wrap the fresh rounds. It'll be a handful more days before they're done wicking out the last of the whey and are safe for waxing. At that point, it'll be just as well to have two people there, to make the work go faster. All hands will be needed for the full harvest, so the sooner we're done with that, the sooner we can help the rest of the holding. Erm, holdings. Traver still owes his kin his service, until Tellik is old enough to take over all of his chores."

"Mm-hmm," her mother agreed, reaching for the jug of distilling spirits. She grunted, lifting the large, heavy, glazed jar onto the table, then spoke. "You know, if I recall correctly, when your father and I waxed the cheese in that cave, that stone floor was awfully hard. You might want to take a couple of blankets."

"*Mother!*"

"I'm just saying . . ." Reina muttered, shrugging blithely. She relented with a glance at her glaring daughter. "Oh, fine. I apologize, and I'll drop the subject. If only to make sure your face doesn't pop like a blister, it's holding so much blood. Help me lift this thing, will you? It's a fresh bottle of mash-spirits, and it's a bit heavy for tilting and pouring accurately on my own. I'm making more of my wound cleanser, since we used up so much on that ax accident. After that, I'll want to prepare several batches of tea sacks for sunburns. People will be out and about in the harvest sun, and too many of them will forget to wear their shade hats."

Grateful the subject would be dropped, Solyn moved to help lift and support the jug. Her mother's words made her think about her own future. "Mother . . ." She stopped, almost saying the wrong name. Starting again, she said carefully, "My husband and I did a lot of talking, last night."

"Oh? I trust this isn't another euphemism," Reina added, carefully filling the smaller jar with the strong-smelling brew. She quickly capped the jar with a piece of cork and pulled the next bottle over. "I promised I'd drop that subject."

Solyn rolled her eyes. *So much for dropping it.* She supported the jar as her mother guided its contents into the next glazed bottle. "I meant, we talked about the future. He wants me to go to a proper school. At some point, that is. He doesn't know what he'll do in town, but he does want to go with me."

"I thought you were firmly set against leaving the valley and leaving me . . . all alone in my efforts as Healer," her mother hedged carefully, helping her set the bottle upright again.

"I think things are looking up. Or will be, soon," she added as her mother gave her a sharp look. Solyn smiled at her mother but didn't elaborate. She didn't dare. The herb-room had windows that looked out on the broad yard that connected a handful of the holding's homes and outbuildings, plus her father's forge.

It was the closest their part of the valley had to a village square, and anyone could be out there during the day, walking past or working within hearing range. Only when Traver—and now her Shifterai husband—had been with her, had she been able to tell when no one was near. Kenyen, however, had gone off to tend to Traver's chores, wearing Traver's face.

Thinking of him and his ring made her think of the feel of it, last night. It had been subtle; the pain of her first coupling and the newness of all the various sensations had distracted her. By the second one, the pain had faded enough that she could focus on identifying just what she liked or didn't like about twining. The ring . . . had been an interesting sensation. It wasn't large, but it was a distinctly different sort of hardness from the rigidity of his manhood, and she kind of liked . . .

". . . Are you done gathering wool?"

Solyn came back to her surroundings with a jump. She blushed, realizing her mother had been trying to get her attention. "Yes, Mother. You, uh, wanted something?"

Her mother nodded at the heavy jug. "Decant that into a smaller set of jugs, will you? I'd like this batch of mash-spirits to last longer than the previous one, and the more air it comes in contact with, the faster it'll go sour. And no drinking it," Reina added tartly. "You're drunk enough as it is on the spirits of your wedding night."

Blushing, she reached for empty, clean bottles. "No more so than *you* were, Mother, I am quite sure."

The Healer chuckled. "I *know* I'm sure."

"When you're done with that, Traver, I want you to take all the scythes and sickles up to the forge. I'll give you some coins to pay Ysander," Ysal Trud Hen, Traver's father, told the shapeshifted Kenyen. "I'll not be beholden to the man even if we're now kin. We're wealthy enough to pay and proud of it . . . but if he's busy, you use the grinding stones yourself. We'll need those tools sharp for the harvest."

"Yes, Father," he agreed, not looking up from the cart harness he was mending. Seated on a bench outside the family home, a broad, conical sun hat shading his head, he set another pair of stitches through the small holes he had punched in the straps.

Traver still "owed" his family's holding his efforts for the next three or so years. Kenyen sincerely hoped he wouldn't be stuck here that long. As nice and friendly as most of these Corredai were, being stuck here, pretending to be Traver Ys Ten, would mean that the

Mongrels were still on the loose. That would mean his wife and new kin would still be in danger from them.

Traver's father lingered. Sensing he had something more to say, Kenyen looked up politely.

"You've done well, boy," Ysal told him gruffly. "Making a wife out of your friend. You've been a bit strange since your fall, but . . . you've grown up some. It's about time you took on some responsibilities of your own. Any chance you'd convince that girl to move into our holding?"

Kenyen could guess from Ysal's tentatively hopeful tone that he was more interested in how the holding's standing would rise in the valley, having its own on-hand Healer. He also could guess what Solyn would have to say about that. "She needs more training, Father. We've been talking about going to a city, one with a Healer's school."

"Would you go with her?" Ysal asked, his tone neutral.

"Yes. I'll find some work while she's studying. If nothing else, I'd hire out as a laborer for the nearest fields," he said. The words were true, too; Kenyen knew enough about farming from Family Tiger's obligatory farming year every so often back home that he could hire out as a laborer. He just hoped it wouldn't come to that; he was a man of action, even if he was still learning how to think through the mess entangling him.

"You'd leave us short one hand?" Ysal scoffed. "Just to follow 'er to a city?"

"A husband and wife should be together, whatever may come," he stated, knotting the last of his stitches. "And she does need more training before she's ready to work on her own. Besides, if the holding's so prosperous that you can pay to have the blacksmith sharpen the scythes, you can pay the wages of a laborer to replace me when I go."

At that bit of factually delivered impertinence, Ysal chuckled. "Yes, you've grown up, boy."

Snipping the waxed cord, Kenyen examined his work on the cart harness one last time and nodded, satisfied by his repair. He might not be the real Traver, but he wouldn't let the other man's family down. "This should hold a good long time." Tucking the leather-working tools back into their pouch, he stood up. "I'll go get the barrow cart and load up the tools."

"When you're done with that, you bring her over for supper," Traver's father ordered him as he headed for the barn. "You may be a part of her family now, but she's a part of ours, too."

"I will," he promised.

It was no surprise to Solyn that her aunt Hylin was the first to bring gossip to their door. Her aunt had been doing that for as long as she could remember. That she brought it so early in the morning, when Solyn and her face-changed husband were still hauling in the second set of water pails after breakfast, that was a surprise. Usually her aunt didn't have anything juicy until at least midday.

"Reina? You won't *believe* what happened!" the older woman called out, bustling into the house ahead of the two. "That Tarquin boy? Remember how he was all after Solyn, and then moped around after she got married?"

"I'd have said sulked, not moped, but yes, I remember," Reina countered calmly. She lifted a hand from the tub of dishes she was cleaning and gestured at the cistern, addressing her daughter and son-in-law. "Pour most of it in there, you two. I'd also like the boiling kettle refilled and the fire stoked for the day. You'll need more clean cloths for the cheeses, after all." She glanced at her sister. "So? What about Tarquin?"

"Well, from what I've heard, he's been missing since that night, and *all day* yesterday. We all thought he was just off twining with some girl in the tea fields, looking for consoling," Hylin added dismissively, "but he didn't even come back last night! And apparently this morning Tunric woke up early, found the boy missing, and has been tearing up and down the valley, knocking on doors and demanding to know which 'harlot' his boy's been twining with all day!"

Solyn blushed, though not as much for her aunt's choice of words. A glance at Kenyen, wearing her best friend's face and body, showed he was keeping his own expression shuttered. Wordlessly, they took their time filling the water tank and the kettle, by unspoken agreement wanting to linger and hear whatever other news there might be.

Her mother, calm as ever, rolled her eyes. "I'm sure *that* caused a stir," Reina said. "They may have been twining with the boy, but that doesn't make them harlots. Their families won't be too happy to hear such language aimed at their girls."

"Oh, well, he stirred up quite a few of them, barging in barely at dawn, riding his horse up and down the valley until it was lathered," Hylin agreed.

"So which girl was it?" Reina asked.

"That's just it; nobody knows! Every girl in the Nespah Valley seems to be accounted for. When he finally realized that, Serilla told me that Tunric swore up a storm and took off down the valley, whipping his horse and headed for who knows where," Hylin gossiped. "Such a fine new mare, too. It'd be a shame if he broke and foundered the poor beast so soon after buying her—I hear the mare was traded all the way from the Plains, so you know it's good horseflesh."

A muscle clenched in her husband's jaw. Solyn had already heard about how the Mongrels had demanded the horse as a "tribute" and could guess the rest of his thoughts. Even if locally her fellow Corredai didn't know much about the Shifterai, the horses of the Shifting Plains were known for their quality, said to be second only to the ones raised on the Centa Plains somewhere far to the east.

The care with which the Shifterai treated and raised those horses was also known. It didn't take her much effort to connect everything together. Silently, she nudged him into finishing the task of stirring the coals and adding more wood to the fire. Her aunt's gossip turned to speculation on when one of the younger women would finally have her baby, and her mother gave measured, experienced answers about babies coming in their own due time. The interesting part of the morning was over.

Pouring the last of the water into the kettle, Solyn followed her husband outside. But they weren't alone, out there. One of her other cousins lifted his scythe from one of her father's grindstones and called out, "Hey, Solyn! Did you hear the news about Tarquin?"

"That he ran off somewhere yesterday?" she called back. "Aunt Hylin just told Mother all about it."

"Do you think he's upset you didn't marry him?"

She rolled her eyes. "Considering how often I turned him down, he had no right to be—mind what you're doing with that blade!"

He lifted his chin in acknowledgment and went back to work. Solyn followed Kenyen partway down the path toward his family's holding, until they were away from prying ears, though not prying eyes. Embracing him, she whispered, "Do you think we can get your horse back?"

That was not what Kenyen expected her to say. He chuckled and hugged her closer. "Maybe. I'd like to, for sure, but I'm more worried about Tunric getting nervous and making some foolish, potentially dangerous move against us before we have reinforcements."

"I'm worried about that, too," she murmured, kissing his throat. "I'll try to study some more spells when I have a spare moment. Hopefully no one gets careless and needs an extra Healer today." She hugged him extra hard, then relaxed. "I'll see you after you've done your morning chores."

He lifted her chin, brushed his lips over hers, then kissed her deeply. When they parted, it was with a sigh from her and a soft groan from him. ". . . At least I have something to look forward to today, besides mucking out goat stalls."

She blushed, thinking of the coming night. Last night, their lovemaking had started much earlier, allowing them to get up at a reasonable hour this morning. Watching him head across the valley, she sighed. *Tonight, we'll not want to exhaust ourselves. Maybe not even make love at all, even if we're both looking forward to it. We'll want to be vigilant.*

I just wish I knew *if my paper birds made it to their targets—and, stupid me, I should've sent one with Traver! Or rather, two, one for "we found the Magister" and one for "we're in trouble" . . . though I didn't know it'd be a "we" until we rescued that poor woman. At least she's free, now,* Solyn consoled herself, turning back up the path toward home. *Hopefully we can find and free more of their victims. Or . . . or at least tell their families what really happened to them . . .*

Solyn wasn't overly devout. She prayed to Cora during holy days and festivals, but rarely outside of those moments. As she walked back up the path, she prayed now. *Goddess of Mountains and Valleys, thank You for the glorious luck we had in Traver running across Kenyen, allowing us to free him before he could be killed. Please, help us to stop the rest of these madmen? You know I don't ask You for much, but we could really use some help in wrapping up this matter . . .*

There was no reply, of course. Cora could have Manifested, as in physically appeared beside her—as all gods could, if the need were great enough, or at the deity's divine whim—but Solyn didn't need that kind of help. *Just a bit more of good luck on our side will do, that's all I'm asking You.*

Kenyen half-feared, half-expected a confrontation with the Mongrels. The trick with the lanolin might disguise some of it, but not all of it. His scent could be explained away from previous visits, but Solyn had never been to the cottage before. Of course, most of the shifters didn't come in close, daily contact with her, so it was possible her scent wasn't that familiar. But he did expect some sort of confrontation, particularly after Tunric had raced off to go looking for his so-called son.

He just didn't expect it the moment he descended for breakfast.

He stopped on the next to last step, staring at the sight of Zellan holding on to an upset-looking Luelyn on his lap, one arm wrapped around her torso and the other hand clamped tight over her mouth, fingers damp from her tears. Beyond the two of them, Reina was being held on the cushion-strewn settee by a shifter he only vaguely remembered from the bonfire night, while Ysander was being held next to the hearth by a third. Each adult had a knife at their throat. Thumps, rustlings, and a faint crash could be heard from somewhere beyond the front hall, no doubt a result of the herb-room being ransacked.

Before Kenyen could do or say anything, Solyn descended the stairs behind him. She stopped and stared as well. Zellan lifted his chin, though whether to signal Kenyen to back off and not attack like the real Traver would, or if he meant for the younger man to grab Solyn, Kenyen didn't know. One of the other two called out.

"Tunric!" the one holding Reina snapped. "He's awake!"

Kenyen descended the last step and rested his hands on his hips. Shaped like Traver, wearing Traver's clothes, he knew from the way Ysander and Reina narrowed their eyes in sudden suspicion that his pose was very un-Traver-like. It wasn't meant for them, though. The power and confidence implied in his stance, along with a touch of impatience, was meant for the Mongrel curs who had invaded the house.

"About time you woke up, boy," Tunric growled, coming into the parlor from the front hall. He stalked up to Kenyen and slapped him. "You're Gods-be-damned *useless*! Like that boy of mine! You've had all that time in this household to find the Gods-damned thing, and you're *useless*!"

Thankfully, the blow came without claws. The force of it did rock him a little, but aside from a sting and a slight bit of bruising, Kenyen wasn't harmed. Ignoring the throbbing, he asked, "What do you mean, useless? I'm here, aren't I?"

"But you never *found* it!" Tunric accused him, pointing a finger at Kenyen. "I *knew* I should've killed you, the moment I saw you!"

"*You* never told me *what* I was supposed to find!" Kenyen lifted his own hand and poked the older man in the chest, hard enough to make him flinch. "*You* kept it a Gods-be-damned secret! That means it's *your* damned fault I couldn't find whatever 'it' is! So, unless *you* don't even know what you're looking for, *what* in the flaming Netherhells *am* I supposed to be finding in this place?"

"You're working with *them*?" Ysander demanded. He tried to lunge forward, glaring at Kenyen. The Mongrel shifter holding him increased his muscles, making the linen of his tunic creak with the strain. Subsiding, Ysander continued to glare at the Shifterai by the stairs.

Solyn realized she needed to react, too. Affecting a hint of confusion and rising accusation in her voice, she asked, "Traver, what's going on? You know what's going on, don't you?"

Reaching back, Kenyen caught her by the arm, dragging her down the last few steps. A spin wrapped his arm around her throat, pulling her against him at an awkward angle. He didn't actually hold her hard, but she did pretend to choke, and "clawed" at his arm, as if the pressure on her neck was too much.

"A *good* wife," he growled, "doesn't question her husband." A quick flex of his arm muscles produced more mock-choking sounds. At least, Kenyen hoped they were faked. He looked back at Tunric, who was smirking. "Now, since you seem bent on ruining my secret, *what* are you looking for? And make it quick. I haven't had breakfast yet, and it's been a very long time since I had someone to chew on."

Tunric narrowed his dark eyes at the order. He did move, though, turning to face Reina. The Healer was glaring stoically at him, unmoved by the blade at her throat. "Greensteel," he growled. "The antithesis of that accursed bluesteel, which marks us all. The one thing which can un-scar our bodies, and allow us to completely blend in wherever we want to go. And *this* bitch and her cur-pup know how to make it!"

Reina frowned at the first insult, but Ysander only blinked in confusion at his. Kenyen decided to enlighten them as to the slander. "He means you're not only the lowest of the low, being a cur, you're at the bottom of all hierarchies, following along in the wake of a woman, of all things."

That news only received another bemused blink.

The man holding the blacksmith snorted. "Too stupid to know when he's been insulted. Can I cut 'im, now?"

A muffled wail interrupted any answer their leader might have made. Luelyn sobbed against the hand smothering her mouth, fresh tears trickling onto her cheeks. Caught in her husband's fake stranglehold, Solyn quickly started humming. It was the same tune she had used the other night, with the same soothing energies pouring out of her. This time, she didn't just touch one distraught female, her sister, but extended it to the Mongrel shifters in the room.

It was all Kenyen could do to prevent a sneeze, at that. He even reshaped the interior of his nostrils, trying to quell the damnable itch her magics stirred. Half a dozen tries, plus some thick-scaled skin, cut off both his sense of smell and the itch, save for its after-effects. Eyes watering, he watched some of Tunric's belligerent tension ease. Some, but not all.

Thankfully, none of the other four shifters looked inclined to sneeze. That did, however, make him think of an alternate plan to distract the Mongrels in their quest. *Now to find the right moment to tell them.*

"No. Not yet," Tunric muttered. "We still need something that'll remove our permanent scars—and will you shut her up?" he added, turning to scowl at Kenyen. His gaze strayed briefly to the humming woman. "She's beginning to annoy me."

"Why?" Kenyen countered. "She's keeping the brat quiet."

"It's annoying me, that's why!" Tunric snapped. "Either you shut her up, you damn pup, or I'll slit her throat! *She* doesn't know the secret to making it!"

Solyn jumped at that threat, losing the thread of her hastily cobbled spell. She recovered fast, though. A quick, hard look at her sister, and Luelyn widened her eyes. A heartbeat later, the little girl wailed again, this time even louder and more frenetically.

"Oh, for sodomizing a Netherdemon—shut up, you little brat, or I'll tear out your throat *myself*!" Tunric ordered the young girl. She shrieked at that thought and sobbed wildly.

"You do *that*, you Netherdemon *spawn*, and I will pull your body to pieces with my powers!" Reina snarled, losing her calm at the threat to her child. She grabbed wildly at the arms holding her prisoner, forcing the shifter to actually struggle to contain her. "By Cora, I *swear* I will!"

THIRTEEN

"Oh, dear. I think you got the little bitch mad," Kenyen quipped, unable to resist the opportunity to rattle the criminal shifter even more. "You know, it's really not a good idea, making a mage foreswear her Healer's Oaths *not* to do harm."

Solyn quickly began humming again, and Luelyn obediently quieted down again. She extended her spell toward her mother, but only enough to help lull the man holding her into relaxing again. Back aching from her position, she shifted a little to take some of the strain off her spine. Thankfully, Kenyen moved his arm to accommodate the subtle change, or it really would have been pressing against her throat.

"As for *you*, young pup—" Tunric snarled, whirling to face him. Kenyen cut him off before he could say anything else.

"—*I* suggest you shut up, *old dog*, and let this 'young pup' teach you a new trick. Now that I *know* what you're after, I can actually *help* you," Kenyen countered. "All *you* have to do is shut up and *listen*."

"Solyn, you didn't tell him," the blacksmith muttered, staring at what he could see of his still humming eldest daughter, given she was on the far side of her husband from him. "Tell me you didn't!"

Tunric seized on that news, his scowl switching to a fierce grin. "Oh, so you *did* get some news out of your 'fresh meat' after all?"

Affecting a smirk, Kenyen mock-kissed his wife on the head. "Plow a bitch good and hard, and she'll tell you anything you want."

Solyn growled at that, but only because she figured it was expected. The two of them had fallen into an unspoken accord on trying to treat Kenyen as if he were a real Mongrel shifter, instead of an honorable one. His words provoked a coarse chuckle from the other shifters in the room. Figuring they were sufficiently distracted, she resumed her soft humming, putting more of her magic than her voice into her spell.

"So? Where's the blade, boy?" Tunric ordered impatiently.

Kenyen rolled his eyes. "It's *not* a blade. The knife is just a decoy. A distraction. *Any* knife will do."

Tunric narrowed his eyes at that. "What do you mean by that?"

"The power to heal scarlessly doesn't lie in steel, whether it's green or red or purple," Kenyen lied. Behind Tunric, he could see the eyes of his in-laws widening in comprehension of what he was actually doing. Only he and Solyn could see, however, because the other shifters were looking at him. He affected a slight but smug smile. "The *real* power lies in the *cheese*."

All four Mongrels blinked. Zellan frowned at Kenyen, his hand loosening a bit more over Luelyn's mouth. Wisely, the young girl didn't bite him or try to escape. "The *cheese*?" he asked. "What do you mean, the power is in the cheese? *What* cheese?"

"Greenvein, of course." Behind his primary audience's back, he could see Reina narrowing her eyes in thought. So did Tunric.

"I've *had* greenvein, boy," he growled. Reaching up, he tugged on the braid at the top of his scalp, reshaping the locks free so that he could pull down the flap of skin guarding his double-stroked Banished mark. "Do you see *unmarked* skin, here?"

"Did you ever eat greenvein while that particular scar was wounded?" Kenyen countered calmly.

Tunric scoffed at that. "You expect me to *believe* this? That eating *cheese* will remove a bluesteel scar from my head?"

With a brief shake of his head, Kenyen shrunk his hair down to stubble, unweaving the braid that had been holding his bangs out of the way ever since encountering the Mongrel holding on to little Luelyn Ys Rei. He tipped his head and smirked. "Do you see a bluesteel scar on mine?"

Mouth sagging, the man pretending to be Tunric Tel Vem stared at Kenyen's head. In the near-silence following the younger shifter's claim, broken only by Solyn's faint humming, they all heard a knock at the front door of the house. Whoever it was knocked again. Heart skipping a beat, Kenyen managed another tight smile.

"*I'll* get that. This is now my house, too, after all. All of you, stay *quiet*, so I can get whoever it is to go away. Come along, *dearest*," he growled, flexing the muscles around Solyn's throat. She gurgled as if he had actually tightened his grip. "Say one wrong word, make one wrong look, and I'll eat your little sister alive, feet first. She looks *tasty*, doesn't she?"

Solyn hastily put a bit more magic behind her humming as Luelyn started to cry for real. Since she was still blanketing the others, Tunric merely nodded, letting them move. Shuffling at his side, she righted herself as her husband's arm shifted to her shoulders, holding her close. A second shake of his head regrew and re-braided his hair into curly, Traver-style locks.

He nudged the door to the parlor almost completely shut as they entered the front hall. But when she drew in a breath to speak, Kenyen quickly lifted a finger to her lips, silencing her, then tapped it against his ear. That ear briefly grew long and large like a horse's before returning to normal again, silent warning that the Mongrels behind them were no doubt doing the same so as to eavesdrop on them. Releasing Solyn, he opened the front door just as whoever it was knocked again.

Manolo Zel Jav, middle-aged Shifterai of the South Paw Warband, Family Tiger, politely lowered his hand, smiled, and asked, "I've been told you sell the best cheese in the land?"

Kenyen quickly flung his finger to his own lips, silencing his friend before Manolo could say *which* kind of cheese. Manolo narrowed his dark brown eyes, giving both of them a wary look. Considering Kenyen still looked like the absent Traver, he couldn't blame his friend for being cautious.

"Yes, we do. Or at least, we like to think so," he stated calmly. A glance showed three others in view: Ashallan Nur Am, the lead princess of their expedition; Anaika Ell Tu, the other princess from Family Lion; and Bellar Sil Quen. The shifter whose brother had been exiled from the Plains, and who had warned him to keep the members of Kenyen's expedition away from the back of the cave, where the remains of the original, true Tunric Tel Vem had been hidden.

There were also two members of the local holding in sight, mainly his nosy aunt-in-law and one of the younger cousins, each poking their head out their front door in curiosity at the visitors. Ignoring them, Kenyen quickly unbuttoned his tunic, pulling aside the front panel. It wasn't easy, speaking and drawing on his flesh in dark-hued scales, but he did his best.

"We have several types of cheeses for sale, at this holding. Soft ones, fresh ones, hard ones, crumbly ones . . . do you have a particular type in mind?" he asked, while on his chest he painstakingly wrote, *Four Mongrels, three hostages*, and the words, *Side doors, upper windows. Go.*

Manolo blinked. So did Ashallan. She narrowed her eyes and dismounted from her horse. A ripple of flesh left her clothes in a puddle on the ground. Launching upward in hawk form, she flew off to the side of the house. Off to one side, Hylin gasped; to the other, the cousin gaped.

Bellan swung out of his saddle, catching the reins for Ashallan's horse, then hastily grabbed at Anaika's. The other princess had dismounted as well, but she didn't take the form of a hawk. Instead, she shifted into the shape of a lioness and headed for the other side of the building. Plains-bred as they were, none of the horses snorted as she slunk off, ears pricked forward and tail lashing in hunt-mode.

Recovering from the shock, Manolo smiled ingratiatingly and said, "Oh, we've heard of several delightful cheeses. There's one called 'golden delight' . . . and 'mautzoa' . . . and 'greenvein.' Do you have any of these?"

"Ah, we don't have mautzoa on hand," Solyn offered. "We could make some by the end of the day, though. It's a fresh cheese. Perhaps if you came back later?"

"Yes, we haven't even broken our fast yet," Kenyen said. "We could also fetch you some greenvein by then."

"I suppose we could wait—could we wait with you, perhaps?" Manolo asked.

"I'm afraid not. The youngest of the family has developed a fever," Kenyen lied smoothly, rebuttoning his tunic. "We don't want it to spread to the rest of the holding."

"Oh, well, we wouldn't want that, no," the older shifter agreed mildly. He questioned Kenyen with his gaze, glancing to either side. Kenyen shook his head subtly.

"Feel free to make use of the benches," he offered politely. "Or even draw water from the well. When we have eaten, we will come back out and discuss quantities and prices and start making the mautzoa for you."

"Cora bless you," Manolo said, though he lifted his gaze toward the rising sun, rather than to the peaks of the mountains around them.

"Goddess bless you," he returned politely. His fellow Shifterai bowed and moved off to the side. Kenyen nudged Solyn inside ahead of him and shut the front door. Pasting on a smile, he grabbed Solyn again and nudged open the inner door, dragging her back into the sitting room. "Good news! We have customers waiting to buy some greenvein cheese. I can easily head down to the storage cave and bring up several *extra* rounds."

Zellan stood, setting the little girl on her feet. "Wrong. *You* will stay here. I know the cave in question, so *I'll* fetch the cheeses. Here, Tunric, you hold the little bitch-pup."

Something slithered out of the kitchen. It paused on the threshold next to the hearth, lifted its head toward the stairwell, then darted forward. Kenyen, recognizing the grass viper and his silent signal, grabbed Solyn and ducked down. The serpent struck the foot of the shifter holding Reina on the settee just as a tawny shape leaped down from the stairs, striking Tunric in the chest.

Pushing his wife away, he rolled into Zellan's legs, knocking down the shapeshifter. As much as he feared for Solyn's safety, he had to trust she could protect herself with her magics. Her little sister had no such protection. Pain lashed up his side as the older shifter reacted, lashing out with claws. The piercing shriek of a hawk and the pain-filled cries of the Mongrel holding his father-in-law mixed with the frightened screams of his young sister-in-law.

A hard kick toppled the older shifter, and a wrenching twist allowed him to grab and fling Luelyn through the door into the front hall. The throw was awkward, considering he was rolling across the floor. One shoulder seam of his tunic ripped from growing his arms to the right length and muscle mass for the job, but it did get Luelyn out of the way. Righting himself with another twist, he shifted everything back to proportion. That stemmed the worst of the bleeding from the gashes in his side.

The feel of Solyn casting a spell, or maybe it was one of her mother's, triggered a hearty sneeze in him. Doubling over with the explosion, Kenyen felt Zellan's second vicious, clawed swipe catch in his braid, instead of his throat. Sidestepping, he ducked his head low, pulling the older shifter down by his own hair, and heaved up under the man's abdomen with double-strength legs. More stitches popped and gave way, since the trousers were more fitted than the gathered style favored on the Plains, but there wasn't time for him to shift out of the garments. Fingers warped into talons, skin hardened into thick, protective scales, he gouged and stabbed at his opponent.

Across the room, Ysander had grabbed the fire tongs and was smacking his own former captor while the hawk had shifted, revealing Ashallan clad in feathers and striking with claws. Reina was flushed and wide-eyed, grappling with an overgrown serpent, her hands glowing with power.

Ashallan, the lioness, had changed forms yet again, this time into an amalgamation of woman and bearlike beast, dodging Tunric's own brutish claw swipes. Zaps of light burst from Solyn's jabbing finger, like miniature, concentrated sun rays without the clouds. The serpent holding her mother flinched and hissed with each smoldering strike.

Zellan slithered around Kenyen, readjusting mass and shape to try to gain leverage of his own. Out of the corner of his eye, Kenyen saw the Mongrel open his jaws beast-wide, huge fangs sprouting. He protected his shoulder with shell-like scales and tensed, building up enough muscles to throw the man at the nearest wall.

"What in Cora's sweet . . . ?" a new, male voice exclaimed from the front entry. "*Omina dormud!*"

Deep blue light washed through the house. Several bodies slumped insensate to the floor, without even the time to sneeze.

Flesh reshaped, knocked out cold by the spell; some of that flesh still bled. Some of it stood on two legs and blinked. Both Solyn and her mother stared at the fallen bodies and hesitantly relaxed, their personal shields dissipating the energies of the mass-sleep spell swirling around them. Whirling to face the entrance, Solyn eyed the man staring at the mess in her family's sitting parlor.

"Oh, thank the Goddess . . ." she breathed, panting from the adrenaline of the fight. The man was clad in an ornately embroidered tunic. She recognized a few of the rune-symbols among those stitchings from her mage books, though she didn't know what they meant. "Please, tell me you're the Magister that Traver Ys Ten flew off to find?"

"I am," the mage stated. Behind him, several armored men bearing the blue and brown tabards of the King's Guard cautiously picked their way into the house. "With the ability to shield against my spell, that would make you . . . Solyn Ys Rei, budding young mage, correct? And the woman behind you would be the Healer Reina?" At Solyn's nod, he introduced himself with a little bow. "I am Magister Caros Nii Veth, and I am here to take all of these shapeshifters prisoner for interrogation."

"Oh, no! Not all of them," Solyn hastily interrupted, fluttering her hands in negation. She explained quickly as he lifted one brow. "Only *four* of them, if you please. The ones with the Banished scars on their heads. They're all the criminal shifters, the face-stealers, the ones who call themselves members of Family Mongrel. The rest are real Shifterai, from the Plains. They all came to Correda to track down the Mongrel shifters when they realized their outcast criminals were banding together to cause trouble for us. Oh, and the extra man by the hearth is my father. He's not any sort of a shifter."

"You mean *five* of them are Mongrels," Reina corrected her daughter. She eyed the bodies on the floor, three of which were naked, and flopped her hands. "I can only say for sure that the two women *aren't* our attackers, but rather our attempted saviors. I wouldn't think Tunric or his bastards would stoop to treating women that way if they actually were members of their group."

"No, Mother, I do mean *four* of them," Solyn corrected. Kenyen's form was the one she was sure of. Picking her way over the two bodies between them, she crouched by his half-clothed form. His side was a little bloodied, but a quick check showed the wounds were no longer seeping. "*This* one is Kenyen Sin Siin, Clan Cat, Family Tiger. He was asked by Traver in a rather hastily made arrangement to *pretend* to be Banished from the Plains . . . and to pretend to *be* Traver.

"The Mongrels guessed that Traver—the real one—knew something about them, and hunted him down when he tried to flee to get help." She looked up at the Magister, who was studying her with a shuttered but attentive expression, absorbing her words. "Kenyen found Traver on the way here, because *his* people had found a body they believed to be the *real* Tunric Tel Vem long dead in a cave somewhere to the north, with a message giving the identity and location of its former owner.

"They didn't have more than a few minutes together before *that* one . . . um . . . I think it was that one," Solyn said, pointing at one of the men nearest the door, "the one pretending to be the mine laborer, Zellan Fin Don, attacked Traver. It was all Kenyen could do to pretend to be a fellow criminal, and convince the Mongrels to let him pretend in turn to be Traver, to infiltrate *my* family for our greatest secret."

"*Solyn!*" her mother snapped. "Don't you dare!"

Pushing to her feet, Solyn faced her mother. "No, Mother. I *do* dare. I'm tired of hiding the truth. I did a lot of thinking over the last couple of days, and Traver is right. People *need* to be told. The *only* way to make us safe is to spread this secret far and wide—Mother, the *good* we can do with greensteel, to heal wounds that even the best of spells cannot keep from scarring, that far outweighs a few rogue shifters carving off their Banished scars!"

"If they carve off those scars with greensteel," Reina argued back, "they could become anyone! They could even try to become the King!"

"Maybe they *could* try, but even after a dozen years of practicing, they *couldn't* hide their true nature," she retorted, pointing at the slumbering body in question. "We all saw how Tunric—what we thought of as the real one—how he turned from a good man and a good master of his mines into a heartless, callous, woman-hating *cur*. And you saw how *Kenyen*, portraying Traver, couldn't hide the fact that he *is* a good man at heart. Everyone's been remarking on how, when 'Traver' fell into the ravine, he may have lost his memory but he gained a lot of maturity and good sense? Well, that's because *my husband* has that maturity and good sense."

Reina planted her hands on her hips, staring down her daughter. "And did you *know* he wasn't Traver when you married him?"

Proudly, Solyn lifted her head. "Yes, I did. And it was by *my* choice, fully knowing who he is, and the mess we were in, that I chose to wed him. He's a *good* man, Mother. Which you'll see for yourself, if you bother to open your eyes and get to know him."

"And the real Traver? Where is he?" Reina demanded next.

A male voice cleared itself by the front hall. Both women looked that way, and spotted the real Traver Ys Ten in the doorway, peering around the shorter but still imposing figure of the Magister.

"Um, right here. And yes, I know she married someone else . . . and if Solyn's happy, and Kenyen makes her happy, then I'm happy for her, too. For both of them." He blushed, rubbed at the back of his neck, and shrugged. "The whole betrothal thing was just a ruse to get Tarquin to back down and stop bugging her. Which was a good thing, since it ended up part of the whole tangle of everything that led to Solyn and this Shifterai fellow saving my life, rather than leaving me to die at these Mongrels' hands."

Solyn smiled at him. She craned her neck, trying to see past both men. "Is Parma with you? I hope she's safe."

The Magister answered her question. "Milady Parma is safe in the protection of a fellow Magister, back at the capital. Her testimony, and specifically her memories, are being examined under spell, both truthful and temporal, in the hopes of getting clear identities of all the shapeshifter invaders she knows about. His Majesty has already awarded her a pension as a war heroine in compensation for her suffering . . . though we will be discussing with the Shifterai how to fund her pension," he added dryly, "given that it was their habit of Banishing their criminals in our direction that started this mess."

"How did you get here so fast?" Solyn asked, glancing between him and Traver.

"We mirror-Gated here to the Nespah Valley, of course, to begin the cleanup of those 'Mongrels' we do know about." Magister Caros nodded at the body slumbering at Solyn's feet. "If this man is indeed the same Kenyen Sin Siin mentioned in her and Traver's testimonies, then he will be set free. After he is questioned, of course. I presume he can corroborate the identities of his fellow Shifterai, if you cannot, young lady?"

"Uh . . . I only saw the Shifterai briefly at the front door a few minutes ago, myself, but yes. He does know his companions," Solyn agreed. "I enchanted paper birds with messages he wrote to them, which is why they finally showed up this morning—we weren't sure if Traver would reach you in time, Milord Magister."

Magister Caros smiled wryly. "Well, bureaucracy has been known to move slowly at times. But not when such serious injustices and crimes are at stake. Stand aside, and I'll awaken your husband.

He'll have to be questioned with one of my Truth Wands, but given the testimony so far, he should be able to confirm it and exonerate himself and his true companions quickly enough."

"Of course." Bowing, she stepped out of his way. Edging toward the front door, she reached Traver's side. Impulsively, she hugged him. "I'm glad you're safe," she whispered, while the Magister crouched to begin his counterspell. "And *very* glad you arrived when you did. I think I knocked one of them out with one of my own spells, but it was very hard to concentrate when everyone started fighting."

Traver nodded, hugging her back. "We were a bit distracted when Luelyn raced out of here screaming just as we arrived—don't worry, she's run off to your aunt Hylin's. *She* looked positively *livid* with curiosity, wanting to know what's been going on over here. The King's Guards are keeping her away for the moment, but you know how long that'll last."

She sighed in relief, then chuckled weakly. "I'm glad some things are still the same."

Magister Caros held the interrogations outside, under a set of shade tents hastily set up by the curious valley residents. This was done, he explained in a voice enchanted to be heard by all who gathered in the broad yard around the forge, so that they could see the King's Justice being done openly, and to let the truth of the matter be known to all so that no false speculations could proliferate.

Ysander, the cut on his neck healed by his wife, only had bluesteel barstock on hand. The Magister, in a show of magic, awakened each shapeshifter and imprisoned him or her in two spells. One that bound their hands and feet together in glowing gold lines—making Kenyen sneeze repeatedly when they were applied to him—and a second one that confined each of them to their natural shapes.

Under the glowing crystalline tip of the Truth Wand held over their hands, the two Shifterai Princesses—hastily re-dressed in their sleep by Solyn and her mother, along with the male shifter, Manolo—explained why they had come with their warband into the Correda Mountains. Ashallan added that most of the others had scattered to track down rumors of yet more residents who had, at one point or another, started acting very much unlike themselves, turning arrogant, callous, even cruel toward those around them. She stated that the Queen of the Shifterai wished to stop the wrongs caused by their former, expelled citizens, and how her band was prepared to cooperate with the Corredai government in doing so.

The Magister duly noted down that information and moved on to her companions. When he came to Kenyen, and Kenyen relayed how he had taken over the life of Traver Ys Ten, the residents of Nespah Valley shouted and glared, until Caros shouted back. His was backed by a spell, one strong enough that his demand for silence echoed off the far side of the valley. Pausing the questioning of the Shifterai male, the Magister ordered Traver to speak of his own ordeals.

The young man did so with an honest eloquence that pleased Solyn. Once Kenyen was allowed to continue, corroborating his side of things, the Magister called upon her for her own testimony. Her words on the subject of her "husband" impersonating her best friend and supposed betrothed were more politely phrased than the ones she had given her mother, but no less firm and truth-filled.

When her questioning was through, Solyn marched over to where Kenyen and Traver had both taken a seat on a bench outside the forge, and sat on Kenyen's lap. Silently proclaiming to all that she would stay with him, rather than her best friend . . . who merely grinned at the couple.

The Mongrels were far less cooperative. One and all, they glared silently, sullenly at the Magister instead of answering his questions.

Even when warned that their silence would be viewed as an acceptance of the charges levied against them, they refused to speak. The crystal-tipped Truth Wand, and the white marble Truth Stone which Ashallan offered to the Magister to use if he needed it, would have revealed any falsehoods . . . and they knew it.

". . . Very well, then," Magister Caros stated at the conclusion of his interrogation attempts. "By the truthful testimony of these witnesses, by the truthful depositions of Milady Parma Nol Vyth, and by the condemnation of your own silence, it is my judgment that the four of you are indeed guilty of the crimes of which you have been accused. You shall be remanded into the custody of my fellow Magisters for further, spell-wrought interrogations and confessions."

That caused a stir. Usually when a verdict of guilty was determined, a punishment was given. The law was the law across the Empire, however shattered and fragmented it now was. Those whose guilt was determined by honest Truth-spell were guilty, and that was that.

Caros held up his hand, quieting the murmurs of the Nespah Valley holders. "Normally they would merely be punished as befits their crimes. But these men have actively instigated a series of kidnappings, murders, lies, deceits, and other lawbreaking activities in an organized fashion the likes which we have not seen in ages, with a kind of magic that is difficult to detect, once they have stolen someone's face and identity.

"There are many more of these evil Mongrel shifters out there. Milady Parma estimated she had met at least forty of them over the years, if not more. That means roughly forty lives have been stolen away, and roughly thirty-six criminals are still at large." He paused, then added with a wrinkle of his nose, "As distasteful as it is to force a confession, not to mention against the spirit of the law . . . there are times when it is necessary to stop further criminal acts.

"The Mongrel shifters who stole the lives of the men you knew of as Tunric, Zellan, Nilpah, and Gromman, will be taken by mirror-Gate back to the capitol. The Shifterai shifters, being Their Highnesses Ashallan and Anaika, Bellar, Manolo, and Kenyen, are free to go about their business—and I will remind you that it is my judgment as a Magister of the Corredai that Kenyen Sin Siin has committed no crimes in this kingdom, since he had the permission of Traver Ys Ten to assume his identity, and the woman Solyn Ys Rei knew his true identity before entering into marriage with him.

"Treat our northern visitors with every courtesy. Assist them as you would me in the investigation of these Mongrel shifters' crimes, as I have Her Highness' Truth-sworn vow that she and her people will share their findings with the Magistrate. If anyone knows of any further information for my investigation, you may bring it to me or to the Guardsmen I will be leaving here to protect this village from possible repercussions by the criminals. Another Magister will take my place before the end of the day, to ensure your people also have adequate magical protections.

"Justice has been met, and so justice shall be served. Thus say I, Caros Nii Veth, Magister of the Corredai and Speaker of the King's Laws. This trial is at an end." Gesturing for the soldiers to gather up the four prisoners, the Magister rose from the writing desk that had been brought out for his use and bowed to the people gathered in the forge yard.

Breaking off their mutterings, most everyone bowed back to him, barring only the elderly, the children who were too young to know courtesy, the Guardsmen, and their prisoners. The Magister pulled a small mirror from the pouch at his waist and began casting spells, no doubt to summon the mirror-Gate that would take him and the prisoners away. The distance between them was enough that Kenyen's nose stung only a little. Hugging his wife, he glanced around the clearing. Many of the valley's residents were still eyeing him warily, but between Traver's and Solyn's testimony and acceptance, it looked like most of them were going to forgive his deception.

A figure stepped between him and the rest of the assembled Corredai. Ysander planted his hands on his hips and looked down at the seated couple. "Well. I suppose since your intentions were *noble*, we're supposed to just forget all your days of lies and deceit and just forgive you, like that?"

"No," Kenyen replied calmly. As far as father-in-law attacks went, the blacksmith's version was fairly mild. "I know that I deceived you and damaged your trust in me, and that means I've thrown away your respect for me. But the Magister did request that there be courtesy between us. If you can, in your graciousness, give me that much . . . then that will be enough."

"Not for *me*," Solyn snorted.

"Hush," Kenyen countered, looking at her. "You will respect your father. You cannot force him to like me. Either he does or does not, but either way, he has the right to his own opinion on the matter."

She made a face at him, so he kissed her, distracting her from her irritation at her father.

A chuckle broke them apart. Ysander gave them a rueful smile. "Well. If she trusts you after all this, and if you can handle her so well . . . and with such *courtesy*," he mocked lightly, "then I'll give you a chance to prove yourself. But only *as yourself*. No more of this face-stealing nonsense."

"Even if I wanted to join an entertainment troupe and become an actor?" Kenyen asked, daring to tease his father-in-law.

The glower he received quashed that notion. "We are upstanding members of the Nespah Holdings, and I will *not* have an actor for a son-in-law! You'll learn an honest trade and make an honest living, or I'll thrash you black and blue!"

"Father!" Solyn protested.

"Does he even *have* any trade skills?" Ysander countered. "Or does he plan to live on your wages as a Healer?"

"She'll be a properly trained mage, not a Healer," Kenyen countered. "I'm quite sure that Family Tiger will gladly pay for her education, particularly if she agrees to come live among us, since real mages are so rare and treasured among my kind—and as for trade skills, I've made enough money as a traveling warrior and a merchant-trader that the marriage bowl I bought was no more than the cost of loose change to me . . . and I am *not* the wealthiest of my kin."

"He's telling you the truth." The support came from Manolo, who had approached the small group next to the forge entrance. "Family Tiger is much like one of your larger holdings, in that it is comprised of many kin-based families who pool their resources together," the middle-aged shifter explained. "Tiger is one of the smallest Families in Clan Cat, but we are the wealthiest, because we train our warbands to be shrewd negotiators as well as effective warriors. Your daughter will be well-supported by her husband and his kin."

"That's assuming she'll move to the Plains," Ysander countered, turning to face the other man. "When in fact, she will come back from her training to live *here*, with *us*."

"*She* will decide where she wants to live, and what she wants to do with her life," Kenyen asserted, frowning at his father-in-law. "Not you, and not anyone else!"

"Wrong," Solyn quipped tartly, capturing the attention of all three men. All four, if one counted her silently amused best friend. "My *husband* and I will decide what *we* want to do with *our* lives. So, Husband," she said, looping her arms around Kenyen's neck. "What should *we* do, next?"

"Well, I suggest *we* politely ask your family to sponsor you to a mage school," Kenyen offered, thinking quickly. He didn't have to think hard about it, though, since they'd already discussed something along these lines. "At least until such time as Manolo can head back to the Plains, explain what's been happening, and return from Family Tiger with my share of funds to support us while you get the training you need. The Magister has promised to protect your family."

"Yes, well, the whole valley will need it, thanks to her talking so much about the secret of greensteel just now," her father groused. "Even if we're kept safe from the evil shifters, everyone will be wanting greenvein cheese for making Healer's blades."

"Not to mention *my* people will want to do some heavy trading in the cheese so those of us allergic to magic going off in our presence will stop sneezing," Kenyen muttered.

"Father, stop complaining," Solyn ordered, rolling her eyes. "We're finally getting rid of the bad shifters, and we're going to make a very nice profit selling all those blades."

"Knowing your mother, she'll want me to sell them at barely above cost, so every Healer for a dozen kingdoms around can afford one," Ysander muttered, glancing at his wife, who was chatting with her sister and several other women of the valley, discussing the events of the day.

"Well, there's always the sale of the cheese," Kenyen pointed out. "You've already been selling us the special tea for making bluesteel and made a good profit on that."

The blacksmith eyed him in suspicion. "Cheese, cheese, cheese! I suppose *you'll* want to be one of the ones making all that profitable cheese . . . and *waxing* it, too?"

Of the five of them, only Manolo and Traver didn't get the joke. Kenyen and Solyn first quivered, then choked, and finally howled with laughter, clinging to each other. Even Ysander gave up and chuckled. As far as euphemisms went, Solyn's mother was more than right: Waxing the cheese was one of the worst, if not also one of the best.

Then again, Gods willing, Kenyen thought, snickering into her shoulder, *we'll have the chance to "wax the cheese" for many more years to come.*